EX LIBRIS

VINTAGE **CLASSICS**

# CHI ZIJIAN

Chi Zijian was born in Mohe in 1964. She started writing while at school and had her first story published in *Northern Literature* magazine when she was at college. She is the only writer to have won the Lu Xun Literary Award three times. *The Last Quarter of the Moon* also won the Mao Dun Literary Award. Her work has been translated into many languages.

Bruce Humes is an American literary translator and critic of Chinese literature, specialising in non-Han authors and their works.

CHI ZIJIAN

# The Last Quarter of the Moon

TRANSLATED FROM THE CHINESE BY
Bruce Humes

VINTAGE

5 7 9 10 8 6 4

Vintage Classics is part of the Penguin Random House group of companies
whose addresses can be found at global.penguinrandomhouse.com

First published in Great Britain by Harvill Secker in 2013
First published in Vintage in 2014
This paperback first published in Vintage Classics in 2022

English translation rights arranged in an agreement with The
Grayhawk Agency, through Georgina Capel Associates Ltd.

penguin.co.uk/vintage-classics

A CIP catalogue record for this book is available from the British Library

ISBN 9781784877897

Typeset in 11.5/16pt Fournier MT Std by Jouve (UK), Milton Keynes
Printed and bound in Great Britain by Clays Ltd, Elcograf S.p.A.

The authorised representative in the EEA is Penguin Random House Ireland,
Morrison Chambers, 32 Nassau Street, Dublin D02 YH68

Penguin Random House is committed to a sustainable future
for our business, our readers and our planet. This book is made
from Forest Stewardship Council® certified paper.

# THE LAST QUARTER
# OF THE MOON

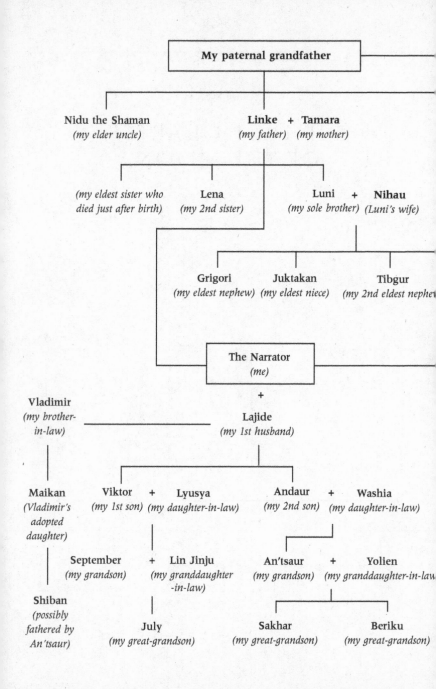

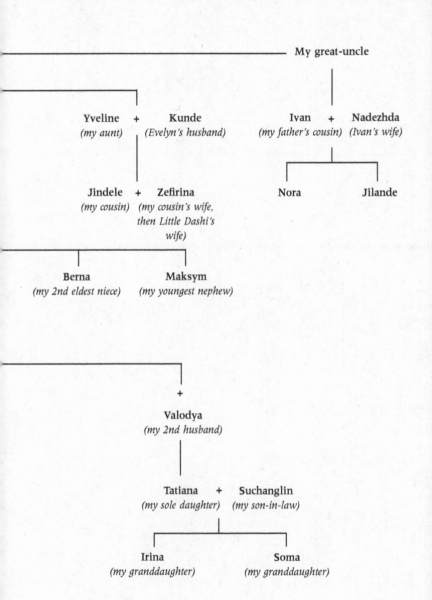

My great-uncle

Yveline + Kunde
*(my aunt)* *(Evelyn's husband)*

Ivan + Nadezhda
*(my father's cousin)* *(Ivan's wife)*

Nora        Jilande

Jindele + Zefirina
*(my cousin)* *(my cousin's wife,*
*then Little Dashi's*
*wife)*

Berna        Maksym
*(my 2nd eldest niece)* *(my youngest nephew)*

+

Valodya
*(my 2nd husband)*

Tatiana + Suchanglin
*(my sole daughter)* *(my son-in-law)*

Irina        Soma
*(my granddaughter)* *(my granddaughter)*

# PART ONE

# DAWN

*A* long-time confidante of the rain and snow, I am ninety years old. The rain and snow have weathered me, and I too have weathered them.

Nowadays the summer rains are more and more sporadic, the winter snows lighter by the year. They're like my roe-deerskin under-bedding, which has shed its hairs from constant rubbing. Its thick undercoat has vanished with the wind, leaving behind scars accumulated over many moons. Seated on the deerskin, I'm like a hunter watching over a salt lick, but rather than deer with their beautiful erect horns, fierce winds swirling with sand await me.

When Shiban and the others left moments ago, the rain arrived. For more than two weeks the sun has appeared red-faced each morning, and in the evening descended yellow-faced into the mountains, never draping itself in clouds.

The blazing sunlight has licked the river water thin, and the grass on the hillsides that face the sun bows in submission.

I don't fear drought, but I fear the sound of Maksym crying. When the moon was full Lyusya wept, but Maksym covered his face and bawled as soon as he discovered the zigzagging crevices in the earth due to the great dry. They were like poisonous snakes out to kill him. I'm not afraid of crevices like that. In my eyes, they are the earth's thunderbolts.

An'tsaur is cleaning up the campsite in the rain.

Is Busu a place that lacks for rain? I ask An'tsaur. Did Shiban have to take the rain with him when he left the mountains?

An'tsaur straightens up, sticks out his tongue, licks the raindrops and laughs in my direction. When he smiles, the wrinkles at the corners of his *eyes and on his cheeks smile too — the corners of his eyes in chrysanthemum patterns, his cheeks in sunflower patterns. The rain nestles like drops of dew among his wrinkled blossoms.*

Only An'tsaur and I remain behind in our urireng. The others descended the mountains this morning in trucks with their belongings and their reindeer. We used to leave the mountains years ago, travelling to Uchiriovo and, more recently, to Jiliu Township where we would exchange our antlers and pelts for items like liquor, salt, soap, sugar and tea. Then we would return to the mountains.

But this time they've left for good. They're going to a place called Busu. Beriku told me Busu is a big town at the foot of the mountains where many white-walled, red-topped houses have been built to serve as fixed residences. There are reindeer pens ringed by barbed wire, and from now on the reindeer will be cooped up.

I won't sleep in a room where I can't see the stars. All my life I've passed the night in their company. If I see a pitch-dark ceiling when I awake from my dreams, my eyes will go blind. My reindeer have committed no crime, and I don't want to see them imprisoned either.

If I can't hear those reindeer bells ringing like rippling water, I'll certainly go deaf. My legs and feet are accustomed to the jagged mountain paths, and if I have to walk the narrow, flat walkways of the town, my legs will become so flabby that they'll no longer support my weight, and I'll become a cripple. I've always breathed the fresh air of the mountain wilderness, and if I have to inhale the farts emitted by the cars in Busu, I'll suffocate.

My body was bestowed by the Spirits, and I shall remain in the mountains to return it to the Spirits.

Two years ago, Tatiana called the urireng together to vote on whether to leave the mountains. She gave each person a square of white birch bark, and those in favour of departing were to place their square on the Spirit Drum left behind by Nihau.

The Spirit Drum was quickly covered by birch bark, as if the Heavens had snowed goose feathers.

I was the last to rise. Unlike the others, I didn't walk towards the Spirit Drum but towards the fireplace, and I cast my birch bark there. It quickly turned to ash in the golden flames. As I emerged from the shirangju, I heard Tatiana crying inside.

I'd expected Shiban would gobble up his birch bark. Even when he was very young he liked to munch on bark, and he can't leave the forest behind. But in the end, he placed his square on the Spirit Drum like the others. I felt like it was his very sustenance that he put there. If he's taking such a bit of food with him, sooner or later he'll starve. I suppose Shiban must have agreed to leave the mountains on account of pitiful Vladimir.

An'tsaur put his square on the Spirit Drum too, but his action didn't mean anything. Everyone knew he didn't comprehend what he was called to do. He just wanted to get rid of the birch bark sooner so he could get back to his chores. An'tsaur likes to work. That day a wasp sting had swollen a reindeer's eye, and he was busy applying herbs to it when Tatiana called him for the vote.

An'tsaur entered the shirangju, saw Maksym and Suchanglin place their squares on the Spirit Drum, and so he did too. The only thing on his mind was that reindeer's swollen eye.

But unlike the others, An'tsaur didn't lay the birch bark down reverently. He released it from his hand nonchalantly as he exited the shirangju, like a soaring bird oblivious to the loss of a feather.

Even though only An'tsaur and I are in the camp, I don't feel a bit lonely. As long as I'm living in the mountains, even if I'm the last human being, I won't feel lonely.

*I return to the* shirangju, *take a seat on my deerskin under-bedding, drink tea and watch over the fire.*

*Whenever we moved camp, we always took along the live cinders. But this time Tatiana and the others abandoned them here. Days without fire are cold and dark, and I truly feel sad and worried for them. They say that every house in Busu has a fire, so they won't need those coals any more.*

*But I imagine fire in Busu doesn't originate in the forest with the striking of a stone against flint. There will be no sunlight or moonlight in Busu's fire. How can a fire like that illuminate your heart and eyes?*

*This fire I watch over is as ancient as me. In the face of fierce winds, heavy snow or torrential rain, I never let it die out. This fire is my beating heart.*

*I'm not a woman who excels at storytelling, but at this moment, as I listen to the swishing of the rain and watch the dancing flames, I long for someone with whom to speak.*

*Tatiana has gone, Shiban has gone, and even Lyusya and Maksym have gone, so to whom shall I tell my story? An'tsaur isn't keen on talking or listening.*

*Then let the rain and the fire listen to my tale. For I know these foes, like human beings, have ears too.*

\* \* \*

I am an Evenki woman.

I am the wife of our people's last Clan Chieftain.

I was born in the winter. My mother is called Tamara, and my father Linke.

The day Mother gave birth to me, Father killed a black bear. He located a hollow tree trunk where a bear was hunkered down in his winter storehouse, and he provoked him with a birch pole. Anger spurs bile production, swelling the gall bladder, so Father waited until the hibernating bear was enraged before he raised his hunting rifle and shot him dead.

That was Father's lucky day. He reaped a double harvest: a bear's plump gall bladder and me.

The first sound I heard as I came into the world was the screeching of ravens. But they weren't real ravens. Because a bear had been killed, the entire *urireng* had gathered for a feast. We worship the bear, so when we eat its flesh we shriek like ravens – *Ya! Ya! Ya!* – to convince the bear's soul that these jet-black birds – and not human beings – are dining on its carcass.

Children born in the winter often take sick and die because of the bitter cold, and I had an elder sister who perished like that. The day she was born the sky was heavy with snow, and Father was out searching for a lost reindeer.

It was very windy, and a fierce gust lifted up one corner of the *shirangju* that Mother had constructed especially for giving birth. My sister caught cold and lived just two days.

When a fawn dies, at least it leaves a pretty hoof print on the forest floor. But my sister departed like the wind that ravaged her. Just a split second's sigh and then a deafening silence.

She was placed in a white cloth bag and flung on a southeastern hillside facing the sun. Mother was devastated. So when she bore me, she wrapped the animal hides good and tight around the *shirangju*, fearful that another gust of frigid wind would stick out its man-eating tongue and make off with her infant.

Of course, Mother only told me all this when I was grown. 'The night you were born,' she said, 'they lit a bonfire on the snowy ground, and the whole *urireng* feasted on bear meat and danced. Nidu the Shaman danced right into the flames, but though his buck-skin boots and roe-deerskin coat were covered in sparks, they weren't even singed.'

Nidu the Shaman was our *urireng*'s Headman. I addressed him as *Egdi'ama* – Uncle – since he was my father's elder brother. My memories commence with him.

Besides my sister who vanished with the wind, I had another elder sister, Lena. One autumn Lena grew sick. She lay in the *shirangju* on the deerskin under-bedding with a high fever, not eating or drinking, drifting in and out of sleep, and talking gibberish.

Father built a four-pole shelter outside the south-east corner of our *shirangju*, slaughtered a white reindeer, and requested that Nidu the Shaman perform a Spirit Dance for Lena.

*Egdi'ama* was a man, but since he was a Shaman, he was obliged to dress like a woman. When he performed a Spirit Dance, his chest was padded. He was very stout, and after he donned the weighty Spirit Robe and Spirit Headdress, I thought he wouldn't even be able to turn around. But he whirled about with great agility as he struck the Spirit Drum.

He danced and chanted from sunrise until the stars appeared, all the while searching for Lena's *umai*, her fledgling soul. Suddenly he collapsed.

The instant he dropped, Lena sat up. She asked Mother for water, and she even said she was hungry.

When he came to, Nidu the Shaman told Mother that a grey fawn had gone to the dark realm on Lena's behalf.

Mother took my hand and led me out of the *shirangju*. In order to entice the does to return rather than gorge on mushrooms far away, we tied up their fawns in the campsite. In the starlight I saw one of these fawns – bursting with playful energy just a while before – motionless on the ground. I grasped Mother's hand tightly and felt a ghostly shiver run down my spine. That shiver is my earliest memory. I must have been four or five.

* * *

The only dwellings I ever saw as a child were our *shirangju*, which are shaped like umbrellas. We have another name for them too: Abode of the Immortals.

They're easy to construct: you chop down twenty or thirty larch trees, saw the trunks into poles about twice a man's height, peel off the bark, sharpen one end, and gather the poles together with the sharp ends pointing to the sky. The poles are evenly spaced in the soil, like countless dancing legs forming a big circle, and then a covering is wrapped around them to protect against the wind and the cold. In the early days we covered them with birch bark and animal hides, but later we used canvas and felt.

I like living in a *shirangju*. It has a tiny opening at the top that serves as an exit for smoke from the hearth. At night I gaze at the stars through this tiny opening. Only a handful of stars are visible from there, but they are exceptionally bright, like oil-lamps held aloft by the *shirangju*.

Father preferred not to go to Nidu the Shaman's dwelling, but I loved to visit, for inside lived more than just a human being; Spirits lived there too. We call our Clan Spirits *Malu*. They were packed inside a leather bag, and the shrine was directly opposite the entrance. Before the adults went hunting they often kowtowed to the *Malu*.

This made me very curious. I begged Nidu the Shaman to untie the bag and let me see the Spirits. Were They made of flesh? Could They speak? Did They snore in the middle of the night like humans? Whenever Nidu the Shaman heard me speak like that about the *Malu*, he grabbed his drumstick and chased me out.

Nidu the Shaman and Father didn't act like blood brothers at all. They rarely spoke and never hunted together. Father was very lean, but Nidu the Shaman was pudgy. Father was a master hunter, while Nidu the Shaman often returned empty-handed. Father was talkative, but even when Nidu the Shaman summoned everyone in the *urireng* to discuss a serious matter, his words were few and disconnected.

It is said that the night before I was born, Nidu the Shaman dreamed that a white fawn would arrive in our camp. This was auspicious, so he showed unmatched joy at my birth, drank more than his share of liquor and that was what made him dance right into the bonfire.

\* \* \*

Father loved playing jokes on Mother. In the summertime he often pointed at her and warned: 'Tamara, Ilan is nipping at your dress!'

Ilan was our family's hunting dog. *Ilan* means 'ray of light', so I especially loved to call for him when the sky grew dark. I thought when he came running he might bring some brightness along. But he was just like me, a shapeless shadow in the darkness.

Mother's yearning for summer wasn't born of a desire to see the forest flowers blossom – she just wanted an excuse to slip on one of her dresses, for she loved to dress up. When she heard that Ilan was chewing on her dress, she'd leap up and Father would chortle gleefully. Mother liked to wear her grey dress, which was embellished with a green waistband, wide in the front and narrow at the back.

With her strong arms and sturdy legs, Mother was the most capable woman in our *urireng*. She had a wide forehead, and she squinted as she smiled, giving her a very gentle expression. Other women always wrapped their heads in blue headscarves, but she left hers uncovered, coiling her thick, jet-black hair in a chignon fixed with a moon-white hairpin of polished deer bone.

'Tamara, come quick!' Father often summoned her just like he summoned us. Mother would saunter over, and Father would give her lapel a tug, pat her on the behind, and announce: 'It's nothing. Off you go!' And Mother would purse her lips and silently return to her chores.

Lena and I learned chores from Mother: how to tan a hide, smoke meat-strips to make jerky, milk reindeer, make a birch-bark basket or canoe, sew roe-deerskin moccasins and gloves, make a reindeer saddle, and how to bake *khleb*, our unleavened bread.

Father felt envious when he saw us flutter about Mother like butterflies bewitched by a flower. 'Tamara,' he would say, 'you must give me an *utu*.' A son, that is. Like other Evenki girls, Lena and I were *unaaji*. Father dubbed Lena his big *unaaji*, so I became his little *unaaji*.

Deep in the night, we could often hear the sound of wind

blowing outside our *shirangju*. In winter it was mingled with the cries of wild animals, while the summer wind carried the hooting of owls and the croaking of frogs.

Inside our *shirangju* there were wind-sounds too, ones that were created from Father's panting and Mother's murmuring. Ordinarily, Mother never called Father by his name, but deep in the night when they made their wind-sounds, she would call out fervently, her voice quivering: 'Linke! Linke!' As for Father, he would struggle for breath like a strange beast on the verge of death.

I thought they must both be gravely ill. But they would wake and go about their chores with warm, rosy faces the next morning. In the midst of one of those flurries, Mother's tummy grew bigger and bigger, and not long after, my brother Luni was born.

Tamara loved Luni. She could have easily left him in the birch-bark cradle when working, but no, she carried him on her shoulder. This meant she couldn't wear her polished deer-bone hairpin, since Luni was forever trying to grab and chew it. The hairpin was pointed, and my mother feared that he would cut his mouth on it. But I liked her best with that hairpin in place.

Lena and I adored Luni too, and we competed to hold him. He was good and plump, like a roly-poly bear cub, and he gurgled and dribbled saliva onto my neck, which felt like a creeping caterpillar. How it tickled! In the winter we liked to run a squirrel's tail across Luni's face, and he'd giggle uncontrollably. In the summer we carried him piggyback down to the riverside and snared dragonflies in the reeds to show him.

Once when mother was feeding salt to the reindeer, Lena and I hid Luni outside the *shirangju* in a big grain barrel. Mother came back and discovered that Luni was missing. She became frantic. She looked everywhere, but Luni was nowhere to be seen. When she asked Lena and me, we shook our heads and said we didn't know. She broke down in tears.

It seemed that Luni and Mother were connected at the heart. At first he lay quietly in the barrel, basking in the sunlight. But when she cried, he began to wail. Luni's cry was laughter to mother's ears. She followed that sound to its source, held him close and gave us a fierce scolding. That was the first time she lost her temper with us.

Luni's arrival forever changed the way we spoke about our parents. Before, like other obedient children, we addressed Mother as *Eni*, and Father as *Ama*. But because Luni was our parents' favourite, Lena and I grew jealous, and we secretly ridiculed them by referring to them as Tamara and Linke. Sometimes I still forget to correct myself when I mention them now. May the Spirits forgive me!

In our *urireng*, every adult male had a woman at his side. Linke had Tamara, Hase had Maria, Kunde had Yveline, and Ivan had his blue-eyed, golden-haired Nadezhda.

But Nidu the Shaman was all alone. I figured that one of the *Malu* we prayed to inside the deerskin bag must be female. Otherwise, why wouldn't he want a woman of his own? The fact that Nidu the Shaman was together with a female Spirit didn't seem strange, but since they couldn't have a child, it was a pity. A camp without children was like trees short of rain – a bit cheerless.

Ivan and Nadezhda, for example, were always teasing their son and daughter, Jilande and Nora, and laughing. Jindele, the son of Kunde and Yveline, wasn't particularly lively but he was like a midsummer cloud that brings a hint of coolness, and this calmed their spirits.

But Hase and Maria were childless, and their faces were always covered in dark clouds. When Rolinsky the Russian *anda* came to our camp, liquor, tea and sweets weren't all he brought to Hase's *shirangju*; there were medicines, too. But after Maria took them to treat her infertility, her tummy still looked the same. This upset Hase so much that sometimes he looked as helpless as a cornered elk bull.

Maria often covered her face in a scarf, lowered her head and went to Nidu the Shaman's *shirangju*. It wasn't a human being to whom she was going to pay her respects; it was the *Malu*. She fervently hoped that They would favour her with a child.

Yveline was Father's sister, and she was keen on storytelling. She's the one who told me all of our folk tales, and about the bad blood between Father and Nidu the Shaman. Of course, I heard the legends when I was very young. But the stories of romance and revenge between adults were recounted to me only after Father died, when Mother and Nidu the Shaman went mad, first one, then the other. By that time, I was almost a mother myself.

* * *

I've seen many a river in my lifetime. Some narrow, others wide; some winding, some straight; some swift flowing, others free of wind and wave. And it is we Evenki who bestowed names upon them: the Delbur Béra, Hologuya Béra, Bischiya, Bistaré, Iming Do and Talyan. Most are tributaries of the Argun, or tributaries of tributaries.

My earliest recollection of the Argun has to do with the winter. That year the snow fell until it obscured the sky and blanketed the earth at our northern campsite. The reindeer couldn't find food, so we were forced to relocate to the south. We hadn't caught any game for two days, and one-legged Dashi sat atop his reindeer cursing those men blessed with a pair of good legs for their uselessness. He announced he had fallen into a dark world where he was going to starve to death. We had to approach the Argun, he said, and bore an opening in the ice cover with an ice pick in order to catch fish.

The Argun was immense. Frozen over, it looked like a massive, freshly made snowland.

A skilled fisherman, Hase drilled three 'eyes' in the ice, and waited, spear in hand. The big fish that had kept their distance from the ice now assumed that spring had returned at last. Their heads and tails wiggling, they briskly approached the holes where natural light was pouring in. When Hase saw the water whirling around the holes, with his sharp eyes and nimble hands he thrust his spear and quickly pierced fish after fish. There were black-spotted pike and even Siberian salmon with fine stripes.

Each time Hase speared a fish, I jumped up and down for joy. But Lena, Jilande and Jindele were afraid to gaze down into the holes. Those ice-eyes exhaling steam looked like traps, and all three kept their distance.

Nora was a few years younger than me, but just as daring. She bent down and stuck her head over the holes. Hase warned her to stay back: 'If you slip and fall in, you'll be food for the fish!'

At this, Nora took off her deerskin hat, shook her head energetically, stamped her feet and cursed. 'Throw me in right now,' she said, 'and I'll swim here every day. When you want fish, just knock on the ice and call "Nora". I'll butt through the ice and give you a live one! And if I can't, then just leave the fish to eat me up!'

Her words didn't bother Hase, but they spooked Nora's mother Nadezhda who came galloping towards her, making the sign of the cross over her chest again and again.

Nadezhda was Russian. Her union with Ivan not only produced two golden-haired, fair-skinned children, it also brought us Eastern Orthodox doctrine. In our *urireng*, Nadezhda prayed to the *Malu* and worshipped the Virgin Mary too.

This made aunt Yveline look askance at Nadezhda. I didn't mind that Nadezhda believed in an extra Spirit or two, for back then I believed they were invisible, but I didn't like it when she made the sign of the cross over herself. For all the world it looked like she was about to cut out her heart with a dagger.

* * *

At dusk, we lit a bonfire on the frozen Argun. We fed the pike to the hunting dogs, but we sliced the meaty Siberian salmon into sections, sprinkled them with salt, skewered them with birch branches, and rotated them over the fire. The aroma of roasted fish spread quickly throughout the camp.

The adults ate fish and drank while Nora and I raced each other along the shore, leaving queues of dense paw prints like a pair of hares.

I still recall how Yveline called us back when Nora and I reached the opposite bank. 'You shouldn't just go over there like that,' she warned me, 'that's not our territory any more.'

But gesturing at Nora, Yveline added: 'She can go because that's her homeland. Sooner or later, Nadezhda will take her and Jilande back to the Left Bank.'

To me, a river was a river and there was no distinction between a right and a left bank. Just look at the bonfire: it was burning on the Right Bank, but its flames tinted the snowy wilderness of the Left Bank scarlet too.

Nora and I paid no heed to Yveline and kept right on running from one side of the river to the other. Nora deliberately relieved herself on the Left Bank, and then returned to the Right Bank and told Yveline loudly: 'I took a pee back in my homeland!'

Yveline threw Nora a scornful look, as if eyeing a newly born deformed fawn.

That night Aunt Yveline told me that the Left Bank of the Argun was once our territory – our homeland – and that we had been the masters of that land.

More than three hundred years ago, Russian soldiers invaded our ancestral territory. They provoked war, and stole the marten pelts and reindeer of our forefathers. With their swords they chopped in two the men who resisted their violence, and used their bare hands to strangle the women who wouldn't submit to rape.

The once tranquil mountain forests, shrouded in dark smoke, descended into chaos. Quarry became less abundant year by year, and our ancestors were forced to migrate from the Lena River Valley in Yakutia, cross the Argun, and begin their lives anew on the Right Bank. So we became known as 'Yakuts'.

When we lived by the Lena River, we were twelve clans strong, but by the time we relocated across the Argun, we were just six. Many clans scattered as the years flowed and the winds blew. And so I do not wish to utter the name of our clan. That is why the people in my story have only first names.

The Lena is a blue river. Our legends say it is so vast that even a woodpecker cannot fly across its expanse. Upstream from the Lena is Lake Lamu, known to others as Lake Baikal, a blue-green lake fed by eight great rivers. Because it lies close to the sun, sunlight floats atop its waters year-round, turquoise aquatic grasses grow thick, and pink and white water lilies abound. Towering mountain peaks surround Lake Lamu. Our Ancestor – a long-braided Evenki – once dwelt among them.

'Does winter come to Lake Lamu?' I once asked Yveline.

'The birthplace of our Ancestor has no wintertime,' she replied.

But I couldn't believe that there was a world where it was forever springtime, forever warm, because each year brought a long winter and bitter cold.

So after Yveline recounted the legend of Lake Lama, I went straight to Nidu the Shaman to get to the bottom of it. Nidu the Shaman didn't confirm the legend, but he attested to the fact that we once hunted freely throughout the Left Bank. He even said that the reindeer-herding tribe that lived in Nerchinsk presented marten pelts as an annual imperial tribute to our Manchu court.

It was those big-nosed, blue-eyed Russian soldiers who forced us over to the Right Bank. I didn't know the exact locations of the Lena River and Nerchinsk, but I did grasp that those lost lands were all on the Left Bank – a place where we could never again go. This filled me with hostility towards big-nosed, blue-eyed Nadezhda when I was young. She reminded me of a she-wolf tracking a reindeer herd.

Ivan was *Egdi'aya*'s son, the son of my great-uncle, that is. He was rather short, his face very dark, and he had a reddish mole that stood out like a 'love-pea' on his forehead. Black bears adore eating those sweet red peas. Whenever Father spotted bear tracks on a hunt, he joked with Ivan to be extra careful for fear a bear would attack him. But there was something to Father's words. For some reason, the sight of Ivan agitated bears more easily than other people, and he had two narrow escapes from a bear's mammoth paws.

Ivan's teeth were rock-hard and he loved to eat raw animal flesh. Whenever we went without game, Ivan was the most miserable one in the clan for he wouldn't eat jerky and turned his nose up at fish. Fish was for children and old people whose teeth weren't in good shape.

Ivan's hands were gargantuan. When he spread them over his lap, they wrapped around his knees like thick tree roots. And those hands of his were mighty. They could crumble a cobblestone and snap larch trunks in two, so we could construct a *shirangju* without an axe. Yveline said that it was Ivan's uncommonly powerful hands that made Nadezhda his woman.

Over a century ago gold deposits were discovered in the upper reaches of the Argun. Knowing there was gold on the Right Bank, Russians often crossed the border to prospect illegally. Back then Emperor Guangxu was on the throne. How could he watch as the grand Qing Dynasty's gold poured into the hands of blue-eyed foreigners?

So the Emperor ordered Li Hongzhang to put a stop to it, and Li dreamed up the idea of operating a gold mine in Mohe City near the river. But six months of every year snowflakes fall on this desolate and sparsely inhabited land, so Li Hongzhang, a Senior Minister in the Court, wouldn't deign to set foot here. In the end, he selected Li Jinyong – the Jilin Deputy Magistrate demoted for opposing Empress Dowager Cixi – to establish a gold mine here.

Once the Mohe Gold Mine opened, stores appeared left and right. But just as fruit follows where there are flowers, brothels also popped up. Those gold-miners located south of the Great Wall hadn't set eyes on a woman all year, and when at last they did their eyes glowed brighter than when they saw gold.

In exchange for an instant of intimacy and pleasure, they'd sprinkle nuggets of gold over a woman's body, and so the brothel business abounded like raindrops in the summer. The Russian *anda* realised that the whorehouses paved the way to riches, and so these merchants brought their women – some hardly more than girls – and sold them into prostitution.

Yveline said that one year when they were hunting on the move in the Keppe River region and the autumn frost had already dyed the forest leaves in patches of red and yellow, a Russian *anda* crossed the Argun with three young ladies in tow. Riding through the dense forest, they proceeded towards Mohe City.

Ivan came across them while hunting. They had caught a pheasant, lit a fire and were eating and drinking. Ivan had seen that bush-bearded *anda* before, and he knew that whatever the trader had with him was for sale. It looked like the gold mine needed more than goods and foodstuffs – it needed women too.

Thanks to years of contact, most of us can speak basic Russian, and the *anda* can understand Evenki. Of the three young women, two had winning looks, big eyes, high noses and slim waists, and they laughed raucously as they drank. They looked like experienced women of pleasure.

But the one with petite eyes was different. She drank quietly, her gaze fixed firmly on her grey-chequered skirt. Ivan surmised she must have been forced into prostitution or she wouldn't appear so despondent. The thought of men lifting up that grey checked skirt, again and again, made his teeth chatter. Never had a girl made his heart ache so.

Ivan returned to the *urireng*. He rolled up two otter, one lynx and a dozen or so squirrel pelts, mounted a reindeer and set out in pursuit of the *anda* and those three young ladies. When he caught up with them, he set the pelts on the ground, pointed to the maiden with the petite eyes, and told the *anda*: the girl belongs to Ivan, and the pelts belong to *anda*.

The *anda* judged the pelts too few, and announced he couldn't engage in unprofitable business.

Ivan strode over to the *anda*. He extended his big hand and plucked the iron flask from the *anda*'s chest. Ivan placed it in his palm, squeezed it hard, and it bent. When he gripped it more forcefully, the liquor squirted out in all directions. Now the flask formed an iron sphere.

The *anda*'s legs turned to jelly, and he let Ivan go at once with the petite-eyed girl. That was Nadezhda.

* * *

Yveline said that Ivan enraged *Egdi'aya*, my great-uncle, to the point of death. Early on he had chosen a marriage for Ivan and planned to welcome the bride into their family that winter. Who'd have imagined that Ivan would bring his own bride back in the autumn?

Ivan's assumption was not wrong. Nadezhda had indeed been sold by her black-hearted stepmother. Along the way she had tried twice to escape, and when the *anda* discovered this, he raped her to force her to accept her whore's fate. So when Ivan took her off with him, she went willingly but with a guilty conscience.

She didn't tell Ivan about being violated by that *anda*, but she revealed it to Yveline. Telling Yveline a secret was like recounting it to a songbird; no one in the *urireng* remained uninformed. At first my great-uncle was ill disposed towards Nadezhda simply due to her Russian extraction, but when he learned that she was a soiled woman, he ordered Ivan to banish her from the mountains. But Ivan didn't. He married her and the following spring she gave birth to a son, Jilande.

Everyone suspected the child was the offspring of the bush-bearded *anda*. As soon as blue-eyed Jilande was born, *Egdi'aya* began spitting blood. He ascended to the Heavens three days later. It is said that when he passed away, the morning clouds turned the east bright pink. He must have taken the blood he coughed with him.

Nadezhda had no experience of living in the mountain forests. At first she couldn't sleep inside a *shirangju* and often wandered about in the forest. She couldn't tan hides, smoke meat-strips or knead thread from tendon. She couldn't even make birch-bark baskets. Ivan noticed that, unlike Yveline, Mother was not hostile to Nadezhda, so he asked Tamara to teach her how to do chores. Among the woman of our *urireng*, Nadezhda was closest to Tamara.

This woman who liked to make the sign of the cross over her chest was clever. In just a few years' time, she mastered all the tasks that our people's women do. And she was extraordinarily good to Ivan. When he came back from the hunt she was always waiting there in the camp to welcome him, hugging him tightly as if she hadn't seen him for months.

Nadezhda was a head taller than Ivan. When she hugged him, it was like a big tree embracing a small tree, a mother bear hugging her cub. It made us laugh. But Yveline said that she acted like a whore.

It was Nadezhda who least liked the sight of the Argun. Each time we arrived there, Yveline addressed her with icy sarcasm, as if she were dying to transform Nadezhda into a gust of wind that would blow back to the Left Bank. Nadezhda eyed the Argun's waters as if she were looking at a greedy master, her face filled with angst, terrified of being exploited again.

But we were unable to leave this river. We always treated it as our centre, living alongside its many tributaries. If the Argun is the palm of a hand, then its tributaries are five open fingers. They extend in different directions, illuminating our lives like flashes of lightning.

\* \* \*

I've said that my memories began with Nidu the Shaman's Spirit Dance for Lena's *umai*, when a fawn went to the dark realm on her behalf. So my earliest recollection of reindeer began with the death of that fawn.

I remember holding Mother's hand when I saw it lying motionless under the stars. I felt so terrified, so heartbroken. Mother picked up the fawn that had ceased breathing and cast it on a south-eastern slope. The infants of our people who don't survive are usually tied up inside a white cloth bag and thrown onto a hillside that faces the sun too. The grass there is the first to sprout in the spring, and wild flowers open the earliest. Mother treated the fawn as her own child.

I still recall the next day when the reindeer herd returned to the camp how that doe couldn't find her offspring. She lowered her head and kept looking at the tree trunk where her fawn had been tied, and her eyes were filled with grief. From then on, this doe – whose milk had been the most abundant – just dried up. It was not until later, when Lena went to the dark realm in pursuit of that fawn, that the doe's milk gushed forth again like water from a spring.

Legend has it that during the Lena River Era our ancestors herded reindeer. The forest was lush with the moss and lichen that we call *enke* and *awakat*, providing reindeer with rich foraging. Back then reindeer were known as *sugju*, but now we call them *oroong*. They have the head of a horse, antlers of a deer, body of a donkey and hooves of a cow. And because they resemble these four animals yet are distinct from them, the Han dub them *si bu xiang*, 'The Four Dissimilars'.

In the past, reindeer were mainly grey and brown, but nowadays they are multicoloured: mixed grey-and-brown, grey-black, white or dappled. I like the white ones the best. In my eyes, white reindeer are clouds fleeing across the face of the earth.

I've never encountered another animal that possesses the docile temperament and endurance of the reindeer. Despite their size, they are extremely nimble. Loaded down with heavy goods, they traverse mountain forests and cross marshes effortlessly. Their bodies are a treasure chest: their coat resists the cold, and their antlers, tendons, penises, placentas and even blood extracted from the heart after death are all precious medicinal ingredients, which *anda* gladly put in their pouches in exchange for the manufactured goods they bring.

The reindeer-milk tea that we drink in the morning is like sweet spring water flowing into our bodies. When we hunt, the reindeer is the hunter's helper: just place the game you've killed on top of a reindeer, and it will transport it safely back to the camp on its own. When we move camp, they not only carry the things we eat and use: women, children and the old and weak also ride them.

Yet they don't need much attention from people. They search for food on their own, and the forest is their granary. Besides moss and lichen, in the spring they also eat green grass, brambles and pasque-flowers. In the summer, they chew birch and willow leaves. In the autumn, tasty forest mushrooms are their favourite.

Yet reindeer forage very delicately. When they pass through a meadow, they nibble lightly so that hardly a blade of grass is harmed, and what should be green remains green. When they eat birch and willow leaves, they just take a few mouthfuls and move on, leaving the tree lush with branches and leaves.

As long as we tie a bell to their necks we needn't worry where they go. Wolves are frightened away by the sound of the bell, and we know their location by its ringing, carried to us by the wind.

Reindeer were certainly bestowed upon us by the Spirits, for without these creatures we would not be. Even though they once took my loved one away, I still adore reindeer. Not seeing their eyes is like not seeing the sun in the day or the stars at night – it makes you sigh from the bottom of your heart.

I can hardly bear to watch the cutting of reindeer antlers, which is done with a bone-saw. Reindeer grow antlers regardless of gender. Typically, a buck's antlers are robust while those of a castrated stag are more delicate. Every year between May and July their antlers mature, and this is the time when their horns are severed. Unlike hunting, both men and women carry out this task.

When its antlers are severed, the reindeer must be tied to a tree and held in place by two wooden poles. Antlers are flesh too, so sawing one off is so painful that the reindeer's four hooves stamp to and fro and the bone-saw is steeped in fresh blood. After the antler has been severed, the base of the antler must be cauterised with a hot iron to staunch the flow of blood. But that is the old way: nowadays we just sprinkle a bit of anti-inflammatory powder on it.

Maria would cry when antler-cutting time came. She couldn't stand to see the bone-saw tainted with blood. It was as if the blood flowed from her own body.

'Maria, don't go!' Mother would say, but Maria would insist. She didn't normally cry, but as soon as she saw blood, her tears would begin to fly – *bzz, bzz* – like a swarm of honeybees. Mother said Maria cried because she couldn't get pregnant. Month after month she saw blood emerge from the lower part of her body and immediately realised that her efforts and those of her husband Hase had come to naught, and she wailed despondently.

But the one who craved a child even more than Maria and Hase was Hase's father Dashi. Dashi had lost a leg in a battle with wolves, so at night when he heard their howling, Dashi gnashed his teeth. He was wizened and scrawny, and his eyes couldn't stand the sight of sunlight or snow, filling with tears constantly. He normally stayed inside his *shirangju*. When we moved camp, he would sit on his reindeer, his eyes blindfolded even when the sky was overcast. It seemed he not only couldn't stand the sunlight, he also couldn't bear the sight of trees, brooks, flowers and little birds.

Dashi had the greyest expression and was the untidiest person in our *urireng*. Linke said after Dashi lost his leg he never cut his hair or shaved. His sparse, salt-and-pepper hair and equally sparse beard intertwined, covering his face with a layer of grey-white lichen. It made you wonder if he was a rotting tree.

Dashi was taciturn, but if he spoke, it was always something about Maria's belly. 'Where's my *omolie*?' he'd ask. 'When will he bring back *Aya*'s leg?' In our language, *omolie* means grandson, and *Aya*, grandfather. Dashi believed that if he only had an *omolie*, the child would slay the wolf that had left him lame. *Omolie* would recover *Aya*'s leg and render him fleet-footed again.

Dashi would cast his eyes on Maria when he spoke, and Maria would cover her stomach, exit the *shirangju*, lean against a tree and weep. So whenever we saw Maria leaning against a tree in tears, we knew what Dashi had said.

Later on, the arrival of a hawk altered Dashi's fate. Originally he had no companion in his *shirangju*, but the hawk's arrival revived his spirits. He trained that hawk to be a fierce hunter, and gave him a name: *Omolie*.

Hase caught the hawk with a bird-trap he set on a towering mountain cliff. Hawks that like to soar in the sky would spot the netting on the cliff and, mistaking it for a resting place, swoop down, only to be taken prisoner, entangled in the trap. Hase brought the grey-brown hawk back home and entrusted its training to Dashi. You could say he was looking for something to keep Dashi busy.

The rims of the hawk's eyes were golden and its eyeballs emitted a glacial light. Its pointed beak hooked downwards, as if prepared to snatch something at any time. Its chest had black stripes upon it, and its soft and graceful wings shimmered with silky lustre.

Hase fastened its claws tight and placed a deerskin cover over its head so the eyes were blinded but the beak exposed. It was very fierce. Head held high, with its sharp claws it scratched one deep gash after another. We children ran over to observe the hawk, but cowardly Lena, Jilande and Jindele ran away, leaving just Nora and me.

When Dashi first saw the hawk he became extremely excited and uttered an '*ululu*' noise. He limped over, bent down with great effort, picked up a stone from the hearth, and threw it. *Paa!* It smashed against the hawk's head. The hawk was enraged. Even though its eyes were covered, it knew where the stone had come from.

Like a whirlwind it took flight, bound for Dashi. But it couldn't fly far because of the cord. It screeched in fury while Dashi chortled. The sound of Dashi's laughter was uglier than the howl of a wolf in the depths of night. The hawk didn't frighten us, but Dashi's laughter sent Nora and me scurrying away.

Every day Nora and I went to watch Dashi train the hawk. He let the bird go hungry for the first few days, and it grew visibly thinner. As thin as the hawk was, Dashi said he only intended to scrape off the oily layer in its abdomen. He chopped fresh rabbit meat into chunks, bundled them in coarse *ula* grass, and fed them like that to the mountain hawk. But since the bird couldn't digest them, it spat them back out whole, and you could spot the oily droplets that now dotted the *ula* grass.

Dashi used this method to thoroughly clean out the hawk's innards, and then he gave him a small amount of food. Afterwards, Dashi had me fetch a cradle. Luni could already scamper about and didn't need one any more, so I carried ours over to Dashi's. As Hase helped Dashi hang the cradle in their *shirangju*, Maria's eyes shimmered with tears.

I've never seen a hawk in a cradle except at Dashi's. Dashi bound the hawk's legs and wings with straw so it couldn't move. With one hand leaning on his cane and one hand crazily rocking the cradle, Dashi's whole body was contorted. I'm sure that even a young child would have been rocked senseless. As he pushed the cradle to and fro, he continued warbling '*ululu*', as if the wind had crept into his throat.

'Why are you doing that?' I asked.

'I want to make the hawk completely forget his past and live obediently with human beings.'

'Are you trying to make him forget the clouds in the sky?'

Dashi spat out a mouthful of phlegm, and thundered: 'Yes, I want to transform this creature of the skies into a creature of the land. I want to turn this cloud into a bow and arrow to devour my enemy – that cursed wolf!'

Once the hawk's intestines had been cleansed and it had been tossed about in the cradle for three days, it did seem somewhat rehabilitated.

Next the deerskin cover was withdrawn, and I discovered that the hawk's gaze was no longer glacial, but softer and a bit blank. 'Now you're really an obedient *omolie*,' Dashi said contentedly.

To ensure it couldn't fly, Dashi fastened a leather strip to its leg and tied a bell to its tail. Then he put on a leather coat, placed the hawk on his left shoulder, left his *shirangju* and walked towards us. He said this was in order to familiarise the hawk with humans. Once it recognised us, it could accustom itself to life among people.

Dashi leaned on his cane, and he held out his left arm to serve as the hawk's perch. As he limped on one leg and leaned on the other, the hawk limped and leaned too, and all the while the bell on the hawk's tail rang. It was a hilarious sight. Dashi had always been so sensitive to the light, but when he took the hawk out for a walk, he wasn't at all timid in the face of the sunlight that enveloped him, even though tears cascaded from the corners of his eyes.

As soon as people heard the bell ringing they knew that Dashi and his hawk were coming.

'Tamara, take a look at my *omolie*,' he said when he encountered Mother. 'Isn't he dashing?' Tamara quickly dropped whatever work she had in hand, greeted him, looked at the hawk and nodded her head repeatedly.

Pleased with himself, Dashi then took the hawk over to Yveline. 'Put that cigarette out right now!' he ordered. He said if the hawk were surrounded by smoke, its sense of smell would suffer.

Yveline discarded her cigarette, fixed her eyes on the hawk, and asked Dashi: 'Does your *omolie* address you as *Aya*?'

Dashi was annoyed. 'No, it shouts, "Yveline!" It says: "Yveline's nose is crooked!"'

Yveline had a good laugh. She really did have a crooked nose. Yveline was very naughty in her childhood, Linke said. When she was four, she saw a grey squirrel in the forest and chased it. The squirrel climbed a tree and Yveline ran straight into the trunk and smashed the bridge of her nose. But I found her crooked nose pleasant, because she had one large eye and one small eye. Her nose leaned towards the smaller one, which rendered her profile more balanced.

Dashi continued to parade the hawk among people regularly, and then he began to feed it meat. Each day he gave it just a bit to keep it half-sated. He said that if the hawk were full, it wouldn't be keen to catch game.

Dashi built a hawk stand outside his *shirangju*. The stand could turn freely. Worried that the horizontal wooden bar would injure its claws, Dashi wrapped the bar in deerskin. 'A hawk's claws are like the rifle in a hunter's hands. They have to be well protected.'

Although the hawk was already very familiar with Dashi, to prevent it flying away he attached a long, thin lead with a swivel loop to the hawk's leg so that when it turned around it wouldn't get tangled.

Each day, Dashi petted the hawk's head and chest softly, always making that *ululu* sound. I suspected that Dashi applied green colouring to his hands, because with each day the hawk's wings not only stood out, they also changed colour. It was a dark green tint, as if someone had draped a robe of green moss over the hawk's body.

Thereafter when we moved camp, Dashi rode a reindeer with his hawk perched on his shoulder. Along with his hawk, it seemed as if Dashi's lost leg had returned and he was reinvigorated. The domesticated bird of prey no longer needed to be tethered. Even when it looked up at the sky, it had no intention of flying high and far. It seemed Dashi's cradle rocking had not been in vain: the hawk had completely forgotten the sky in which it once soared.

Only when moving camp could we enjoy the sight of the hawk capturing prey. Hase often wanted to take the hawk on the hunt, but Dashi wouldn't hear of it. *Omolie* had become his personal property.

I can still recall my first sight of the hawk chasing down a hare. It was early winter when the mountain forests were not yet shrouded in white snow, and we were proceeding south along the banks of the Pa Béra. The moss in that area was especially abundant and wild game copious, and everywhere you could see hazel grouse in flight above the treetops and hares racing on the ground.

Quietly perched on Dashi's shoulder at first, the hawk grew

restless. It raised its head, fluttered its wings slightly, and looked as if it would take flight at any second. Dashi spotted a wild hare running out of a pine grove. He tapped his hawk and shouted: *'Omolie, jü! Jü!' Jü* means 'Give chase'.

The hawk spread its wings and took off, overtaking the wild hare in the blink of an eye. At first, it used a single claw to grasp the hare's bottom, and when the hare turned back to struggle, the hawk clapped its other claw onto the hare's head and, with both claws, quickly suffocated it. Then, using its keen beak, *Omolie* ripped open its catch in no time. The hare's innards spilled on the forest floor like a fresh red blossom emitting sizzling plumes of steam. Dashi warbled his *ululu* excitedly.

On the way to our next campground we didn't expend a single bullet. The hawk caught five or six hares and three pheasants for us, so when we lit our bonfire at night there was always the scent of meat wafting in the air.

But when we got to the new site and erected our *shirangju*, Dashi wouldn't allow *Omolie* to chase game. Instead, he laid a grey wolf pelt on the ground, and yelled *'Jü! Jü!'* again and again, and forced the hawk to pounce on it.

The year that Dashi battled the wolves, when he killed the she-wolf with his bare hands, it was the wolf cub that bit off his leg and ran away. Dashi skinned the adult wolf and always kept her hide with him. Whenever he saw that wolf-skin he gnashed his teeth, as if beholding his mortal enemy. Yveline said it really seemed that Dashi was going to dispatch his hawk to exact revenge.

At the beginning, *Omolie* was very resistant to being forced to attack a lifeless wolf-skin. It retracted its head, and when it heard the *'Jü! Jü!'* command, it backed away. Dashi became very agitated.

He clutched the hawk by the head and dragged it over to the hide. But the hawk just remained planted there listlessly.

Dashi cast aside his crutch, threw himself down on the wolf-skin with a grunt, patted his only leg and cried. After a few rounds of tears, the hawk seemed to comprehend that this wolf-skin was his master's hated foe, and soon began to treat it as a living thing. Not only did the frequency of its pounces increase, but each was fiercer than the last. Whenever Dashi noticed its neck bending and head drooping, he patted its wings immediately to keep his *omolie* vigilant.

So Dashi didn't get enough sleep and his eyes were often pink like a hare's. Whenever we passed by his *shirangju*, Dashi pointed at *Omolie* and said: 'Hey, take a look! This is my bow and arrow, this is my rifle!'

When he spoke like this to others, almost no one contradicted Dashi. But when he spoke like this to Father, Father asked: 'I use a rifle to kill a wolf. Can *Omolie* do that?' Father loved his rifle second only to Tamara. He took a rifle on his back to hunt and he was always fiddling with it in the camp.

When Dashi heard Father speak sarcastically about his *omolie*, he ground his teeth as if he'd heard a wolf howl. 'Just you wait, Linke. You wait and see if *Omolie* doesn't help me get revenge!'

* * *

In the earliest times the gun we used was called '*Ulmuktu*', a flint-lock rifle that fired small bullets. This was a short-range gun, so sometimes you also had to use a bow and arrow and a spear too. Later we bartered with the Russians for a flintlock with bigger bullets, the '*Tuluku*'. Then came the '*Berdanka*' which was considerably more powerful.

But following the *Berdanka* came an even more lethal rifle: a repeating rifle that fired several bullets in succession. Once we possessed the *Berdanka* and the repeating rifle, flintlock rifles were reserved for squirrel hunting. So to me, the bow and arrow and the spear were the hares and squirrels of the forest, the flintlock rifle was a wild boar, the *Berdanka* was a wolf, and the repeating rifle was a tiger – each fiercer than the last.

Linke possessed two *Berdanka* and one repeating rifle. When Luni was just three or four, Linke taught him how to hold a rifle. All those guns came to Linke through bartering with Rolinsky.

Rolinsky was a Russian *anda* who came to our *urireng* at least twice a year, and sometimes three or four times. When we moved camp, we always left tree markers, that is, after we'd walked a certain distance on our way we would cut a notch in a tree trunk with an axe to indicate the path we were taking. That way, no matter how far we travelled, *anda* could find us.

Rolinsky was a short fat fellow with a red beard and puffy bags under his big eyes. He always came to our *urireng* on horseback. Typically, he arrived with three horses, two laden with goods. He came up into the mountains with liquor, flour, salt, cloth, bullets and descended with our pelts and antlers. And Rolinsky loved to drink.

Rolinsky's arrival was a festive day. Everyone gathered to hear him recount news of other *urireng*: Which *urireng*'s reindeer had been ravaged by wolves, which had shot the most squirrels, which had added a new member or lost an elder who had ascended into the Heavens. Since this *anda* had been in contact with six or seven *urireng*, he couldn't help but know the details.

He was very sweet on Lena and each time he came into the mountains he brought something just for her, like an engraved copper bracelet or a tiny wooden comb. He loved to hold Lena's delicate hands, sigh and ask: 'When will Lena grow up into a big *unaaji*?'

And I'd reply: 'Lena is already a big *unaaji*. I'm the little *unaaji*!' And Rolinsky would whistle in my direction as if teasing a little bird.

Rolinsky lived in Jurgang where the Russian merchants gathered. He had travelled to many places like Bukuyi, Jalannér and Hailar on business. Just mention shops like Yushenggong and Jinyintang in Bukuyi or the Ganjur Temple Fair in Hailar, and Rolinsky's eyes would sparkle, as if the loveliest sights on the earth were to be found in these emporiums and fairs.

He liked to bare his arms whenever he drank his fill, and then you could see the tattoo on his shoulder: a coiled snake, greenish, with head cocked. Father said Rolinsky must be a bandit on the run from Russia. Otherwise, why would he have a tattoo on his body?

Nora and I loved to look at that green snake and we treated it like a real one. We touched it, withdrew our hands and ran away as if it might actually bite us.

'I don't have a woman with me now,' he said once, 'so this snake is my woman. In the cold winter it gives off heat, and in the hot summer, it exudes cool air.' The men who had women all laughed. But Nidu the Shaman frowned and left the noisy gathering.

Whenever Rolinsky came, no matter what the season, we always lit a bonfire at night and danced the '*Uubchu*'. At the beginning, the women held hands and circled the bonfire, while the men joined hands to form a circle surrounding them. The women danced to the right and the men to the left. This simultaneous rotation to the left and the right seemed to set the bonfire gyrating too. The women yelled '*Gey!*' and the men shouted '*Gu!*', and soon shouts of '*Geygu! Geygu!*' echoed like swans flying over a lake.

Mother said that long ago our ancestors were sent to guard the border. One day, enemy troops surrounded the outnumbered Evenki soldiers who had depleted their provisions. Suddenly, a powerful wave of cries of '*Geygu! Geygu!*' was carried to them on the wind – a flock of swans flying past! Mistaking the birdcalls for the arrival of Evenki reinforcements, the enemy troops retreated. To commemorate being saved by the swans, our people invented the 'Swan Dance', the *Uubchu*.

Since Nidu the Shaman rarely danced and lame Dashi couldn't take part, the men in the outer circle danced with outstretched arms to keep the women within the inner circle. But as they danced and danced, the women gradually moved into the outer circle, and in the end they all formed one large circle. Everyone held hands, dancing until the bonfire dimmed and the stars dimmed too, and only then did they retire to their *shirangju* for sleep.

Mother loved to dance, but she couldn't sleep afterwards. On those nights I'd often hear her whispering to Father. 'Linke, Linke, my head's awash in cold water. I can't get to sleep.' He wouldn't say anything, but he'd give her the gift of the wind-sounds to which I had become accustomed, and then Tamara would fall asleep.

Each time Rolinsky left the camp, he always gave Lena a kiss, which made Nora and me infinitely jealous. Normally I played with Lena, but when Rolinsky came, I took Nora as my playmate. As soon as he left, I abandoned Nora again, because Lena always gave me the things that Rolinsky had brought for her. I lost the bracelet and bent the comb he gave her, but Lena never complained.

As for which goods and how many to barter, it was Nidu the

Shaman who had the last word. He based his decision on the goods brought by the *anda*. If he brought fewer things, then naturally he was given somewhat inferior pelts. Unlike other *anda*, Rolinsky didn't examine the quality of the fur on the pelts one by one and pick fault with them. He just rolled them up and fixed them on his horse's back.

Even though Nidu the Shaman wasn't so accustomed to the fun-loving ambience that Rolinsky brought with him, he often praised him in his role as an *anda*. He must have seen hard times, said Nidu the Shaman, or he wouldn't be so kind-hearted. But we didn't know his past. He simply mentioned he had herded horses when young, and not only had he known hunger, he had known the sting of a whip. Just who had let him go hungry and who had used a whip on him, only he knew.

October to November was the best season for hunting squirrels. And once the squirrels in one locale were hunted, we'd move on to another site. So we changed places every three or four days during this period.

With their big fluffy tails cocked and patches of long black fur sprouting next to their tiny ears, squirrels are very sweet. They're nimble and love to hop between tree branches. Their grey-black fur is very soft and fine, and it makes very durable collars and cuffs. *Anda* are very keen to barter for squirrel pelts.

Women also take part in squirrel hunting. Set a *charka* – a trap with a small clamp – where they range and when one passes over it, the trap will clench the squirrel. Lena and I loved to lay the traps with Mother.

Squirrels like to store away foodstuffs for winter and they especially love mushrooms. If there are a lot of mushrooms in the autumn, they gather them and hang them from tree branches. Those withered mushrooms look just like frost-covered blossoms, and you can use them to estimate the snowfall in the coming winter. If there will be a lot of snow, the squirrels hang the mushrooms from higher branches; if the snowfall will be lighter, they hang them lower down.

If we can't find squirrel tracks in the snow when squirrel hunting, then we look for mushrooms among the branches. And if we can't find any mushrooms there, then we relocate to the pine forests, since squirrels love pine nuts.

Squirrel meat is quite fresh and tender. Skin it and rub in a bit of salt, put it over the fire and lightly roast it, and it's ready to eat. There isn't a woman alive who doesn't like squirrel meat. Oh yes, and we like to swallow squirrel eyeballs whole. Our elders say this brings us good fortune.

\* \* \*

It was in the midst of a squirrel-hunting season that Lena left us. Mother's health and spirit were poor because she had just given birth to a baby girl who died the same day. She had lost a lot of blood and this, plus her grief, left her face ashen. She didn't leave our *shirangju* for days.

So when Nidu the Shaman announced that since there were few squirrels in the area we should move on, Linke opposed the idea. He wanted to wait until Tamara's health had recovered before moving, worried that she couldn't withstand the cold.

Nidu the Shaman was most displeased. 'What kind of Evenki

woman can't withstand the winter?' he asked. 'If she's afraid of the cold, then she should marry a Han outside the mountains, and live in a grave every day. There's no cold there!' Nidu the Shaman always referred to Han-style houses as 'graves'.

Linke was very angry. 'Tamara has just lost our baby. She's too frail. If you want to go then you can all go. I'll stay behind with her!'

'If you hadn't given her a child,' sneered Nidu the Shaman, 'she wouldn't have lost one.' His words made Yveline emit an odd laugh, and I couldn't help but think of the wind-sounds Tamara and Linke made at night in our *shirangju*.

In the midst of Yveline's cackle, Nidu the Shaman rose from the deerskin under-bedding, clapped his hands, and said: 'Prepare yourselves. We'll leave good and early tomorrow morning!' His head held high, he exited the *shirangju* before the others.

Linke's eyes were scarlet with anger. He raced after Nidu the Shaman and very soon we heard Nidu the Shaman's howl. Linke had knocked him down onto the snow-covered forest floor and stepped on him. Nidu the Shaman resembled a wounded quarry now under a hunter's foot. His shrill, doleful cry was excruciating.

Mother wobbled out and after she learned the details from Yveline, began to cry. Ivan pushed Linke away from Nidu the Shaman. Father walked towards Mother, panting heavily. 'Linke, how could you do that?' Mother said. 'You make me ashamed! How can we be so selfish?'

That was the first time I witnessed Father confront Nidu the Shaman, and the first time that I heard Mother reproach him. Knowing how Nidu the Shaman could bring about the death of a fawn through his ritual dance, I worried that one night he would use the same means to silence Father for ever.

I confided my fears to Lena. 'Let's sleep at *Egdi'ama*'s,' she said, 'so we can watch over him and make sure he doesn't do a Spirit Dance.'

That night Lena and I entered Nidu the Shaman's *shirangju*. He was drinking tea and watching over the hearth. Seeing his pale face and grey temples, I suddenly pitied him. We said we'd like to hear him tell a story, and sure enough, *Egdi'ama* let us stay the night.

The wind was very strong and very cold, and the flames crackled constantly as if sighing. And Nidu the Shaman's story was about fire.

Once upon a time there was a hunter who rushed about the forest all day long. He saw many creatures, but he couldn't kill even one. All his prey escaped before his eyes and he was very vexed. He returned home that night with a troubled look on his face. He lit a fire, but when he heard the kindling go *pee-paa pee-paa* as it burst into flames, he felt someone was mocking him. In a fit of pique, he grabbed a knife and stabbed at the vibrant flames, snuffing them out.

The next day the hunter arose from his sleep and tried to light a fire but to no avail. Unable to drink anything warm or make breakfast, he left home for the hunt. But once again he had nothing to show for his efforts, and when he returned home he was unable to light a fire. He found this strange, and spent yet another long night cold and hungry. For two days running, the hunter had eaten nothing and gone unwarmed by fire.

On the third day, he entered the mountains again to hunt when he suddenly heard mournful crying. Following the sound, he discovered an old woman leaning against a pitch-black withered tree and covering her tearful face.

'Why are you crying?' asked the hunter.

'Someone cut my face with a knife, and the pain is hard to bear,' she replied.

When she put her hands down and the hunter saw her bloody, mangled mien, he realised he had offended the Fire Spirit. He knelt down and begged her forgiveness. He swore that from that day hence he would venerate her for ever. But when he finished kow-towing and stood up, the old woman had vanished. Perched on the withered tree was a gaily-coloured pheasant. He drew back his bow and shot the bird. The hunter took the pheasant back to his quarters and discovered that the fire, lifeless for three days, had rekindled itself. The hunter knelt by the hearth and wept.

We deeply revere the Fire Spirit. From my earliest memories, the fire in our camp has never gone out. When we move camp, the white buck at the very front, the *Malu* King, transports the *Malu*. Normally, it cannot be ridden or used for mundane tasks.

Following it is the reindeer that transports the live cinders for our fire. We place the coals inside a birch-bark bucket and bury them under a thick layer of ash. No matter how arduous the path we take, light and warmth always accompany us.

We often drip animal fat on the fire, for it is said that our Ances-tral Spirits like its aroma. There is a Spirit inside the fire, so we must not spit or sprinkle water on it, or throw unclean things into it. Lena and I learned these customs when we were young, so when Nidu the Shaman recounted the Fire Spirit's tale, we were enchanted.

When the story ended, Lena and I both had something to say.

My words were for Nidu the Shaman: '*Egdi'ama*, does the Fire Spirit jump out from the flames each night to speak to you?' Nidu the Shaman gazed at me and then the flames, and shook his head.

Lena's words were for me: 'In the future you must be sure to protect the live cinders. Don't let the rain quench them, or the wind snuff them out!' I nodded as the setting sun nods to the mountains and the valleys into which it descends.

The next morning the reindeer came back from a night of foraging, and we awoke too. Nidu the Shaman was already up and preparing reindeer-milk tea. Its fragrance licked our cheeks and Lena and I took breakfast there. Lena yawned several times, her face a pale yellow.

'I didn't sleep all night,' she whispered. 'I was afraid that Nidu the Shaman would rise at midnight to perform his Spirit Dance, so I did my best to keep my eyes open. Listening to you snore, I felt as envious as someone who hasn't eaten for days when she smells a squirrel roasting!'

Lena's words made me deeply ashamed. She had remained alert all night for Father's sake, while I slept sweetly through to the morning.

When we left Nidu the Shaman's, he was busy taking the *Malu* down from the shrine and hanging them on a triangular wooden stand. Then he lit some *kawaw* grass whose smoke purifies the *Malu* Spirits. This was something that Nidu the Shaman did each time before we moved camp.

We left the old campsite as Nidu the Shaman wished. The white *Malu* King walked at the very front, followed by the reindeer transporting our fire source, and then the reindeer loaded with our household possessions. The men and able-bodied women normally walked with the herd, riding reindeer only if truly tired. Hase held the axe and after we had covered a certain distance, he hacked a tree marker into a big tree trunk.

That day mother was lifted onto a reindeer. Using a rabbit-hair hat and a scarf, she wrapped her face good and tight. Linke followed her reindeer closely. Dashi, Nora, Lena and I also rode.

Since *Omolie*, perched on Dashi's shoulder, only exhibited its hunting skills when we moved camp, Jilande and Luni tagged along on either side of Dashi's reindeer. But Jilande was yellow-hearted and afraid that the hawk might suddenly attack him. So after a while, he ran over to Luni and walked at his side. They gazed at the hawk like a hero, bursting with admiration. But the hawk eyed Luni and Jilande menacingly, as if they were a pair of hares.

Lena normally loved to ride a particular white-spotted brown reindeer, but that day when she went to saddle it, it shrank away and darted off, as if unwilling to carry her. Just then the grey doe whose milk had long dried up came over to Lena of its own accord and lowered its body submissively. Without a second thought, Lena placed the saddle on it.

At first Lena's reindeer went ahead of mine, but as we moved along it fell behind. When Lena was ahead of me, I saw her head nodding as if she were napping.

No matter how bright, the winter sun always gives one a chilly, solitary feeling. The snow cover in the forest was quite thin, and the withered yellow of the wild grass and fallen leaves on the hillsides facing the sun was naked to the eye. Birds in their twos or threes darted over the treetops, leaving crisp calls in their wake.

Ivan walked and chatted with Nadezhda. He had heard from Rolinsky about how gold was discovered in the Xikouzi Mine: one day a Daur tribesman caught some fish, lit a fire on the riverbank, and cooked them. When he had finished eating, he washed the pan. As he scrubbed and scrubbed, he discovered sparkling grains of sand at the bottom of the pan. He put them in his hand, rubbed them and, lo and behold, they were gold!

'So the next time you scrub your pan with river water,' said Ivan, 'pay attention to the grains of sand, and check to see if they're the colour of gold.'

Nadezhda made the sign of the cross over her chest and prayed out loud for the Virgin Mary's protection. 'Heaven forbid we should discover gold! My brother lost his life prospecting with a partner. Since ancient times gold has never been a good thing, it only invites disaster,' she said.

'As long as people aren't greedy for money,' said Ivan, 'there won't be any disasters.'

'When people see gold it's like a hunter spotting his prey,' Nadezhda retorted, 'they can't help but be greedy.' When she finished speaking, she gave Ivan a pat on the head.

Yveline noticed this gesture and angrily reproached Nadezhda. 'Our women don't casually touch a man's head! We believe you'll enrage the Spirits that live there and invite punishment.'

'Watch out ahead, everyone!' shouted Yveline. 'Nadezhda rubbed Ivan's head.'

We started out when the sun was high in the sky, and only when we had walked it to the corner of the sky did we arrive at our new camp. This was a dense pine forest and we could see squirrels darting back and forth in the thickets. Nidu the Shaman's face lit up in a smile. Just when the men were preparing to erect *shirangju*, and the women had gathered dry branches to get the fire going, I discovered Lena was not in the camp. I called her name but there was no response.

When Father heard Lena was missing, he immediately went

looking for the grey doe she had been riding. He found it at the tail end of the queue, its head hung low and looking sad.

Linke and Hase realised that Lena was in trouble. Each rushed to mount his reindeer and search for her along the trail we had taken. Mother looked at the reindeer that Lena had been riding, probably recalling how this doe's fawn had departed from our world on behalf of Lena. Now, Lena had gone missing while riding this very doe; this could not be a good omen. Mother felt a shiver run down her spine.

We in the camp were fervently hoping for Lena's return.

Our hope turned the sky black and brought out the stars and the moon, but Linke and Hase still hadn't returned.

Except for Dashi, none of us was in a mood to eat. Dashi roasted up a hare that his hawk had caught along the way, and downed it with liquor. When the food and drink got him excited, he began warbling *ululu* again. That's the first time I've ever detested anyone. I could have cut off his tongue! In my eyes, Dashi's chomping mouth was as filthy as a spittoon. If only that wolf had gobbled him up!

The night grew late but Lena had still not appeared. Mother began crying. Yveline held her hands and reassured her, but Yveline's own eyes were filled with tears.

Maria cried too, but she wasn't just worried about Lena, she was worried about Hase too, for Hase had forgotten his rifle. What if he ran into a wolf pack?

Dashi poured oil on the fire. 'That idiot Hase! He goes searching for someone without even taking a weapon. Does he imagine that his arms are made of iron that can serve as a rifle? The wolves needn't worry about tonight's dinner, I'd say!'

Nidu the Shaman had been sitting silently by the open fire, but Dashi's words brought him to his feet. 'If you say one more word tonight,' he said to Dashi, 'your tongue will be as hard as stone tomorrow!' Dashi knew about Nidu the Shaman's powers so he didn't dare continue his babbling.

Nidu the Shaman sighed. 'There's no use spilling your tears,' he said to the women. 'Linke and Hase will be back soon, and Lena is already together with the birds in the sky.'

His words made Mother faint. Yveline's face was covered in tears, Maria stamped her feet in anguish, and Nadezhda's hand — in the midst of crossing herself — froze over her chest.

Soon Father and Hase returned on their reindeer. But Lena didn't return, she would never return. Father and Hase had found her long-since-frozen body and buried her on the spot.

I ran into Nidu the Shaman's *shirangju* and shouted: '*Egdi'ama*, please save Lena! Go and retrieve her *umai*!'

'Lena can't come back,' Nidu the Shaman said. 'Don't call for her!'

I kicked the water flask next to the hearth so hard it banged *kwang-lang kwanglang*. I cursed and swore that I was going to burn his Spirit Robe, Spirit Headdress and Spirit Drum. 'If Lena doesn't stand up again, I'll lie down beside her and never get up again either!'

But I didn't lie down, and Lena didn't stand up again.

Father said that when he found Lena, her eyes were closed tight and the corners of her mouth were creased in a smile, as if she were having a beautiful dream. She must have been fast asleep to fall from the reindeer. Drowsy, once she fell into the soft snow, she just kept on sleeping. She froze to death while dreaming.

And so Lena departed, taking with her the sound of Mother's laugh. Tamara had lost two daughters in succession, and her face was ashen throughout the winter. One long night after another passed without Tamara and Linke making wind-sounds in our *shirangju*. How I missed hearing her call out 'Linke! Linke!' passionately in the midst of those wind-sounds.

Snowfall that winter was light, and squirrels were numerous and our hunting garnered an exceptionally bountiful yield, but Linke and Tamara didn't cheer up.

In the spring, Rolinsky arrived in our camp on his horse. When he learned that Lena was no more, his face instantly darkened and he was struck dumb. He wanted to see the doe that had taken Lena into the valley of death, and Linke took him.

By this time that grey doe once again had milk, but for Tamara this was just a reminder of bad tidings. Every day she yanked at its teats with all her might, despising her inability to milk it dry on the spot. Day in and day out the grey doe withstood Tamara's mistreatment, even though its legs trembled. But Rolinsky understood why Tamara's milking was so crazed.

He patted the reindeer affectionately. 'You know how much Lena cared for the reindeer,' he said to Tamara. 'If she saw you treating a doe like this, she'd feel bad.' Tamara released her grip on the doe's teat, and wept.

During that visit Rolinsky didn't join in our Swan Dance or drink with us.

As he took leave of the camp with bundles of squirrel pelts, I spied him hanging something on a little pine tree. After he had mounted his horse and moved away from the sapling, I discovered the tree was twinkling. I ran over to take a look. It turned out to be a tiny round mirror.

It must have been a gift Rolinsky had brought for Lena! In the mirror were reflected the balmy sunshine, pure white clouds and green, green mountains. But it couldn't contain all the abundance and moist freshness and brightness of springtime – it seemed as if the mirror were going to burst into pieces.

Although I felt horrible the night Lena disappeared, I just couldn't cry. But the spring scenery condensed onto the surface of that tiny mirror set free the tears accumulated deep within my heart. I finally let loose with a wail and bawled, causing the birds perched on the trees to take flight in fear.

I took down the tiny mirror and hid it away. It's still in my possession, but the glass is hazy. I once gave it to my daughter Tatiana as part of her dowry. She gave birth to her daughter Irina, and noticing that she too liked the mirror, when Irina married she also included it in her dowry. Irina loved painting, and she often reflected her own paintings in it, for she said her paintings in the petite mirror were like a lake veiled in a thin layer of mist, hazy and delicately beautiful.

A few years back Irina departed from this world. Tatiana was putting her daughter's things in order, and just when she intended to smash the mirror on a rock, I took it back. This mirror has witnessed our mountains, trees, white clouds, rivers and many women's faces. It is an eye on our lives – how could I stand by and let Tatiana blind it?

I kept this eye, even though I know that because it has witnessed too much scenery and too many people, its eye, like mine, is no longer so limpid.

* * *

I discovered springtime is a medicine capable of healing.

In the winter following Lena's departure, Mother languished in depression. But with the return of spring, a smile's shadow appeared on her face. It was that spring when I discovered blood flowing from my body. Seeing Mother's complexion was ruddy once again, I felt certain that blood from my body had flowed into hers.

'I'm bleeding,' I told Mother. 'I'm going to die! But my blood isn't flowing in vain – it's gone to your face.'

Excited, Mother drew me into her bosom and yelled to Father: 'Linke, our little *unaaji* has grown up!'

Mother brought some fine strands of dried willow bark and swathed my groin with them. Then I understood why she gathered willow bark on the riverbank each spring: to absorb our youthful spring waters.

Whenever the wind softened the willow trees on the riverbank, mother would strip off pieces of bark, fill long baskets on her back with them, and return to camp. She singed the bark to render it malleable. Then she tore the pieces into fine threads, kneading them on her legs to make them fluffy, dried them under the sun and stored them. Back then I had no idea of their use, and when I asked Mother she always smiled. 'When you're grown up you'll understand.'

I think the fact that I used those strands of willow bark so early was related to my love for birch sap. In this I was definitely influenced by Mother, for she drank even more birch sap than us. The liquid we imbibed was white, but what flowed out was red.

White birch are the most brightly garbed trees in the forest. They're draped in a white silken gown festooned with black blossom-shaped decorations. All you have to do is cut a shallow opening at the root with a hunting knife, stick a straw in it, position the birch-bark bucket, and the sap flows naturally through the straw into the bucket like spring water. The liquid is pure and transparent, fresh and sweet. Take a sip and your mouth feels clean and cool.

I used to tap birch sap with Lena, but after she departed, I went with Luni. He would kneel at a root, dangling a straw from his mouth. Luni drank his fill first and then let the sap flow into the bucket.

I never saw anyone who loved white birch trees as intensely as Tamara. She often stroked a fuzzy tree trunk and said admiringly: 'Look at how she's dressed, so pristine, just like snow! Look at her waist, so slender and straight!'

Whenever Luni and I brought back birch sap, Tamara wouldn't touch reindeer milk. She'd ladle out a bowl of the sap and down it in one go. When she'd finished, she'd squint deliriously, like someone encountering the sunlight after a long spell in total darkness.

And when she stripped the bark from a birch tree, she liked to scrape the viscous liquid straight off the trunk and eat it. Her bark-stripping technique was even better than a man's. Sharp hunting knife in hand, she selected a birch with a trunk of a consistent width and a top layer of lustrous bark. First she cut an opening down the thickest part of the trunk, then she made a horizontal cut around the top, circling the whole tree, repeated the circular motion at the bottom, and then she could neatly lift off a whole piece of birch bark.

Since the bark is removed from the tree trunk, during the first year it is essentially naked. The next year it turns grey-black as if it had slipped on a pair of dark trousers. One or two years after that, the stripped area grows a fresh layer of tender bark as if it has donned an eye-catching white gown. In my eyes, the birch tree is a fine tailor who cuts clothes to suit herself.

The bark stripped from a birch tree can be made into all sorts of things. Just warm it slightly over a fire until it becomes soft and pliable enough to make a bucket or a box. A birch-bark basket can be used to fetch water, and boxes of various shapes to store salt, tea, sugar or tobacco.

Birch-bark canoes are made from big pieces of bark. That sort of birch bark must be put in a large iron pot and cooked for a short while and then removed. Once the water is drained, it's ready to make a boat.

We call our birch-bark canoes '*jawi*'. To fabricate a *jawi* you need to use pine for the frame and wrap the birch bark around it. We fasten the joints using thread made from red pine fibres. Then we seal the openings with glue made by simmering a mixture of pine and birch oils.

*Jawi* are very narrow, but very long too – the height of four or five people combined. Its ends are pointed and there is no head or tail, so whichever end you stand at, that is the bow. When you put it in the water it's as nimble as a silver carp.

Every *urireng* possesses three or four *jawi*. Normally they're kept in the camp, and they're light so they can be easily transported when needed. If we stay at a campsite for a long time during the summer, we keep our *jawi* by the riverside for the sake of convenience.

My memories of birch-bark *jawi* are associated with the elk, the largest creature in the forest. A mature *kandahang* can weigh two hundred and fifty kilos! Its head is big and long, but its neck is short, and it has grey-brown fur, slender limbs and a small tail. Antlers grow on the head of the bull. The upper portion of the antlers are shaped like a shovel and look like a pair of square scarves hanging out to dry atop its head, one on the left and one on the right.

*Kandahang* love to eat the *jungu* grass that grows in marshes at bends in the river, so to kill one a hunter often must keep watch on the bank. During the daytime *kandahang* hide away in a shady place in the forest, emerging only at night to look for food, so our men hunt them after the stars come out.

Father was determined to shape Luni into an outstanding hunter, so when my brother was eight or nine, as long as the hunting ground wasn't too far from the camp, Father took him along.

One cool summer night I was kneading thread from deer sinew with Mother by the fireside when Luni came running in. Bubbling over with enthusiasm, he told me Father was going to take him in a *jawi* to a cove for *kandahang* hunting.

I wasn't so keen on *kandahang*, but I really wanted to ride in a *jawi*. I begged Mother to ask Father to bring me along. I knew that taking a girl on the hunt was a big taboo. But as long as Mother told Father to do something, I was confident he could only say 'yes'. So when Mother walked out of the *shirangju* to look for Father, I jumped up from the fireside, knowing that I would go with them to the cove.

Rifle at his back, Linke took us through the forest to the riverside. On the way he instructed Luni and me: once in the *jawi*, we mustn't speak loudly or spit in the water.

Back then the forest on the Right Bank of the Argun not only had big trees that blotted out the sun, it also had tributaries everywhere, so many of the small rivers were nameless. Like shooting stars that slide across the Heavens, most have now disappeared. So let me call that unnamed waterway *Kandahang River*, because it was there that I saw my first ever *kandahang*.

As if he were dragging a lazy child against his will, Linke pulled the canoe out from the underbrush where it was hidden, and pushed it into the river. He watched Luni and me get aboard and then he jumped in. The canoe didn't displace much water. It was a dragonfly alighting on the water almost mutely, rocking slightly. As the craft moved languidly along, gusts of cool wind caressed my ears.

I watched the trees on the bank as we advanced and it seemed as if each one had sprouted legs and was in steady retreat. The river was a courageous warrior and the trees were vanquished soldiers.

There wasn't the hint of a cloud around the moon. It was so luminous that I worried that the exposed moon might suddenly tumble down to the earth.

At first the river flowed straight as an arrow, and then it bent a wee bit and as the curvature increased, the flow accelerated and the river widened. At last we reached a big bend on the Kandahang River that overflowed into a small, oval lake to one side, while the main stream rushed single-mindedly ahead.

Linke swung the canoe into the lake, and we rowed towards a low-lying part of the mountain opposite us. Linke went ashore but didn't allow Luni and me to debark.

As soon as Father left, Luni tried to scare me. 'Look!' he said. 'There's a wolf in front of us. You can see the light shining in his eyes!'

I was just about to scream when Father called back to Luni: 'What did I tell you? A good hunter mustn't talk nonsense!'

Luni immediately quietened down. He tapped his fingers lightly against the body of the canoe several times as if he were rapping his own head in self-criticism.

Linke returned to the canoe quickly. He whispered that he had discovered the faeces and hoof marks of a *kandahang* in the undergrowth on the bank. The faeces were very fresh, which meant the *kandahang* had been there a few hours previously. Based on its hoof marks, it was a mature and sizeable one.

Linke said we should go to the willow grove opposite to keep watch for it. We rowed towards the grove, and once the *jawi* was squeezed into the grove, it served as a piece of dry land. We concealed ourselves in the canoe, and Linke had Luni load the bullets into the rifle chamber. Then Linke held his finger up to his lips, signalling that we mustn't make a sound.

We waited with bated breath. At the beginning I was very excited, expecting the *kandahang* to arrive at any second. But when even the moon had shifted its body in the water, I still hadn't heard a single sound. I was drowsy and couldn't help yawning. Luni put out his hand and tugged on my hair to keep me alert. But that hurt my scalp, and I was so annoyed that I hit him on the shoulder. He tilted his head and smiled at me. I can still recall Luni's smiling face in the moonlight. Those two rows of neat teeth twinkled like silver, as if he had a treasure stashed away in his mouth.

To stay awake, I kept my head moving constantly. First I gazed at the moon in the sky, and then I lowered my head and gazed at the moon in the river. After I gazed at the moon in the water, I raised my head again and gazed at the moon in the sky. One moment I felt the moon above was bigger and brighter, and the next I felt the moon below was larger and more luminous.

A breeze began to blow. The moon-in-the-sky looked the same as ever, but now the moon-in-the-water had grown a wrinkle-covered mien, as if it had suddenly aged. It was then and there I realised that it is the things in the sky that are eternal; no matter how lovely the things reflected in the water, they are all short lived. I recalled Nidu the Shaman said Lena was together with the birds in the sky, so I felt she had gone to a nice place and I didn't need to avoid thinking of her any more.

As I was remembering Lena, Father forced down a mouthful of spit. I heard a *cha-cha*, like someone chopping a tree with an axe. It wasn't a sharp axe. It was a bit dull because that *cha-cha* wasn't crisp.

But *cha-cha* quickly changed into *pupu*. Following the sound, I discovered a grey-black shadow moving on the other side of the lake! Evidently that *'pupu'* was the sound of an animal's hooves sinking into the lakeside marsh. Father was so excited that he couldn't resist exclaiming *'Uh!'*, so I knew that shadow must be a *kandahang*! My heartbeat quickened, my palms sweated and my drowsiness vanished.

The *kandahang* advanced unperturbed in the night. Its huge body looked like a shifting sand dune. It walked towards the lake, lowered its head, and drank for a moment. When it lifted its head, Father took aim but missed his chance when the *kandahang* suddenly plunged into the water.

I had imagined it would be very clumsy, but the *kandahang*'s entry was unexpectedly graceful. It must have gone underwater to eat *jungu* grass, its head appearing now and again. Doubtless it deemed itself master of the lake and didn't linger at any one spot; one moment it was on the southern side of the lake, the next it was swimming to the east, roaming freely throughout its kingdom. We could see its traces from the bubbles that broke the surface of the water.

As the *kandahang* approached the centre of the lake, it shattered the moon-in-the-water. The golden fragments rippled and made my heart ache for the moon.

As the *kandahang* drew closer to us, I became very anxious because it certainly looked as though it had a big appetite. If Father didn't shoot it spot on, it would pounce. Our *jawi* would be trampled to pieces and we'd have to flee. And if we ran slowly and it caught up to us, we'd be lucky to escape with our lives.

Linke was a genuinely fine hunter. When the *kandahang* submerged itself and the moon appeared perfectly round on the lake surface once more, he remained very composed and waited patiently. Only when the *kandahang* stood up, shook its head with satisfaction and made ready to go ashore did Linke fire his rifle. When the rifle sounded, my heart leapt out of my chest too. I saw the *kandahang* totter as if it were going to collapse in the water, but it quickly righted itself and charged in the direction of the rifle shot.

I screamed, ignoring Linke's earlier instructions. Only after Linke fired another two bullets into the *kandahang* did it cease its charge. But it didn't fall immediately. It staggered for a long moment like a drunkard, and finally collapsed – *gudung*! – in a gargantuan splash. In the silver moonlight, the spray glowed a dark greenish-blue.

Luni cried out with joy, and Linke let out a long sigh and lowered his gun. We waited two or three minutes to confirm that the *kandahang* wasn't breathing, and then rowed the canoe through the willow grove and quickly swept over to the lake centre.

The *kandahang*'s head was immersed in the water and only a corner of its body showed, like a bluish sandstone whose edges had been worn away. The moon next to it was full again, but was no longer silvery white; it had become a black moon, for the *kandahang*'s blood had dyed the lake's centre night-black.

Recalling how just a moment before it had been leisurely

chomping on *jungu* grass under the water, my teeth chattered and my legs shook. But Luni was in high spirits. I knew then that I would never be a true hunter.

We didn't transport the *kandahang* back to the camp since it was too heavy. Linke rowed and whistled cheerfully as he took Luni and me back home. But when we passed by the tree that touched the skies, Linke didn't dare keep whistling, fearful he would disturb *Bainacha*, the Mountain Spirit.

It is said that a long, long time ago a Clan Chieftain took his clan on a 'surround hunt'. They heard all sorts of wild animal cries emerging from a big mountain, so they surrounded it. The sky was already dark, so the Chieftain ordered everyone to pitch camp on the spot.

Under the leadership of the Chieftain they tightened the encirclement the next day. Time passed very quickly, and at dusk he queried his kinsmen: 'How many sorts of wild animals have we encircled? And how many are there of each sort?'

No one dared answer because guessing how many wild animals were surrounded in the mountain was like trying to guess how many fish are swimming in a lake.

Just when everyone remained speechless, a genial, white-bearded old man opened his mouth to speak. He not only stated the total number of wild beasts that were inside the hunting circle, he also classified them and specified the numbers of deer, roe-deer, hares and so forth.

When the hunt was over the next day, the Chieftain personally accompanied the others to count the number of beasts, and lo and behold, they numbered exactly as foretold! The Chieftain sensed the old man was someone unusual and went looking for him. He had unquestionably seen the old man sitting under a tree a moment ago, but now he'd vanished without a trace.

The Chieftain was amazed and dispatched people in all directions to search for the old man, but no one could find him. The Chieftain reckoned that the old man must be the Mountain Spirit who ruled over all the wild animals, so he carved his likeness – the *Bainacha* Mountain Spirit, that is – on the big tree under which the old man had been seated.

When a hunter is hunting and sees *Bainacha* carved on a tree, he must not only respectfully make offerings of tobacco and *baijiu* to it, he should also lay down his rifle and remove the bullets, and kowtow to pray for the Mountain Spirit's protection. If the hunter has made a kill, he should smear the animal's blood and fat on the image of the Spirit.

Back then in the forests on the Right Bank, numerous big trees sported a carving of the Mountain Spirit's image. When a hunter passed by *Bainacha* he had to remain silent.

All along the way home I was lethargic, and Linke asked if I was sleepy. I didn't answer. Even though a bullet hadn't struck me, I was lifeless like the *kandahang*. After we returned to the camp, Father explained where we had killed the *kandahang*, and Ivan, Hase and Jindele left in the middle of the night to fetch it.

Like a hero justly recognised for his feat, Linke stayed behind to rest and must have been very content. Tamara and he made very passionate wind-sounds in the *shirangju*, and Mother called out his name again and again.

But in the midst of those wind-sounds, that round black moon flashed before my eyes. It tore apart my dreamland, and I fell into a heavy sleep only when light appeared in the east.

By the time I got up the sun was already high in the sky, and Mother was busy cutting the *kandahang* into strips on the wooden chopping block. I knew she was preparing to dry the meat. Those crimson meat-strips looked like red lily petals blown to the ground by the wind.

Because a *kandahang* had been killed, the campsite took on a joyful air. I saw Maria and Yveline cheerfully drying their meat-strips like Tamara. A smile hung on Maria's face, and Yveline was humming a tune.

Yveline saw me from afar. 'Come over,' she yelled. 'I've gathered *shirimmooyi*. Have a taste!'

*Shirimmooyi* are the fruit of bird cherry plants that grow in river valleys. Before deep autumn its fruit, hackberries, aren't sweet. 'I don't like sour berries,' I answered loudly and walked past her *shirangju*.

Yveline chased after me. 'It's the first time you've hunted with Linke, and you killed a *kandahang*. From now on we'll dress you up as a boy and send you out on the hunt!'

I pursed my lips in contempt and said nothing.

I was going to Nidu the Shaman's. I knew that when a bear or a *kandahang* was killed, he made offerings to the *Malu*. We would build a triangular shelter in front of Nidu the Shaman's *shirangju*, remove the animal's head, and hang it facing the direction in which we would next relocate our camp. Then we would take the head down and set it, along with the animal's gullet, liver and lungs, before the *Malu* shrine inside the *shirangju*. From the right to the left, branches would be placed on top of the innards, and covered with an animal hide as if to block them from view and allow the *Malu* to enjoy them in privacy.

The next day, Nidu the Shaman would dissect the heart of the bear or the *kandahang*, taking out each of the *Malu* from the leather bag, smearing their mouths with blood from the animal's heart, and then replacing them in the bag.

Afterwards he cut a few slices of fat off the hunted animal and threw them into the fire. When the fat sizzled and oozed oil, he covered the slices with *kawaw* grass. As its aromatic smoke suffused the air, he took the leather bag containing the *Malu* and swayed it repeatedly over the smoke, as if he were placing an item of clothing in a stream to cleanse it. Then he hung the Spirits back in their shrine, which was directly across from the entrance to the *shirangju*, and the memorial ceremony was complete.

Now we could divide and eat the animal's heart, liver and lungs. Since Dashi's eyesight was poor, the liver was generally given to him. He sliced it with a knife and ate it raw and bloody. The corners of his lips were soaked in blood, and his chin was soiled with bits and pieces of blood too. It was revolting.

The animal's heart is distributed equally according to the number of *shirangju*, and it's basically eaten raw too. I eat uncooked meat but I don't eat organs raw, because they are receptacles for blood, so eating them is like sucking blood.

Many times I wanted to go and look at the Spirits inside the leather bag during a ritual, but each time I missed my chance. I wondered: after a Spirit's mouth is smeared with blood, does it pucker like a human's?

Since the women had begun drying meat-strips, it was obvious that the *kandahang* had been transported back to the camp last night, and the ceremony was over. But I went to Nidu the Shaman's to try my luck anyhow.

An unfamiliar grey-white speckled reindeer stood outside his *shirangju*. It was fitted with a saddle, which meant someone had been riding it. It looked like a stranger had arrived in our camp.

All those who came in search of Nidu the Shaman were from neighbouring *urireng*, but they weren't our clansmen. They had but one goal in seeking Nidu the Shaman: to request he perform a Spirit Dance.

Not every *urireng* had its own Shaman. Whenever someone became seriously ill, they would follow the tree markers until they found an *urireng* with a Shaman and entreat the Shaman to exorcise the illness. They came bearing gifts, like a wild duck or a pheasant, to be presented in tribute to the *Malu*. When a Shaman returned from performing a Spirit Dance, he typically brought back a reindeer, a gift of gratitude. Only rarely would a Shaman refuse.

In my memory, Nidu the Shaman had twice been requested to perform a Spirit Dance outside our *urireng*. Once was to treat a middle-aged man who had suddenly gone blind, and the other was to cure a child with scabies. To treat the man's blindness he left for three days, but he came back same day after dancing for the child. It is said that Nidu the Shaman restored vision to that man who had been in darkness a dozen days; as for the boy, in the midst of Nidu the Shaman's trance dance, scabs formed over the blisters and the pus ceased flowing.

When I entered the *shirangju*, Nidu the Shaman was putting his ritual items in order. A big-mouthed man, stooped over, his face covered in dust, waited beside him.

'*Egdi'ama*,' I asked, 'are you leaving to treat someone's illness?'

He lifted his head and gave me a look but didn't say anything about leaving to perform a Spirit Dance. 'The *kandahang* you killed yesterday is very big, the meat is good and the hide will be fine too. I told your Aunt Yveline that after she tans the skin, she should make you a pair of boots.'

Yveline's handiwork was the finest. The boots she made were both light and solid, and she embossed all sorts of eye-catching decorations on the bootlegs. It seemed he knew that I had gone *kandahang* hunting with Linke and considered my behaviour commendable, or else he wouldn't have instructed Yveline to make me boots.

But I wasn't interested in boots. I wanted to accompany Nidu the Shaman to another *urireng* and observe his Spirit Dance.

I watched him gather the Spirit Robe, Spirit Headdress, Spirit Trousers, Spirit Skirt and Spirit Cape, wrap them in a Tibetan-blue cloth, and place them together with the Spirit Drumstick, made from a roe-deer leg, in a leather bag.

When he took them outside, I spoke up. *'Egdi'ama*, I want to go with you.'

He shook his head. 'The road will be long and it won't be safe or convenient to take you. And I'm not leaving home just for fun. Some day soon I'll take you to Jurgang. There's lots to see there – shops and horse-drawn carriages and inns.'

'I just want to watch you perform your Spirit Dance for someone. I don't want to go to Jurgang.'

'This time I'm not going to do a Spirit Dance for a person, it's for some sick reindeer,' he said. 'Nothing worth watching. You stay here and help your mother make jerky.'

'But Tamara has already dried the meat-strips!' I said angrily.

Nidu the Shaman stared at me. He couldn't believe that I didn't address my mother as '*Eni*', and called her 'Tamara' like Linke.

'Did the *kandahang* you killed last night run off with your memory? Have you forgotten how to say "*Eni*"?'

His scornful tone irked me. 'If you don't let me go,' I said spite-fully, 'no matter what Spirit Dance you perform, it won't cure anything! It won't cure anything at all!'

My words made the hand in which Nidu the Shaman held the leather bag quiver.

If you asked me if I have ever spoken wrongly in my life, I would answer that on that summer's day over seventy years ago, I shouldn't have cursed those sick reindeer. If Nidu the Shaman had cured them, perhaps the fate of Linke, Tamara and Nidu the Shaman might have been otherwise, and I wouldn't find my recollections so painful.

Nidu the Shaman returned three days later. We all assumed the reindeer in that *urireng* had been saved, because the men who accom-panied Nidu the Shaman on his return brought two reindeer to thank him. One was brown and white-spotted, the other grey-black.

The men told us that during the spring a yellowish snow fell around their *urireng*, and it was said that reindeer that ate such snow would catch a deadly infectious disease. The snow fell late at night when their herders were deep in sleep, so the reindeer – who forage at night – ate the tinted snow without their knowledge.

They feared the reindeer would grow sick and every day they prostrated themselves before *Alung*, the Spirit that protects rein-deer, but the reindeer still took ill. After Nidu the Shaman's dance, the reindeer that had been lying on the ground for days were able to stand up. Oddly, while the man recounted all of this, Nidu the Sha-man's face showed no joy.

At that time the reindeer had not fully moulted, so the fact that the two newly arrived reindeer had what looked like small scars on their backs didn't arouse anyone's suspicions, as some reindeer have such marks when shedding intensely.

Reindeer are naturally gregarious, and the next day the newly arrived reindeer went out with the others to forage, departing at dusk and returning at dawn. When they returned to the camp, their bodies carried a balmy scent of morning dew.

To ward off the mosquitoes and horseflies that harass reindeer, we lit a fire using fresh grass, which gives off a lot of smoke. Some of the animals lay resting on the ground while others licked salt. It was when Tamara fed salt to the reindeer that she discovered there was something amiss with the two new arrivals. Unlike the other reindeer, which licked the salt greedily like parched plants sucking up rain, the pair showed no appetite whatsoever.

Tamara thought that since the reindeer had just arrived they were being shy like humans, so she put her salted palm right up to their lips. Perhaps they didn't want to disappoint good-hearted Tamara, and they stuck out their tongues and licked a bit, but very reluctantly. When they finished licking, they even began to cough.

Tamara sensed there was something odd with these two reindeer. 'The new reindeer aren't very lively,' she said. 'Let's keep them in the camp rather than letting them go out with the others.'

But Linke joked with Tamara. 'Those two bucks have been gelded. Now they've come and discovered all the lovely does here and it's almost mating season but they can't do anything. They're nostalgic for their virility, so they're a bit depressed.'

Tamara's face turned red. 'Do you suppose reindeer are like you, obsessed with such thoughts all day long?' Father chuckled and so did Mother, and their laughs tempered their worries.

But not long after we discovered that most of the reindeer were shedding very heavily. Patches of scars appeared like a pot-holed road eroded by torrential rains. And they didn't care to lick salt either. The time of their daily return was delayed until noon, and when they arrived back in the camp they simply collapsed on the ground.

One day, after it returned to camp and lay down, the white-spotted newcomer was unable to right itself again. And then its companion, the grey-black one, died. The departure of these two reindeer suddenly awakened us to the truth: they had brought the much-feared epidemic with them, and our reindeer were fated to suffer. Nidu the Shaman had not only failed to cure the reindeer in the other *urireng*, he had brought our lively herd of reindeer to the brink of death!

Overnight, Nidu the Shaman's cheeks caved in.

He gloomily donned his Spirit Robe, Spirit Headdress, Spirit Skirt and Spirit Trousers, and began his trance dance to save our reindeer. My memory of this Spirit Dance is extraordinarily clear: Nidu the Shaman began as the first brushstrokes of black appeared against the sky, and until the moon rose and myriad stars filled the sky, his feet didn't stop moving. Beating the drum, he raised his head and cried loudly, then lowered his head and moaned. He danced until the moon sank in the west and the east turned white, and then he collapsed.

He had danced for a full seven or eight hours, and his feet had stamped a big hole inside his *shirangju*. He collapsed in that hole, and no breathing could be heard. But not long after, a '*wuwa wuwa*' cry rang out. From his wailing, we realised that our reindeer were doomed too.

That bout of the reindeer plague continued for almost two months. In front of our eyes, our beloved reindeer lost their coats, collapsed on the ground and died, day after day. The weather cooled, the leaves yellowed, grass dried and mushrooms appeared, but there remained only thirty or so reindeer capable of eating them.

Linke painstakingly selected those thirty head from among the sick. He herded them to a place bordered on three sides by mountains and one by water, restricting their activities to that area and isolating them from other reindeer. As for those that stayed behind in the camp, each and every one died. During that time, we buried reindeer virtually each day. To prevent the spread of the epidemic to other *urireng*, we dug deep, deep pits.

The ravens were extremely active. They circled above our camp, screeching, '*Ya! Ya!*' Dashi released his hawk to banish those horrific creatures but they were too numerous. As soon as you drove away one throng, another arrived. They were oppressive jet-black clouds. When Dashi saw us burying the reindeer, he wailed '*ululu*' until teardrops criss-crossed his face. But no one heeded him, because our hearts were teeming with tears too.

During the reindeer epidemic we didn't move camp or hunt. We didn't move because we didn't want the plague to spread and harm the reindeer of other *urireng*.

When Linke brought those thirty or so reindeer back among us, many of us cried, for Linke had managed to preserve the 'fire source' upon which our lives depended.

Those reindeer had already begun to grow their winter fur. Even though they looked frail after surviving the pestilence, they liked to eat salt again and could go out on their own to forage reindeer moss. Everyone treated Linke like a hero. He looked gaunt but his eyes were radiant, as if the gazes of the dead reindeer had gathered in his eyes.

But over the course of the epidemic Nidu the Shaman aged radically. Never fond of speaking, he became even more taciturn. When the reindeer were buried, he removed the bells from their necks, and they occupied two whole birch-bark baskets. He put them in his *shirangju* and often gazed absentmindedly at them. His eyes were spiritless, and those bells looked like spiritless eyes too.

Except for Dashi, no one reproached him. One day Dashi asked Nidu the Shaman: 'Do you know why your Spirit Power has grown useless? I'll tell you. It's because you don't have a woman at your side. Without a woman, how can you have power?'

Nidu the Shaman's lips quivered, but he made no retort. Sitting right beside them, Ivan was very angry that Dashi could be so brazen. 'You don't have a woman either. Does that mean you are powerless too?'

'Of course I have power,' yelled Dashi. 'I have *Omolie*!'

Ivan denigrated the hawk. 'It survives off animals killed by others. All it knows how to do is open its trap and gobble up meat. It's damn useless!'

Dashi was so angry that his eyes almost popped out of their sockets. 'My *Omolie* is a Spirit Hawk used to exact revenge. It needs to conserve its energy. You can't expect it to behave like an ordinary hunting bird.'

From that day onward, Dashi refused food. At mealtimes, he placed the hawk on his shoulder and went to Ivan's *shirangju*. 'Ivan,' he yelled in a hoarse voice, 'come out and take a look! I haven't eaten anything. I gave my portion to my *Omolie*!'

Ivan paid him no heed. But when Nadezhda came out and saw

Dashi with his red eyeballs and bushy moustache that gave him a demonic look, she was so frightened that the blood drained from her face, and she couldn't help but cross herself.

Dashi fasted for three days. On the fourth, the hawk suddenly flew away. 'You've been good to him in vain, eh?' Hase said mockingly. 'He's just an animal after all. He left just like that, didn't he?'

Dashi maintained his calm. 'Just wait. My *Omolie* will return!'

That dusk the hawk did return with a noisy flap of the wings. But it didn't return alone; a pheasant dangled from his beak. It was a handsome cock with dark green plumage and a long, long tail. It placed the pheasant before Dashi. The old man's tears flowed at once, for he knew his *Omolie* had noticed he wasn't eating and made a kill for him.

If our *urireng* had previously thought Dashi's faith in his *Omolie*'s ability to avenge him was wishful thinking, the sudden departure and return of the bird convinced us that it was truly a Spirit Hawk, and we stopped mocking Dashi.

That evening Dashi was surely the most contented man on the face of the earth. He sat by the hearth and plucked the pheasant's feathers. He severed the head, wings and tail with a knife, and along with the innards he had removed, wrapped them all inside a bunch of soft branches. Then with his characteristic limp and a twist he hobbled over to a pine tree outside his *shirangju* and hung them there – a wind-burial ritual for the pheasant that he had never bothered to perform in the past.

When we ate pheasant, we never plucked the feathers on its head, wings and tail. Instead, we cut these parts off and hung them from the tree, feathers and all. But Dashi looked down upon people who did this, saying that only a bear or a *kandahang* was worthy of such ritual. When he ate pheasant sometimes he didn't even pluck the feathers. He just removed the organs, roasted it and ate it whole.

So Dashi always ate pheasant by himself – others wouldn't touch it – since meat that had not undergone the burial ritual was not pure.

When Dashi had finished the rite on behalf of the pheasant, he roasted the meat until it was cooked through, tore off a few strips of meat to feed his hawk, and then he ate. Perhaps because he had fasted for three days and felt somewhat distant from the act of eating, Dashi ate languidly. He ate from the moon's rise in the east to its descent in the west.

When he finished, he rambled about the camp leaning on his cane with *Omolie* perched on his shoulder until he finally stopped in front of Ivan's *shirangju*. He made his *ululu* cooing sound, a signal for Ivan to come out. Ivan stepped out of his *shirangju* to find Dashi grinning at him. 'That's the most chilling smile I've ever seen,' Ivan told me later.

\* \* \*

That was the winter we relocated most frequently. Squirrels aside, game was uncharacteristically rare. We saw many dead roe-deer in the valleys. Linke said they had caught the epidemic for sure.

Game were sparse, but not wolves. They probably couldn't find anything to eat, so they often followed us in packs of four or five. We and our remaining thirty or so reindeer were the foodstuff of their dreams. At night's onset, the howling of the wolves surrounding our camp sounded exceptionally shrill and mournful. We had to keep the bonfire outside our *shirangju* alive through the night. As fierce as a wolf's eyes are, they fear the fire's eyes.

When Dashi heard the wolves howling, he clenched his fist and gnashed his teeth noisily. He trained his hawk even more frequently using the she-wolf's hide. Indeed, *Omolie* looked more vigilant than ever, full of fighting spirit, poised to exact revenge on Dashi's behalf.

It was in the coldest time of that year that Dashi and his beloved *Omolie* took leave of us for ever.

Dashi reacted to any wolf howl with anger, but his hawk would just raise its head yet remained unruffled. But Hase said the night that Dashi met with his doom even the hawk was agitated, taking wing and alighting inside the *shirangju* as if disturbed by something. Seeing the hawk in that state, Dashi roared with laughter. 'The time for revenge has arrived at last!' he said, over and over.

Maria and Hase had long ago grown accustomed to Dashi's peculiar behaviour and went to sleep without taking any notice.

Hase awoke the next morning, and seeing neither Dashi nor his hawk, assumed they'd gone over to Ivan's. Ever since he and Ivan had squared off over Nidu the Shaman's Spirit Power, Dashi loved to go to Ivan's and swagger.

But he wasn't at Ivan's. Hase went looking around other *shirangju*, but Dashi was nowhere to be found. Knowing that lame Dashi couldn't have gone far and was probably in the nearby forest with his *Omolie* searching for prey, Hase wasn't too anxious.

The *Malu* King that transported the carvings of the Spirits and the reindeer that carried the live cinders had both survived the epidemic. For us, they were two fireballs burning bright in the middle of our dark night.

After the plague, when the reindeer finished foraging they would return in a queue, with the white *Malu* King at the very front and the grey fire carrier at the tail end. They were like the parents of an extended family, faithfully guarding their few surviving offspring.

That morning the reindeer returned with the *Malu* King at the front as usual, but when Linke came out to meet the reindeer he noticed there was something dangling from the *Malu* King's mouth: a wing. Finding this odd, he took the wing in his hand, examined it closely, and his heart filled with foreboding.

Grey with hints of white spots and dark-green stripes, wasn't this the very wing of Dashi's *Omolie*?

Wing in hand, Linke rushed to find Hase. With one glance Hase realised this was ominous and ran to inform Nidu the Shaman, but he wasn't in the camp either. Hase and Linke went to search for him, but before they'd gone far they saw him linking wooden poles between four straight pine trees. Hase collapsed on the spot, for he knew that Nidu the Shaman must be constructing Dashi's wooden burial platform.

People who died back then all underwent wind-burial. Four very erect trees at right angles to one another were selected and wooden poles were laid horizontally on top of a branch of each tree, forming a four-sided platform. The corpse was placed on it with the head to the north and feet to the south, and then covered with branches.

Nidu the Shaman had read from the stars that Dashi would be leaving us. In the middle of the night he saw a shooting star pass over the camp, and from the chorus of wolf howls, he ascertained that the one who would be leaving was Dashi. So he arose early in the morning to select the location for Dashi's wind-burial.

Everyone followed the reindeer's tracks and found Dashi in a birch grove near the camp. Or more accurately, we found a battle-ground. Many white birch saplings had been snapped at the trunk and their branches speckled with blood; the wormwood in the snow had been trampled flat, and we could imagine how savage the strug-gle had been.

Sprawled sideways on the battleground were four incomplete skeletons: those of two wolves, one human and a hawk. Linke said that one of the two wolves was most certainly the cub that had escaped from Dashi's hands years ago. It had followed Dashi's scent, and accompanied by its own offspring, the now grown-up cub had come to avenge its long-dead mother.

Yveline and I saw Dashi at the wind-burial site, or should I say, we saw a pile of bones. The largest of them was the skull. There was also a pile of bones of unequal thicknesses and lengths with pink flesh stuck to them, like a pile of dry firewood.

Based on traces left behind, Linke and Ivan surmised that the hawk had indeed helped Dashi exact revenge, but they were ser-iously injured during their struggle against the wolves and eventually immobilised. The wolves died, but neither Dashi nor his hawk could return home. The stench of blood attracted a handful of voracious wolves. They came running and devoured Dashi and his hawk. They didn't eat their own kind, but those two dead wolves didn't escape being eaten either: in the wee hours of the morning, a throng of ravens and hawks made a sumptuous breakfast of them.

On their way back to camp, the reindeer saw the swathe of white bones. From the remnants of the hawk they sensed Dashi must be dead too, and so the *Malu* King returned with *Omolie*'s wing dan-gling from its mouth as a sign of the calamity.

Whenever it occurs to me that it's likely Dashi and his hawk were gobbled up by wolves while still breathing, I can't help but feel shivers run down my spine. In our lives, wolves are gusts of icy wind that assault us. But we can't exterminate them any more than we can halt the onslaught of winter.

Nidu the Shaman buried the hawk's skeleton with Dashi. Dashi was indeed fortunate, because he finally witnessed the annihilation of his despised enemy, and he was buried together with his beloved *Omolie*.

Standing before the pile of bones that was Dashi, Yveline told me that he was actually crippled in an attempt to protect our reindeer. In the summertime, wolves love to attack the fawns at the rear of the reindeer herd. Once three fawns had strayed and Dashi went to search for them. He found them trembling, cornered on a cliff by a pair of wolves, one old and one young.

Dashi didn't have a rifle on him, just a hunting knife, so he picked up a rock and threw it, hitting the old wolf squarely on the head. Its face bloodied, it pounced on Dashi in all its rage. Dashi struggled against it bare-handed, but during the struggle the young wolf bit into Dashi's leg and wouldn't let go. At long last Dashi beat the old wolf to death, but the cub escaped with Dashi's leg in its jaws.

Those three fawns were safe and sound and returned to camp with Dashi. But they returned on foot while Dashi crawled back, dragging a blood-soaked wolf-skin.

Now the hawk and Dashi were gone. The hawk's home is in the Heavens and Dashi went with it, with no worries about their future abode.

After Dashi departed, Maria suddenly took ill. She vomited everything she ate and became so weak she couldn't stand up.

Everyone thought Maria's days were numbered. Only Yveline said that in the future, when Maria saw fresh blood run from severed antlers, she wouldn't cry any more. Everyone understood that Yveline thought Maria was pregnant.

But based on Maria's symptoms, both Tamara and Nadezhda surmised that she wasn't pregnant, she must be seriously ill. Who had seen a pregnant woman who even threw up the water she drank? Maria grew thinner by the day, and even she thought her days were numbered.

'Hase,' she said, 'after I die you absolutely must promise to take another wife, an able-bodied woman capable of bearing a child!' Hase cried. He told Maria if she left him, he'd turn into a swan goose and chase after her into the Heavens.

But Hase didn't transform into a swan goose, for one day Maria suddenly sat upright and could drink and eat. As spring approached her belly grew big and her face full and bright. It seemed Yveline had surmised correctly. From then on Maria and Hase were always smiling.

Yveline concluded that Maria had been infertile for years because Dashi had skinned the she-wolf and kept that unlikely hide with him. Now Dashi and the wolf-skin were no more, and an air of darkness and gloom no longer occupied their *shirangju*, so Maria had become pregnant.

But Hase and Maria didn't see things that way. On the contrary, they believed that it was Dashi's soul that ensured they could have a child, because Dashi had always yearned for his own *omolie*. They even settled on a name for their unborn child: Dashi.

Yveline pursed her lips. 'Anyone named "Dashi" can't help but be ill-fated. Wasn't one lame Dashi enough for our *urireng*?'

When spring came the does bore fawns, but of each ten born, eight or nine died. 'The epidemic weakened the constitution of the reindeer,' explained Linke. 'The fawns born of their coupling are naturally inferior, so many will die. We must hurry to barter for a few head of strong, healthy bucks before the next mating season in late autumn. Otherwise, next spring's fawns will be just as unlikely to brighten our spirits.'

Later that year Linke decided to go to the *Shituruyiche Inengi* on the banks of the Pa Béra and trade for reindeer. This festival was our traditional day of celebration for a season of bountiful hunting, and it coincided with the beginning of the rainy season.

Before I was born, people crossed the Argun to Pokrovka for the celebrations. They gathered to sing, dance and trade the goods they had obtained through hunting. Some married across clan lines, and it was there that Hase and Maria met and became engaged.

But later the celebrations were relocated to Jurgang Village on the banks of the Pa Béra. Many *anda* brought their horse caravans that transported rifles, ammunition and all sorts of manufactured goods, and traded with the hunting peoples during the festival. And the various *urireng* traded among themselves too.

Rolinsky was our trusted *anda* and we normally exchanged our entire catch with him. We rarely lacked for anything, so even though our clan always sent people to celebrate the *Shituruyiche Inengi*, our *urireng* rarely did. My impression is that during those years Nidu the Shaman and Kunde each went once.

Nidu the Shaman went to perform a ritual dance for a shaman who had lived on the banks of the Pa Béra and ascended the Heavens just before the festival.

Kunde went in the hopes of exchanging birch-bark buckets for four horses. He transported several dozen buckets of various shapes and sizes on reindeer, but returned with just one scrawny nag.

When Yveline made fun of him, Kunde's jowls trembled like a skirt in the wind. 'If only those *anda* weren't there on the Pa Béra. I'd have bartered direct with the Mongols, and I could've got at least three horses. Those *anda* are all wolves!'

But that skinny horse was with us short of a year when it dropped dead.

It was a dreary day that Linke set out for the river with his catch and extra bullets to trade for a few robust bucks. Mother had a premonition of some sort, and just before Father was to depart, she gave orders to the hound that would accompany him: 'Ilan, you must protect Linke and make sure that he comes back safe and sound with our reindeer.' Ilan always followed Father around and understood us well. When Tamara finished speaking, he put his paws on her legs and nodded.

Having obtained the dog's promise, Mother's face lightened and she leaned over and petted Ilan's forehead. Her tenderness made Ilan a bit giddy, and he barked, delighting Luni and me.

'Put your heart at ease,' Father said. 'With you back here, even if my body doesn't want to return, my heart won't agree!'

'Linke, your heart alone won't do,' Tamara protested. 'I want your body too!'

'My body and heart will both return!'

When the rainy season arrives, lightning often flashes over the forest, accompanied by the rumbling of thunder. Nidu the Shaman said there are two Thunder Spirits, one male and one female, who govern the weather in the mortal world. On his Spirit Robe were round pieces of iron representing the Sun Spirit and crescent-shaped ones for the Moon Spirit, and forked tree branches symbolising the Thunder Spirits. When he performed his Spirit Dance, those metallic totems of every shape and hue clanged against one another, and I reckoned it was a Thunder Spirit speaking, for the Sun and the Moon are mute.

When thunder sounded, I took it for the Heavens coughing. When the cough was slight, it was light rain that fell; when the cough was deeper, it was heavy rain that fell. When it rained lightly, it must be the Female Thunder Spirit appearing; when it rained heavily, it must be the Male Thunder Spirit appearing.

The Male Thunder Spirit's prowess was great. At times He propelled balls of fire, sundering the big trees in the forest and leaving them pitch-black. So typically when thunder rumbled, we stayed in our *shirangju*. If we were outside, we would certainly choose a flat area near a body of water and avoid big trees.

Not long after Father left the camp, the sky turned even gloomier, the thick clouds of deep autumn gathered and the air was oppressive. The birds flew low, and the breeze grew into a gale that made the forest vibrate with a *hwa-hwa* sound.

Mother glanced at the sky. 'Do you think this rain is going to fall?'

I knew she was worried about Father on the road and hoped it wouldn't rain. 'It looks to me like this wind will blow the clouds away,' I said sympathetically. 'The rain won't fall.'

Tamara seemed reassured and cheerfully went off to gather the wormwood drying in the shade outside the *shirangju*. When it was in season, we'd collect a lot, dry some and use it to stew meat in the winter.

Just as mother was bringing the wormwood into the *shirangju*, a clap of thunder suddenly roared. The forest shuddered and lit up for an instant, and then came the pitter-patter of raindrops. They began falling from the south-east, and rain from that direction often grows into a storm.

The Male Thunder Spirit probably felt the rain wasn't heavy enough, so He cleared His throat more forcefully, and coughed up bolts of lightning that danced like golden serpents in the sky. When they disappeared, the woods reverberated – *wa-wa, wa-wa*. The rain was so heavy that it seemed to have lost its soul, flying and dashing in all directions. What appeared in the air was no longer a rain curtain comprised of fine braided raindrops, but a downward-surging river.

Mother listened, so frightened that her mouth remained agape. If she believed in the Virgin Mary like Nadezhda, I thought to myself, she'd certainly cross herself over and over.

When the lightning lit up our faces, Mother's blanched face wasn't all I could see; the terror deep within her eyes was also illuminated. It was such an extreme terror that all my life I've never forgotten her gaze.

Mother's gaping mouth closed only when the rain ceased. She looked utterly fatigued, as if she had transformed into the Female Thunder Spirit during the storm, and gone and fabricated wind and rain.

'Your *Ama* won't run into trouble, now, will he?' she asked me feebly.

'Why would he be in trouble?' I said. 'It's just another rainstorm. He's seen plenty of them.'

Mother relaxed noticeably. 'That's right,' she reassured herself. 'What hasn't Linke been through?'

Rainbows appeared in the sky after the rain. The first was hazy, but then another appeared, distinct and brightly coloured. When the second rainbow emerged, the first grew vivid too. The two rainbows were curved and gaily hued, like a pheasant flaunting a pair of kaleidoscopic feathers: reds, yellows, greens and purples were all on show. The entire *urireng* came out to view the rainbows, and everyone was enchanted.

But even as we watched, the colours of one rainbow suddenly paled and vanished. The other, although still complete, aged abruptly and lost its vivid colours; it seemed as though dust had flown into it, rendering it murky. The rainbow's altered hues changed the colours of our faces. Everyone knew this was an unfavourable omen, and Mother went back to our *shirangju* ahead of the others.

Only when the virtually black rainbow vanished did she come out again. Teardrops hung from her face. She was already mourning for Father.

Ilan came back at dusk. When he saw mother, he put his paws on her lap, eyes moist. His forlorn gaze convinced mother that Father was gone. She patted the hound's forehead roughly. 'Ilan, what did I tell you? How come you didn't bring Linke back with you?'

Father was struck by lightning while passing through a dense pine grove. Two big, muscular trees were also hit. They were split in two at the waist, and there were scorch marks at the point of cleavage.

It was already deep in the night when Ilan led us to the scene of the accident. Father's body was hunched over, laid out against a severed tree stump, head and arms dangling as if he had grown tired of walking and was resting. The night sky was exceptionally bright after the storm, and the moonlight lit up each tree, and Father.

I cried and Mother cried too. I called '*Ama*' over and over, while Mother wailed, 'Linke, oh my Linke!'

Nidu the Shaman was in the pine grove throughout the night where he selected four big trees at right angles to one another, chopped a few poles, and placed them on branches to construct Father's wind-burial platform especially high up. Nidu the Shaman said that the Thunder Spirit took Linke away, and since thunder comes from the Heavens, it should be returned there, so his grave had to be a bit closer to the sky.

In the early morning we wrapped Father in a white cloth and raised him up to his final bed. Nidu the Shaman cut two shapes from birch-bark – a sun and a moon – and placed them on Father's head. I suppose he intended for Father to have light in the other-world. Even though the reindeer that remained with us were few, Nidu the Shaman still had Hase bring a reindeer and slaughter it. I think he wanted Father to have a reindeer to ride in the other-world. Father's clothing, hunting knife, tobacco case, hanging pot and flask were also placed with him for his wind-burial.

But before the burial, each of these objects was damaged by Luni according to Nidu the Shaman's instructions: he bashed the hunting knife against a stone to make the blade crooked; he poked a hole in the birch-bark tobacco box with a tanning knife; he cut off the collar and cuffs of Linke's upper garment with scissors; and he used a stone to smash an opening in the pot and kettle. It is said that if these things are not done, those who live on will meet with disaster.

These defective objects made me immeasurably sad. If his clothing lacked collars and cuffs, wouldn't Father's neck and arms feel cold? If the blade on his hunting knife were bent, how would he skin the game he caught? If his hanging pot and kettle leaked, what would he do when he cooked meat and the soup dripped, putting out the fire? When it occurred to me that none of the things Father was taking with him was still intact, I really wanted to cry. But I stifled myself, because I was afraid if I cried then Mother would lose herself in tears.

Ilan was Father's most beloved hunting dog, and it seemed he wanted to depart with Father. He kept using his paws to scrape the forest soil as if to dig his own grave. But when Nidu the Shaman steadied Ilan and was about to put his knife to the dog, Mother stopped him. 'Leave Ilan for me,' she said. Nidu the Shaman put away his knife.

Mother took Ilan and left Father before the wind-burial began. Nidu the Shaman feared Mother would take her own life, so he told Yveline to follow her. Afterwards, Yveline told everyone that along the way back to camp, Tamara walked and played like a little child; when she came upon a butterfly she caught it, when she came upon a bird she imitated its cry, when she came upon wild flowers she stuck one in her hair. So when she arrived back at the camp she had a basketful of flowers on her head.

She refused to enter our *shirangju*. Instead, she sat down and sobbed, and called out Father's name. 'You're not here any more. I won't go in, it's cold and lonely inside.'

Father was gone, taken away by thunder and lightning. From then on, I liked to listen to the thunder's rumble on dark, rainy days. It felt like that was Father speaking to us. His soul was surely hidden there, emitting earth-shaking thunder and blinding rays of light.

Father was not only unable to trade for the bucks of which he dreamed, he also took Mother's laughter and dresses away with him. Before, Tamara so loved to laugh and dress up, but after he left, these pleasures vanished from her person. She still liked to milk the does, but she'd squeeze and squeeze and then her hand would stop abruptly, and she'd be lost in vacant thought. When she cooked *khleb*, tears splattered on the hot stones that baked the bread. She didn't wear her deer-bone pin any more and her hair became a frizzy mess. When winter came her hair had the chilly ambience of winter cold. Not just dry and coarse, but also much whiter than before.

* * *

Mother was elderly now, but Luni and I had grown up. Shouldering the repeating rifle and *Berdanka* that Father left behind, Luni often went hunting with Ivan and Hase. He really was Linke's son, hitting his target with virtually every shot.

Our *urireng* had two big harvests that winter. One was a bountiful hunting season. We exchanged our many pelts for flour, salt and bullets, and also for twenty reindeer to replenish our troop with much needed fresh blood. The reindeer bells that we had saved from the time of the plague came in handy, and once again the bells accompanied the reindeer in song among the rivers and valleys.

The other harvest: Maria gave birth to a son at last. He was very lively, and Hase and Maria did name him 'Dashi.' Little Dashi loved to laugh and brought us much happiness.

After Father departed, Nidu the Shaman was a changed man. His chin used to be covered in stubble, but now he shaved it as smooth as silk. Before, he dressed like a woman, but now he resumed his manly appearance. 'Seems your *Egdi'ama* doesn't want to be a Shaman any more,' Yveline said sarcastically to Luni.

Besides his changed looks, the formerly reticent Nidu the Shaman took to inviting everyone to his *shirangju* to discuss even the pettiest matter. This was a big departure from his former style of deciding everything on his own. But Mother didn't like going to his abode, so if there was something to talk about, I was the one to go.

At those times Nidu the Shaman would ask me: 'Why doesn't Tamara come?'

'Why must she be the one who comes?' I'd ask him in return.

Ever since Linke's departure I felt an indescribable antipathy towards Nidu the Shaman. After all, if he hadn't brought the reindeer plague back with him to our *urireng*, Linke wouldn't have gone to trade for reindeer and wouldn't have been struck by lightning. Thinking of Nidu the Shaman's power to make a fawn die, I even wondered if he had beckoned that day's thunderbolt. He had always envied Father, so perhaps he made use of his Spirit Power to eliminate him with the arrows and knives of thunder.

When we moved camp Nidu the Shaman often trailed behind Mother. I think he secretly wanted to watch her back. In his eyes, perhaps Mother's backside was the sun and the moon. Otherwise, why was he forever pursuing her?

Reindeer don't always move at the same pace, and sometimes his would catch up with hers. As soon as Nidu the Shaman's reindeer came alongside Mother's, he'd cough, and he could even cough himself red.

'Nidu the Shaman, why don't you ride facing backwards?' Yveline said once. 'If you ride facing backwards the wind won't make you cough. But of course, then you'd be looking at me and not Tamara.'

Nidu the Shaman and Tamara got flustered, and Tamara gave

her reindeer a kick, urging it forward, while Nidu the Shaman stopped straight away and filled his pipe with tobacco. It was then that I had an inkling perhaps something was going to occur between Mother and Nidu the Shaman. When I recalled the wind-sounds that Tamara and Linke had made in our *shirangju*, I felt very wary of Nidu the Shaman. I certainly didn't want mother and him to kick up wind-sounds like that.

Those two years we moved camp especially frequently, and I wondered if that wasn't related to Nidu the Shaman's pleasure in watching Tamara's backside. Gradually, I realised just how important Tamara was to Nidu the Shaman. One time we were just about to pick up camp – we'd even disassembled our *shirangju* – when Mother lightly voiced a lament about the scenery: 'The flowers here are truly beautiful. It makes you hate to leave!'

Nidu the Shaman decided then and there to remain camped until those vibrantly coloured flowers had wilted.

One day Mother and I were milking the reindeer and she told me she had dreamed of a silver hairpin. Blossoms were engraved on the hairpin, and it was absolutely lovely. So I asked her: 'Is it as lovely as a hairpin made from deer-bone?'

'Many times over!' she said.

Nidu the Shaman, who was removing the halter from the reindeer next to us, overheard our conversation. 'What do we see in our dreams that isn't lovely?' he asked.

Even though he teased Tamara like that, on Rolinsky's next visit to our camp Nidu the Shaman told the *anda* to trade us a silver hairpin. I knew Nidu the Shaman had Tamara in mind. But ever since Lena's death, Rolinsky never brought women's goods for us, and each time he left in a rush.

'If you'd like to barter for a silver hairpin,' he answered good-naturedly, 'you should look for another *anda*, because I don't handle women's finery any more.'

His reply enraged Nidu the Shaman. 'In that case you needn't bother coming again to our *urireng*!'

Rolinsky didn't get angry, he just breathed a long sigh. 'That's fine, just fine. When I come to your *urireng* nowadays, I always feel very sad. My heart doesn't want to come, but when I remember you need to trade and we're old acquaintances, my legs bring me here. Beginning today, I don't have to come again, and my heart won't ache so.'

Everyone understood that it was Lena who made his heart ache. Just like that, an invisible silver hairpin pushed our most trusted *anda* away from us.

From then on, Turkov entered our lives. He was also a Russian *anda*, and behind his back we called him *dahé*, meaning 'catfish'. Not just because his mouth was big like a catfish's, but his temperament was also similar – his entire body seemed to be coated with a slippery gel.

For the first two years, the enthusiasm that Nidu the Shaman devoted to Tamara elicited no response whatsoever. But the appearance of a bird-feather skirt changed Tamara's attitude towards him. I discovered that, face to face with an object she loves, a woman finds herself hard-pressed to resist the temptation to possess it. But when she accepted that skirt, it was equivalent to accepting Nidu the Shaman's affection, and our clan does not permit that sort of relationship. Thus they were fated to go mad from the torment.

None of us had noticed that whenever Nidu the Shaman ate pheasant he carefully selected feathers from those he had plucked.

He collected them, and quietly sewed a skirt for Tamara, and his handiwork was exquisite.

The skirt lining comprised several pieces of coarse, dark-blue cloth, and it was shaped like a lily, with a tight waist and wide hemline. The size and colours of the feathers were not uniform, but they were all sewn with the quill pointing upwards and the pointed tip of the feather downwards. The thread used to set the feathers in place was made of fine *kandahang* tendon.

Nidu the Shaman first wrapped the thread around the shaft at the centre of each feather, and then stitched it onto the cloth so the feather itself was completely unharmed and intact, giving it a soft and delicate appearance.

Nidu the Shaman was a master at positioning the feathers. Smaller ones with finer barbs and subtle grey tones were placed at the waist; next came mid-sized feathers that were mainly green set off by wee bits of brown; and down where the skirt widened and at the hemline, he employed lustrous blue feathers speckled with yellow.

So the skirt comprised three parts: a grey river at the top, a green forest in the middle, and a blue sky at the bottom. When Nidu the Shaman presented it to mother, you can imagine her amazement, joy and gratitude. She held the skirt out in her arms and said this was the prettiest thing she had ever seen.

At first she laid it out on top of her bedding, gently caressing it. Then she carried it outside and hung it on a white birch, stood back from it and then went near, gazing at it all the while. The warm spring sun illuminated the feather skirt, and it was truly magnificent.

That sort of beauty can make a woman's heart flutter and her flesh tingle. Tamara's face reddened. 'Your *Egdi'ama* has a pair of magical hands. How could he ever have fashioned such a beautiful skirt?'

Mother was a squirrel racing about with its bushy tail held high. Nidu the Shaman was a master hunter, and that feather skirt was the *charka* he laid to snare her.

Deep in my heart I was glad that the skirt was created just for her. Her long-departed youthfulness and vitality reappeared, rendering her incomparably elegant and noble. But I still replied icily, 'You'll look like a big pheasant with that on!'

Mother's face went white. 'Am I really so unpresentable now?' she asked meekly. I gritted my teeth and nodded.

Tamara cried all afternoon and finally stored the skirt away in the evening. 'Let's keep it for you to wear when you get married. In another few years you can probably put it to use.'

Although Tamara never wore that feathered skirt formally, from time to time she would hold it in her arms, utterly enchanted for an instant, and her eyes would look so very tender.

She often hung about Nidu the Shaman's *shirangju*, perhaps unwittingly. But if he suddenly came out, she'd utter a frightened 'Oh!' and turn to run away. Only a woman whose heart has been conquered by a man fears the very sight of his shadow.

Tamara painstakingly crafted two items for Nidu the Shaman: roe-deerskin *beri* – gloves – and a *kabtuk*, a tobacco pouch.

Back then we wore mittens that were easy to make. But what Tamara crafted for Nidu the Shaman were five-fingered gloves of short-furred roe-deerskin. She spent half a month executing the needlework, embroidering three circles at the wrist: one contained fire, one water, and one clouds. I still recall the one in the middle was fire, while water was above and the clouds below.

When she finished, she asked me what I thought of the patterns. Since I knew she was making them for Nidu the Shaman, I ridiculed her: 'Clouds and water together makes sense, but where on earth can you find water and fire together?' My words turned Tamara's face pale, and she said 'Ow!', as if she'd been pricked with a needle.

So when she next handcrafted a *kabtuk*, she didn't apply any pattern. The pouch was made from the skins of a pair of roe-deer legs in the shape of a calabash. She sewed trimming onto the opening and seams, and a sac containing a flint dangled from it.

At first Tamara tied one of Father's flints to the *kabtuk*, but when Luni and I discovered this, we stole it, so in the end the tobacco pouch Tamara gave to Nidu the Shaman had no flint.

It's strange to say, but that winter when Nidu the Shaman put on those roe-deerskin gloves, his fingers became very nimble and he shot two animals that are tough kills, a fox and a lynx. Their pelts are the most valuable and this made him unspeakably happy. He treated that tobacco pouch like a talisman and always hung it from the right side of his waist.

More than once I told Yveline that I hoped Nidu the Shaman and Tamara wouldn't end up together in the same *shirangju*. But Yveline always replied that that would be impossible, because they could not live together. 'Nidu the Shaman is Linke's elder brother. According to our clan's customs, if your elder brother dies, you can take his widow as your wife. But an elder brother cannot marry the widow of his younger brother.'

Yveline gave me an example: if Nidu the Shaman died and Linke were still alive, then Linke could marry *Egdi'ama*'s widow.

'But *Egdi'ama* doesn't have a woman, so if *Ama* wanted to marry the woman his brother left behind, it would have to be a *Malu* in the deerskin pouch! But how could *Ama* father a child with a Spirit?'

It turned out that like me, the matter of Nidu the Shaman and Tamara had also troubled Yveline, but my words made her burst out laughing. She rubbed her crooked nose, chortled '*Aiyo, aiyo!*' and called out my name repeatedly, as if trying to retrieve my soul. 'You're old enough to get married but you still talk like a child!'

Yveline didn't usually talk about Linke, but when Tamara and Nidu the Shaman began to gaze at each other, she began to mention Father when everyone was sitting together discussing affairs. How Linke learned to shoot a bow when just five, how Linke could make snowshoes when just nine, how Linke was faster than a squirrel, or how he caught a hare on foot when he was ten.

Then she'd turn towards Mother and say: 'Tamara, if you'd seen Linke when he was young, you would have wanted to grow up as quickly as possible so you could marry sooner!' Mother would cast a doleful glance at Nidu the Shaman, and he'd lower his head as if he'd done something wrong.

Gradually Nidu the Shaman and Tamara stopped sitting together, for they sensed everyone's hostility towards their affection. From then onwards, each time Tamara opened up the bird-feather skirt, she'd break out in waves of odd laughter.

That laugh reminded me of the strange emotion that swept across Dashi's face when he spread out the wolf-skin and urged his hawk to pounce on it. Her laughter made your hair stand on its end, and it drove Luni and me out of our *shirangju*. We looked dumbly at the sky, longing for a gust of wind that would whisk away her cackling.

I had become a young lady, and Luni had also grown up and

begun to grow a beard. We watched Tamara wither day by day, her back bent over.

One time little Dashi came to our *shirangju*. He looked at Mother and suddenly said, 'Your head is covered with snow. Aren't you cold?'

Tamara knew little Dashi was referring to her increasingly numerous grey hairs. 'I'm cold indeed,' she said bleakly. 'But what's to be done? Perhaps a thunderbolt will take pity on me, carry me away and put an end to my suffering.'

From then on, each time there was a thunderstorm Mother would run off into the forest. I knew what she sought. But the thunderbolts would not serve as a noose around her neck. They just wanted to strike her with the raindrops they had brought to life.

Soaked and shivering, her hair dishevelled, she would return safely to the camp, and then Nidu the Shaman would begin to chant. As soon as he began, little Dashi would rush into Maria's embrace and wail. That song was too sorrowful.

Then the Japanese made their appearance. The year of their arrival, two major events occurred in our *urireng*: Nadezhda fled with Jilande and Nora back to the Left Bank of the Argun, an act that pushed lonely Ivan into an abyss. And I married a man, with hunger playing my matchmaker.

# PART TWO

# MID-DAY

*O*nce the flames in the fireplace grow faint, the coal's face is no longer red but grey.

I spot two embers that stand tall. A bellyful of tales seems to be smouldering within them, waiting for me to divine what they might be.

Traditionally, if you see an upright ember in the morning that means someone will arrive today – you should hurry to bow and offer a greeting, otherwise you're neglecting your guest. If you see an upright ember in the evening, you should knock it over because it foreshadows a ghost's arrival. But it is neither dawn nor dusk. So what's coming: a human or a ghost?

It's noon and the raindrops are still falling. An'tsaur walks in.

An'tsaur isn't a ghost, but he doesn't resemble a human either. I've always felt that the one to remain with me to the very end would be a Spirit.

When An'tsaur came into the shirangju just now, the embers collapsed. Perhaps they really do live and die for him.

An'tsaur puts a birch-bark basket in front of me. It contains several items he has picked up while tidying the campground: a roe-deerskin sock, a small iron hip flask, a colourful handkerchief, a deer-bone necklace and several white reindeer bells, all unintentionally left behind when Tatiana and the others moved this morning.

In the old days, when we relocated we always used soil to fill the holes we had dug for the fireplace and to fix the shirangju poles in place. Then we put all the rubbish together and buried it deep to avoid the stench, and so as not to scar the place that hosted us.

Even though they began taking stock of their possessions several days before departure, when the moment came to set out early this morning, *they still showed signs of confusion. From what they left behind, it seems not only were our people confused, so were our reindeer. As they jostled and butted one another, their bells fell to the ground.*

*But that makes sense. As Beriku said to me, the reindeer will be cooped up in pens with barbed-wire fences. They know they won't be free to roam in the mountains, so what use would bells be? They might just as well be dangling mute bells from their necks.*

*One look at the deerskin sock and you know it's Maksym's. It's so big.*

*The hip flask is Vladimir's. In the wee hours of the morning I saw him drinking, his mouth open, guzzling the* baijiu *while cooing 'ululu' as if he were very gay, or maybe very sad. It reminded me of old Dashi's throaty birdcall.*

*Vladimir forgot his flask. He'll be agitated when he gets to Busu, won't he? When Vladimir gets upset, it's Shiban who suffers because Vladimir takes it out on him. Vladimir either curses him for no reason or throws rocks at him and threatens to stone him to death. Busu is a town and perhaps stones aren't so easy to come by, so Vladimir won't be able to hit Shiban, he'll just swear at him. But cursing doesn't hurt the flesh, so Shiban won't have it so bad.*

*The coloured handkerchief is Beriku's. He loves to toy with girls' knick-knacks, and once I saw him wrap that handkerchief around his head, jerk his head up and down and shout 'Hey! Hey!' as he danced, like a woodpecker hammering 'tuk tuk' against a tree.*

*Beriku loved to dance as a youngster, and he used to dance quite handsomely too. His waist and neck did not shake as violently then. But after he bummed around in the city for a year and returned to the mountains, his dancing wasn't fit to watch. His waist rocked erratically and his neck gyrated madly. It made me feel like his neck was attached by a single tendon.*

*I hate the way he makes his voice hoarse and yells 'Hey! Hey!' when he dances. He was blessed with a crisp, clear voice, but he insists on making it raspy.*

*This deer-bone necklace is Lyusya's and she has worn it for several decades. It was polished by Viktor, my eldest son, and he strung it just for her. When Viktor was alive she wore it daily, but since he died, she only wears it to weep under the full moon.*

*When she left early this morning, I saw her clutching the necklace. She must have thought leaving it elsewhere was risky. Most probably a few reindeer weren't willing to get on the truck, and as everyone scrambled higgledy-piggledy to grab them, Lyusya helped out and lost the necklace in the midst of it all. It seems the thing you least want to lose slips out of your hands most easily.*

*An'tsaur adds a few pieces of firewood from wind-felled trees to the hearth. We never chop live trees for firewood. There are many things in the forest that can feed a fire, like naturally shed dry branches, trees struck by lightning, and those blown down by strong winds. We aren't like the Han who station themselves in the mountain forests. They chop down trees that are perfectly healthy, hack them into little pieces of firewood and stack them all around their houses.*

*It hurts just to look at those piles. I still remember many years ago when Valodya passed by a Han hamlet for the first time and saw mounds of firewood in front of every household. He came back and said anxiously to me that they didn't just cut the trees down and transport them to the outside world. They burned live trees every day! Sooner or later all the trees would be chopped down and burned, and then how would we and our reindeer survive?*

*Valodya was my second husband, the last Clan Chieftain of our people, and he was far-sighted about such things. The day that Tatiana summoned all the members of our* urireng *to vote on whether to leave the mountains, I recalled Valodya's words. When I cast my piece of birch-bark into the hearth – and not towards the Spirit Drum left behind by Nihau – I saw Valodya's smile there in the firelight.*

*An'tsaur adds water to my tea mug. 'We'll have meat at noon, Até,' he says. I nod.*

*Ever since Beriku told An'tsaur to address me as 'Nainai' – 'grand-mother' in the Han fashion – and not 'Até' in our language, An'tsaur stopped calling me anything. He probably thinks that now those who addressed me as 'Eni' and 'Bergeng' for 'sister-in-law' in Evenki and 'Gugu' for 'aunt' in the Han tongue have all left, and no one requires that he use 'Nainai' any more, so he can call me 'Até' again.*

*If I am an old tree that has lived through the wind and the rain with-out falling to the earth, then the children and grandchildren at my knees are branches on that tree. No matter how old I am, those branches con-tinue to flourish. And of all those branches, An'tsaur is the one I most adore.*

*An'tsaur's speech is often rather curt. After he said we'd have meat for lunch, he went to fetch half a pheasant left over from yesterday.*

*Knowing they were departing for good, the mountain-leavers wanted to treat us to a feast. As the time for departure approached, Maksym, Suchanglin and Shiban went hunting daily, but invariably returned empty-handed.*

*In recent years, like trees, wild animals have become increasingly scarce in the mountains.*

*Fortunately, Shiban killed two pheasants yesterday, and Suchanglin used a* lenz *– a contraption with sharp wooden stakes that allows fish in but not out – to corner a few fish in a cove, so last night there was a pleas-ant aroma wafting around the bonfire.*

Maksym told me that one day when they were searching for prey they spotted two grey cranes flying over a low-lying marsh in the forest. But just when Maksym was about to open fire, Shiban stopped him. Shiban said they'd be leaving the mountains soon, so they should save those birds for An'tsaur and me. If not, we couldn't gaze upon the loveliest fowl, and our eyes would suffer. Only my Shiban could say something so adorable.

I slice a piece of pheasant and throw it on the fire in veneration of the Fire Spirit, and only then do I sprinkle it with salt, spear it with a willow branch, and put it over the fire to roast. As An'tsaur and I eat the pheasant, he suddenly says: 'Look, Até, it's raining. Will there be water again in Rolinsky Ravine?'

Rolinsky Ravine was once a mountain stream with a plentiful source, and the children all loved to drink from it. But it ran dry six or seven years ago.

I shake my head, for I know one rainfall can't revive a mountain stream. Disappointed, An'tsaur puts down his food, stands up and walks away.

I put my food down too and sip my tea. Seeing the flames burning vigorously again, I'd like to continue recounting our tale. If rain and fire, this pair of foes, have tired of hearing me rattle on this morning, I'll have An'tsaur bring in the items that are inside the birch-bark basket, and they can lend an ear.

They must have been left behind for some very important purpose. So let the roe-deerskin sock, coloured handkerchief, hip flask, deer-bone necklace and reindeer bells come now and listen to my tale!

\* \* \*

If you had arrived in the forests on the Right Bank of the Argun seventy years ago, you'd have frequently encountered two things hanging between the trees: wind-burial coffins and *kolbo* for storing goods.

Actually, it was beneath a *kolbo* that I first encountered Lajide. Prior to that, a *kolbo* had just been a cache hanging high above the forest floor, but once Lajide and I became engaged under one, in my mind a *kolbo* became a square-shaped moon, because it lit up and warmed my formerly gloomy and solitary heart.

In the autumn of the twenty-first year of the Republic of China, what is now called 1932, Turkov the *anda* brought news to our *urireng* of the arrival of the Japanese. He came on horseback, bringing only a small amount of ammunition, flour, salt and liquor. He said the world belonged to the Japanese now, and that they had established the state of 'Manchukuo' in the historical homeland of the Manchu. Rumour had it that they intended to launch an attack on the Soviet Union very soon. Many Russian *anda* in Jurgang feared persecution by the Japanese, so they returned to the Left Bank. Trading became difficult and goods were in short supply.

Hase was furious that these measly items were all Turkov could offer us in exchange for more than one hundred squirrel pelts and our high-quality velvet antlers. 'Don't try to use the Japanese as an excuse to cheat us!' he said. 'Rolinsky was never so black-hearted!'

Turkov became hostile. 'I risked my neck to bring these things to you! Look around you now. How many blue-eyed *anda* still dare to do business under the eyes of the Japanese? If you think you're getting a raw deal, I'll take my things and be off. You can find somebody else to trade with!'

Back then with only a few remaining, our bullets were like the stars in the sky at dawn, the bags we used to store flour were shrivelled stomachs; and the salt our reindeer loved to lick was like snow on the ground in the spring wind, sparser by the day. The items that Turkov brought were lifesaving straws to be grasped no matter how high the price. In our hearts we cursed him: sly *dahé*! But we still traded with him.

Turkov appeared quite pleased as he readied his departure. 'Word has it that the Japanese are going to come in the mountains and eradicate people with blue eyes.' He looked to Jilande. 'Start running now – don't wait here to die!'

Jilande had always been chicken-hearted, and Turkov's words turned his face white and set his teeth chattering.

'I've lived here in the forest all my life,' he said tearfully. 'Why do the Japanese want to "eradicate" me?'

'The colour of your eyes! If they were black like the soil here, that'd be fine. You could take root. But they're sky-blue, and that's a dangerous colour indeed. You wait and see!'

Then Turkov turned to Nora. 'And if you don't flee, you'll be even more unlucky. The Japanese like to bed pretty blue-eyed maidens!'

Nadezhda's hair was already mostly grey, but she still looked quite sturdy. 'What's to be done?' she said to Ivan, crossing herself. 'Let's ask for Nidu the Shaman to help us turn our eyes and hair black!'

At crucial times like this, Nadezhda turned to our Spirits for aid. Perhaps because Nidu the Shaman was very close, while the Virgin Mary was far, far away.

'What's wrong with blue eyes?' said Ivan. 'My wife and children just happen to be blue-eyed! If any Japanese dares "eradicate" them, I'll "eradicate" what's sandwiched between his legs first!'

Ivan's words made everyone break out in laughter, everyone but Nadezhda, that is. She looked wistfully at Jilande and Nora, like a starving person who has picked two lovely mushrooms but — suspecting they're poisonous — just stares at them.

Jilande was listless, like grass suddenly covered in frost. As for Nora, she regarded her hands vacantly. Since she had dyed her fingernails in various hues, they weren't pink. They were purple and blue, yellow and green. Perhaps she was wondering if she could dye her fingernails, couldn't she dye her eyes black?

Jilande wasn't as rugged as his father Ivan. The frail boy had no interest in hunting and preferred women's chores like tanning hides, making birch-bark containers, sewing leather gloves, or gathering wild vegetables.

All the women in the *urireng* were fond of Jilande, but Ivan lamented that his son didn't act like a boy. 'How can a man who can't hunt win a wife?' he'd say.

The thing Nora most loved was dyeing fabric. She extracted liquid from fruits or blossoms, using blueberries to dye white cloth blue, and red love-peas for a bright pink tint.

She even coloured one piece with lily extract. Nora first picked a summer's worth of pink lily blossoms. She mashed them into a paste, squeezed an extract from it, which she salted and diluted with water, then let it stew in a pot all afternoon. In the evening, she rinsed the dyed cloth in the river, and spread it out on a blue-green poplar.

The first to see the cloth was Maria who thought it was the sun setting on our camp, and she shouted for everyone to come out. It really did resemble the sky at sunset, the rosy clouds after the rain, so lively and fresh. We all thought it was the Spirits revealing themselves!

If not for the distant sound of Nadezhda scolding Nora, no one would have realised what it was. 'You didn't clean the pot you used to dye your cloth. How am I to cook dinner?'

Only then did everyone gazing from afar realise that it was just a piece of dyed fabric, and they all left with a sigh.

But I didn't leave, I treated it as a genuine swathe of sunset, for that's what it seemed. Those watery pink hues weren't consistent, as if there were tiny beads of rain and wisps of cloud mixed up inside. This very cloth later served as the decorative border for my wedding gown.

Nora liked to bring her batik to our *shirangju* to show Luni. Like Ivan, however, Luni was fond of his rifle. 'If there's no game to hunt, people will starve,' he said. 'But if you've got one set of thick clothes and another single-layered one made from animal hides, that's enough for a lifetime. Cloth is something you can do without.'

When Nora heard Luni say that, she fumed. 'How could you raise a son as idiotic as Luni!' she said to Tamara who was lost in thought.

But despite this reproach, Tamara didn't get angry. She gave Nora a glance, looked at the cloth in her hands, and sighed. 'Even if you keep on dyeing, it still won't be as lovely as my feather skirt! Who dyed those feathers? The Spirits! Can your colours compare with Theirs?'

Nora stomped off, vowing never again to show us her batiks. But the very next time she dyed a cloth, she still brought it over triumphantly.

After Turkov left, Nadezhda didn't focus so intently on her

chores. More than once she cut her finger slicing meat. I frequently saw her talking about something with her daughter until Nora's eyes brimmed with tears.

One day when Yveline and I were fastening bells to the fawns, Nora suddenly came running over. 'Where do the Japanese come from? The Left Bank or the Right?' she asked Yveline.

'What have the Japanese got to do with the Argun?' Yveline said indignantly. 'Neither bank is their land! You have to cross the sea to get to where they live. People crossed to Japan on rafts once upon a time, but the ones who arrived there never returned!'

'If they have nothing to do with the Argun,' said Nora, 'why would they come here?'

'Wolves will flock to any place that has game but lacks good hunters,' said Yveline.

The germ of Nadezhda's idea to flee may have been planted by Turkov, but it was a strange encounter on Hase's part that finally prompted her to take action.

One day when Hase was searching for two stray reindeer, he came across an old Han man with a birch-bark basket on his back. He was gathering astragalus root. Hase asked him if he was collecting it for deer foetus extract, because when we decoct it in a metal pot, we often add medicinal herbs like palm-shaped ginseng and astragalus root.

'How could I be lucky enough to shoot a pregnant doe?' replied the old man. He was just collecting astragalus root to take to a herbalist in exchange for a meal. 'Now that the Japanese have come, getting food is even tougher.'

'Are the Japanese really going to wipe out blue-eyed Russians?' Hase asked.

'How would I know? But as soon as the Japanese show up, the blue-eyed people all start running!'

Hase related his encounter with the old man to everyone over supper. Nadezhda's eyes filled with alarm. She wolfed down meat and began to hiccup, but she continued stuffing herself. His meal unfinished, Jilande left looking preoccupied.

Watching Jilande's back as he walked away, Ivan sighed. 'He doesn't look at all like my son. Not a defiant bone in his body!'

Yveline had always doubted Jilande's parentage. 'Hmph,' she snorted contemptuously. 'Jilande's eyes are so blue, of course he doesn't look like your son!'

Nora resented Yveline speaking that way about her brother. 'You shouldn't "hmph" so much,' she said. 'Your nose is already crooked, and if you keep snorting at people like that, it will bend all the way over to the Left Bank of the Argun!'

Everyone laughed heartily. But Yveline was so angry she jumped up and said, 'Even if my nose is bent, it won't bend all the way to the Left Bank. It stinks of your piss over there, and I wouldn't want to dirty my nose! I'd rather my nose bent to the right, all the way into the Sea of Japan!'

Back then whenever anyone mentioned the word 'Japan', Nadezhda reacted as if she'd heard a thunderclap. Yveline's words made Nora storm off, but Nadezhda remained seated right where she was, wolfing down one huge mouthful of meat after another.

The sight of her eating like that spooked Ivan. 'Nadezhda, you've only got one stomach!'

Nadezhda just kept bolting her meat. Perhaps Yveline realised she had gone too far. She sighed, stood up and left.

That night two sounds could be heard intermittently throughout the camp. One was Nadezhda vomiting, and the other was Nora screeching '*Ya! Ya! Ya!*', like a raven. Those were the last sounds they left behind in the camp.

The next day Ivan behaved as usual, taking an early-morning breakfast and then going out on the hunt with Hase and Luni. That evening when he returned to camp he discovered his *shirangju* was vacant. The deerskin bedding and quilts, usually piled haphazardly, were neatly folded; his cigarette case was full of tobacco and placed next to the fireplace; and his mug was at his bedside, sparkling clean and free of thick tea stains. This unusual orderliness gave Ivan the jitters.

He realised something was not right, and he went to look at the buckskin bag for storing clothes. Half the contents were missing. Only one of the pink cloths that Nora had dyed remained, and most of the jerky stored in the bucket was gone. It looked like they'd fled with food and clothing in tow.

I had actually seen Nora at the riverside that morning when I was washing my face. She rolled some grass together to serve as a rag, and was using fine grains of sand from the riverbed to wipe clean the mug.

'Why are you scrubbing it?'

'There's a lot of tea stains,' said Nora, 'so the brewed tea doesn't look transparent.'

When I had washed my face and was about to leave, Nora suddenly spoke. 'My batiks are so pretty. Why doesn't Luni like any of them?'

'Didn't you call Luni an idiot? It's no wonder an idiot doesn't appreciate beauty!'

Nora pursed her lips. 'How can you say Luni's an idiot?' she said. 'Of all the people in our *urireng*, he's the cleverest!'

Nora asked me which of her dyed cloths I liked best. 'The pink one,' I said. 'When that one appeared, we all thought the sun was setting right in our camp.'

As for the pink cloth that Nora left behind, I do believe it was intended for me. After I left the riverside, it occurred to me that I'd forgotten to ask: 'We didn't eat bear meat last night, so why were you imitating a raven's call?'

That night when we gathered round the bonfire for dinner, Ivan came all by himself, head bowed. His footsteps were very heavy.

'Nadezhda and the children?' asked Maria.

Ivan sat down in resignation. He rubbed his face with those massive hands of his, let them fall, lifted his head a bit, and said forlornly: 'They've made their escape. You shouldn't go looking for them. There's no holding back someone who wants to leave.'

All who heard the news kept dead silent, except Yveline.

'*Ya!*' she exclaimed. 'Just like I said long ago, sooner or later Nadezhda was bound to take her children back to her homeland! That woman is black-hearted! She took both the children, but she should have left one for Ivan. Maybe it was fitting to take Jilande. But Nora – she's definitely Ivan's child. Only a whore could be so vicious!'

'If anyone dares call Nadezhda a whore, I'll rip her tongue out!' roared Ivan.

Yveline shuddered and shut her trap.

I returned to our *shirangju* and told Tamara the news about Nadezhda's flight. But she surprised me by laughing. 'Good for her! How fine it would be if everyone in our *urireng* ran away!'

'You should run away too!' I said, to get her goat.

'If I ran away, I'd go to Lake Lama! There's no winter there, and

lotus flowers bloom all year round. How nice that would be.' Then
she tore a lock of grey hair from her head and cast it into the fireplace. Her crazed look made me extraordinarily sad.

I went to Nidu the Shaman's. 'Nadezhda has run off with Jilande
and Nora. You're our Headman. Aren't you going to go after them?'

'Chasing after something that has run away is like clutching at
the moonlight,' he said to me.

I looked down on this Headman who, because his own romantic
ardour had been snuffed out, had no compassion for others.

'If we pursue them, we can catch them and bring them back!'

'You'll never bring them back!' said Nidu the Shaman.

Ivan didn't search for Nadezhda. It was Hase, Luni, Kunde and
I who did. We struck a big tree with a wooden club so the reindeer
roaming nearby would realise that a task awaited them. Six or seven
reindeer soon returned to camp. We chose four that were in good
shape, mounted them and set out.

We knew that Nadezhda was fleeing towards the Argun, so the
direction of our pursuit was certain.

Under the clear autumn night sky, a blue glow floated above the
mountains, and a milky glow above the river. Since we were searching for her in great earnest, as we started out I yelled 'Nora!' and an
owl perched on a tree took off in flight, spooked by my shouting. It
flew right past us, its eyes tracing two luminescent lines like shooting stars. Those inauspicious rays of light pricked my heart like
a needle.

'When travelling at night you shouldn't speak loudly, you'll disturb the Mountain Spirit,' Kunde said. 'Besides, Nadezhda is trying
to escape, and if they hear our calls it'll just drive them further away.

'They aren't riding reindeer, so they'll need at least two days to get to the Argun. And even when they arrive, they might not be able to find a ferry. They'll have to wait on the bank.'

At the outset we were a group of four. But after we crossed one mountain, Hase said there was a shorter path to the Argun, and although it was a hard route to follow, with reindeer to forge the trail it shouldn't be a problem. So we separated, Hase taking Luni while I went with Kunde. It was agreed that if Kunde and I couldn't find Nadezhda and her children, we'd return to camp at dawn and Hase and Luni would press on to the Argun.

As soon as they left and we had put a mountain behind us, Kunde spoke up. 'Nadezhda and her children have already walked for one day and they'll be very hard to overtake. We'd better head back. Hase and Luni will keep searching for them anyhow.'

'Maybe they haven't gone so far,' I said. 'Nadezhda might regret leaving, and there's no saying for sure that they aren't hiding somewhere!'

'I didn't bring much ammunition, so we'd better turn back. What if something happened to you. How could I explain myself to Yveline?'

'Since we've come this far, we should search a bit longer.' Kunde didn't respond, but he wasn't enthusiastic, and kept the reindeer moving at a very leisurely pace.

Looking for someone in the forest is a daunting task, like fishing for a needle. We were both drowsy as the night drew on. Kunde came to a halt, wanting to have a smoke to perk himself up, and I needed to relieve myself.

'I'll be right back,' I said. Kunde knew what was on my mind and reminded me not to go far away. He and the reindeer would stay put.

I jumped off my mount. My legs felt sore and weak. At my back

I heard Kunde grumbling. 'The tobacco's so moist, it's sure to rain tomorrow. That Nadezhda is a load of trouble!'

In the silence of the night the slightest sound is amplified. I was worried Kunde could hear me peeing, so I walked deeper into the dense forest. It was a towering pine grove, and I could hear the light breeze brushing against the branches, mimicking the wind relieving itself.

I walked until I was certain Kunde was out of earshot, and then I crouched down. I hadn't slept enough, and I lost my bearings with the act of crouching and rising. When I stood up again, I felt the earth spin, my eyes blur and I tumbled back on the ground.

But when I rose again my feet took the wrong direction. I walked for a moment in a daze, but when I didn't see any sign of the reindeer, I realised I was in trouble. I glanced at the moon. It seemed to make sense to walk towards it, because as we rode here our campground was at our backs. To the west, that is.

But it turned out this too was a mistaken conclusion. At first I had gone a little off course, but now I was actually walking in the opposite direction to the path that brought us here.

I walked for a long time but still didn't see Kunde, so I yelled his name. Later I learned that after Kunde had finished his smoke, he lay down on his reindeer and dozed off. Otherwise, when he realised I hadn't returned after such a long time, he'd have gone looking for me. But then, if he had found me, I wouldn't have encountered Lajide.

If it weren't for the gusts of chilly wind that roused Kunde, he might have kept on sleeping. There were already rays of light in the sky when he awoke. He discovered I wasn't there and knew I was in trouble. He fired his rifle and yelled out my name, but by that time I was further and further away from him and couldn't hear a thing.

After I'd passed a dreadful night, I was greeted by a dawn without a sunrise. Thick lead-grey clouds covered the sky. Without the sun, I was even more clueless about which direction I should take. I began to look for a path, one of those snaking paths we and our reindeer tread. If you follow those paths, you're bound to happen upon signs of human habitation.

With no food on me, I picked some mushrooms to ward off hunger. Having lost my way, the thing I most feared was confronting a wild animal. Except for the time Linke took Luni and me *kandahang* hunting, I had no experience dealing with them.

I hadn't walked long when it began to rain, and I rushed to take shelter under a tawny boulder with green moss growing on it. The shapes formed clouds and trees, rivers and blossoms – like a painting.

The rain had no intention of stopping, and I felt that if I remained under the rock to avoid it, my situation would only worsen. I began to search for one of those pathways again. At last, in the middle of a thicket I found a small winding path. It was like seeing the sunrise, and I went mad with joy. But my joy was uncalled for, because the path vanished at the foot of a mountain.

Now I was desperate. I wanted to cry, but the tears didn't come. I struck my leg with my fist, and facing the mountain forests, I cursed Nadezhda and Kunde, Tamara and Nidu the Shaman. They were the ones who had pushed me into this hopeless situation!

Curiously, when I finished cursing them the panic in my heart had largely subsided.

I stood up and decided to go looking for a river. If I could only find a river, I'd follow its banks and find a way out of my predicament. First I found a stream and took a drink, and then I followed the water forward, reckoning the stream would eventually feed into a river. Full of confidence, I walked the sky till it was pale, but I suddenly found that the stream terminated in a lake, not a river. Struck by raindrops, the surface bubbled like a pot of boiling water. I wanted to throw myself in.

Many years later, Valodya, who loved to read, pointed at a circular symbol in a book. 'That's a full stop,' he said. 'If someone in the book has finished a sentence, they draw this symbol.'

'When I lost my way in the mountains I saw a symbol like that,' I said. 'It was written in the forest, the lake that I saw. But the full-stop lake didn't draw an end to my life.'

I was afraid of encountering a wolf or a bear in the darkness, so I sat all night on the shore, imagining that if one appeared, I'd dive into the lake. I would've preferred to be swallowed by the lake than have a wild beast drink one drop of my blood.

The rain stopped and stars appeared, and I was soaked, cold and hungry.

It was on that night that I happened upon two deer that had come for a drink. One adult and one young, they appeared on the opposite side of the lake. The fawn was gambolling in front as its mother followed at a leisurely pace. The fawn drank playfully, lapping the water and then insinuating its head between its mother's legs. In reaction, the doe turned and licked her fawn's face.

At that instant a burst of warmth began to flow at the bottom of my heart. I longed for someone to lick my face so tenderly. My breathing quickened and my cheeks flushed, and the pale world before my eyes suddenly shone brightly. When the two deer left the lake, one behind the other, my heart brimmed with joy and happiness. I told myself: I haven't yet experienced the sensation of being licked by someone who loves me. I can't leave this world – I have to keep on living!

The sky lit up and the sun rose. I picked some button mushrooms and a few handfuls of red love-peas as a makeshift breakfast and climbed a ridge to survey the land below, but I was disappointed. A string of mountains stretched before me like a series of burial mounds, and this put me in a desolate state of mind. How badly I yearned to see the silhouette of a sparkling silver-white river!

Descending the ridge, my legs felt even feebler. With no path or river, which direction should I take? I looked to the sun for guidance. One moment I thought I should walk towards the rising sun, but then I thought I should walk where the sun would set. My brain buzzed like a bee snared in a spider's web, circling frantically to no avail.

Suddenly, I heard 'ka-CHA ka-CHA' ahead. I thought I must be hallucinating so I stopped to listen carefully. Yes, it really was the sound of a tree suffering under the impact of an axe. Delirious with excitement, I raced towards the noise.

Sure enough, there was a clearing ahead. A few pine trees with trunks as wide as the mouth of a bowl were piled there. I charged towards the clearing, but all I saw was a black shadow uprooting a sapling. Its furry body made me scream in terror. This was no human being – it was a black bear!

Hearing my cry, the bear turned around, lifted its two front paws, stood erect and walked towards me just like a human. The way that black bear walked made me believe what my father had once told me: the ancestor of the bear was a human being, but because the bear had done wrong, the Spirits transformed it into a beast on all fours.

But at times it could still behave like a human, stand erect and walk. I watched it approach step by step, as if it were taking a stroll and enjoying the scenery, its head rocking smugly to and fro.

I suddenly recalled something Yveline had told me: a bear wouldn't harm any woman who bared her chest. I cast off my upper garment. I felt I was a tree, and my naked breasts were a pair of pom-pom mushrooms sprouting on it thanks to the rain's nourishment. If the bear truly wanted to devour these mushrooms, I had no choice but to sacrifice them.

So the first being in the world to set eyes on my breasts wasn't Lajide, but a black bear.

The bear stopped for an instant, startled, as if recalling something. Then it quickly put its front paws down, took a few steps on all fours, turned around and continued uprooting trees.

I realised that the bear had abandoned me, or I should say, abandoned my breasts. I wanted to flee as quickly as possible, but I couldn't take a single step. I just stood there in a daze, watching it uproot the saplings one by one. Only when it detached the third tree did strength return to my legs, and I left the clearing.

At first I proceeded very slowly, but then the sense of terror assaulted me again. I feared the bear would start following me, and I began to run. I remembered what Father had told me: when you're dealing with a bear, above all don't run against the wind, or else the wind will blow open the hairs on the bear's eyelids and improve its vision. So I halted, gauged the wind's direction, and then began to run with it.

When I could run no further, the sun was in the middle of the sky. I fell to my knees in a thicket, and then I realised my breasts were still exposed. I'd forgotten to grab the top I'd taken off. But even if I had it I wouldn't have dared put it on again, for how could I be sure I wouldn't encounter another bear?

Lajide later told me that bears have a habit of creating a clearing where they can amuse themselves. Personally, I think they have no other outlet for their great strength.

Remembering the bear, I decided to continue moving with the wind. At least I could avoid becoming food in a bear's mouth. In that season the wind blew from the south-west, so I proceeded towards the north-east.

I walked until the sun set in the mountains when I, weary and famished, finally discovered a path. I followed it and suddenly found myself before a *kolbo*.

Virtually every *urireng* constructs a *kolbo* in the mountains, as few as two or three, or as many as four or five. To build one, you need to choose four pine trees of similar thickness at the right distance from one another, break off the branches, sever the tree crown, and use the four tree trunks as 'pillars' for the *kolbo*. Between the pillars, a base and a rectangular frame are constructed with pine poles. We cover the frame with birch-bark and leave an opening at the bottom for storing and removing goods.

When we move camp, we store temporarily unused or extra items there, like clothing, hides and foodstuffs to retrieve as needed. Since this cache is way above the forest floor, wild animals can't destroy it. But if you have a *kolbo*, you have to make a ladder too, because it's as high off the ground as the height of a good two people combined. The ladder is generally placed flat on the ground in the woods nearby.

In earlier times, our *kolbo* were often raided by Siberian weasels and lynx that clambered up the pillars to pilfer food. Later, we stripped the bark from the trunks, and once they were smooth they weren't easy to climb.

Still later, we wrapped each pillar with a thin sheet of iron and cut it so that jagged saw-tooth edges protruded. Even nimble thieves weren't willing to injure their claws in the ascent. Except for bears that were able to move the ladder to reach the *kolbo*, other animals could only lick their lips and gaze longingly at that rich cache suspended in the air.

I found a ladder under a birch tree near the *kolbo*, stood it on end and climbed up.

Even in my earliest memories, I recall the grown-ups reciting two proverbs to us:

*When you leave home you don't take your house, and a traveller doesn't lug his cauldron on his back.*

*Guests only enter houses with a warm hearth, and birds only alight upon trees with branches.*

So we never locked our *kolbo*. Even if the *kolbo* you happen upon doesn't belong to your clan, if you urgently need something, you're free to take it. Of course, having removed something, you should return one later. But even if you don't, no one complains.

There weren't many things in the *kolbo*, just a few disused cooking utensils and bedding, and no valuable pelts. But there was a birch-bark basket of badly needed roe-deer jerky and two tins of snow-white bear fat. Recalling that a bear had just spared my life, I respectfully declined to eat it.

I chewed the dried strips of venison at first, but perhaps because of the rain, they weren't very crisp and chewing was laborious. I began by eating slowly, but as I ate my hunger intensified and eventually I was wolfing down huge mouthfuls.

I knew I was saved. I not only had food, I also had a place where I could temporarily rest and shelter from the wind and rain. Huddled over, I sat there chewing on jerky and feeling like I was the most fortunate woman on the face of the earth. After I had finished eating I decided to nap first and then search for a campsite. I guessed that there must be people not far from the *kolbo*.

The sun had descended towards the mountains, and between the cracks in the *kolbo*'s pinewood poles I could still feel the cosy warmth of its afterglow. With a full stomach, I felt even drowsier. I lay down, bent my legs and prepared to sleep.

I heard a sudden crunch of footsteps, followed by a thud – the ladder hitting the ground. I reckoned that the clever bear had followed me all the way and intended to keep me cooped up in this *kolbo* for ever.

I stuck my head out for a look. But it wasn't a bear. It was a man, and he was pointing his rifle at me and glaring fiercely!

That 'he' was Lajide, and this *kolbo* belonged to his *urireng*. He was passing by, spied the ladder, and hearing sounds coming from up above, thought it was a bear ransacking the *kolbo*. He dislodged the ladder to cut off its escape route, and was just about to kill it with a single bullet.

Who'd have imagined that when I popped my head out, my breasts would pop out for a look too? Lajide said his first sight of me left him breathless. My hair was dishevelled, and my cheeks and upper body had not only been scratched raw by branches, my skin was also swollen from insect bites.

But it was my eyes that touched him. He said they were limpid and moist. Just one glance won his heart.

Lajide could tell that I was in this pitiful state because I'd lost my way in the mountains. He didn't ask me anything, but put the ladder up again and motioned for me to come down.

Once on the ground, I collapsed weakly into his embrace. I had long forgotten that I was naked above the waist. Lajide said that when my soft, warm breasts buried themselves in his chest, a feverish wave surged through his body. Since her breasts have found their way into my embrace, he said to himself, I can't let them ever again be embraced by another.

It was then and there – at sunset, the most beautiful instant of the day – that the idea of marrying me germinated in his heart.

\* \* \*

Luni and hase chased Nadezhda, Jilande and Nora right to the Argun, but they didn't bring them back, for they had disappeared without a trace. I wonder if they found a birch-bark canoe and made it to the Left Bank, or were they carried away by the swirling waters while trying to swim across? After they left us, whenever we went to the Argun everyone was silent as if mourning lost relatives.

On their way back, Luni and Hase ran into Kunde and Yveline who were searching for me. They thought I must be dead since I'd lost my way for three days. But on the fourth day I returned not only safe and sound, but with a man too.

Lajide's *urireng* was the biggest in their clan with some thirty-odd members, and his extended family numbered sixteen mouths. Besides his father, three elder brothers, two younger sisters and a younger brother, his elder brothers had each taken a wife and already had their own children.

The year we married, Vladimir, his youngest brother, was just three. Lajide told me his mother loved raising children, but she had died at fifty due to Vladimir's difficult birth. After a glance at her wailing newborn, she died smiling. When I met Lajide, he had just completed the third year of mourning for his mother, or else our marriage would have been delayed.

I told Lajide I couldn't leave our *urireng* because my mother had lost her senses and needed someone to care for her.

'Then I'll join your *urireng*,' Lajide replied. 'I have many brothers who will stay with my father anyhow.'

Lajide's father was a kind old man. He not only agreed that his son could *ru ƶhui* – marry into the wife's *urireng* – but on our wedding day he led an entourage to formally deliver Lajide to us. And he brought twenty head of reindeer as a marriage gift.

Yveline made my marriage gown in a rush. Ivan gave me the pink batik dyed by Nora as a present, and I asked Yveline to use it to trim my gown. The round collar of the long blue gown, the horsehoof cuffs and waist – all were edged with that pink fabric. I wore that gown twice as a bride.

I still have it but I can't wear it any more. I'm old and wizened, and the gown is too big for me now. The colours look old too, particularly the pink that aged faster than the blue. It is so faded that you simply cannot imagine its original lustre and enchanting aura.

Our marriage ceremony was a simple affair, just a gathering of two *urireng* taking a meal around a bonfire. The gathering lacked a festive ambience. Ivan got drunk and vomited his food and drink on the bonfire, and this left Yveline frowning. I knew she interpreted it as an inauspicious omen. Tamara and Nidu the Shaman appeared indifferent, and neither offered a blessing.

But I felt incomparably happy. That evening when Lajide and I embraced tightly in our newly constructed *shirangju* and we made our very own vibrant wind-sounds, I felt like the luckiest woman under the sky. I recall that a full silver moon was visible from the tip of our *shirangju*.

I buried my head in Lajide's chest and told him I had never felt so warm. 'I'll make sure this warmth accompanies you for ever,' he said.

He kissed my breasts, dubbing one his Sun and the other his Moon. He said they would bring him eternal brightness. That night he uttered the word 'eternal' many times, and that sounds like an oath, but oaths are rarely for ever.

\* \* \*

Lajide liked to hunt, and in order to spend more time together I frequently went with him. Generally, it's taboo for a woman to accompany a hunter, especially during her moon period, as it is thought to bring bad luck. But it wasn't taboo for Lajide, and provided he was hunting near the camp, he would leave the others to take me along.

We crouched together by salt licks to await wild deer, caught otter in their dens amongst shrubs, and shot lynx dead in pine groves. But when we encountered dormant black bears, I always advised Lajide to let them be.

Many people say the most cunning animal in the forest is the fox, but I reckon it's the mountain cat. The lynx is shaped very much like a cat but much bigger. Its entire body is brownish-yellow with grey spots. It has a very short frame and tail, slender limbs, and two long tufts of fur extend from its ears.

Lynx are terrific tree-climbers and can reach a treetop in the blink of an eye. They prey upon hares, squirrels, pheasants and roe-deer. To launch an attack on these animals, the lynx typically uses a tree as a stronghold. Hidden in the tree, it leaps down on its quarry, severs the throat, sucks the blood and then uses its claws to rip open the skin and enjoy the flesh in a leisurely fashion.

I find their bloodsucking cruel, that's why I despise lynx. But they're not just cruel, they're cunning too. If suddenly threatened by a black bear or a wild boar, the lynx quickly darts up a tree. And if the bear or boar rushes to the bottom of the tree, the lynx will unleash a stream of urine on its foe below. Stinking of piss, the animal is no longer in the mood to mess with the lynx, and slinks away, utterly defeated. So I've always felt that, like a human hunter, the lynx has bullets – its pee.

In winter, lynx like to stow their prey to allay their hunger when they haven't made a recent kill. This creature always has something up its sleeve.

When Lajide hunted lynx, he rarely employed a rifle and bullets. He used the ancient bow and arrow. Just when a lynx was climbing a tree, Lajide, who lay in wait in the forest, shot his arrow, and virtually every time the arrow would pierce the animal's throat, throwing it off balance and bringing it to the ground with a somersault.

One time we discovered a lynx climbing a tree in pursuit of a pheasant. Lajide, quick of eye and deft of hand, pulled back his bow and released his arrow. It was truly 'One arrow, Two eagles' – the arrow pierced both the lynx and the pheasant!

I believe that it was because of water dogs that I was able to become pregnant with Viktor, my first child. From then on, I never hunted them again.

Otters love to eat fresh fish, so their lairs are always connected to a waterway. If you discover a hole near a river and there are fish bones scattered next to it, the chances are you'll find a water dog there.

These are very leisurely creatures. In the daytime they swim in the river and eat small fish, and at night they return to their lair to rest. Typically I located the lair, and it was Lajide who captured and killed them.

It was the third spring after I married Lajide that we discovered four pups whose eyelids were still closed. Lajide said that water dogs open their eyes very slowly, about a month after birth. We knew their mother must be nearby so we didn't touch the pups.

At dusk an adult water dog swam back from the river to the lair, but when its shiny head surfaced and Lajide was about to shoot it, I stopped him. 'These four pups haven't even seen their mother,' I thought to myself, 'and if the first thing they see upon opening their eyes is mountains, the river and hunters pursuing them, they'll be heartbroken.'

We let them go. Not long after, following three childless years, there were signs of a new life in my belly. This changed the way that Yveline looked at Lajide and me. During the first two years, Yveline noticed my stomach was always shrunken, and she often ridiculed us.

'Lajide has the air of a tiger,' she would say, 'but deep in his bones he's as soft as a squirrel. Otherwise, why doesn't his woman become pregnant?'

She even reproached me for hunting with Lajide: 'How can a woman who hunts have a child?'

One night she couldn't sleep and wandered about the camp. Suddenly she heard my groaning and Lajide's huffing coming from our *shirangju*. The next day she pursed her lips, tweaked her nose to one side and asked me: 'You two spend so much energy doing that sort of thing. How come no child comes of it?' Her words made my cheeks blaze like coals in a fire.

After I became pregnant, I did stop hunting with Lajide.

Both in looks and temperament, Lajide closely resembled my father. Though lean, his shoulders were broad, his arms long, and his frame rugged. Unlike other men's sparse eyebrows, his were very dense. This made it seem as if his eyes were veiled in a lush, dark forest, which gave him an air of serenity.

Like Linke, he liked to play jokes. In the summer, he stuffed ladybirds down my back. In the winter, he furtively grabbed fistfuls of snow and stuck them down my neck, chilling me so badly that I'd jump up. When I screamed '*Aiyo!*' he broke out in laughter. I could stand the ladybirds, but snow was another matter. Whenever it snowed and I noticed Lajide coming into the *shirangju* with his hand closed in a fist, I giggled and rushed to take cover.

'If you say something nice,' he cajoled, 'I'll spare you.' Since I hated the cold, I mouthed all sorts of sickly sweet things to melt the snow in Lajide's hand.

Mother's marriage gift to me was the live cinders of a fire, the very fire that I am watching over now. This flame is the one that *Naajil'aya* – my mother's father – gave her when she was joined in marriage with Linke. She never permitted it to go out. Even after she went mad, when we moved camp she never forgot to bring the fire source with her. When she saw me put on the marriage gown sewed by Yveline and realised that I was going to be a bride, she touched my cheeks.

'You're going to have a husband of your own. Let *Eni* give you a fire.'

From the fire given her by *Naajil'aya*, Mother gave me a burning coal, and I embraced her and wept. I suddenly felt how pathetic and lonely she was! Perhaps we had been wrong to forbid the affection between her and Nidu the Shaman. Although we were abiding by our clan's rule, in reality weren't we extinguishing the flame in her heart? We rendered her heart completely cold, so even now when she watched over the fire her days were glacial.

Gazing at this flame that is even older than I, I see Mother's silhouette.

Perhaps it was because Lajide so resembled Father that my mother loved to watch him – watch him eat, watch him drink tea, watch him polish his rifle, watch him play jokes on me. She seemed lost in reverie as she watched, contented. But after my belly grew big, she didn't like to watch him any more and even displayed a certain loathing towards him. Yveline said that Tamara saw Lajide as Linke's phantom. When she discovered that Lajide had got me pregnant, she felt Linke had been unfaithful to her, so she began to hate him.

It was shortly before Viktor's birth that I learned of the bad blood between Father and Nidu the Shaman.

Lajide had built a separate delivery shed for me. We call it a *yataju*, and males are not allowed to enter. It's also taboo for a woman to help deliver a baby, because it is said this may cause the early death of her husband. But when the labour pains hurt so badly that I began howling like a wild beast, Yveline came inside.

To pacify me, Yveline recounted two legends. She thought those wonderful tales would ease my pain, but they did just the opposite. 'Those damn stories are a pack of lies!' I yelled. The pain was torturing me so badly that I had lost my wits.

'I'll tell you a true story,' Yveline said reluctantly. 'But this is no tall tale, so don't you dare scream again!'

As soon as Yveline began her narration, I stopped my howling, because it was a story about two men and a woman, and Linke, Tamara and Nidu the Shaman were the protagonists. I was enthralled.

It was a painful story, but it made me forget my own pain. When I had heard it all, Viktor was already safely born and his cry marked a full stop to the tale.

One summer, when my grandfather was still alive, he led his clansmen towards a new campsite. When they came to the banks of the Yuksagan River, they encountered members of another clan also on the move. The two clans halted and began revelries that lasted three days and three nights. All the hunters brought the game they had killed and surrounded the bonfire, drinking and eating, singing and dancing.

It was there that Linke and Nidu the Shaman came to know Tamara. Yveline said Tamara loved to dance more than any other maiden in her clan, and clad in a long grey skirt, she danced from dusk to deep night, and then from deep night to dawn. She looked especially fetching as she danced and skipped wildly, and both Linke and Nidu the Shaman fell for her.

At almost exactly the same moment they told Grandfather that they liked that girl named Tamara, and wanted her hand in marriage. This was awkward for Grandfather. He hadn't imagined that his two sons would fall in love with the same maiden.

Grandfather quietly raised the matter with Tamara's father, intending that he ask his daughter which one she preferred. If she wasn't keen on either, the matter could be easily resolved.

But the dance-loving maiden unexpectedly told her father that both of these fellows pleased her: the stout one appeared pleasant and faithful, while the thin one looked clever and cheerful. Either would do.

This put both Grandfather and Tamara's father in a difficult position, but not Tamara. She had enticed the very souls of Linke and Nidu the Shaman, but she herself remained calm. She continued to dance her dance and even smiled sweetly at others at the end of each tune.

Grandfather eventually came up with a solution. He summoned Linke and Nidu the Shaman. 'You are both my beloved sons. Since you have fallen in love with the same maiden, and she has said that either of you may be her groom, one of you must yield.'

Grandfather first asked Nidu the Shaman: 'Are you willing for Tamara to pair with Linke?'

Nidu the Shaman shook his head. 'Unless a thunderbolt transforms into a rope, ties itself around Tamara and places her before Linke, I will never agree.'

Then Grandfather asked Linke: 'Are you willing to let Tamara be taken in marriage by your elder brother?'

'Unless the earth is submerged in a huge flood and the raging torrent carries me away and washes my brother and Tamara up onto an island together, I will never agree.'

'So be it,' said Grandfather. 'I have prayed to the Spirits, and it is Their wish for you to speak with your arrows.'

It was the rainy season when a white mushroom that we call 'Monkey Head' makes its appearance. It's as big as a fist and soft and velvety. Stew pheasant with Monkey Head mushrooms, even the most finicky eater will praise your cooking. They grow on oak trees, but it's an odd sort of fungus that generally occurs in pairs. If you discover one on a tree, another Monkey Head mushroom will often be facing it on a nearby oak.

Grandfather found a pair of Monkey Head mushrooms growing opposite one another in the woods on the banks of the Yuksagan, and he instructed Linke and Nidu the Shaman to contest their archery skills there. He whose arrow pierced his Monkey Head mushroom would take Tamara's hand in marriage. If the arrows of both parties struck their mushrooms in the first round, then another pair of Monkey Head mushrooms would be found to serve as targets until a victor emerged.

The two oak trees were separated by a distance the length of a *shirangju*, said Yveline, so they looked like a pair of brothers. When Linke and Nidu the Shaman arrived before the trees with their bows and arrows, everyone from the two *urireng* came running to watch.

Except for Tamara, that is. Dressed in her beautiful skirt, she was dancing by herself on the riverbank.

The brothers were fine archers. That pair of Monkey Head mushrooms lit up under the sun like glittering, crystalline ear lobes protruding from the tree trunks. When the brothers released their arrows simultaneously upon Grandfather's barked order, Yveline said she covered her eyes.

All she heard was the *shwa-shwa* of two gusts of wind passing by. But that sound mutated in a split second. The *shwa-shwa* split into a *chaa* and a *tuk*, and then stopped abruptly. Everything was still.

Yveline opened her eyes to discover Linke's Monkey Head had been pierced by his arrow, while Nidu the Shaman's arrow was stuck in the tree trunk wide of the mark, leaving his Monkey Head perfectly intact.

And so it was that in full view of the two clans, Linke won Tamara's hand. Once an exceptionally good marksman, from that time onwards, whether shooting an arrow or firing a rifle, Nidu the Shaman rarely hit his target.

Yveline said she suspected that Nidu the Shaman intentionally yielded to his younger brother, because when Nidu the Shaman looked at that failed arrow, his gaze was very composed.

But that's not what I thought. He had told Grandfather that he wouldn't give up Tamara, and agreed to a winner-takes-all duel, so Nidu the Shaman would surely have done his utmost. If he did change his mind, it could only have been at the last instant. Perhaps he couldn't bear to see his younger brother's disappointed gaze.

When everyone brought the news that Linke had won Tamara, she was sitting on the riverbank teasing two black ants in her palm and watching them joust. When she learned that she was to be Linke's bride, she stood up, tossed the ants away, smoothed out her skirt, and smiled. Her smile convinced everyone that, deep in her heart, she had preferred Linke.

The following year when it came time to sever reindeer antlers, Linke married Tamara and brought her into our *urireng*. She came bearing live cinders and fifteen head of reindeer.

The moment the couple wed, Nidu the Shaman cut his finger

with a knife. You could see the blood flow drop by drop. But when Yveline went to get Deer Grass to staunch the bleeding, Nidu the Shaman stopped her. He simply held up his bleeding finger, blew on it, and miraculously the bleeding stopped.

Once upon a time a hunter encountered a deer in the forest. He shot two arrows but neither struck a fatal blow. The wounded deer took flight. The hunter followed the trail of blood, reckoning that once it bled enough, it would naturally drop in its tracks. But as his pursuit lengthened, the hunter discovered that the traces of blood disappeared. The deer had made good its escape.

It turned out that this was a Spirit Deer, and as it fled it used the grass on the forest floor to treat its wound. Ever since, hunters gather tufts of this herb we call 'Deer Grass', or hellebore, that can staunch bleeding. Yveline said when everyone noticed that Nidu the Shaman didn't apply hellebore to his cut, and used his own breath to stop the bleeding instead, it was more terrifying than seeing the blood itself.

From then on Nidu the Shaman's behaviour became ever more strange, said Yveline. He would go for several days and nights without food or water, and then walk energetically for an entire day. He could pass through a patch of thistles barefoot, his feet unscathed.

One day he stumbled on a rock by the riverside. He was so angry that he gave it a kick, and – who'd have imagined? – the huge rock took to the air like a bird in flight, made straight for the river, and *tung!* sank to the bottom. From his extraordinary strength, everyone knew that he was destined to be a Shaman.

Three years had passed since the death of our clan's Shaman but a new one had not yet been born. Generally speaking, the new

Shaman comes into being three years after the death of the old one, but it is uncertain into which *urireng* he will be born.

Yveline said that when the newly prepared Spirit Robe, Spirit Hat, Spirit Drum, Spirit Skirt and other ritual items used in the Spirit Dance were presented to *Egdi'ama*, he cried for one day and one night. He wept so bitterly that all the birds around the campsite flew away.

Afterwards, a Shaman from another clan came to our *urireng* to preside over the Initiation Ritual for Nidu the Shaman, and they performed a three-day Spirit Dance. My grandfather passed away during that Spirit Dance.

My son Viktor was born and a new image of Nidu the Shaman was also born in my heart. I began to sympathise with him and Tamara. It seemed that fate had returned to him his own arrow that had gone awry in the duel for Tamara, and he had every right to transform it into an arrow of happiness.

I no longer resented Tamara's spreading out her bird-feather skirt, or the way Nidu the Shaman rode behind Mother when we moved camp. But that view of her backside was all he ever got.

If lightning transformed itself into a sharp arrow and spirited away Linke, then the arrow that Nidu the Shaman received was already spotted with rust, because it came bound together with our clan's antiquated customs. Confronted with this arrow, the withering and lunacy of Tamara and Nidu the Shaman were only natural.

\* \* \*

It was in the fifth year of the reign of Manchukuo Emperor Kangde, that Luni took Nihau as his wife. And next to the spent grey ashes of the wedding bonfire, just as the day dawned, Tamara left us for eternity. She died dancing in the bird-feather skirt stitched for her by Nidu the Shaman.

It was because of Ivan's iron-forging skills that Luni met Nihau.

Nadezhda's departure turned Ivan into a taciturn man, and in just a few years he went bald. Yveline busied herself finding another wife for him. Once she commissioned a matchmaker but when Ivan learned of it, he lashed out at her.

'I've just one woman in my life, Nadezhda, and just one pair of children, Jilande and Nora,' said Ivan. 'No one can change that.' Yveline was forever reducing others to tears, but this time Ivan made her cry.

Ivan was our *urireng*'s blacksmith. In the springtime, he often lit a fire in the camp and crafted tools for everyone. Forging iron usually took four or five days, and under no circumstances could the fire be extinguished.

Whenever Ivan did his forging, Jilande, Nora, Luni and I loved to run over and watch. One time, naughty Luni peed on the roe-deerskin bellows. For Ivan, this was utterly taboo.

'The tools forged with this bellows are cursed for sure. They won't be any good.'

Indeed, that batch of tools was all flawed: the machete handle snapped when hammered; the tip of the fish spear was blunt, and the point of the hunting spear was curved like the head of a white crane. From then on, we were not allowed to watch, and even less were we permitted to touch the hammer, bellows, tongs, sizing block or the furnace.

It was not only we children who weren't allowed to approach the furnace during forging, it was even more strictly forbidden for women to do so. Women are made of water, and if they stand too close, they will put the fire out.

People in other *urireng* knew that Ivan was a skilled blacksmith, and in the spring they often followed the tree markers to our camp and asked Ivan to forge for them. They brought liquor or meat as a reward, and Ivan never disappointed. Those hands of his that could crush a stone seemed to have been made for shaping metal. So the visitors always left fully satisfied, new tools in hand.

After Nadezhda's departure, Ivan changed the time for forging to the autumn. The falling leaves danced like yellow butterflies in the forest, falling on the bellows and on Ivan too. His smithery was still so sonorous and forceful, and each item that he hammered into shape was so fine that his services remained much sought after.

In autumn of that year, a hunter named Alek rode a reindeer to our campsite with his daughter and asked Ivan to make two machetes for him. Alek's daughter looked to be just thirteen or fourteen, and although she had inherited the flat face of our people, her chin was a bit pointed and this gave her a sweet and mischievous air. Two curly locks covered her high cheekbones, and her slender eyes were radiant and jet-black. She had fixed purple chrysanthemums in her sole plait, and she smiled very sweetly. This was Nihau.

Yveline took a liking to the girl. She said one day she must bring Nihau into our *urireng* as a bride for her son Jindele.

But Luni had just reached marriageable age and, like Yveline, he took a fancy to Nihau at first sight. Originally he had intended to ask Yveline to serve as his matchmaker, but when he heard that Yveline wanted to marry Nihau to Jindele, Luni seized the initiative. Just as Nihau was about to leave with her father, Luni proposed to her in front of everyone in the *urireng*.

'I adore your smile,' he said to Nihau. 'I'll put you inside my heart and protect you as I would my own. Marry me!'

Alek hadn't imagined that in requesting Ivan to forge a pair of machetes, he'd get a son-in-law in the deal!

He had known Linke and could see Linke's good looks and courage in Luni, so naturally he was willing to give Nihau to him. 'But Nihau is still too young, so you'll have to wait another two years to marry,' Alek said.

Jindele had also taken a fancy to Nihau, so Luni's public marriage proposal brought tears of hopelessness to his eyes.

Yveline, however, remained unruffled. 'Indeed, Nihau is still too young and shouldn't marry so soon,' she announced. 'Even if she is to be engaged, the matter should be formally agreed through a matchmaker. For such a fine maiden, marriage arrangements shouldn't be made hastily.'

The night Nihau left our camp, Yveline bound Jindele to a tree and lashed him with a branch. She detested his spinelessness. How could he cry in front of others? Wasn't that tantamount to admitting defeat at Luni's hands? What future is there for a man who sheds tears over a woman?

Jindele was truly spineless. Each time Yveline struck him, he moaned, *'Aiyo! Aiyo!'* This ignited her rage, and she lashed him even more harshly. She cursed Jindele for taking after his father Kunde. Worthless, gutless creatures, no wonder they were trampled upon by women.

She didn't stop lashing him until the branch snapped. The sound of Yveline beating Jindele echoed throughout the camp, but no one interfered. Everyone knew Yveline's temper, and trying to dissuade her would only have resulted in heavier punishment for Jindele.

Yveline's behaviour made Luni feel that the wolf pursuing him had already chased him to the edge of a precipice. So he took an even bolder action. The next day Luni left camp, explaining he was going hunting and would return in three days.

Three days later Luni did indeed return, but his catch was Nihau herself. Her father Alek led the entourage to see the bride off, and it was a merry party that arrived in our *urireng*.

Just how Luni convinced Alek to marry his daughter to him – when she was not yet fully grown – we never learned. But what we saw was a young Nihau, attired like a gorgeous flower swaying in the wind, with an enchantingly shy and joyful smile. She was doubtless exceedingly happy to be with Luni.

Nidu the Shaman presided over the marriage ceremony. After a glance at Tamara, who was shivering despite her seat by the fire, he stated eloquently to Luni: 'Henceforth, Nihau shall be your wife. A man's love is a flame. You must ensure that your woman never knows the cold and lives happily in your warm embrace!'

Then he turned to Nihau, and said to her: 'Henceforth, Luni shall be your husband. Love him well, for your love endows him with eternal strength. The Spirits shall bestow upon you the finest sons and daughters on the earth!'

Nidu the Shaman's words transformed the expressions of several women. Nihau smiled. Yveline pursed her lips. Maria nodded her head in affirmation. Tamara ceased shivering. Her moist eyes focused on Nidu the Shaman, and her face seemed to reflect the sunset, displaying a tenderness long absent.

The sun descended into the mountains, hand held hand, and while dancing began about the bonfire, Tamara appeared with Ilan. Our hound was listless, but to our surprise Tamara was in high spirits.

I'll never forget Mother's attire that day. She wore a short, beige blouse, and the bird-feather skirt crafted for her by Nidu the Shaman. On her feet were knee-high deerskin boots. She pulled her grey fringe and the hair on her temples into a chignon, giving her an exceptionally neat and serene look.

When she made her appearance there were gasps of surprise. Those in the party that had come to send off the bride, and were thus unfamiliar with Tamara, exclaimed at her beauty, while the rest of us marvelled at a certain new aura about her.

For so long, she had carried herself stooped, her neck bent like a criminal, and buried her head in her chest. But at that moment Tamara held her head high, back straight, and her eyes shone brightly, and we wondered if we weren't looking at someone else. Rather than say she was wearing a bird-feather skirt, you might say her lower body was decorated in a swathe of autumn. Those dappled colours seemed to have undergone a baptism of frost.

Tamara began to dance and she was as lithesome as ever. She laughed as she twirled and I'd never heard her laugh with such a light heart.

Old Ilan lay next to the fire, his head at an angle, watching his mistress with utter devotion. Seeing Ilan so well behaved, naughty Viktor sat down on him like a pillow.

As soon as he was seated, he yelled at Lajide: '*Ama, Ama*, this leather cushion is hot!' Viktor picked up a straw and poked around Ilan's eyes with it. 'Tomorrow your eyes will shine,' he said. 'I'll feed you meat and you'll be able to see again!'

One day not long before, Viktor had thrown a piece of meat to Ilan, but Ilan paid it no heed whatsoever, lowered his head and walked away. Little Viktor thought this meant that Ilan's eyes weren't working right. But I understood. He didn't want to eat meat any more. He just wanted to deplete his reserves of energy more quickly.

Nihau adored Tamara's skirt, and like a butterfly flitting about a flower, she circled Tamara, admiring the skirt. Perhaps Luni thought that mother's dancing in that bird-feather skirt was undignified, and he told me to urge her to leave.

But I hadn't the heart to do so. She looked so full of vitality, and I was unwilling to stifle it. Even more so, since everyone was happy about the marriage of Luni and Nihau, except for Yveline and Jindele. When you're happy you can indulge yourself a bit.

The bonfire gradually paled and the number of dancers dwindled. Members of the entourage from Nihau's *urireng* went to rest at Ivan's. Only Tamara remained, circling the fire. At the beginning I kept her company, but I grew so drowsy I couldn't carry on and I retired for the night. When I left, only slumbering Ilan, a dismal bonfire and the waning moon remained to accompany Mother.

I was a bit worried about Luni and Nihau. I feared he was rash and, because she was so young, he'd hurt her. So I didn't return directly to my *shirangju*. Instead, I headed to Luni's to listen for anything amiss. But even before I got there Nihau came running out. She was crying, and she threw herself into my arms.

'Luni's a scoundrel,' she said. 'He has a spear attached to his body and he wants to pierce me with it!' I couldn't help laughing when I heard this.

I consoled Nihau while I reproached Luni. 'If he dares use that spear to harm you, I'll punish him myself.' Only then did Nihau go back inside their *shirangju*, mumbling, 'Marrying a man is a load of trouble.'

Outside, Luni looked at me sheepishly. 'You were in a rush to wed her,' I said, 'and now she's yours for real. But she's so young! At first, you'll have to look after her as she grows up, and after that you can be her husband.'

Luni sighed and nodded. So during their first two years, even though Luni and Nihau lived in the same *shirangju*, their relations were as innocent as brother and sister.

I returned to our *shirangju* thinking of mother dancing all alone, and my entire body felt cold. My teeth chattered, and in the darkness Lajide pulled me into his warm embrace. But I was still cold no matter how tightly he held me, and I kept trembling. I couldn't get to sleep. Again and again images of Mother's dancing silhouette flashed before my eyes.

When the morning's first light appeared in the sky, I arose, wrapped an upper garment around my shoulders and walked to where everyone had gathered in revelry last night. I saw three piles of ashes: a bonfire's, for it had burned itself out; a hound's, for Ilan was deathly still; and a woman's, for Mother had fallen to the ground, her face to the sky. Her eyes were open, but they were already fixed in place. Only the bird-feather skirt and her white-speckled hair fluttered in the morning breeze. The sight of those piles of ashes is engraved on my heart for ever.

Linke had died, and now Mother too. One parent departed in thunder, the other in dance.

We buried Mother in the trees and selected birch for her wind-burial, not pine as we had for Father. Her bird-feather skirt served as her shroud.

As Nidu the Shaman presided over Tamara's funeral, a flock of southbound wild geese passed in the sky, in the shape of a forked tree branch, or perhaps a bolt of lightning. The difference is that lightning is white against dark clouds, while the geese were a black line against a clear sky.

Nidu the Shaman intoned a dirge for Tamara that made me recognise the profound love he had for Mother.

Our ancestors believe that when a human leaves this world she proceeds to another, happier one. On the way there, she must pass a very, very deep River of Blood where her previous actions and character undergo scrutiny. If a kind-hearted person arrives here, a bridge will emerge from the river, allowing her to pass safely; if a person who has committed wicked acts arrives here, a stone will leap out of the river. If she shows remorse for bad conduct in her former existence, she can step on the stone and jump across the river. Otherwise, she will be utterly submerged by the River of Blood and her soul will vanish.

Did Nidu the Shaman sing this dirge for Mother because he feared she might fail to cross the River of Blood on her own?

> *O raging River of Blood*
> *Pray raise up a bridge*
> *For she who treads before you*
> *Is a kind-hearted woman!*
>
> *If fresh blood stains her feet*
> *It is no one's but her own.*
> *If there be tears in her heart*
> *They too are her very own!*
>
> *If you disdain a woman*
> *With blood-stained feet*

*And tear-filled heart*
*Pray fix a stepping stone*
*And let her jump safely across!*

*If you must assign blame*
*Then assign blame to me!*
*If only she reaches*
*Yonder shore of happiness*
*Even if doomed to melt*
*In the River of Blood*
*I shall not protest!*

As Nidu the Shaman sang, Nihau shuddered, as if each word in the lament had turned into a stinging wasp.

Back then we didn't realise that in her former existence she had forged an affinity with Spirit Songs. In reality, she was a fish swimming in a river invisible to us. Nidu the Shaman's Spirit Song was bait cast to snag her. But at the time we thought she was shuddering out of fright from Tamara's death. Luni was distressed for her and held her hands.

'One day her bones will drop from the trees,' said Nihau abruptly as she left the wind-burial site, 'and the bones that fall upon the ground will germinate.'

\* \* \*

After Tamara's death, Nidu the Shaman became even more disinterested in the life of the *urireng*. When to go on the hunt, when to sever reindeer antlers, when to move camp – he was utterly indifferent now. He lost weight more and more quickly. Everyone felt he was no longer fit to be Headman, so Lajide was chosen to replace him.

Lajide's first act as Headman was to split the *urireng*'s big family into several smaller ones. Everyone still hunted together, but when they transported their catch back to the camp, except for items such as pelts, antlers and bear galls, which belonged to the *urireng* and were to be bartered for manufactured items, the meat was evenly divided according to the number of mouths in each household. This meant that except for festivals, each family ate on its own.

The most ardent supporter of this decision was Luni, and I understood why. He didn't want to hear Yveline ridicule guileless Nihau in front of everyone day in and day out, and even less did he want to see the avaricious and spiteful gaze that Jindele cast upon her.

But Yveline was staunchly opposed. Lajide's decision was inhumane and would lead to the break-up of the *urireng*, she said. Ivan and Nidu the Shaman were the loneliest people on the earth, and if they didn't even have the chance to sit with others and eat, to whom would they speak? Didn't this mean that Nidu the Shaman could only converse with the *Malu*, and Ivan with his reindeer?

It was clear to me that Yveline was using the excuse of their loneliness to bemoan her own. She didn't like to dine alone with Kunde and Jindele, and she often revealed her loathing for father and son. But I didn't understand the origin of this loathing. I went to ask Maria, and she helped me unravel the mystery.

Maria said Kunde was once a lively and bold young man. One year he went to the bazaar on the banks of the Pa Béra to barter his catch. There he fell in love with a Mongolian maiden, but Kunde's father didn't approve of their marriage because he had already settled the matter of Kunde's future union with Yveline. Compelled to take Yveline's hand in marriage, Kunde was forever downcast.

Yveline despised dispirited, apathetic men, and she often enumerated Kunde's shortcomings, describing him as devoid of virtue. Kunde's father found this offensive. 'If I'd known you would treat my son like this, I'd have broken his engagement to you and allowed him to marry that Mongolian maiden!'

It was then that Yveline comprehended why Kunde was always so lukewarm toward her. Strong-willed Yveline was furious, and in a fit of anger she came running back to our *urireng*, swearing never to return to Kunde. She was already with child then.

At his father's insistence, Kunde came to retrieve Yveline on several occasions, but each time her cursing chased him away. After Yveline gave birth to Jindele she realised that the child couldn't grow up without a father, so she took Kunde back, on the condition that he move to our *urireng*.

Having joined us, Kunde passed his days obediently. But whenever Yveline was displeased, she vented her anger on him. For Jindele's sake, Kunde swallowed her insults in silence.

But no one had imagined the lengths to which Yveline went to chastise Kunde. Maria said that one time Kunde had drunk too much when hunting with Hase, and he cried as he told Hase that he wasn't living like a real man. She said that having borne him one mongrel was sufficient.

Maria felt that Yveline was going too far, so she had a few conciliatory words with her in private. But Yveline flew into a rage and declared that she, Yveline, would never sleep with someone who didn't love her. Whenever it occurred to her that, in the darkness of night Kunde might treat her as someone else, she felt nauseous.

Maria told me that the young Kunde was like a blade of emerald grass teeming with thick sap. But having undergone endless kneading in Yveline's hands, he had become a wizened straw. I understood why Yveline displayed a certain envy and contempt for the happiness and true affection of others.

I sympathised with Kunde, but I also sympathised with Yveline because, like Nidu the Shaman and Tamara, she had suffered on account of love.

Since Yveline's heart concealed awkward secrets, and Nidu the Shaman and Ivan were truly lonely, I suggested to Lajide that it would be better if everyone sat together and ate as we used to.

'If you allow lonely and jolly people to sit together,' replied Lajide, 'the lonely ones will just feel even more miserable. It's better to let them be by themselves – that way they still have pleasant memories for company. No other women in our world can completely occupy the hearts of Ivan and Nidu the Shaman like Nadezhda and Tamara once did.'

As for Yveline, despite her loathing for Kunde they needed to live in each other's company, and forcing them to spend more time alone together was the only way to break down the wall between them.

'If two people are always seated side by side,' continued Lajide, 'they grow older and more feeble with time. As they observe one another's old and feeble faces, their hearts will eventually soften.'

And so, the new Headman's decision was implemented amidst Yveline's curses and protests. At dinner time, she often lit a fire in the campsite, and sat outside her family's *shirangju* eating by herself. Sometimes she let loose a stream of abuse at the hovering ravens that hankered after the food in her hands.

Everyone understood that when she cursed the ravens she was cursing Lajide, but he didn't mind. 'After a while when Yveline realises that there's no joy to be had in this, she'll go and sit with Kunde and Jindele.'

With the arrival of the snowflakes, Yveline eventually ceased lighting a fire outside, and learned to gather round the fireplace and eat in her family's *shirangju*.

But she was still resentful of Lajide and often found fault with him. Either the share of the meat allotted to her family was too small or there were too many bones in the meat. Lajide didn't argue. Instead, whenever he divided the catch, he would call Yveline over and let her have first pick. At the beginning Yveline self-righteously selected the choicest parts, but soon she realised that Lajide always left the most inferior meat for himself, and she was embarrassed and stopped being so fussy.

Turkov hadn't visited our camp since the previous spring, and flour was running short now it was winter. Just when Lajide and Hase were preparing to go to Jurgang – also known then by its Russian name, Uchiriovo – to barter for food supplies, a stout Han on a Mongolian Three River Horse came into our camp. A native of Shandong named Xu Caifa, he owned two stores in Jurgang and appeared good-natured.

Lajide's elder brother missed him, so he had divided up some flour, salt and liquor and asked Xu Caifa to bring them to our *urireng*. He told us that the Japanese had founded the Manchurian

Livestock Company in Jurgang, and in the future we'd have to exchange our pelts there.

'But the Japanese can really fleece people,' he said. 'Take squirrel pelts, for example. One squirrel pelt can only be exchanged for a box of matches, three pelts for a box of bullets, six pelts for a bottle of *baijiu*, and seven pelts will only get you a small box of tea leaves. Most *anda* realise that's no way to do business, so those who can have left.'

'Are these Japanese even more black-hearted than Turkov?' asked Yveline.

Xu Caifa had news of that sly *anda*. 'Turkov has gone back to the Soviet Union. When a black-hearted fellow encounters another of his kind, it's the worse of the two who remains!'

I remembered Rolinsky fondly, so I asked about him. 'Rolinsky was a fine fellow, but unlucky! These last few years he fell in love with booze, and last winter while transporting a consignment from Jalannér to Uchiriovo, he ran into a pack of wolves,' recounted Xu Caifa. 'His horse took fright and went on a mad gallop. The goods weren't damaged, but Rolinsky was dragged to death.'

'Hmph,' groaned Yveline. 'Of course the goods weren't damaged. They were dead to start with!'

'In the future the Russian *anda* won't dare enter the mountains to deliver goods. If the Japanese find out, who knows what's in store.'

After he unloaded his goods, he took a few swigs of liquor, ate two pieces of meat and set off. Lajide gave him a few squirrel pelts and deerskins in gratitude.

\* \* \*

One snowy day not long after Xu Caifa left, three men arrived on horseback: a Japanese, Lieutenant Yoshida; a Han interpreter for the Japanese, Wang Lu; and their Evenki guide, Ludek.

That was the first time I heard Japanese spoken. That *jeelee-wala* of theirs resembled someone speaking with a stunted tongue. I was so amused that I chuckled, and little Dashi and Viktor laughed along with me. Noting our laughter, Yoshida frowned and looked very displeased.

Wang Lu was a kind fellow, and seeing Yoshida express his hostility towards our mocking laughter, he made up a white lie. 'When the Evenki like what someone says, they make a laughing noise.'

Yoshida's brows relaxed. 'Last year most of the hunting peoples were called down from the mountains for a meeting to select their new leaders. You were all neglected then, but we haven't forgotten you. Now that we've come, all of you will enjoy happy lives. All Soviets are bad, and in the future you're not to deal with them! We Japanese are your most reliable friends.'

Wang Lu interpreted Yoshida's speech, and we could see that he didn't understand our tongue either.

'When a wolf wants to eat a hare, it's bound to compliment its beauty!' said Yveline.

'If the Japanese are our friends,' said Hase, 'how come they just exchange one box of matches for a squirrel pelt? Rolinsky would give us at least five boxes!'

'It seems the Japanese have only brought a pan,' said Lajide, 'and they're waiting for our meat to start cooking!'

'But their tongues are so short I'll bet it's not so easy for them to eat meat!' Luni's words made everyone howl with laughter.

But Ivan, his head hung low, didn't laugh. He stared vacantly at his huge hands like a pair of iron tools gone rusty. Emptiness was written all over his face.

Yoshida noticed that his interpreter and guide were laughing, and assuming this meant that they approved of what he was saying, he laughed and raised his thumb.

When we were summoned earlier for Yoshida's speech, Nidu the Shaman hadn't come. But just when Yoshida asked Wang Lu if any *urireng* members were absent, Nidu the Shaman made his entrance in the *shirangju*. In his hands was the Spirit Drum, and the Spirit Robe was draped over his shoulders, but he hadn't donned his Spirit Hat so his grizzled hair hung loose.

His demonic appearance gave Yoshida such a fright that he shuddered and took a step back. Tongue-tied at first, he pointed at Nidu the Shaman, and asked Wang Lu: 'Who is this man?'

'A Shaman,' said Wang Lu, 'a Spirit!'

'What does a "Spirit" do?'

'The Spirits can make rivers run dry,' I told him, 'or make waters overflow when rivers run low. They can make roe-deer flourish or wipe out all the wild creatures.'

'The Spirit cures human illness,' was Wang Lu's translation.

Yoshida's eyes lit up. 'So he's a doctor?'

'Yes.'

Yoshida rolled up his trouser and pointed to a bloody scar on his leg. 'Can you make this scar disappear right now?' he asked Nidu the Shaman.

Wang Lu's face displayed panic, but Nidu the Shaman was quite calm. He instructed Wang Lu to inform Yoshida: 'If he wishes his wound to vanish, then the horse he rides must be sacrificed.' As he pronounced these words, he altered his typically depressed mien, and looked extraordinarily composed.

Yoshida thought Nidu the Shaman intended to kill his horse. He became enraged. 'This is a battle steed selected from more than one hundred horses. It is my good companion and under no circumstances can it be put to death!'

'If you wish for your war-horse to survive, then your eyes shall not see your scar healed. And I, Nidu the Shaman, need not kill your war-horse with a knife. I shall terminate its life with a dance.'

Yoshida laughed. He didn't believe Nidu the Shaman possessed that sort of power.

'If Nidu the Shaman can really make my wound vanish without a trace, I am willing to sacrifice my battle steed,' Yoshida said merrily. 'But if he fails, Nidu the Shaman must burn his ritual vestments and Spirit Drum in front of everyone, kowtow before me and beg my forgiveness.'

When Wang Lu finished translating these words, there was dead silence within the *shirangju*. It was dusk just then, the sun midway on its downward path.

'We must await the night's arrival before commencing the Spirit Dance,' said Nidu the Shaman.

'What you await,' said Yoshida in words pregnant with meaning, 'is most certainly your own dark night.'

Wang Lu translated Yoshida's words, and then said to Nidu the Shaman: 'Perhaps it would be better not to dance. Just say that your body is not strong enough today, and you will dance another day.'

Nidu the Shaman sighed. 'I want him to comprehend that I am capable of summoning a dark night, but it will not be mine. It will be his!'

Darkness fell and Nidu the Shaman struck his drum and began to dance. We huddled in the corners of the *shirangju*, apprehensive. Ever since the deer plague, we had begun to doubt his powers.

At times he raised his head to the sky and laughed heartily, at times he lowered his head and moaned. When he neared the fireplace, I saw a tobacco pouch hanging from his waist, the one Mother had sewn for him. He didn't look his usual feeble self. His back straightened miraculously, he made the Spirit Drum emit intense drumbeats, and his feet were so nimble that I found it hard to believe that someone could take on such a different demeanour when dancing. He appeared full of vitality, just like the Nidu the Shaman of my youth.

I was pregnant with Andaur then. It wasn't time for labour to begin, but after I anxiously watched Nidu the Shaman perform the Spirit Dance for a while, I began to feel a wave of stomach cramps. My palms and forehead sweated profusely. I held out my hand to Lajide. He thought the sweat was due to fright, and kissed me tenderly by my ear to placate me. And so I withstood the severe pain and watched Nidu the Shaman complete his performance. It never occurred to me that, like watching Mother at Luni's marriage celebration, I was witnessing his ultimate trance dance.

When the dancing stopped, Yoshida came over to the fireplace and lifted his leg. We heard him emit a bizarre cry: a moment before his wound was a vividly coloured blossom, but now it had dispersed in the wind fabricated by Nidu the Shaman.

Following Nidu the Shaman, we left the *shirangju* for a look at the horse. On the snowy ground illuminated by the stars in the camp's pine grove, we found just two horses standing. Yoshida's mount had already collapsed and no longer drew breath.

This made me think back to my earliest memory of the grey fawn that had collapsed in our summer camp. Yoshida caressed his dead battle steed, its corpse free of the slightest wound. Then he turned to Nidu the Shaman and began to shout his *jeeleewala* Japanese. 'Spirit Man, we need you!' translated Wang Lu. 'Come with me to serve Japan!'

Nidu the Shaman coughed a few times, turned and walked away. He hunched over again and discarded first his drumstick, then the Spirit Drum, and then the Spirit Robe and Spirit Skirt. The Spirit Robe was decorated with many metallic totems, and they jingled as they hit the snow.

We remained around the dead war-horse, as if keeping watch over a gigantic boulder that had dropped from the sky. We observed Nidu the Shaman's back in a daze. No one stood up.

Only Nihau followed slowly in his wake, scooping up each item as he discarded it. When there was not one ritual instrument or piece of Spirit Garb left on him, Nidu the Shaman collapsed.

That very night I went to Nidu the Shaman's *shirangju* to give birth to Andaur, since there was no time to construct a *yataju*. I knew that Nidu the Shaman had departed, but our *Malu* were still there, and They would help me get through the difficulties of a premature delivery.

I didn't keep Yveline at my side. In the *shirangju* where Nidu the Shaman had resided, I felt brightness and courage supporting me just like my own legs.

When Andaur came wailing into this world of snow and ice, at the pointed top of the *shirangju* I saw a bright star giving off a blue glow. I believe those rays of light were emitted by Nidu the Shaman.

\* \* \*

Yoshida returned to the Kwantung Army Garrison. He had come on a battle steed but left on foot. He gave us the other two horses. He was spiritless, like someone with a sharp weapon who has done battle with an unarmed man, yet has lost.

Little Dashi liked these two horses and he became their master. That winter he led them to graze on sunlit slopes to ensure they could feed on dry grass. The grass on the northern hillsides was blanketed in thick snow.

Because the scrawny horse that Kunde had traded for long ago had not survived, Yveline had a strong aversion to horses. 'Since the first horse that arrived in our *urireng* didn't bring us good luck, those two horses left by the Japanese will only bring disaster,' she predicted.

The following year spring seemed to arrive unusually early. Andaur couldn't walk yet, and I put him in a cradle. Viktor watched him while Lajide and I went to make a salt lick.

*Kandahang* and deer like to lick salty soil, so in places frequented by their quarry, hunters dig one foot into the ground, bore a hole with a wooden wedge, place salt in it, and fill in the hole with dirt, thereby gradually rendering the soil alkaline.

We conceal ourselves in the nearby woods and wait for deer to pause and lick the briny soil. In a sense, a salt lick is actually a deer killing ground.

There were two salt licks belonging to our *urireng*, one small and one large, and two years running we went there in the evenings after the rain and knelt in wait for our prey, but our efforts were fruitless.

Lajide said our salt licks were too close to water. He said we should build new ones on one of the sunny slopes, where *kandahang* and deer liked to roam. Lajide secretly left the mountains for Xu Caifa's store in Jurgang where he obtained two bags of salt.

We spent two days completing a new salt lick. 'This soft, salty soil is the best bed,' Lajide whispered, nestling up to me. 'We should make a daughter here.'

His words excited me. I could almost see young girls fluttering about us like butterflies. 'That's a wonderful idea,' I said.

The sun was so pleasantly warm. The sunlight gleamed on the new salt lick, and its silky white rays were like sprouts shooting up from the salt-laden soil, fresh and radiant.

We embraced spontaneously, luxuriating like a cool breeze in the spring light. That was our most touching spell of intimacy ever, and the longest. Below me warm salty soil, above me the man I loved, and above the man I loved, blue sky.

My eyes fastened onto an unbroken white cloud wafting from east to west like a heavenly river. And the lower part of my body flowed a river too, a hidden river only a woman knows, surging solely for the man she loves.

One day as summer approached, I rose at dawn and went to milk the reindeer when I suddenly passed out. When I came to I found Lajide grinning broadly at me. 'That new salt lick isn't bad at all,' he said gently. 'Seems your belly is looking after a spotted fawn.' Then I recalled fainting when I was pregnant with Andaur too, which had given Lajide a terrible fright.

Just as we were carrying out the annual severing of reindeer antlers, three men arrived in the camp, two of whom we knew: Ludek, the guide, and the interpreter Wang Lu. The third was a Japanese, but not Yoshida. This was Suzuki. He was short and thin, sported a walrus moustache, wore a military uniform, and had a rifle on his back, and ordered liquor and meat upon his arrival. Once they were down in his gut, he commanded us to sing and dance for him.

Wang Lu said the Japanese had established the Kwantung Army Qilin Forest Brigade Training Camp, which came to be known as the Kwantung Army Garrison, in the eastern part of Uchiriovo. Suzuki had come to gather the Evenki hunters and lead them down from the mountains for training. All males over fourteen were required to participate.

'We are mountain hunters,' said Lajide. 'Why should we leave the mountains?'

'You'll just be gone for a month or so,' said Wang Lu. 'The world belongs to the Japanese now, and defying them is just asking for trouble. Best go down from the mountains and put on a show, shout marching songs in unison, practise your riflery, and treat it as a chance to take in the scenery.'

'Isn't that drafting us to serve in the army?' Lajide asked. 'Even if it is, we can't fight for the Japanese!'

'Who says you're being drafted?' said Wang Lu. 'It's just training, not war. You'll be back soon.'

Lajide sighed. 'If we're really going to be forced to join the army and sent to some far-off land, then we should be soldiers like Hailancha.'

It was my father who told me the story of Hailancha, an Evenki who lived during the early Qing Dynasty. He lost his father in his youth, and his mother died before her time, so he began herding horses for a trader in Hailar while still young. Wolves often attacked the horses until he took up the position. It is said that when he slept, he emitted a roar like a tiger that carried several *li*. So the wolf packs naturally stayed far away from his grazing herd.

Hailancha enlisted during the reign of Qing Emperor Qianlong and was dispatched to Xinjiang where he helped put down a revolt by the Dzungar Mongols. He captured a rebel general alive, an act which brought him lasting fame.

Hailancha was held in high esteem by Emperor Qianlong who later sent him on expeditions to do battle in Myanmar, Taiwan, Tibet and other lands. He became an illustrious Evenki general.

Father said Hailancha was not only exceptionally courageous, he was also handsome and rugged. 'One day when you seek a husband, look for someone like Hailancha!'

I still remember how I shook my head. 'No, that won't do! When he sleeps he roars like a tiger. What if he makes me go deaf?' Father doubled over with laughter.

'Hmph,' snorted Yveline. 'If Hailancha were alive today, would the Japanese dare come here? Hailancha chased away those big-nosed British. Would he fear the flat-nosed Japanese dwarfs? I'd be surprised if he didn't spill their guts!'

Wang Lu was so alarmed that his lips quivered. 'This Japanese understands a little Evenki now,' he told us. 'Don't talk nonsense in front of him whatever you do. Heads will roll.'

'A person only has one head,' said Yveline. 'If no one cuts it off, in the end it'll rot on the ground like a piece of overripe fruit. What's the difference if it's cut off early or later?'

Suzuki sensed that the tone of the conversation was a bit tense, so he questioned Wang Lu closely. 'What are these savages saying?' He didn't refer to us as 'hunting peoples' like Yoshida.

'The savages say that leaving the mountains for training is a good thing,' said Wang Lu. 'They're keen to go.'

Suzuki wasn't convinced. He pointed at Yveline. 'Then why does this woman look so unhappy?'

'She's incensed that the training is just for men,' said quick-thinking Wang Lu. 'She says mountain women are just as strong as the men, so why not permit women to go too?'

Suzuki smiled. 'A good woman. A good woman indeed, and if her nose weren't crooked she'd be even better!'

When Wang Lu interpreted this entire exchange, everyone chuckled.

Yveline laughed too. 'You tell him that if my nose weren't crooked, he couldn't find me here in the mountains. I'd have left to reign as the Empress!'

She glanced at Kunde and Jindele and sighed. 'I'll be happy to see them leave so I can get some peace and quiet. If the Japanese can hammer them into shape in the barracks, so much the better!'

Yveline was willing for Kunde and Jindele to leave her, but Maria was quite the opposite. Dashi was just old enough to receive military training. Maria could stand for her husband Hase to leave, but not Dashi. At the very thought that he might have to undergo hardship, Maria couldn't hold back her tears.

Suzuki pointed at Maria and asked: 'Why is this woman crying?'

'Whenever this woman is happy she cries,' said Wang Lu. 'She's thinking how fortunate her son is. He's just turned fourteen, otherwise he couldn't take part in the training. And if he doesn't undergo training, he won't be a real man!'

'The women in this *urireng* are amazing,' said Suzuki admiringly. Then his eyes turned to Nihau. Nihau was a lamp, and Suzuki's gaze was a moth inescapably attracted to her flame.

Nihau was grown up now. Nourished by Luni, she had grown into a full-figured woman. She couldn't bear for him to leave the mountains either, because she was pregnant and they were enjoying a period of great passion and intimacy.

Nihau was very astute, so when she realised that Suzuki kept glancing at her, she placed her arm on Luni's shoulder affectionately to indicate that this was her man.

The men gathered and left for training in Uchiriovo. As we saw them off from the campsite, the forest was filled with dancing white butterflies. Though the sun was bright, it seemed that the men were veiled in white and walking in snow. A summer with an abundance of white butterflies foreshadows a snowy winter.

I still recall how Lajide stretched out his hand and snatched a butterfly. 'Here's a snow blossom for you,' he said. Smiling, he opened his fist and the butterfly fluttered towards me, which made all the women seeing off their men laugh merrily.

\* \* \*

In the first days, those of us who remained in the camp felt very happy. With the severing of antlers now behind us, every day we gathered simply to drink tea, eat and do our chores. But we quickly learned that the men's absence meant certain tasks became difficult to handle. For example, when the herd returned each day a few reindeer were always missing. Normally, the men would search for them, but now this chore fell to us. Just locating two or three reindeer could eat up half a day.

We feared wild animals would enter the camp and harm our young in our absence. So I carried Viktor on my back, and placed Andaur in a cradle up in a tree in spite of his wailing.

Once we came back and brought Andaur down only to find his face covered with blisters. Wasps had taken his delicate pink face for a flower and stung him repeatedly, and he had long ago cried himself hoarse.

But that wasn't all. When there are no men, there's no one to go on the hunt, and Yveline – who was accustomed to eating fresh meat – found it especially trying. The men had taken their rifles with them, but even if we had guns they'd have been useless in our inexperienced hands.

Remembering that Lajide and I had built a salt lick, Yveline decided to go hunting on her own. She took a spear from Ivan's *shirangju*. Nihau and I, both pregnant, were to remain behind while she and Maria went to lie in wait at the salt lick.

They went three nights in a row but came back empty-handed, their faces as pale as a sunless dawn. But Yveline wasn't downcast. She was determined, and on the fourth day, she went with Maria once again. That day a light rain fell, and deer love to come out the night after a rainfall. So when they set out Yveline was bursting with confidence. 'Bring out the pot for stewing meat. My spear will come in handy today for sure!'

And Yveline was true to her word. At dawn next day, she and Maria brought back a fawn. The spear had pierced the fawn right at the throat. Knowing how deer like to move against the wind, Yveline and Maria had hidden in a thicket downwind. Towards dawn they heard the *cha-la cha-la* sound of chomping, and a doe and a fawn appeared at the salt lick.

Yveline decided to go for the fawn because it had its side to her, making its throat a natural target, while the doe's rump faced her.

Maria said Yveline sent the spear flying like a thunderbolt — *shwa* — and the fawn flipped onto the salt lick. While Maria was recounting all this in high spirits, I felt a wave of painful spasms. I had conceived a child at that salt lick, and I didn't like to imagine a doe losing her young offspring there.

We constructed a three-sided hut, severed the deer's head, and hung it for a wind-burial. Then we removed the organs, took them inside the *shirangju* and offered them as a sacrifice to the *Malu*.

After Nihau retrieved Nidu the Shaman's ritual items and Spirit Garb, they remained with her. Lajide said you could tell from Nihau's behaviour that she might become a Shaman, so the *Malu* formerly worshipped by Nidu the Shaman were placed in Nihau's *shirangju*.

The *Malu* I had longed to see as a child were finally revealed to me during the rite for the fawn that Yveline had killed. The twelve Spirit Figurines were stored inside a deerskin pouch. First among them is '*Shewek*', our Ancestral Spirit. Actually, it's a single wood carving of a male and a female. They have hands and feet, ears and eyes, and are even dressed in a set of tiny deerskin clothing. Their lips have been coated in so much animal blood that they've turned purple.

All the other Spirits are related to the Chief Spirit, *Shewek*. *Shewek* likes the sound of drumbeats, so a small deerskin drum has been made for It; *Shewek* likes to fly atop a *Gaahi* bird, so a *Gaahi* hide keeps It company; and *Shewek* likes to ride reindeer, so a halter and reins have been given to It.

Inside the deerskin pouch were also squirrel, teal and *kerunacha* pelts; a Snake Spirit crafted from sheet iron; a sparrow-shaped *Umai* Spirit of white birch, which looks after young children; a Bear Spirit; and an *Along* Spirit of curved larch branches, which protects our reindeer.

As Nihau explained the Spirit Figurines to me, a *shwa-shwa* wind-sound echoed in my ears. It came from the Spirit Figurines.

'How come you understand so much about the Figurines?' I asked her.

She told me she saw her grandfather carve such statuettes when she was very young, so she knew the domains of each.

I gazed at those figurines made of wood and animal hides for a long time. They all originated in the mountain forests where we lived. This gave me faith that if they could really protect us, our happiness must lie within the mountain forests, not elsewhere. Although they weren't as beautiful or mysterious as I'd imagined, the magic gusts of wind they fabricated made my ears flutter like birds' wings, and filled me with reverence. It is surely because I once heard wind-sounds like those that my ears and eyes remain sharp today.

That evening we lit a bonfire in the camp, ate meat and drank *bai-jiu*, the clear distilled liquor we love. Yveline and Nihau drank too much, but they expressed their drunkenness quite distinctively: Yveline wept while Nihau sang. Because it was accompanied by Yveline's crying, Nihau's spur-of-the-moment song was bleak. One lost herself in tears, the other in song.

This crying and singing made the two horses whinny in fright. Maria was so anxious that she rushed over to them, afraid they'd snap their tethers and leave the camp. When Dashi left for

Uchiriovo, he hated parting with his horses. Again and again he told Maria to look after them attentively, where to take them for grazing, and at which ravine they should drink. He gave specific instructions for everything. After Dashi left, Maria cared for those horses as lovingly as if they were her very eyes.

I've had many lovely nights during my lifetime, and this one in which the sounds of weeping and singing melted together counts among them. We waited until the campfire grew faint before retiring to our *shirangju*. That night the wind was very cool. Andaur slept while Viktor cuddled up against me and pestered me for a story. So I told him a tale Lajide had told me.

Lajide said when his grandfather was young he once went into the mountains to engage in a traditional 'surround hunt'. The men couldn't return to their campsite the same day, so they constructed a *shirangju*. All seven slept inside, each occupying his own space.

Lajide's grandfather awoke in the middle of the night needing to pee and discovered it was very bright inside. A round moon hung at the top of the *shirangju*. He looked at the moon, then at the sleeping men, and noticed that each had struck a distinct pose: a crouching tiger, a coiled snake, or a squatting bear in hibernation. Lajide's grandfather realised that under a full moon humans reveal their true colours. From their sleeping positions, you can tell what they were before – a reincarnated hare or lynx or tiger, and so on.

'What was *Ama*'s grandfather in his former life?' Viktor asked.

'When he's awake he hasn't any way of knowing what he looks like when asleep,' I said.

'Then I'm not going to sleep tonight,' said Viktor. 'I want to see what *Eni* was reincarnated from.'

I smiled. 'It's not a full moon so you won't be able to see *Eni*'s former self.' I held Viktor tight, looked up at the stars over the *shi-rangju*, and yearned for Lajide.

We'd assumed the men would return in the autumn, but they'd been gone two months and there was still no news. We moved three times in the vicinity of the old camp, but eventually we had to undertake a major relocation because there were no longer any reindeer moss or fungi nearby. The reindeer roamed further and further afield, and at times didn't return for two days. Even tethering their fawns at the campsite to bring back the reluctant does was of no use, and we had a very tough time searching for those stray reindeer.

'We must leave here,' said Yveline. So we all put our possessions in order and followed the Bistaré River south-west.

The things we didn't need urgently we stored in a *kolbo*, taking just the necessities for survival. With two horses and more than seventy reindeer, we set off.

I walked at the very front and hacked tree markers with an axe. 'Let's not leave any markers behind,' said Yveline mischievously. 'The men will be frantic when they return if they don't know where we've gone.'

'Winter is almost here,' I said. 'If they can't find us, who'll hunt for us? How will we get meat?'

'It looks like it isn't deer or bear meat you want,' said Yveline loudly. 'You crave the meat on Lajide's body, eh?'

Yveline's words made Nihau chuckle so hard that she swayed back and forth on her reindeer and just about fell off. And they made Maria, who was the furthest behind leading her horse by the reins, tumble onto her bottom with laughter.

The *Malu* King was right behind me, then the reindeer transporting coals for the fire, followed by a large herd of reindeer.

Viktor was also riding a reindeer. Seeing everyone laughing so heartily, he said loudly to me: '*Eni*, if you eat *Ama*, don't eat his feet. They stink!' Viktor's words made us laugh even more hysterically.

After we'd travelled a few hours, Yveline took the axe from my hand, helped me up on a reindeer and let me rest. Each time she hewed a marker, she grunted 'Oh!', as if the hacked tree had opened its mouth wide to speak.

Moving camp without the men was already very tough, and given that our destination was undecided, our progress was slow. What originally should have been one day's journey became two.

In the end, it was the reindeer that helped us settle on the new camp's location. They discovered a Fairy Ring – a circular growth of mushrooms – at the foot of a mountain near a river, and came to a halt. When they stopped, so did we.

We constructed just two *shirangju*. Nihau and I stayed in one, and Maria and Yveline in the other. Once they'd arrived in the new camp the reindeer no longer strayed far and came back promptly each day.

In the northern forests, autumn resembles a thin-skinned person. If the wind utters a few less than complimentary words about him, he pulls a long face and beats a retreat.

It was late September, and you could still spot the odd wild chrysanthemum blooming here and there on the south-east slopes. But two days of sudden fierce winds blew away the last vestiges of that world once so full of vitality.

Having shed their every leaf, the trees were bald and fallen leaves massed under them in a thick, thick layer. A frigid wind began to blow, and the weather altered in a flash.

The snowflakes arrived early. Usually the first snow is not a heavy one and melts as it falls. So when we saw the snow-blossoms dancing in the air we weren't alarmed. But it snowed all day. At dusk, when we collected kindling around the camp, we discovered the snow was already very thick and a heavy layer of cloud had massed in the sky. Worried about the reindeer that were out searching for food, I asked Yveline: 'Will it snow through tomorrow?'

Yveline glanced proudly at the sky. And then eyeing me as if I were a scruffy half-wit, she said with conviction: 'The first snowfall is never heavy. Don't be fooled by how nasty it looks.' Yveline had years of experience, so I trusted her judgement and returned relieved to my *shirangju*.

Nihau was busy sewing a pair of mittens for her unborn child. Naughty Andaur occasionally stretched out his hand and grabbed the thread, hindering her progress.

'When there are lots of white butterflies in the summer,' said Nihau, 'the winter snow tends to be heavy.' I sighed and so did Nihau. We were both consumed with worry for our men. Did they feel the sting of a whip during their training? Did they have enough to eat? Now that the weather was cold, would the Japanese issue them heavy clothing? What if they caught cold?

In the slightly yellow light of the hearth, I could see the snow-flakes floating towards the *shirangju*. They stuck their furry heads inside for an exploratory look through the small flue at the top. But they weren't hard grains of sand; delicate and unable to withstand a wee bit of warmth, they melted almost as soon as they entered the *shirangju*. I watched the snowflakes for an instant and then placed a few pieces of damp firewood on the flames, for I wanted the fire to burn steadily until dawn. Then I fell asleep hugging Andaur.

The following day we were surprised to find that not only had the snow remained but it was falling more and more heavily. Outside the *shirangju* it was already above the knee, and the temperature had dropped dramatically. The mountain forests were a boundless mass, and the river had iced over.

As I came out of my *shirangju*, Yveline came staggering over. 'What are we going to do?' she said, stunned. 'Is this going to turn into a "White Calamity"?' That's what we called a life-threatening snowstorm.

A White Calamity would not only interfere with our hunting, it would threaten our reindeer, which was an even more frightening prospect. Reindeer can't break through the thickly accumulated snow to search for moss, and they starve.

We awaited the return of the herd apprehensively. The morning passed without any sign of them, the snowflakes continued to flutter and the wind picked up. If you stood outside just for an instant, the biting wind made you shiver uncontrollably.

Yveline decided to go looking for the reindeer with Maria and told Nihau and me to stay behind in the camp. At a time like that, two big-bellied women were a burden. Yveline had no inkling where the reindeer had gone. Normally we'd follow their tracks, but the heavy snowfall had buried any trace of them.

Nihau and I waited anxiously, but when the sky turned dark, there were no signs of either the reindeer or Yveline and Maria. At the outset we were just worried about the reindeer, but gradually the two worries combined, and Nihau and I became very restless. Again and again we left the *shirangju* to try to catch sight of them, but each time we returned disappointed.

Just when we were on the verge of tears, Yveline and Maria finally returned. Their bodies were clad in snow, and icicles had formed on their hair like a pair of snowmen. Yveline said all afternoon they had covered less than two *li*. The snow was simply too thick. You couldn't even move. Unable to find any sign of our reindeer, and worried we might go out looking for them, they had returned.

We passed a sleepless night kneeling before the *Malu*, praying that the reindeer would emerge from this crisis unscathed.

At such a time we missed our men more than ever. If they were here – even in the event of a White Calamity – they'd find the means to cope. Yveline consoled us, explaining that during a big snowstorm the reindeer would take cover under a cliff. The wind and snow there are not only less intense; there is also edible moss. They can remain there safely three, four or maybe even five days. Once the snow ceased, they would naturally find the path back to the camp.

I reckon that snowfall was the heaviest of my life. It fell for a full two days and two nights. On the third day, just as we were preparing to go out and search for the reindeer, our men returned. Hase told us later that the Japanese still wanted them to train for a few more days, but Lajide could see from the clouds that the weather was about to undergo a big change. He was worried about the women left up in the mountains, and so he asked Wang Lu to tell Suzuki that they had to return to the mountains.

Suzuki wouldn't allow it, so Lajide went looking for Yoshida who was in charge of the Kwantung Army Garrison. Perhaps because Yoshida's own eyes had seen his wound disappear and his battle steed die, he had a certain reverence for Nidu the Shaman's *urireng*. So he instructed Suzuki to return their rifles and allow our men to re-enter the mountains.

Snow had already begun falling when they set out. But before they reached the old campsite, they discovered the tree markers we had left behind. They realised we had moved camp and followed the markers along the Bistaré until they tracked us down.

It had been two days since they last rested, and on their way they had caught just one hare. After they arrived at the *urireng* and Lajide heard that the reindeer had been away from the camp for two days, he gulped a few mouthfuls of water, and they split into three groups for the search: Hase, Dashi and Ivan in one, Kunde with Luni and Jindele, and Lajide on his own. The others wore snowshoes but Lajide went on horseback. He said the horse had been with the reindeer for so long that it was familiar with their scent, so it could help him track them down.

Our *urireng* possessed a dozen or so pairs of snowshoes. They were made of pinewood with *kandahang* hide attached to the underside. Each snowshoe was nine hand-spans long, curved at the front, sloped at the back, and in the middle were leggings with leather straps. The men often wore snowshoes when hunting after a snowfall: you could cover three days' walk in just one day in snowshoes.

The men had no time to make idle conversation. They strapped on their snowshoes and left the camp straight away. Lajide was the last to depart. As he mounted his horse, he noticed that he and I were alone in the snow. He gestured to my belly. 'Soon, eh?'

I nodded. Lajide winked at me and chuckled. 'When she comes out I'll send another in. Can't have you idle!'

At dusk the next day, Lajide's horse returned bearing Lajide. But Lajide didn't greet me. He lay head-down on the horse, motionless. The horse was panting and collapsed upon reaching the camp. It appeared that Lajide, who had been dashing about for several days, had simply overdone it. He probably intended to take a short nap, and didn't expect to doze off stretched out on his horse. He froze to death while dreaming. As its master didn't move or shout commands, the horse must have realised that something was wrong, so it brought him back to the camp.

How I regretted not urging Lajide to search on foot with snow-shoes like the others! Then he wouldn't have fallen asleep, and I wouldn't have lost him and the child he and I created at the salt lick.

Seeing Lajide frozen stiff, I fainted. When I came to, my belly was empty. Yveline had already placed the premature infant in a white cloth bag and thrown it on a south-east slope. It was a baby girl as Lajide had foreseen.

Yveline cried. She was crying for Lajide and the child. Maria was crying too, but besides Lajide, she was also crying for the horse. She had seen how thirsty and weary it looked and given it a bit of water. But after finding the strength to right itself and drink, it had suddenly hit the ground with a thud and stopped breathing. Imagining how upset Dashi would be over the horse's demise, Maria's heart ached.

I wept too. A small part of my tears surged down my cheeks, but most surged towards my heart, because what flowed from my eyes were tears, and what flowed towards my heart was blood. It was the thick, tender drops of blood that Lajide had implanted in my body.

The other men all returned to the camp on the third day. Our reindeer had separated during the White Calamity and two-thirds had strayed beneath a hillside facing the sunless north-west. The snow was already falling very heavily, and combined with the north-west wind, a towering wall of snow had formed, trapping the reindeer inside. Unable to exit or find food for three or four days, most had frozen or starved to death, and only four were fortunate enough to survive.

The remaining third of the herd, led by the *Malu* King, sheltered under a cliff facing a gulch. The snowfall was lighter and there was food on the rocks, so except for some fawns that froze to death, the remainder survived. But altogether our herd was vastly reduced now to thirty head or so, equalling the losses we suffered during the Year of the Reindeer Plague.

We conducted a wind-burial for Lajide near the camp. With him gone, we chose Ivan to be the new Headman.

* * *

That winter was an endless night for me. Even in the daytime when the sky was clear and bright, I still felt a swathe of darkness before my eyes. As soon as the steps of the men returning from the hunt sounded in the camp, I used to run out of our *shirangju*, full of expectation, to greet Lajide.

The other women welcomed their men and took them back while I stood there all alone in the winter wind. Those icy gusts awoke me to reality: Lajide truly was no more. I yearned for the wind to take me to his soul, but the sound of Viktor and Andaur playing in the *shirangju* summoned me back to the hearth.

Nihau gave birth to a baby boy in the spring and Luni named him Grigori. We all adored Grigori, except for Yveline. Every time she saw the baby in his swaddling clothes, she looked at him askance and said the reddish mole on his forehead resembled Ivan's. 'Ivan was ill-fated,' she said, 'and Grigori will be no better.' Of course, she spoke these words in Ivan's absence.

Luni paid no heed to Yveline. He knew that she nursed a grudge because of Jindele.

Indeed, not long after Grigori's birth, Yveline arranged a match for her son. Named Zefirina, the bride was a very capable and mild-tempered girl, but her mouth was a tad crooked, as if she were always vexed about something or other.

Jindele clearly didn't care for the girl. 'Do you mean it's not bad enough to have a mother with a crooked nose, and now I have to take a girl with a crooked mouth for a wife?' he said.

At this, Yveline exploded with anger. 'You don't have the means to marry the ones you like, and the ones you don't show up at your *shirangju*,' she roared. 'That's your father's fate and yours too!'

'If you force me to marry her, I'll jump off a cliff!' said Jindele.

Yveline smiled icily. 'If you really have the guts to do that, then you're my son after all!'

When the rainy season arrived, the men went to Uchiriovo again. They took their catch with them, planning to barter them for the manufactured goods we lacked.

Hase said when they received training at the Kwantung Army Garrison, every day they had to run in formation, practise bayonet charges and wrestling, and they also had to learn how to conduct reconnaissance. Clever Dashi was assigned to the reconnaissance class where he mastered photography.

The Japanese also taught them their language, but Ivan refused to learn. 'Whenever they told him to speak Japanese, he'd stick out his tongue at an angle for Suzuki to see,' said Hase. 'Ivan meant that his tongue was useless and he couldn't say anything.'

And so, when it was time to study Japanese, Ivan went hungry. 'Since your tongue can't speak, I assume it can't eat either,' said Suzuki.

This training session lasted just forty days and the men returned in the autumn, but the goods they obtained for their pelts were meagre. Hase said if it hadn't been for Ivan's foresight in hiding twenty or so squirrel pelts and six roe-deerskins in a cave near the garrison – instead of exchanging them all at the Manchukuo Livestock Company – then they would have returned with even fewer goods.

When the training was over, Ivan ran to the cave under the cover of darkness and took the pelts to Uchiriovo where he located Xu Caifa who exchanged them for ammunition, salt and *baijiu*. Otherwise, that year – when our livelihood was already threatened due to the loss of our reindeer – would have been even more trying.

In the thirty-first year of the Republic of China, that is, in the spring of the ninth year of the reign of the Manchukuo Kangde Emperor, two big events took place in our *urireng*: Nihau became a Shaman, and Yveline fixed a date for Jindele's marriage without his consent.

Just after that year's *Ané* Festival – or 'Spring Festival' to the Han – Nihau started behaving oddly. One day at dusk when it was snowing, out of the blue she told Luni she wanted to go out and watch the sunset. 'It's snowing!' said Luni. 'What's there to watch?'

Nihau didn't reply and ran out barefoot. Luni grabbed her boots and chased after her. 'You'll freeze your feet off without your boots!'

Nihau just laughed loudly and kept running without a backward glance. Luni was the fastest runner in the *urireng*, but he couldn't overtake Nihau that day. The further she went the faster she ran, and soon there was no trace of her.

Luni panicked. He called Ivan and me over, and just when we were ready to split up and look for her, Nihau returned like a whirlwind. She was still running bare-footed, as light on her feet as a nimble fawn.

Back in their *shirangju*, she took Grigori in her arms, lifted up her blouse and nursed him as if nothing had happened. And her feet weren't chilled at all.

'Nihau, where did you go just now?' I asked.

'I've been right here, nursing Grigori.'

'Aren't your feet cold?'

'I'm next to the fire. Why would my feet be cold?'

Luni and I looked at one another, our hearts comprehending: perhaps Nihau was going to become a Shaman. It had been three years since the death of Nidu the Shaman, so it was time for our clan's new Shaman to emerge.

Not long afterwards, Nihau took sick. She lay next to the hearth, eyes wide open day and night. She did not eat, drink or speak for seven entire days. Then she yawned and sat up as if she had merely dozed off.

'Has the snow stopped falling?' she asked Luni. It had been snowing when she lay down seven days before.

'The snow stopped a long time ago,' he said.

Nihau gestured at Grigori. 'I only took a nap. Why's he looking so frail?' Nihau hadn't breast-fed Grigori for seven days and all Luni could feed him was reindeer's milk. It was only natural that the child had lost weight.

Meanwhile Maria came running in all flustered and delivered the news: the *Malu* King had died. He had lived twenty years and died of old age. We were grief stricken.

Traditionally, after the *Malu* King dies the pair of copper bells around his neck are removed and placed in the Shaman's *shirangju* where they remain until a successor has been chosen. It is the Shaman who hangs the bells on the new *Malu* King.

We walked into the reindeer herd only to find the *Malu* King collapsed on his side. His fur, worn away by years of wind and rain, resembled patches of lingering snow.

As we knelt before him, Nihau nonchalantly walked up to the *Malu* King, removed the reindeer bells, and abruptly placed them in her mouth.

'Nihau, why are you eating the bells!' exclaimed Luni. No sooner had he said that than she swallowed them in a single gulp. Each bell was as a big as a wild duck egg, and even a bull's coarse gullet couldn't ingest one so effortlessly.

Luni was appalled. But Nihau appeared quite unaffected, and didn't even burp.

Every year at the end of April and throughout May it was the fawning season. At that time we normally began to look for a place by a river or a gully with abundant lichen where we could deliver the fawns. We'd corral the bucks and the castrated males in a crude pen to ensure that the deliveries went smoothly.

When the *Malu* King died, the does were due to fawn in a month but we were lingering at our old campsite and still hadn't selected an ideal location. But just a few days later, Nihau announced: 'A new *Malu* King is about to be born!'

And her pronouncement was not mistaken. A white-spotted doe suddenly cried out and then gave birth to a snow-white fawn! It resembled an auspicious cloud that had just fallen to the earth.

As we ran towards the fawn, Nihau suddenly halted, opened her mouth, and effortlessly coughed up the copper bells. One bell in each hand, she proceeded slowly towards the new *Malu* King. Those bells looked so pristine and shiny that they seemed to have just been forged. There must have been a crystal-clear river flowing inside Nihau to have scrubbed those dusty bells so thoroughly!

That fawn became our *Malu* King the moment Nihau attached the bells to its neck.

When we buried the old *Malu* King, Nihau intoned the first of her Spirit Songs:

> *Your snow-white mantle*
> *Melted in springtime.*
>
> *Grass burgeons green*
> *From your blossom-shaped spoor . . .*
>
> *And that pair of silver clouds*
> *Are your ever-shining orbs!*

While Nihau sang the Spirit Song, two round, snow-white clouds appeared in the dark blue sky. Gazing at them was like gazing into the luminous eyes of the *Malu* King we had known so well. Luni held Nihau against his chest affectionately, and stroked her hair lightly, so gently and sorrowfully. I understood. He longed for our clan to have a new Shaman, but he was also unwilling to see the woman he loved racked by the physical pain of being possessed by the Spirits.

\* \* \*

The grass grew green, flowers bloomed, swallows flew back from the south, and the waves shimmered again on the river. The ceremony marking Nihau's designation as our clan's Shaman was set to take place amidst the sights and sounds of springtime.

According to established practice, a new Shaman's initiation should take place at the *urireng* of the former Shaman. But Nihau was pregnant again, and Luni was worried that it would be hard for her to travel to Nidu the Shaman's old *urireng*, so Ivan invited a Shaman from another clan to come and preside over the Initiation Rite.

She was known as Jiele the Shaman. Past seventy, she still had a straight back, a set of neatly spaced teeth and a head of jet-black hair. Her voice carried far, and even after downing three bowls of *baijiu* without a pause her gaze didn't waver.

We erected two Fire Pillars to the north of our *shirangju*, a birch tree on the left, a pine on the right, symbolising the co-existence of mankind and the Spirits. They had to be big trees. In front of them we also placed two saplings – once again, a birch on the left and a pine on the right. We stretched a leather strap between the two big trees, and attached sacrificial offerings – reindeer hearts, tongues, livers and lungs – to show reverence to the Shaman Spirit. Blood from a reindeer heart was smeared onto the saplings. Besides all this, Jiele the Shaman hung a wooden sun to the east of the *shirangju*, and a moon to the west. She also carved a wild goose and a cuckoo out of wood, and suspended them separately.

The Spirit Dance Ceremony commenced. Everyone in our *urireng* sat next to the blazing fire observing Jiele the Shaman as she taught Nihau the Spirit Dance. Nihau was wearing the Spirit Robe left behind by Nidu the Shaman, but Jiele the Shaman had adapted it because he had been fat and taller than Nihau, so the Spirit Robe was too loose for her. That day it seemed that Nihau was a bride again. Clothed in a Shaman's costume, she was lovely and dignified.

Attached to the Spirit Robe were small wooden replicas of the human spine, seven metal strips symbolising human ribs, and lightning bolts and bronze mirrors of every size. The shawl draped on her shoulders was even more resplendent with teal, fish, swan and cuckoo bird adornments fastened to it. Twelve colourful ribbons symbolising the twelve Earthly Branches hung from the Spirit Skirt she wore, and it was also embellished with myriad strings of tiny bronze bells.

The Spirit Headdress she donned resembled a large birch-bark bowl covering the back of her head. Behind it draped a short, rectangular 'skirt', and at the top rose a pair of small bronze reindeer antlers. Several red, yellow and blue ribbons were suspended from the branches, symbolising a rainbow. In front of the Spirit Headdress dangled strands of red silk that reached the bridge of her nose, endowing her gaze with a mysterious air, since her eyes were visible only via the gaps between the strands of silk.

As Jiele the Shaman had instructed her, before the Spirit Dance Nihau first addressed a few words to the entire *urireng*. She proclaimed that after she became a Shaman she would unquestionably use her own life and the abilities bestowed upon her by the Spirits to protect our clan, and ensure that our clansmen would multiply, our reindeer teem, and the fruits of our hunting abound year after year.

With her left hand holding the Spirit Drum and her right hand grasping the drumstick made from the leg of a roe-deer, she followed Jiele the Shaman and began her Spirit Dance.

Although Jiele the Shaman was very elderly, as she began to perform the Spirit Dance she was full of energy. When she beat the Spirit Drum, birds came flying from afar and alighted on the trees in our camp. The drumbeat and the chirping of the birds blended poignantly. That was the most glorious sound I've heard in my life.

Nihau danced with Jiele the Shaman without pause from high noon until the sky went dark. Luni lovingly brought Nihau a bowl of water to get her to take a sip, but she didn't even glance at it. Meanwhile, the rhythm of Nihau's drumbeats grew more compelling, and her dancing more skilful and eye-catching with every step.

Jiele the Shaman stayed in our camp for three days and danced the Spirit Dance each day, and she used her drumming and dancing to transform Nihau into a Shaman.

As Jiele the Shaman prepared to leave, Ivan presented her with a gift of two reindeer. Just then Yveline appeared among those who had come to see off the Shaman. In her black attire, Yveline looked just like a raven. 'I've set the date for the marriage of my son, Jindele,' she explained. 'When he returns from Uchiriovo, he'll take Zefirina as his wife. My son's marriage ceremony must be presided over by a virtuous and prestigious Shaman.'

Yveline admired Jiele the Shaman, so she was extending this invitation ahead of time, and requested that the Shaman consent now.

I still recall how Jiele the Shaman's lips twitched. Then, without a nod or shake of her head, she simply mounted a reindeer, waved to us and told Ivan that she should be on her way. As they departed, the crisp sound of a woodpecker hammering at a tree travelled towards us, like the lingering sound of the Spirit Drum that Jiele the Shaman had beaten in our camp.

No sooner had Jiele the Shaman and Ivan left than Jindele and Yveline began squabbling.

'Even if I marry, I won't live in the same *shirangju* with that crooked-mouthed girl. If that's really how it must be, I'd be better off living in a grave!'

Once he'd had his say, his moist eyes glanced at Nihau. Nihau pursed her lips and hastily looked down. 'Then you go right ahead and move into your grave!' sneered Yveline.

When the men left again for the Kwantung Army Garrison, Yveline really did begin preparations for the marriage. The odd pieces of cloth that she had regularly set aside were all brought out. She planned to sew one set of clothes each for Zefirina and Jindele. I admired Yveline's needlework, so when she was busy with her sewing I took Andaur in my arms and watched.

Yveline had stored a fish-skin blouse and she spread it out to show me. It was pale yellow with a speckled grey pattern, an open collar, straight sleeves, and lapels that met in the front and were knotted in place; simple yet beautiful. My grandmother wore it in her youth. Yveline said Grandmother was of medium height but somewhat thin, while she herself was tall and slightly chubby, so she'd never been able to wear it. She said that clothing made of genuine fish-skin is actually tougher than roe-deerskin.

She held the blouse up against me to gauge the size. 'Looks like it fits you,' she said, pleasantly surprised. 'It's not too tight. I'll give it to you!'

'Zefirina is soon to be Jindele's bride,' I said, 'and her figure is just right, so keep it for her.'

Yveline sighed. 'She's not our flesh and blood. This has been passed down from our ancestors. Why give it to her?'

From her long sigh I could sense that deep down she wasn't too pleased with this marriage either, so I urged her not to be so hard on Jindele. Since he didn't care for Zefirina, why force the matter?

Yveline looked straight at me, unblinking for a moment, and then she said softly: 'You loved Lajide, but where has Lajide gone? Ivan loved Nadezhda, but didn't she take the children and abandon him? Linke and your *Egdi'ama* both loved Tamara, but they almost became enemies. Jindele loved Nihau, but didn't Nihau marry Luni? I've seen through it all. Whatever you love, that's what you end up losing. On the contrary, it's what you don't love that stays by your side for ever.'

When she finished speaking, Yveline sighed again. I couldn't bear to talk about something like the importance of happiness – even if it's short-lived – with this woman who had stored up so much melancholy in her heart. I just let her be.

For Jindele, Yveline sewed a Tibetan-blue *changpao* with openings down both sides. The collar and cuffs were edged with pale green lace.

She even took advantage of originally unusable scraps of deerskin and cloth to put together a wedding gown for Zefirina. It had a tight-fitting, long skirt with a wide hem, a crescent-moon collar, horse-hoof cuffs and a jade-green band inset at the waist. It was very beautiful, and reminded me of the bird-feather skirt Nidu the Shaman made for Mother. Matching this gown was a pair of buckskin boots bordered with lace.

Besides these items, she also made a roe-deerskin blanket and an under-bedding of wild boar fur. She said you couldn't let a new bride sleep on bear fur – she'd be infertile.

When the men came back from training at the Kwantung Army

Garrison, Yveline had already procured everything necessary for the marriage ceremony.

That was the latter part of summer, the time of the year when the plants in the forest were growing most vigorously. When Yveline brought up the subject of his marriage with Zefirina, Jindele no longer objected.

This time when Dashi returned he brought a loess-coloured cotton overcoat and appeared in high spirits. He had not only learned how to ride a horse in the Kwantung Army Garrison, he had also secretly crossed the Argun and gone to the Left Bank on reconnaissance.

When Maria heard that Dashi had been to the Soviet Union, she fell to the ground in fright. 'What if you didn't come back?' she repeated. 'Are the Japanese trying to push my only child off a cliff?' This refrain of hers made everyone fall about laughing.

Dashi told us he and two others used the cover of night to paddle a birch-bark canoe across the Argun and set foot on the Left Bank. 'We hid the boat in a grove on the bank, and followed the road to search for rail tracks, count the bridges and roads in the area, and record how the Soviet army was deployed.'

Dashi was responsible for taking pictures. The team member who was literate took notes, and the other was responsible for observing and calling out numbers. Train types, frequency and the number of individual carriages running on the railway daily – all had to be recorded. On their backs they carried rifles and bags of dry rations, with enough jerky and biscuits to survive for seven or eight days.

'One day when I was taking a picture of an arch bridge on the railway, a Soviet soldier on patrol spotted me. He shouted and chased us. We were scared to death and ran like madmen all the way, escaping into the forest.'

Fortunately the camera was hanging around his neck, he said, otherwise it would have been lost in the panic.

From that day onwards, they discovered that more frequent and better-manned patrols were set up on the roads and bridges, so their reconnaissance work became increasingly arduous.

Dashi and his team remained in the Soviet Union for seven days, and then they returned to the place where they had stashed their canoe and took advantage of the night to return to the Right Bank. The Japanese were very pleased with the results of their reconnaissance work, and rewarded each of the men with a heavy cotton overcoat.

As we listened to Dashi's tale, Yveline suddenly turned to Ivan. 'If you learned how to conduct reconnaissance like Dashi and went to the Soviet Union, you could bring Nadezhda back, right?'

Ivan twisted those two hands of his together, said nothing and walked away, sullen. Kunde sighed. He probably thought about admonishing Yveline with a few choice words, but he didn't dare.

Hase said that since the Japanese were dispatching men to enter Soviet territory and secretly survey those things, it looked like they intended to extend Manchukuo's boundaries.

'They're dreaming,' snorted Yveline. 'This isn't even their territory. They're basically poaching their food and drink over here, and now they're thinking of going over there to the Soviet Union to steal another mouthful? Do they think the Soviets are pushovers?'

We were just about to move from our summer camp to the autumn site, but Yveline said it was absolutely necessary to carry out the marriage ceremony before relocating. So she and Kunde went to the bride-to-be's *urireng* and fixed the date.

It was a bright sunny day when Ivan led the entourage,

including Jindele, which formally welcomed Zefirina into our *urireng*. Jindele was wearing his brand-new long *changpao*, and he appeared very detached. Zefirina wore the wedding gown and boots that Yveline had made for her, sported a wreath of wild flowers in her hair, and smiled cheerfully with her crooked mouth. She looked beside herself with joy.

Yveline had hoped that Jiele the Shaman would preside over the wedding ceremony, but Ivan insisted that our own Shaman host it, so Yveline had to back down. When Nihau blessed the couple on behalf of the *urireng*, Zefirina broke out in a broad smile, and she looked at Jindele. But Jindele's eyes were fixed on Nihau, his gaze so tender and forlorn that I felt a twinge of sadness in my heart.

The marriage ceremony over, everyone gathered round the bonfire and drank and ate roasted meat, and the singing and dancing began. Jindele toasted each person courteously with a bowl of *baijiu*. Then he waved his hand to the revellers and said, 'Go ahead and eat, drink, sing and dance! I'm awfully tired. I'm going to leave you all.'

Everyone assumed he'd been worn out by the marriage ceremony and was going back to his *shirangju* for a rest. Right after Jindele left, so did Dashi. We knew that he was going for his daily horse-ride down by the river.

At dusk Dashi suddenly appeared by the bonfire, his face covered in tears. Everyone was having a ball watching Hase and Luni, both drunk, perform the Bear Fight Dance that pits a man against a bear. With their legs bent, bodies leaning, wobbly dance steps and exaggerated growling, they were terribly amusing.

Dashi's tears gave Maria a fright. She thought something must have happened to his horse. Just as she was going to ask, Nihau stood up from the side of the fire, and a shiver ran down her spine. 'It's Jindele, isn't it?' she said. Dashi nodded.

As Dashi was riding back to the camp, he'd caught sight of Jindele's corpse suspended from a withered pine tree.

I had noticed that tree before. Even though it stood upright, it was all dried up and had no leaves, just a forked branch that stuck out at an angle. At the time I was gathering kindling with Yveline and about to take my axe to the tree, but she stopped me.

'This tree's dead,' I said. 'Why not chop it down?'

'That branch resembles a deer's antlers,' she said. 'We shouldn't chop it down. There's no telling – it might come back to life one day.'

It didn't occur to Yveline that this very tree would claim Jindele's life. That forked branch looked so dry and brittle that it probably couldn't even support an owl. Who'd have imagined that it would prove good and firm, firm enough to hang Jindele? If it wasn't made of steel, then he must have been made of feathers.

'Jindele was very kind-hearted,' said Nihau. Even though he intended to hang himself, he didn't want to hurt a vibrant, living tree. So he chose a dead one because he knew that, according to our folk custom, whoever hangs himself will undergo a fire-burial along with the tree that hanged him.

I still recall when we arrived at the site how that shrivelled tree suddenly cawed like a raven. Its trunk leaned to the west, and Jindele, still suspended, leaned westward too. It was as if the tree was embracing Jindele, and then it fell to the ground with a crash and splintered into several pieces. Oddly, the body of the tree shattered but the branch resembling a set of deer antlers remained perfectly intact.

Yveline marched forward and stomped furiously on the forked branch. 'Ghost! Ghost!' she shouted hoarsely. Try as she might, the branch remained whole, continuing to display its beautiful prongs.

Yveline began to wail, but Kunde couldn't cry, his face twisted in agony. 'Now at last he's your son, eh?' he said to her, his voice trembling.

It's unlikely that any other Shaman has presided over a marriage and a funeral in one day, both for the same person, as Nihau did.

The funeral for someone who has hanged himself must be conducted the same day. So we took Jindele's clothing and the things he had used, and we cremated them along with his body and that tree. When Nihau lit the fire, Zefirina suddenly charged towards it, screaming: 'Don't abandon me here, Jindele! I want to go with you!'

Maria and I joined forces to pull her back, but her feet still reached the fire. She was just too strong for us. Finally, it was Ivan's huge hands that pulled her out. She sat down and wailed.

The flames tore apart the night and shone red on Zefirina's face. Out of the blue, Dashi approached Zefirina and knelt down before her. 'Jindele doesn't want you. Even if you went with him, he wouldn't want you. Pursuing a man who has no place in his heart for you, isn't that foolish? Marry me. I'll take you as my wife, and I promise you, you won't end up throwing yourself onto a bonfire!'

If you asked me how many soul-stirring moments have there been in my life, I'd tell you that the sight of Dashi proposing to newly widowed Zefirina on his knees, right there at the site of the fire-burial, that is my most unforgettable moment. At that instant, meek Dashi was the very incarnation of a mighty warrior.

All present were stunned except the fire's flames. The longer they burned the more vigorous they grew, and a strange odour penetrated our noses. Everyone realised that was the smell of Jindele's flesh being consumed by fire.

Maria stared blankly ahead a good while, and then suddenly came to herself. 'Dashi! Dashi!' she shouted, hugging her son. 'You're drunk. Wake up! Zefirina is much older than you, and she has a crooked mouth. She's a widow now. Are you out of your mind? Don't be a fool!'

Dashi said nothing and pushed Maria away. Still kneeling before Zefirina, he looked tenderly at her like a swallow watching over its nest.

As for Zefirina, she was shocked by the sudden twist of happy fate that Dashi's proposal represented. She stopped wailing, and looked at Dashi like a parched blade of grass beholding long-awaited rain, bursting with yearning and gratitude.

Just when everyone had fallen silent, Nihau began a Spirit Song. Accompanying her was the *pipa-pipa* crackling of the fire.

> *Fear not the black night*
> *You whose soul has gone far away.*
>
> *For here burns a fire*
> *To illuminate your pathway.*
>
> *Pine not for those close to you*
> *You whose soul has gone far away.*
>
> *Upon your arrival there shall sing*
> *The moon, stars, clouds and Milky Way.*

The light of the fire grew faint and died. The wizened tree and Jindele were reduced to ashes, and the night turned its head and returned. We made our way back to the camp. The bonfire for the marriage ceremony was a wilted blossom, and an air of sadness wafted through the campground.

Yveline wept, Maria wept, and I didn't know whom to console. Dashi was walking next to me and I quietly asked him: 'Will you really marry Zefirina?'

'I intend to do what I said.'

'Do you really love Zefirina?'

'Jindele didn't want her but she has married into our *urireng*, so she's one of us now. She's a widow, and a crooked-mouthed one at that. If I don't marry her, who will? I can't bear to see her tears. She's so pitiful.'

Dashi's words made my eyes moist too, but he couldn't see my tears. There was no moon that evening, and the stars were dim. In a night as dark as that, you become the night's darkness.

Our *shirangju* was closest to Jindele's, and the night he died wave after wave of Yveline's cries radiated from there. At first I thought that Kunde blamed Yveline for Jindele's death and was teaching her a lesson. I threw a coat over my shoulder and prepared to dissuade him. But as I approached, I heard Yveline shouting: 'Kunde, I don't want to. It hurts! It hurts! I don't want to!'

Kunde said nothing, but I could hear his heavy, hurried breathing and a wind-sound like someone being lashed. It seemed as if he were firing bullets – *Da! Da! Da!* – at Yveline's body. I understood what means Kunde was using to chastise Yveline.

I returned to my *shirangju* and found Viktor, who had been sleeping, now awake and adding kindling to the fire. '*Eni*,' he said, 'it seems like there are wolves howling. We'd better make the fire fiercer to scare them away. Otherwise, if the wolves come in and snatch Andaur, what'll we do?'

The next morning, Ivan told everyone to pack their things and prepare to transfer to our autumn campsite. I understood. He wanted to leave this campsite that had broken our hearts as soon as possible.

In just one night, Yveline had visibly lost weight. The rims of her eyes were red and puffy, and she walked with a bit of a limp. We all looked at her sympathetically except Maria who cast a hateful gaze at her. This was understandable, for deep in her heart, she blamed Yveline. If she hadn't forced Jindele to take a maiden he didn't love as his wife, Jindele wouldn't have died; if Jindele hadn't died, Dashi wouldn't have pitied Zefirina and the idea of marrying her wouldn't have entered his head. Trying to get Maria to accept Zefirina was like forcing her to cross a frozen river barefoot.

'If you really want to marry Zefirina, you must wait for her to complete three years of mourning for Jindele,' Maria said to Dashi.

'I'll wait.'

'Zefirina still belongs to Yveline's family. During these three years, she'll have to live with them.'

Yveline and Kunde didn't say anything, but they looked Zefirina up and down.

'I'll return to my *urireng* to live,' Zefirina said to Dashi. 'If you're still willing to marry me in three years, come and find me. But if you don't come, I won't blame you.'

'I'll come!' said Dashi.

While we relocated to the autumn campsite, Dashi escorted Zefirina back to her *urireng*. They rode together on one horse.

Although Ivan had told Dashi the direction in which we were relocating, Luni was still worried, and so as we went along he hacked markers with an axe. At the outset Maria was unconcerned, but towards dusk, when the mountain valleys and rivers were bathing in the golden light of the setting sun, Maria lost control and began to cry.

Just then Luni was chopping a marker on a big tree, and Maria charged over and snatched the axe. 'I don't want Dashi to find us!' she shouted. 'Let him go where he likes. Just don't make me see him again!'

Her voice reverberated in the mountains and valleys. The echoes were so melodious that they didn't seem to have been uttered by Maria. Those penetrating sounds must have softened as they collided with the breeze, the clouds and the trees.

\* \* \*

In the autumn of that year, I began to do rock paintings on cliffs by the river.

If it weren't for Ivan's iron-forging, and for the fact that — like the iron itself — the soil where iron is forged is also smelted, I wouldn't have hit upon the idea of using that soil as a pigment for paint.

And if I hadn't made those rock paintings, Irina, who loved to accompany me when she was young, wouldn't have learned how to paint. Then her youthful silhouette wouldn't have floated down the Bistaré so early in her life.

But I don't feel there was any harm in those paintings. They helped me express my yearnings and dreams.

Nowadays you all know about the rock paintings on the banks of the Onion River, a tributary of the Bistaré. You can see a patch of blood-red paintings on the weathered rocks of the cliffs overlooking the river. Our ancestors used the dark red soil there to sketch reindeer, *kandahang*, hunters, hounds and Spirit Drums.

When I was doing my rock paintings, those at Onion River had not yet been discovered, even though they were there long before me.

I left behind many rock paintings on the Right Bank of the Argun. But except for Irina, no one else knew where they were or what I painted. Since Irina is gone now, I am the only person who knows about those paintings. All traces have probably vanished, washed away by dust and rain. Those outlines are like petals that have fallen to the ground in the mountain valleys.

I took the soil left after Ivan forged his iron, rubbed it into strips, placed them inside my *shirangju* and waited for them to dry. Then I used them as drawing sticks.

The first time I did a rock painting was by the Imaqi River. It was a blue rock, so as soon as the reddish-brown lines showed upon it, it was like evening rays of sunlight against a faint sky. I'd never have imagined that the first form I painted would be a man's figure. His head resembled Linke's, and his arms and legs those of Nidu the Shaman, but his broad chest was unquestionably Lajide's. At that instant, those three departed loved ones combined to assume the aspect of a perfect man.

Then I painted eight reindeer around the man: one each to the east, west, south and north, and then one each to the south-east, north-east, south-west and north-west. They were like eight stars encircling the man.

Ever since Lajide left me, my heart no longer contained the tenderness that nourished it. Yet when I finished my painting, once again my heart was flooded with the warm waters of desire, as if those pigments had seeped into my anaemic heart, giving it vitality and strength. A heart like that is surely a bud that will blossom again.

That autumn Nihau bore her second child, a daughter. She named her *Juktakan*, which means 'little lily'.

Late at night you could still occasionally hear Kunde lashing Yveline. Yveline always shouted the same words: 'Kunde, I don't want to. It hurts!' Yveline began to stoop, while Kunde's back straightened.

One time when he was drunk he confided to Hase: 'Yveline must give birth to another Jindele for me. She has to come up with another child to replace the one she went and lost!'

When the winter hunt began, the men were again summoned to the Kwantung Army Garrison for training. Yveline gnashed her teeth. 'Let the Japanese keep them in the army for good and send them far away!'

But Kunde and the others returned. The one who didn't was Ivan.

Dashi told us that one day when the regiment was marching Kunde kept making mistakes. When ordered to turn east, he turned west, and repeatedly fell out of formation. Suzuki was furious. He told Kunde to stand in the middle of the parade ground and unleashed a German shepherd on him. In seconds flat the dog charged over, knocked Kunde down, and gashed his face and arms with its paws.

At first, like everyone, Ivan was dumbstruck, but then the sound of Suzuki's cackling ignited his anger. Ivan raced over, grabbed the dog's tail, twisted it tightly around his hand like a piece of rope, lifted the dog in the air and swung it around in circles.

All you could hear was the German shepherd's pathetic yelping, and its tail was soon severed from its body.

The tail-less dog went crazy and lunged ferociously at Ivan who deftly caught it and stepped on it savagely. Just a few kicks and the dog was motionless, for Ivan's feet, like his hands, were unmatched in their strength.

Suzuki was dumbfounded, beads of sweat gathering on his forehead. He had watched, dazed, as Ivan took a perfectly healthy German shepherd and turned it into a dead rat in the twinkle of an eye.

But when Ivan flung the dog's tail against his chest, Suzuki finally reacted. He shouted for two soldiers who dragged Ivan away and locked him in a cell on the western side of the camp.

That night the sound of a leather whip carried out from the cell, but no one heard Ivan cry. He must have endured the pain and refused to utter the faintest groan.

That very night Ivan took flight. The door to the cell was firmly locked and there were bars on the window, but those iron-forging hands of Ivan snapped them. Like a bird freed from its cage, he easily distanced himself from the Kwantung Army Garrison. Two Japanese soldiers took their German shepherds into the mountains in pursuit, but they found no trace of him.

While Dashi recounted Ivan's misadventure, Kunde crouched next to the fireplace, ashamed. Yveline cast a glance at her husband, and then spat at him with contempt. 'You can't even stand up to one of those dogs the Japanese have,' she said. 'All you've got is a knack for standing up to women. What kind of a man does that make you?'

Kunde kept his head down and put up no argument. All you could hear was the fire fizzing as his tears fell on it.

We no longer heard Yveline's pained cries at night in the camp. No doubt that pain had transferred to Kunde's body. Yveline's back became less stooped, and she spoke loudly and confidently once more. Like a branch under the weight of heavy snow, Kunde's back bent again.

* * *

With Ivan gone, we selected Luni as Headman.

That winter we killed three bears. When Nihau performed the wind-burial for a bear, she always liked to sing a song of veneration. Henceforth this song was passed down among our clansmen:

> *O Bear Grandmother*
> *You have fallen down.*
> *Sleep sweetly!*
>
> *Feasting on your flesh*
> *Are those black, black ravens.*
>
> *Reverently we place your eyes in the trees*
> *As if hanging Spirit Lamps!*

Not long after Dashi returned to the *urireng*, he went off on his horse to see Zefirina. Maria spent the whole day sighing. Yveline knew perfectly well the source of Maria's heartache, but she insisted on goading her.

'Don't worry about Dashi's marriage with Zefirina,' Yveline said to Maria. 'I'll help you prepare her wedding gown.'

The normally docile Maria couldn't hold back her anger. 'If he really does wed that crooked-mouthed maiden, I'll thank you not to make the gown. How could anyone who wears your gown meet with good fortune?'

Yveline laughed coldly and corrected Maria. 'You're wrong. It's not a crooked-mouth maiden Dashi is marrying – it's a crooked-mouthed widow!'

Beside herself with rage, Maria charged over to Yveline and twisted her nose, swearing that she was a reincarnated wolf.

Yveline kept right on smiling coldly. 'Fine, fine. I should thank you for twisting my nose, you might even set it straight!' Maria let go and turned away, sobbing. From that day forward this pair of confidantes were utter strangers.

Another spring arrived, spring in the tenth year of the reign of the Kangde Emperor. That year we delivered twenty fawns next to a crystal-clear mountain stream. Usually a doe gives birth to just one fawn, but that year four does bore twins, and all the fawns were so good and healthy that it brought smiles to our faces.

That nameless stream flowed in a dark-green valley, and we named it Rolinsky Ravine in memory of the Russian *anda* who had been so friendly. Its waters were refreshing and sweet. Not only did the reindeer love to drink from it, so did we. From then on, even if we didn't go to Rolinsky Ravine each fawning season, we brought it up fondly in conversation like a distant loved one.

Viktor, my first son, had become a big boy. He learned archery from Luni, and could easily bring down a hazel grouse that had just landed on a treetop. Luni firmly believed that our *urireng* had reared another fine hunter.

My second son Andaur grew tall too and could play with Grigori. Even though Andaur was fatter than Grigori and a head taller, Grigori bullied him. Grigori was very naughty. He used to play and play with Andaur, and then out of the blue he would knock him down with a punch, expecting him to cry.

But after he fell to the ground Andaur didn't cry, he just looked up at the sky and reported to Grigori how many white clouds were up there. Grigori got so angry that he stepped on him for good measure, but Andaur still didn't cry, he just chuckled. By this time Grigori was so angry that he himself began crying.

Andaur got up. 'Why are you crying?'

'I knocked you down. Why didn't you cry?' said Grigori. 'Then I stamped on you. Why didn't you cry?'

'You knocked me down so I can see the clouds, and that's a good thing,' said Andaur. 'What's there to cry about? I itched all over and you stepped on me. Weren't you just trying to make me laugh?'

Since his childhood people have said Andaur was feebleminded, but I adore him. My Andaur resembles his father, Lajide, a lot.

Andaur and Grigori adored the young reindeer. When the antler-cutting season arrived the fawns could already run about on their own and eat grass. We feared that wolves would attack fawns that separated from the herd, so we tied the slow ones to trees back in the camp. Andaur and Grigori liked to untie them and lead them down to Rolinsky Ravine. Before they went they stuffed their pockets with salt. They put the salt on their palms to get the fawns to lick it.

One day I went to Rolinsky Ravine to wash clothes and discovered Andaur crying there.

'Since fawns like to eat salt and drink water too, wouldn't it be better to sprinkle the salt in the stream and let them drink it like that?' Andaur asked.

Grigori told him that once it was in the water, the salt would flow downstream with the current. But Andaur didn't believe him. He sprinkled all the salt in his pockets into the water and watched the twinkling white droplets dissolve. Then he put his head down to the surface of the stream and stuck out his tongue. But when he couldn't taste the salt, he began to howl. 'The water is a cheat!' he cursed.

From then on Andaur refused to eat fish because he was sure that they contained evil spirits. Once you swallowed them, they'd bite your stomach and leave it filled with holes like a fishnet.

That summer the 'Yellow Sickness' spread in the mountains. The Japanese cancelled training at the Kwantung Army Garrison and didn't force the hunters to leave the mountains. The epidemic won the hunters their freedom for a while.

The footprint of the Yellow Sickness extended into three or four *urireng*. The skin and eyeballs of the sick turned as yellow as frostbitten leaves. They couldn't eat or drink anything, their bellies swelled up like a drum, and they couldn't walk. Luni heard tell that in those *urireng* infected by the Yellow Sickness, no one took the reindeer out to graze, and their losses were great. The injections administered by the Japanese doctors stationed in those *urireng* didn't result in any improvement, and many people had already died.

No one in our *urireng* had caught the illness so Luni would not allow anyone to leave the mountains. He wouldn't even permit anyone to go to neighbouring *urireng* for fear they'd bring back the disease.

During the period when the Yellow Sickness danced in the wind like locusts, Maria was excited. She would have been only too pleased for the epidemic to reach Zefirina's *urireng*. If the Spirits carried away the crooked-mouthed maiden, then Maria would have good reason to seek another match for Dashi.

But Dashi was genuinely worried for Zefirina. More than once he announced to Luni that he was going to ride over and visit Zefirina, but Luni wouldn't hear of it.

'As the Headman, I can't risk your bringing back the Yellow Sickness,' he said.

'I'll wait until it's over and then return,' said Dashi.

'But what if the Yellow Sickness keeps you there for ever. Who'll look after Maria and Hase?' asked Luni.

Dashi was mute. In the end he didn't leave the camp, but his eyebrows remained knitted.

The Yellow Sickness was a poisonous flower, blooming for almost three months and then withering in the autumn. That bout of the disease claimed the lives of thirty people. I couldn't have imagined that the sickness would sweep away all but one member of Lajide's huge brood, Vladimir, his younger brother. When I heard that there were just nine people left in his *urireng*, and that pitiful Vladimir had lost all his relatives, I brought him into ours. Even though Lajide was no longer with us, I felt Vladimir was family.

Vladimir had been a lively teenager, but watching helplessly as one blood relation after another departed like the stars at dawn, he became taciturn. When I went to fetch him, he was crouched like a stone by the riverside. In his hand he held the *mukulén* – a mouth harp left by his father. He simply watched me, motionless.

'Come along with me, Vladimir,' I told him.

'Is the Yellow Sickness a Spirit?' he asked forlornly. 'How can it carry away a person just like that?' When he finished speaking, he put the *mukulén* to his lips, lightly blew a note, and then his tears cascaded.

Zefirina survived. Dashi was incomparably happy but Maria began to moan.

Dashi liked Vladimir a lot. He taught the boy how to ride a horse, and the two rode on a single mount. They looked just like brothers. Once again I heard Vladimir's laughter, and when he played the *mukulén*, it seemed filled with a balmy spring breeze.

It wasn't just the children who liked to listen, even grownups like Yveline and Maria did too. The sound of the *mukulén* in the camp was like a happy little bird that put us in a cheerful mood.

Bucks often battled ferociously to win a mate during rutting season. So every September, to prevent goring, we severed the sharp points of their antlers, and sometimes even covered their mouths with a wire halter. Ivan and Hase formerly handled these tasks, but now they were carried out by Dashi and Vladimir.

The studs aside, the other bucks usually had to be castrated. I dreaded listening when they were neutered because they shrieked wretchedly. Back then, the method of castration was quite cruel. After the male reindeer was pushed down on the ground, a cloth was wrapped around its testicles, and then smashed with a wood pole. At that instant the buck's wail resounded over the mountains and down into the valleys. Sometimes the castrated bucks even died. I wondered if it wasn't simply the wounding that did them in, but perhaps because they had lost their *qi*, their life-force.

Our men were typically a bit hesitant about performing castration. Unexpectedly, Vladimir performed this chore crisply and decisively. He said that he had learned the craft from his father when young. When he smashed the bull's testicles, his handiwork was quick so they didn't suffer too much, and after the castration he played his *mukulén*, consoling them with music to speed their recovery.

Dashi and Vladimir penned the studs up during the day and only let them out at night for foraging and mating. That year not one of our bucks died from castration, and they all looked strong and healthy.

That winter a Han named He Baolin arrived in our camp on a reindeer. He had come to make a request of Nihau. His ten-year-old son was very ill with a high fever and couldn't hold down his food. Baolin begged Nihau to save his child.

In general, a Shaman is happy to rid someone of an illness. Nihau's mouth agreed but her eyebrows frowned. Luni thought she was worried about her children, and to comfort her he assured her that he was capable of looking after Grigori and Juktakan.

Before Nihau set out with her Spirit Garb and ritual implements in hand, she paid no heed to Juktakan who was playing next to the hearth, but she held Grigori to her bosom and kissed him again and again, her eyes shiny with tears. Even when far from the camp, she kept looking back at Grigori as if she hated to part from him.

Ever since his birth, Nihau had kept Grigori close by her. The first two days after her departure, Grigori didn't miss her much. He and Andaur happily learned the Bear Fight Dance from Luni in the snow.

But over the next two days Grigori began demanding to see his mother. '*Eni* is mine,' he said. 'Why did someone take her away?'

'*Eni* has gone to cure a child and she'll be back very soon,' Luni told him.

Grigori began climbing trees like a lynx, saying he wanted to get to the top and see if he could spy some trace of *Eni*. The very day Nihau was on her way back to our *urireng*, Grigori clambered up the tallest pine near the camp. He had just seated himself on a cluster of large branches when a ghostly raven flew towards him, fluttering its wings noisily.

Grigori stretched out his hand to grab the bird, but the raven recoiled and flew off towards the sky while Grigori lost his balance and came hurtling down.

It was early morning, and Maria and I were standing in the camp greeting the returning reindeer. We saw Grigori's descent. He looked like a big bird pierced by an arrow, screaming and falling with his arms open wide. His last call to the living: '*E-n-i!*'

By the time Maria and I carried Grigori's badly mangled body back to the *shirangju*, Nihau had returned. A shiver ran down her back as she entered. She glanced at Grigori. 'I know. He fell out of a tree.'

Sobbing, Nihau told us that when she left the camp, she knew that if she saved the life of that sick child, she'd lose one of her own.

'Why?' I asked.

'The Heavens summoned that child. But I kept him here on the earth, so my child had to go in its place.'

'You could have refused to save the sick child!' sobbed Maria.

'I'm a Shaman,' said Nihau forlornly. 'How can I see someone in death's clutches and not save him?'

Nihau herself sewed a white cloth bag, put Grigori's body in it and cast him on a south-east hillside. She sang Grigori's last ballad there:

> *O child, my child,*
> *You mustn't go down under,*
> *Where the sun shines not,*
> *And the cold reigns.*
>
> *O child, my child,*
> *If leave you must, then go to the Heavens*
> *Where there is brightness and*
> *A shining silver river*
> *And Spirit Reindeer to rear.*

\* \* \*

Cutting river ice to melt for water is an essential winter task. We use a metre-long wooden handle with a sharp iron tip to chisel ice from the river surface, and put the piles of ice in a bag or a birch-bark bucket. If the water source is nearby, we carry them back directly to our campsite, otherwise we transport them on the back of our reindeer.

That winter Nihau and Luni were like madmen. Every day they went to a lake or a river to cut ice, and no matter the distance, they didn't use reindeer to transport it; they insisted on using their own bodies, and they preferred to go out and cut ice after dinner. After one, two or three trips and the moon had set in the west, they returned exhausted to their *shirangju*, laid down their heads and fell asleep at once. It was as if they wanted to use the ice-cutting to find their way through the endless night.

In front of the camp were towering heaps of ice. Under the midday sunshine, those stacks emitted a rainbow that sparkled like gems.

I often saw Nihau shedding tears among the ice piles. When Yveline, who still brooded that Nihau hadn't married Jindele, saw Nihau looking hurt, she'd hum a happy tune. Perhaps Nihau's misfortunes lessened the guilt Yveline felt towards Kunde.

In the eleventh year of the reign of the Kangde Emperor, in the summer of 1944 that is, Ludek the guide and Wang Lu the interpreter brought Suzuki up into the mountains again. By this time Suzuki could speak the Han tongue fairly well, and he summoned the *urireng* members himself.

At first, he asked if Ivan had returned. We told him no. 'If Ivan comes back, you must bring him under guard to the Kwantung Army Garrison,' he said. 'Ivan is bad. He is your enemy. If you conceal his return and do not report it, Commander Yoshida will arrest everyone in your *urireng*!

'The Yellow Sickness is over now, so training will be held as usual. If you don't train well as a unit,' he said, 'how will we handle the Soviets?' I think the Japanese had an inkling that their final days loomed.

Suzuki told Luni to bring the entire catch from our winter hunt. 'After we reach Uchiriovo, I'll personally take responsibility to exchange them for the goods you need. I'll have Ludek deliver them to you up here in the mountains.' You could tell that he was a military man who aimed to make a killing by doing business on the side.

At that time Vladimir was almost fifteen, and having only just survived the Yellow Sickness by the skin of his nose, he was very vigilant about the Japanese. While Suzuki was busy admonishing everyone, Vladimir remained hidden. But he was a naïve lad, and when he began blowing on his *mukulén*, it echoed like the mountain wind and revealed his whereabouts.

Suzuki followed the sound to its source, and asked Vladimir how old he was.

'I'm fourteen,' he replied gingerly.

Suzuki took the *mukulén* from Vladimir's hand and tried blowing on it, but no sound came out. He shook his head, handed it back and told Vladimir to play a tune.

He did so, and Suzuki was very pleased. 'You're fourteen now,' he said, 'and it's time for you to serve Manchukuo. You should go to the Kwantung Army Garrison too.'

Vladimir was inseparable from Dashi, and wherever he went, Vladimir was naturally willing to go. Vladimir nodded to signal his willingness.

Suzuki pointed at the *mukulén* in Vladimir's hand. 'And bring that with you to play for Commander Yoshida!'

Dashi realised that Suzuki wanted Vladimir to bring his *mukulén* in order to ingratiate Suzuki with his commander. And since Dashi couldn't bear the thought of leaving behind his beloved horse, he had a bright idea.

'That's the war-horse Commander Yoshida left behind,' he said, pointing at his beloved mount. 'He hasn't seen it for years and must miss it terribly. Why not take it back to the garrison and show it to Commander Yoshida?'

Suzuki agreed. After all, it would be convenient to use the horse to transport the *urireng*'s winter catch.

Luni knew that after carrying away all the fruits of their winter hunting, Suzuki would probably pilfer a good portion for himself. Putting their catch in his hands was like stuffing a few plump hares in a wolf's mouth. So taking advantage of the moment when Suzuki was indulging in drink, Luni quietly passed three bundles of squirrel pelts and two bear galls to me. 'Stash them in a hollow tree near the camp!' he said.

But as he set out to leave the mountains, Suzuki was noticeably suspicious about the number of pelts. 'Why are there so few?' he asked Luni.

Luni told him that last winter there wasn't much game and bullets were in short supply, so they hadn't killed many animals.

'If you're hiding your catch, I'll confiscate your rifles!' said Suzuki.

'Go ahead and search,' said Luni coolly. 'If you find any hidden, I'm willing to hand over all our rifles to you!'

Suzuki didn't conduct a search. He probably realised that if we had concealed something, searching for it would be as difficult as climbing to the Heavens.

Once again just women and the young were left in the camp. We busied ourselves, for we had to mind the reindeer and attend to the children. A few days later, Suzuki did send Ludek to bring us the goods obtained in exchange: a bag of whole-wheat flour, one box of matches, two packets of coarse tea and a bit of salt. It was *baijiu* that Yveline most longed for, and when she saw that the miserably few items obtained in exchange for our winter catch didn't include even one bottle, she was so angry that she vented her frustration on Ludek. She even insisted that he must have drunk it all on the road.

Ludek was indignant. Suzuki had said since only women and

children remained in the mountains, they wouldn't need spirits. So Ludek hadn't transported *baijiu* for any of the *urireng*.

'If I want liquor, I don't need to snatch it from your mouths. I can buy it any time and anywhere I like back in Uchiriovo!' said Ludek.

'*Pah!*' scoffed Yveline. 'You're just a slave to the Japanese, a walking map. You bring them into our mountains year after year and get your soldier's rations every month, so of course you don't worry about food and drink!'

Ludek sighed again. After he unloaded the goods, he led his horse away without even sipping a bowl of water.

I still had a birch-bark bucket of blueberry wine I'd brewed myself, and I carried it over to Yveline with both my hands. That evening she emptied two bowls in succession and staggered away from the campsite. When she was tipsy she liked to go and drink from the river.

Not long after she arrived there, we heard a sombre sound. At first we just assumed it was the river moaning, because it was the rainy season and the river waters were rising.

But later Nihau could tell that it was Yveline sobbing. It was the first time I ever heard her cry like that. No one went to comfort her. We just sat outside our *shirangju* and quietly awaited her return.

Her moaning continued, and when Yveline finally came staggering back to the camp it was very late. There was a full moon and the night was almost as bright as daytime. The silver moonlight blanketed her, and we could clearly see her loose-hanging hair and a snake twisting in her left hand. She walked to the clearing in front of the *shirangju*. Her feet began to dance to and fro, and the snake swayed too.

Suddenly, the snake miraculously stood up straight on Yveline's hand, raised its head and leaned towards her, as if to murmur something in her ear. An instant later Yveline fell on her knees. 'Tamara, forgive me,' she said. 'Go forth in peace.'

Then the serpent jumped out of her hand and wriggled away in the grass.

I don't know how she caught the snake alive or why Yveline uttered my mother's name. After the snake left the camp, Yveline went back to her *shirangju* and slept.

The next day I asked her why she had called out Mother's name. 'Did I really bring a snake back with me?' she asked. 'Are you sure that's what you saw? I was drunk, I don't remember a thing.'

I assumed she was telling the truth and asked nothing more.

Many years later at Ivan's funeral, we noticed two maidens had suddenly appeared, claiming to be Ivan's goddaughters. As we were trying to guess where they had come from, Yveline – short-sighted by then – told us that this pair of young ladies decked out in white must be the foxes whose lives Ivan had spared.

Everyone in our clan has heard that tale. It is said that one day the young Ivan went hunting on his own deep in the mountains. He walked all day without encountering any prey, but at dusk he suddenly spotted two snow-white foxes running out of a cave. Excited, Ivan raised his rifle and prepared to fire when one of the foxes spoke to him.

'Ivan, we know that you are a fine shot!' it said, bowing respectfully.

When he heard them speaking in a human tongue, he realised the foxes were Immortals who had attained enlightenment, and so he let them go unharmed.

It was at Ivan's funeral, all those years later, that Yveline finally confided what transpired that night at the riverside. She had been sobbing so hard that she wanted to bury herself in the river, but just then a snake quietly crawled up behind her, climbed her neck and wiped away her tears. She realised that the serpent was of a special provenance, so she brought it back to the camp.

But when she began to dance and wave the snake about, it unexpectedly pressed close to her ear and spoke to her in a human tongue: 'Yveline, do you really believe you can out-dance me?' Recognising Tamara's voice, she knelt down and released the snake.

By the time Yveline recounted all this to me, she was already an old woman flickering like a candle in the wind. She had no call to lie. Granted, I didn't hear the snake speak, but I did hear Yveline pronounce Tamara's name, and I saw her kneel before it. From then on, I've forbidden my children and grandchildren to kill snakes.

The training in the summer of 1944 was the last for our *urireng*'s men. The following year the Japanese were defeated and surrendered. That last session was very short, just twenty days or so, and then the men returned. But neither Vladimir nor that horse returned, and Dashi looked especially downhearted. He said Commander Yoshida liked to hear Vladimir play the *mukulén* and kept him to serve as his *mafoo*, or groom, so the horse stayed there too.

I was very worried about Vladimir. 'Why didn't you insist on bringing him back too?' I asked Luni.

'I did,' he replied, 'but Suzuki wouldn't hear of it. Yoshida was fond of Vladimir and his *mukulén* playing, and couldn't do without him.'

'Vladimir wasn't keen to remain behind,' explained Dashi, 'but

Suzuki threatened that if he didn't stay at his post as a *mafoo*, he would slaughter the horse that we both adored, so he had no choice.'

It had never occurred to us that the horse would be the source of Vladimir's lifelong misfortune.

In the first ten days of August, 1945, Soviet planes appeared in the sky and the mountain forests rumbled with the sound of guns. Very soon the Soviet Union's Red Army had crossed the Argun and attacked the Kwantung Army Garrison. We realised that the last days of the Japanese were at hand.

After the event Vladimir told us that even before the Red Army arrived at the Kwantung Army Garrison, things were already in chaos. The Japanese began incinerating documents, destroying goods, and rushing to prepare for retreat. Although the Japanese Emperor had not formally declared defeat, Yoshida knew that the game was up.

As Yoshida withdrew with his troops, he stuffed a map inside Vladimir's shirt. 'I can't guarantee your safety! Get on your horse, go back into the mountains and find your family. You're young, and if you lose your way take a look at this map.

'If you run into the Soviet Army, don't admit you served as a *mafoo* for the Japanese!' He also gave Vladimir a rifle, matches and biscuits.

Just before his departure, Yoshida asked Vladimir to play his *mukulén* one last time. Vladimir chose 'Parting at Night', a tune that his father had taught him. He had played this song when the Yellow Sickness claimed his loved ones. The sad, haunting tune covered Yoshida's face in tears.

As he helped Vladimir up onto his horse, these were his last words: 'You Evenki are amazing! Your dance can kill a war-horse, and your music can heal a wound!'

Vladimir didn't know where we were then, but he guessed we were active within the Bistaré River basin, so he followed the river to find us.

Due to the artillery attacks, the reindeer herds began to scatter, and we spent the better part of each day looking for them. The sound of artillery is a thunder that originates in the land itself, and the arrival of this unwelcome guest threw humans and animals into a panic. We often saw wild animals running scared, but without bullets, our hunting rifles were just scrap metal. Our flour bags were empty and little jerky remained. We were forced to slaughter our beloved reindeer for food.

It was just at this extraordinary time that we encountered Valodya on the banks of the Bistaré.

If my first matchmaker was hunger, then my second was the fire of war.

As soon as the gunfire of the Red Army sounded, the Japanese soldiers stationed in the area took flight. But since all the roads and fords had been occupied by the Soviets, the Japanese could only flee into the forest. They weren't familiar with the mountain terrain and lost their way easily.

Valodya was a Clan Chieftain, but by then his clansmen numbered only twenty or so. He had received orders from the Red Army to track down Japanese who had lost their way in the mountain forest. When I ran into him, he had just captured two deserters.

Axes in hand, the Japanese were felling trees to make a wooden raft that they planned to ride downstream on the Bistaré. When Valodya and his clansmen encircled them, the deserters realised that they were outnumbered, so they threw down their axes and rifles and surrendered.

It was high noon, and the Bistaré was so illuminated by the intense sunlight that it gave off a blinding white light. Swarms of blue dragonflies danced above the river.

Lean Valodya stood on the bank, and there was something extra-ordinary about him. He wore a pair of deerskin breeches, and a buckskin vest that bared his arms. Around his neck hung a purple cord of leather decorated with fish bones, and his long hair flowed behind him.

I guessed he was a Clan Chieftain, because only he would be allowed to wear his hair long. His face was gaunt, and his cheeks marked with several crescent-moon furrows. His gaze was tender and melancholic like the fine rain of early spring. When he looked at me, I could feel a breeze penetrate to the bottom of my heart, and my body felt warm and fuzzy. I felt like crying.

That night our tribes set up our *shirangju* by the riverbank, built a bonfire, and gathered to feast. The men used the rifles and bullets they had seized to shoot a wild boar that weighed more than two hundred kilos. Boar generally move in groups, but the artillery fire had also scattered them. Our catch had become separated from the herd, and it was gnawing at the bark of a poplar tree with its sharp teeth when it met its end.

The two Japanese soldiers eyed the yellow-orange flames hungrily as we roasted the wild boar. They probably thought Valodya wouldn't give them food, so when they were invited to eat the very first slices that had been cooked through, tears rolled down their faces.

They used broken Han to ask Valodya: 'Now that you've captured us, are you going to kill us?'

Valodya told them they'd be taken out of the mountains and handed over as prisoners of war. 'Once we're in the hands of the Soviet Red Army, we're dead for sure!' said one of the prisoners. 'Let us live here in the mountains and herd reindeer for you.'

But before Valodya could answer, Yveline spoke up. 'Wouldn't that be like asking two wolves to be our guests? Go back to wherever you came from!'

Then she went over behind the Japanese and stuck a few of the steel-hard wild boar hairs down their collars. The prickling sensation made them cry out. We were all heartily amused by Yveline's behaviour.

The next day we parted with Valodya's clan there on the banks of the Bistaré. He escorted the prisoners to Uchiriovo while we continued searching for our stray reindeer. I knew he was going in the direction of the Argun, so I asked him to look for Vladimir.

I still recall his reply: 'I'll return to your side with Vladimir.'

I didn't immediately understand the significance of those words. So when he brought Vladimir back ten days or so later and suddenly appeared before me to propose marriage, I fainted.

I want to tell you all something: if a woman can faint out of happiness for a man, she has not lived in vain.

Valodya's wife had departed twenty years ago after a difficult childbirth. He deeply loved her and had never been moved by another. Alone, he led the members of his tribe in their nomadic hunting in the mountains, persuaded that happiness would not occur again in his lifetime.

Yet there by the Bistaré, Valodya said when he saw me standing on the bank his heart trembled. For that I must thank the rays of the midday sun. They clearly illuminated my melancholy, weariness, tenderness and tenaciousness, and it was this complex expression that touched Valodya. He said that if a woman possesses a look that etches itself in his memory, she must be a richly spiritual person with whom he could weather the storms of life.

Although my complexion was pale indeed, he said the sunlight softened that paleness, and if my eyes had a melancholic air, they were also very limpid. For a man, such a pair of eyes are the waters of a lake where he can rest. When he learned from Luni that Lajide had already left me, he decided to take me for his wife.

When I came to I was already in Valodya's embrace. Each man's embrace is distinct. When Lajide held me, I was a wisp of wind weaving through mountains and valleys; in Valodya's embrace, I was a fish in spring waters swimming carefree. If Lajide was a big tree standing tall, then Valodya was a warm bird's nest in a big tree. They were both my loves.

Even though Vladimir returned safely, he was no longer fully intact. When he was searching for us, he passed through a pine grove one day, and a circling Soviet plane dropped two bombs. The violent explosion gave his horse a fright, and it took Vladimir on a mad gallop that jolted him so badly that everything went dark.

When his mount finally came to a halt, Vladimir felt the saddle under him was warm and sticky. And when he looked, he saw a puddle of fresh, purplish blood. His scrotum had been lacerated and his testicles jiggled to pieces.

That aeroplane was a hellish old eagle, and Vladimir's testicles were unborn birds suffocating inside their shells, snatched away by that eagle before they had a chance to sing.

Vladimir said he realised then that he was no longer a real man, and he didn't want to go on living. He braided a straw string, wrapped his *mukulén* in it, tied it to the horse's neck, and let the horse go and find us. He reckoned when Dashi saw the horse and the mouth harp, he'd understand that Vladimir was no longer on the earth.

Vladimir intended to commit suicide with his rifle, but he fired twice without success. The sound of the rifle shots caught the attention of Valodya and his prisoners, however. Valodya rescued Vladimir and took him and his horse all the way to Uchiriovo.

By that time the Kwantung Army Garrison was in ruins, and except for Yoshida who had committed hara-kiri on the banks of the Argun, the Japanese soldiers were now prisoners of the Soviets.

Vladimir came back with that horse of his. When it saw Dashi, its eyes filled with tears. It refused to eat grass or drink water. Dashi understood what was on its mind. They took it to a gully, and killed and buried it there. Dashi and Vladimir wept where the horse was buried, and we knew they weren't crying for the horse alone.

From then on, our *urireng* stopped keeping horses and the task of castrating the reindeer bucks was shouldered by Vladimir alone.

That autumn saw the demise of Manchukuo, and Emperor Kangde was escorted to the Soviet Union.

In late autumn Nihau bore a son, and she named him *Tibgur*, 'black birch tree'. She and Luni hoped he would be as solid, healthy and strong and resistant to wind and rain as a black birch.

After the child was born Nihau looked much more cheerful and presided over two successive marriages: one was Dashi's, and the other was mine.

Dashi didn't go back on his word. He married crooked-mouthed Zefirina and brought her into our *urireng*. At Dashi's marriage ceremony, Maria got drunk and sprinkled a bag of flour over Yveline's head. With her hair and face covered in flour, Yveline looked like she was sprouting mould.

My marriage with Valodya was a grand and bustling affair. Our people and theirs celebrated together, and everyone drank and sang to their hearts' content. Once again I was a bride, and I wore the wedding gown that Yveline had sewn for me. Valodya also loved the pink cloth that edged the collar and sleeves and embellished the waist. He said their rosy hues were rainbows against the gown's sky-blue.

Suddenly, right there during my marriage ceremony, when happiness flowed like the river in springtime, a masked rider appeared in our camp. The date-red horse he rode was swift and fierce, and it made Dashi and Vladimir sigh in envy. The masked man jumped off his horse, walked over to the bonfire, poured himself a bowl of *baijiu*, and drank it all in one go.

The giant hands that held the bowl were so familiar to us that we were shocked. Even before he tore off his mask, people were shouting his name – Ivan!

PART THREE

DUSK

*I*t is dim inside the shirangju, *and it seems dusk has arrived. The warm waves emanating from the hearth and the sombre light in the sky have rendered both my tale and me drowsy. I think I should go out and get a breath of fresh air.*

*The rain has ceased and a few strands of orange-red afterglow drift in the western sky. If the sunset is a golden drum, those strands are distant drumbeats. Cleansed by the rain, the floating clouds are already white, but I discover the campsite has turned green. An'tsaur has transplanted pines in the clearing where the* shirangju *were disassembled today.*

*There remains just one* shirangju *in the camp. An'tsaur must have feared that those empty spaces would make me sad. The fresh air and the suddenly arrived green saplings run towards me like two gentle kittens. They stick out their frisky, moist tongues and lick me, one on the left cheek and one on the right, and sweep away my drowsiness.*

*The herd has already left the camp to go foraging. The smoky daytime bonfire that we fed with fresh grass to drive away the insects that bother our reindeer has burned itself out, but the ashes continue to give off the warm scent of fresh vegetation.*

*Reindeer resemble stars. At night they blink their eyes as they roam, and in the day they return to the camp to rest.*

*Only sixteen head remain with us. Tatiana worried that if she left too many An'tsaur and I couldn't manage them, but if she left too few we'd feel unoccupied. In the end An'tsaur and I selected which reindeer would keep us company.*

*We'll move camp in the forest again in the future so Tatiana left us the* Malu *King and the reindeer that transports live cinders for our fire.*

As for the others, half were chosen by An'tsaur, half by me. An'tsaur is an affectionate and merciful soul, so the six or seven head he chose were old and feeble – and two even have a severe cough.

To ensure that our herd grows in number and strength, I chose two studs, three does in their fawning prime and two bouncy fawns. When I finished my selections, Tatiana's eyes sparkled with tears. 'Eni's eyes are still so bright!' she said.

A bucket of water in one hand and a bunch of purple chrysanthemums in the other, An'tsaur approaches from afar. He knows I adore this flower, and on his way to fetch river water he must have picked some just for me.

He sees I've emerged from our shirangju and smiles. He walks up to me, hands me the flowers and then takes the bucket to water the newly planted trees.

When he finishes watering the trees, he puts the bucket down and, without pausing, enters the shirangju to bring out the dried bats. He places them on a limestone slab and grinds them with a smooth rock from the river. He'll pound them into a fine powder, add water and pour the concoction down the nostrils of the sick reindeer to cure their cough.

I return to our shirangju and discover that the fire in the hearth is burning more intensely than when I left. It seems An'tsaur threw some kindling on the fire when he came inside to get the dried bats. The firelight illuminates the shirangju and I decide to locate the birch-bark vase and arrange the flowers in it.

I haven't used this vase in a long while. Valodya knew I adored purple chrysanthemums, so he crafted it just for me. To set off the purple blossoms, he chose darkish birch-bark with a wavy pattern. The vase is only as high as my hand is long, and seen from the side it's flat and equally wide from bottom to top, except at the neck where it narrows slightly.

*Valodya said that you shouldn't use a tall, slender vase for this sort of flower. Not only would this limit the number of blossoms; they might appear crowded and thus less enchanting. When arranging this sort of small-blossomed flower with luxuriant foliage, you should employ a large-mouthed vase with a short body to make them look vivacious.*

I have a deerskin bag containing objects that I hold dear: the tiny round mirror that Rolinsky intended to give to Lena, the vase crafted for me by Valodya, the deer-leg drumstick used by Nidu the Shaman and Nihau, the deerskin cloth Linke used to polish his rifle, the birch-bark sheath for Lajide's hunting knife, and a handkerchief with a pair of embroidered butterflies. Yveline gave me a mosaic of reindeer and elk hairs left by Irina, and I have a leather satchel inlaid with tree and antler patterns from Zefirina. These are all items left by people who have passed away.

Of course, there are also objects from people who are still alive. For instance, a candelabrum of tree roots made by Maksym; a spittoon shaped like antlers carved by Shiban from wind-dried oak branches; a silver hairpin engraved with a magpie and plum blossom design, purchased by Tatiana; a pair of reading spectacles Beriku had made for me in the city; and a watch from Lyusya that stopped running long ago.

Even though I'm ninety years old I don't need reading spectacles; occasionally I catch cold, but I just cough for a day or two and then it's over, so the spittoon is just for decoration; I prefer moonlight and the light of the fire emanating from the hearth, so the candlestick serves no purpose in the night's darkness. In my eyes the sun and the moon are two round clocks, and I'm accustomed to reading the time from their faces, so in my hands the watch might as well be blind. If you stick a silver hairpin in black hair it's as lovely as a white bird perched on a shirangju, but now my head is covered with grey and the beauty of a silver hairpin perched on hair like this is buried, so it too has been set aside. If only Valodya were here, I'd give the hairpin to him and let it serve as a bookmark, for he loved to read.

I open the deerskin bag and the objects inside are like long-separated old friends who can't wait to shake hands. Just after I touch the drumstick, the birch-bark sheath sticks to the back of my hand. And then when I push away the silver hairpin that pricked my hand, that ice-cold watch slips heavily into my palm.

I dig out the vase, fill it with water, stick the purple chrysanthemum in it, and place it in front of the deerskin bedding. Once in the vase, the flower resembles a maiden who has found a reliable man, and now she looks even more dignified and beautiful.

An'tsaur enters and it appears he has already pounded the dried bats into powder. He gives me a loaf of khleb. I break off half and give the other half back.

Before she departed, Lyusya baked two bags full of khleb and left them for us. This sort of unleavened bread will go unspoiled for a month. She spent two entire days baking it. Her eyes were red and puffy for those two days; perhaps it was the fumes from the fire. As I drink tea and chew on the khleb, An'tsaur goes out again. He's a restless sort.

The sun must have set. From the opening at the top of the shirangju I can see the sky has turned deep grey. But in a summer night's fair sky, this deep grey won't last long. The moon and stars will recast it deep blue.

Ah yes, I haven't finished telling my tale. I imagine that early today the objects inside the deerskin bag pricked up their ears to listen, first in the morning alongside the rain and fire, and then in the afternoon together with the items that An'tsaur picked up while cleaning the campsite.

I'm willing to tell all of you the rest of the story. If you *chrysanthemums don't catch on immediately, don't be anxious. First put your heart at ease and listen along with everyone else. Wait until I've reached the end and then the vase will narrate it again from the start just for you.*

*Now, birch-bark vase, no excuses accepted! After all, who told you to pull the purple chrysanthemums into your embrace and suck their fragrant sap?*

\* \* \*

When Ivan removed his mask at my marriage ceremony with Valodya, the campsite went wild. Luni cheered and jumped about like a child and promptly poured Ivan a second bowl of *baijiu*. Hase cut him a big chunk of fresh roe-deer liver. Ivan swallowed the liver and downed the drink in a flash.

Then he walked over to Valodya and me. 'I heard about your marriage ceremony so I put on a mask to give you a pleasant surprise!'

He poured himself another bowl, finished it off in one go, and wished us happiness in our union. Then I poured a fourth bowl for him, and welcomed him back to our *urireng*.

'I can only stay a day or two,' said Ivan, 'because I'm an enlisted soldier now. The year I escaped from the Kwantung Army Garrison, I ran into a small unit of Anti-Japanese Allied Forces who were battling the devils in the mountains. The situation was precarious, so the forces were preparing to withdraw to Soviet territory where they could preserve their strength.

'I guided them to the Left Bank of the Argun, and then I joined the army there. Now we're coordinating with the Red Army to battle the Japanese. There are still some remnants in the mountains, and I want to wipe them out before I return to our *urireng* once and for all.'

Ivan's unexpected reappearance seemed like an illusion to Maria. '*Tian ah! Tian ah!*' she murmured to the skies above, beating her chest. She couldn't quite believe Ivan was there in the flesh.

Yveline was a bit lost too, as she could no longer blame Kunde for Ivan's death. She suddenly stooped, as if a weighty stone were pulling her downward.

As for Kunde, he was like someone who had long been unjustly imprisoned emerging into the light of day. Tears of relief flowed down his face as he looked at Ivan, for if he hadn't returned, Kunde would have lived out his days in self-reproach.

Vladimir couldn't help himself and began to play the *mukulén* for the first time since his testicles were shattered. Everyone knew that he was not just welcoming Ivan; he was also playing a song of praise for Ivan's beautiful bay horse. He blew and blew on his mouth harp and approached the horse with Dashi close behind. Tears stained their faces, and the animal's eyes, bewitched by the tune, also shone.

When the sound of the *mukulén* disappeared into the forest like water flowing into the distance, Maria posed a tactless question. 'When you went to the Soviet Union, did you find Nadezhda and your children?'

Ivan rubbed his face with those huge hands, and his tone was the same as ten years ago when Nadezhda left him. 'I wouldn't go looking for them. There's no holding back someone who wants to leave.'

Ivan stayed two days and then mounted his bay. As he left, Dashi handed him a map – the one Yoshida had given Vladimir. When Vladimir returned to us he was about to burn it, but Dashi grabbed it from him.

'There's all sorts of scribbling on it,' said Dashi at the time. 'Let's keep it. It might prove useful.'

'The Japanese lost the war. Keeping their things is just courting disaster!' cautioned Yveline. But Dashi quietly stored the map away.

The day Ivan left I heard Kunde castigating Yveline again in the depths of night. Yveline still cried out miserably in pain. If Ivan's rumoured death was once a whip in Yveline's hands, now that Ivan had returned the master of that whip changed, and it was firmly in Kunde's possession.

That winter, ageing Yveline became pregnant and her dry vomiting could be heard in the camp. Kunde treated Yveline with visibly greater tenderness. We understood, for Kunde intensely desired a child. He expressed thoughtfulness toward her as never before; he wouldn't let her touch cold water, chop firewood, or feed salt to the reindeer out of fear one might get naughty and kick her belly, causing his cherished blossom to fall. Even when Yveline did her needlework, Kunde repeatedly reminded her to avoid bending suddenly and disturbing the foetus.

Yveline appeared unmoved by Kunde's attentions and at times even sneered at him, as she kept right on doing her beloved chores. But one snowy day, Yveline suddenly vanished. Kunde was so anxious that his mouth became parched, and he shovelled snow between his lips madly as if flames were licking his stomach.

At dusk, when the snow stopped, Yveline suddenly appeared in the camp like a phantom. Her hair was dishevelled, face muddied with tears, and trousers stained purple. She stood before us with her legs crossed, legs that were like wizened branches blown by a fierce wind. She trembled violently and blood dripped, drop by drop, from between her legs, dyeing the snow with a patch of bright red love-peas.

Fitted in snowshoes, Yveline had criss-crossed the snow-covered mountain ridges and valleys all day in order to terminate the tiny life inside her that Kunde dreamed of day and night. I'll never forget Yveline's expression as she looked at Kunde. Behind that joyous, revengeful glance lay an unspeakable bleakness.

That night the sound of Kunde punishing Yveline echoed throughout the camp. But this time Kunde was using a real leather whip. Yveline didn't cry in pain, no doubt because she had gone numb.

From then on, they rarely spoke to one another. They both grew elderly and taciturn, and in the years that followed, they were just a pair of weathered cliffs facing one another.

* * *

In the autumn of 1946 I gave birth to Tatiana. Valodya adored her. He often sat next to the fireplace, held her close to his chest and read poetry to her, unconcerned whether she comprehended.

Tatiana would squeal *yee-ya*, grab a lock of Valodya's long hair and stuff it in her mouth like a grazing lamb. Her saliva got his long hair all wet and sticky. There was no way to comb it, so I had to rinse it regularly with water.

Valodya had frequent contact with the Han, studied their language when young and could read books in *hanzi*. He liked to compose poetry and he was our people's poet. If you find that there is a certain passion to the way I tell this tale, and that I express myself fairly well, this is Valodya's influence.

After our marriage, Valodya divided his clan in two. He designated a man called Chirala as Headman, and had him take twenty or so clansmen to live in their own *urireng*. They continued their nomadic hunting in the Bistaré River area, but whenever they encountered a major matter requiring a decision, Chirala would pay a formal visit to their Clan Chieftain, Valodya.

A dozen or so of his clansmen came with Valodya and were absorbed into our *urireng*. He was still a Clan Chieftain, but in our *urireng*, he obeyed Luni in all matters. His moderate and magnanimous behaviour incurred the dissatisfaction of a member of their clan nicknamed Puffball, however. He said Valodya had betrayed his clan.

After Dashi married Zefirina, Maria was always brooding and tried to exclude her daughter-in-law. Maria wouldn't look at her, and when she ordered Zefirina to do something, Maria's eyes avoided her gaze, as if Zefirina were a poisonous flower.

Maria had always been very hard-working, but after Zefirina's arrival she became lazy and assigned virtually all chores to Zefirina. If Zefirina showed the least sign of dissent, Maria wouldn't feed her.

One day Maria told Zefirina to comb her hair. But when Maria noticed that the comb was tangled with hair, she didn't admit she was losing her hair at a frightening rate. Instead, she insisted that Zefirina was purposely pulling out her hair to make her go bald.

She summoned Dashi and handed him the comb. 'If you don't poke out Zefirina's eyes with this, I'll tear out all my hair!'

Instead, Dashi turned the comb on his own eyes. Maria rushed forward and snatched the comb back. 'Dashi! Are you trying to end your mother's life?' she sobbed.

Even though Dashi didn't actually pierce his eyes, one was damaged and this made Maria's hatred for Zefirina even more venomous.

Once Dashi was chopping firewood in the camp and Zefirina was helping him stack it. Dashi took a break and laid the axe on the ground. Zefirina didn't notice it and, holding logs in her arms, she stepped over the axe. One of our taboos is that a woman must not step over an axe, for it is said that she will give birth to an idiot.

Maria insisted that Zefirina had done so on purpose. Maria ordered her to kneel down, grabbed a piece of wood and struck her so fiercely that Zefirina had to cover her head.

Watching this scene, Valodya's clansmen were outraged. If it weren't for Dashi picking up the axe and vowing that he was going to cut off his foot and make himself lame, Maria wouldn't have stopped punishing Zefirina.

When Zefirina became pregnant, Maria insisted that since she had stepped over an axe, the foetus was cursed and would certainly be an idiot, and therefore Maria was determined that Zefirina should not keep it. For two days and two nights Zefirina cried, but to avoid making things difficult for Dashi, she slipped away, climbed a hill, rolled down it, and had a miscarriage.

When Zefirina returned to the camp, her face covered in tears and her trousers stained with blood, the scene reminded me of Yveline. But the difference was that one aborted herself out of love and the other out of spite.

Maria's hatred for Zefirina and Yveline's disharmony with Kunde were two dark clouds hovering over our clan. But a dark cloud also loomed over Valodya's kinsmen, and that was Mafenbao.

Real *mafenbao*, or Puffball, is a kind of fungus that grows in the forest. It's round and white at first, but after it matures it turns brown and contains a sponge-like filling. Children love to step on *mafenbao* for fun. When you stamp on it, it shrinks instantly with a 'poof' and a grey, ash-like floss flies out from the opening. *Mafenbao* has medicinal uses. If your throat swells or you're bleeding from an external injury, just apply the *mafenbao* powder and it will get better quickly.

The man nicknamed Puffball was a drunkard, and short and fat. If you saw him walking from afar, you'd think a ball was slowly rolling towards you. He had a daughter named Lyusya who was three years younger than my Viktor. Lyusya didn't look anything like Puffball. She had a lovely figure, arched eyebrows, and a curved mouth that looked very sweet when she smiled.

When Puffball was drunk he vented his anger on Lyusya. He made her remove his shoes and light his cigarette, and if her movements weren't quick enough, he gave her a whack. If Lyusya came running out of their *shirangju* covering her face, everyone knew Puffball had slapped her again.

Valodya said Lyusya's mother was a comely Daur maiden. One year in early spring she and two young Daur female companions were fishing on the Argun when a strong wind began to blow. The ice cover suddenly cracked and splintered into blocks, big and small.

In the midst of the panic, each maiden ended up on a separate block of ice. Even though they were on small blocks, the other maidens drifted towards the bank. The block carrying Lyusya's mother was larger, but it followed the current and was swept towards the middle of the river.

In the blink of an eye it struck another big block of ice, and she fell into the water. There probably isn't a Daur alive who isn't a good swimmer, but the newly melted river was too cold. She splashed about for a moment but got cramps in her leg. The two girls who had just reached the bank shouted for help.

Puffball was passing by on his way back from Uchiriovo where he had been trading for ammunition. He threw off his clothes, dived into the bitingly cold river and rescued the Daur maiden.

Ignoring the fact that his daughter already had a sweetheart, her father insisted she marry Puffball out of gratitude for saving her life. So she left her Daur tribe and followed Puffball to live in the mountains.

Valodya said that right from the start he wasn't optimistic about the union, because they weren't a good match in terms of their looks, personalities or habits, not to mention that the maiden's mind wasn't on Puffball. So not long after she gave birth to Lyusya, she ran off. Fearful that Puffball would come looking for her, she left her clan with her sweetheart and was never heard of again.

From then on Puffball drank to excess and hated all females. He despised Lyusya, and said when she grew up she'd be indecent like her mother. Little Lyusya liked fish, as her mother had. But Puffball would intentionally toss fish into the fire until it was charred.

'You've got to get it through your head,' he said, 'that just because you love something doesn't mean you can have it!'

Viktor was keen on Lyusya, so whenever he found Lyusya running out from her *shirangju*, hands over her tearful face, he knew that Puffball had struck her and he was very angry.

To teach Puffball a lesson, Viktor went with Andaur to the forest and collected a basketful of *mafenbao*. Then they placed lots of round *mafenbao*, big and small, outside the entrance to his *shirangju*. When Puffball came out, he stepped on the fungus, and that ash-like floss flew right in his face, provoking a coughing fit.

Viktor was waiting at the side of the entrance to the *shirangju*. 'Come quick and see – Puffball stamping on puffball!' he yelled gleefully.

Vladimir was the first to come running over to see what the excitement was all about, and when he glimpsed Puffball's pitiful countenance, he couldn't help but guffaw. His laugh infuriated Puffball, who charged at Vladimir, landed a heavy punch on his chest and cursed at him.

'Who are you to laugh at me?' said Puffball. 'You aren't even a real man.'

This wounded Vladimir deeply, but he refused to show it. 'You've got the brains of a child,' he retorted. 'Are you sure you have what it takes to be a man?'

And with that the two went at one another. Puffball grabbed Vladimir by the neck, and Vladimir kneed Puffball in the crotch.

'Everybody come and watch!' shouted Puffball. 'This wimp wants to turn me into a eunuch too!'

After this incident, Puffball stopped speaking with our kinsmen, and we despised him more and more. Not only was he violent towards Lyusya, he didn't even show respect for Valodya. He often mocked him, and said that Valodya had split up his own clan for the sake of a widow, so he was a wrongdoer. But Valodya understood Puffball's deep-seated anguish, so he never quibbled with him.

Lyusya was a talented child who liked to gather wild vegetables and berries. She told Viktor that she liked such chores not only because she could avoid her father's reproaches, but also because she could enjoy the bird chatter and the cool forest breeze all by herself.

One day Valodya and Luni killed a bear. They carried their prey back to the camp and the greeters all stood at attention and pretended to caw like ravens. That day Puffball volunteered to skin the bear himself. Before skinning a bear you must cut off its testicles and hang them from a tree because we believe that only a castrated bear will behave itself.

Puffball severed the bear's testicles, wrapped them in grass, and then unexpectedly gave them to Vladimir to hang from a tree, grinning cruelly as he did so. Vladimir said nothing, but his face went pale and, his hands shaking, he took the testicles, walked unsteadily to a pine and attached them to a branch. When he turned around to come back, his eyes were sparkling with tears.

The feast following a bear hunt is the happiest time for us. After we've eaten bear meat, each person drinks a bit of the bear fat.

But because of Puffball's insulting behaviour towards Vladimir, our clansmen were angry and sullen as we ate. Puffball could sense everyone's resentment, but he intentionally spoke loudly and drank heartily.

Lyusya preferred not to see her father act like that, so she ate a small chunk of bear meat, picked up a birch-bark bucket and went off to pick the blueberries that were just beginning to ripen.

As soon as Lyusya was on her way, Juktakan began making a fuss, saying she wanted to go along too. The weather was very hot, but even under the scorching sun Nihau felt a shiver run down her spine.

'You can't go with Lyusya,' said Nihau.

'But I want to go! I want to!'

Juktakan was on the point of tears. 'The child just wants to play. Let her go along,' said Luni. 'They won't go far.'

'No running off on your own. And stay by Lyusya,' ordered Nihau. 'Do you hear me?'

'I know, I know!' But when Juktakan ran off in pursuit of Lyusya, Nihau shivered again.

There are many taboos about eating bear meat. For example, no matter how sharp the blade used to cut its flesh, we call it *kergingke*, which means 'dull knife'.

But Puffball intentionally brandished the knife and shouted: 'Look here! See how sharp this knife is? If you don't believe me, grab a hair and try it. *Shwaa!* And your hair will be sliced in two just like that!'

We mustn't discard the bones carelessly when we eat bear. But Puffball cast the bones he chewed in every direction. He threw one into the fire, and another off into the distance like a stone.

Valodya was very cross. 'If you dare throw away another bear bone like that,' he scolded, 'I'll chop off your hand.'

'I beg you, if you're going to chop off my hand, then chop off both of them!' said Puffball impudently as he munched on a bone. 'Without my hands I can't do any work, and you'll all have to treat me respectfully like the *Malu*. Just think how comfortable I'll be!'

Just as Puffball completed that sentence, he suddenly uttered a strange, '*Ya!*' The bone he'd been munching was stuck in his throat, and his face abruptly turned into a ghostly grimace. His mouth wide, eyes bulging, his cheeks began to tremble, his lips twitched, and his entire face, such a healthy red a moment earlier, turned green. His arms danced but he couldn't utter a word.

Valodya stuck a finger inside Puffball's mouth and swished it around, but didn't touch any bone. It had to be lodged further down. Puffball grunted a low-pitched choking sound. Beads of sweat broke out on his forehead and he looked imploringly at his clansmen.

First we gave him a spoonful of bear fat and then patted him on the back, thinking that now his mouth was lubricated, with another few pats that bone would slide down into his belly like a slice of overripe fruit. But the bear bone had grown teeth and bitten into his gullet.

As this didn't do the trick, someone suggested hanging him upside down, which would naturally dislodge the bone. Luni brought a rope, wrapped it around Puffball's feet, hung him from a birch tree, and then patted him energetically on the shoulder. But like a seed that has finally found the most fertile of soils, the bone remained firmly embedded.

Everyone scrambled to take him down from the tree. By then Puffball's face was purple and he was barely breathing. He made a big effort to lift his arms in Vladimir's direction, his eyes full of regret, as if begging for forgiveness. Vladimir sighed and shook his hands towards Puffball to signal there was no need to apologise. Then he stood up and gathered the bear bones carelessly discarded by Puffball just a moment ago. Vladimir was so painstaking and sincere that you'd have thought he was searching for someone's soul. Puffball's eyes filled with tears.

But the bear bones gathered by Vladimir didn't loosen the one lodged in Puffball's throat. His breath grew fainter. We had tried every idea but to no avail. That bear bone had probably set its mind on severing Puffball's throat.

Everyone's gaze turned simultaneously to Nihau. Only she could save him!

Trembling, Nihau remained mute and buried her head in Luni's arms. Her behaviour made Luni comprehend that if she saved Puffball, they might lose their beloved Juktakan. Luni also began to shake.

But in the end Nihau draped herself in the Spirit Robe that was certainly heavier than a mountain. She donned the Spirit Headdress that was certainly woven with thorns, for her head was covered with scars. And the Spirit Drum that she brandished was certainly forged of red-hot iron, for it scalded Nihau's hand. While Puffball was carried into the *shirangju*, his breath as airy as gossamer, and Nihau began her dance, Luni was already on his way to find Juktakan.

Typically, the Spirit Dance cannot be performed before the sky has turned dark, so it would be very difficult for the Spirits to descend. Although it was almost dusk, the summer sky was still bright. To fabricate darkness, Nihau had animal hides normally for winter use placed over the *shirangju*'s thin birch-bark covering to keep light out. The entrance that faced the east was tightly bound to hinder anyone's entry or departure, and the fire in the hearth was extinguished. In this way, the only natural light was the slender beam streaming down from the very top of the *shirangju*.

Valodya and I remained inside. His hands were soiled with fresh reindeer blood. When Nihau decided to save Puffball, Valodya had quickly seized a fawn that remained in the camp and sacrificed it to the *Malu*.

Once Nihau began her Spirit Dance, she was no longer herself.

Her air of vulnerability disappeared, and she looked full of passion. When the drum began to sound, my heart beat along with it. At first we could also hear Puffball groaning, but eventually the drum drowned him out. When Nihau rotated to the centre of the *shirangju*, that beam of natural light illuminated her. She became a colourful candle, and that ray of skylight was the spark that ignited her.

After Nihau had danced for about two hours, a gale from the netherworld suddenly began to swirl inside the *shirangju*. It moaned like the midwinter northern wind. The light streaming down from the top of the *shirangju* was no longer white, but dim yellow, as the sun had dropped behind the mountains.

At the beginning that strange wind floated everywhere, but then its moaning massed in one place: around Puffball's head. I had a premonition that this wind would blow the bear bone out. Sure enough, when Nihau put down the Spirit Drum and stopped dancing, Puffball suddenly sat up, yelled '*Aaagh!*' and coughed up the bone.

The blood-tainted bear bone landed right in the centre of the *shirangju*. It looked like a rose cast down from the sky.

Nihau stood with her head drooping while Puffball whimpered. Nihau was silent for a moment, and then she began to intone a Spirit Song. But she wasn't singing for Puffball who was back from the dead, she was singing for her prematurely wilted lily – Juktakan.

> *The sun to slumber has gone*
> *And there is no light in the forest.*
>
> *The stars have not yet emerged*
> *And trees murmur in the wind.*

*O, my lily*
*Autumn is not yet upon us*
*Countless summer days await*
*Why scatter your petals now?*

*You've fallen*
*And the sun has descended too.*
*But still your fragrance wafts*
*And the moon will yet rise!*

When Nihau had finished her Spirit Song and we followed her out of the *shirangju*, we saw Luni with Juktakan in his arms. Behind was Lyusya, weeping.

While Lyusya was picking blueberries she kept Juktakan with her. But later she discovered a thick patch of the fruit and forgot herself. Just when it was that Juktakan wandered away, Lyusya didn't really know.

Eventually Juktakan's plaintive cries interrupted Lyusya's fruit picking. She followed the sound and discovered Juktakan on the forest floor. She had run smack into a big wasps' nest hanging from a birch branch, and wasp stings had already rendered her face unrecognisable. Beyond the birch stood an enchanting cluster of red and white lilies in full bloom. Juktakan must have been galloping towards them.

Wasps in the forest are bigger than your typical honeybee, and their tail ends feature a poisonous sting. Undisturbed, they amuse themselves flying in and out of their nest and collecting nectar; but if by chance you damage their nest, they will swarm and exact revenge. It never occurred to Juktakan that a tiger lay between her and those pristine red lilies. The wasps' nest bumped Juktakan right up into the Heavens.

By the time Luni found them, Lyusya was on her way back, struggling to carry Juktakan in her arms. The venom had already begun to take effect throughout Juktakan's body and she was experiencing wave after wave of shivers.

When Luni pulled her close, Juktakan smiled faintly, called out '*Ama*' weakly, and shut her eyes for good.

That night grief shrouded the camp. Nihau pulled the poisonous stings from Juktakan's face, washed her wounds and changed her into pink clothes. Luni picked a bouquet of those eye-catching red and white lilies near the wasps' nest, and placed them in her crossed arms. Only then did he put her inside the white cloth bag.

After Nihau and Luni each placed a final kiss on Juktakan's forehead, Valodya and I lifted that white cloth bag. As we walked towards a sunny slope, Juktakan seemed as light as a bundle of clouds in our hands.

The moon was still in the sky when we set out, but it was raining upon our return. 'Tell Nihau not to name her child after a flower in the future,' Valodya said. 'How can a flower have a long life here on the earth? If she weren't named Juktakan, perhaps the wasps wouldn't have stung her!'

My heart filled with loathing. If it weren't for Puffball's bad behaviour, Nihau wouldn't have saved someone so worthless, and Juktakan wouldn't have died. 'The flower that was Juktakan withered on account of your clansman,' I said sullenly. 'If you hadn't arranged for a layabout like Puffball to stay with us, we'd all be safe! I don't want to see that disgusting creature again!'

I stood crying in the rain. Valodya reached out to me, his hand so warm. 'I'll arrange tomorrow for Chirala to take Puffball into their *urireng*,' he said. 'I don't want to see my woman in tears.' He pulled me over and caressed my hair.

But before Valodya could enact his plan, Puffball won our forgiveness through an act of self-mutilation.

The day after Juktakan's death, the sky cleared. Early in the morning we heard Lyusya crying. Valodya and I thought it must be Puffball venting his anger on his daughter again and we ran over to dissuade him.

But we were astounded by what we found. Puffball lay on his roe-deerskin blanket, his legs crossed and his face a sickly green. His trousers were unbuckled, and blood had dyed his crotch a purplish black. Next to him were a few shrivelled *mafenbao*. It looked like he had ripped them open to use their cottony floss to staunch the flow of his blood.

When Puffball saw Valodya, he made an effort to grin, but his smile gleamed with an icy light. 'Getting rid of those things is a relief,' he said. 'I feel less burdened and confused now.'

At the crack of dawn Puffball had castrated himself with a hunting knife. Thereafter he became best friends with Vladimir, and Luni and Nihau no longer felt he hadn't been worth saving.

A period of peace and tranquillity followed in the wake of the Puffball incident. We continued to go down from the mountains during the spring and the autumn to trade our furs and deer products for manufactured goods.

In the spring of 1948, Nihau bore another child, and it was Ivan who named her Berna. Nihau had just given birth when Ivan came riding into our camp on horseback. His garb had changed, and now he sported a military uniform.

'The map that Dashi gave me was no ordinary map,' Ivan told us. 'It didn't just show the names of mountains and rivers. Some military installations built by Japan's Kwantung Army were marked too. Using the map, we located a cave where tanks and ammunition were stored.

'Two Japanese soldiers at the cave were still resisting, and they had no idea that their emperor had already conceded defeat.'

The People's Liberation Army had embarked upon a clean-up operation targeting bandits who had taken refuge in the mountains. Ivan had stopped by to inform us that there were both anti-communist bandits and Kuomintang deserters in the mountains. If we discovered them, we should report them promptly and not release them.

Ivan also brought a piece of shocking news: Wang Lu and Ludek had been arrested and charged with treason. If convicted, they could be executed!

We couldn't understand why. Luni in particular expressed himself with great intensity. 'Wang Lu and Ludek didn't help the Japanese do bad things. One of them knows Japanese and the other knows the lie of the land, and that's why the Japanese made use of them.

'If you insist that they did wrong, then Wang Lu's crime was his tongue, and Ludek's crime was his legs. If they have to be punished, isn't it enough to cut out Wang Lu's tongue and sever Ludek's legs? Why chop off their heads?'

Perhaps we only saw superficial things about Wang Lu and Ludek, cautioned Valodya. 'Maybe we were kept in the dark about what else they did for the Japanese, and what they got in return.'

Luni was very unhappy with Valodya's speculations about Wang

Lu and Ludek. 'If you define a traitor like that, then Vladimir is no exception! Didn't he stay behind in the garrison and play the *mukulén* for Yoshida?'

No sooner had Luni spoken than Yveline's long mute mouth opened to speak. 'Vladimir did play the *mukulén* for Yoshida, but didn't his tune sound the defeat of the Japanese?'

Her voice was remote, like an ill-wind blowing towards us from a distant canyon. Startled, we gazed at her, but she continued sewing her leather socks without even looking up.

Luni was a bit displeased with Ivan because of the news about Wang Lu and Ludek, but since Luni had just become a father again, he still felt Ivan was a bearer of good tidings, so he asked Ivan to choose a name for his newborn.

'Why not call her Berna?' said Ivan after a moment of reflection.

Yveline opened her mouth again. 'Ivan has never been able to keep a woman at his side. If he names a girl, that girl is lost for sure.' She kept her head down, busy with her handiwork.

Ivan sighed, and Luni felt a shiver run down his back. 'This name doesn't count,' Ivan said. 'You and Nihau give her another name.'

'She has been named,' said Luni. 'We haven't used the name a single day. How can we discard it just like that? Let's call her Berna.' But even as he said this his voice was tinged with foreboding.

Ivan stayed just one day and departed. Everyone gathered and said their goodbyes and watched him ride his horse down the mountain. Only Yveline, sitting slumped over next to a sapling and playing with a hunting knife, remained unmoved. When the sound of the hooves grew distant like a gurgling stream, she sighed. 'We don't have a blacksmith any more. In the future when our spears and ice picks are broken, and our machetes and axes dull, who will forge them for us?'

Yveline's words reminded me of the 'paint sticks' I had kept, the ones made from the red-ochre soil where Ivan forged iron. That balmy afternoon, I tucked a few of those dried sticks of pigment in my pocket and walked a few *li* to a tiny tributary of the Bistaré. There, I found a stretch of weathered white rock and painted a Spirit Drum with a fire pattern on one side, and seven reindeer fawns circling the Spirit Drum. The Spirit Drum was the moon, and the seven reindeer surrounding it were the stars that comprise the Plough.

That stream had no name. But ever since I left a painting there, in my heart I call it '*Untuung*', 'Spirit Drum Creek'. Today, like Rolinsky Ravine, it has dried up.

That was the most satisfying painting I ever left by a waterway. Spirit Drum Creek was so limpid, and as I stood barefoot in the water, looking towards the white rock face and painting, I could feel tiny fish lightly kissing my ankles. They had never seen two white stone columns standing like that in the middle of the water. Some fish were playful and curious and tried nibbling on me, but when they realised I was not a stone, they swam away with an audible shrug – *paa* – that rippled the surface of the water.

I painted until the sun fell into the mountains. By the time the setting sun draped the rock and water in gold, I had already hoisted a full moon and seven stars for the night that was soon to come.

During those years, I believed that a pair of moons shone upon *Untuung*, one in the sky raised by the Spirits, and one on the rock held up by my dreams.

The moon rose and I returned to camp, and Valodya was

standing outside our *shirangju* anxiously awaiting me. The instant I saw him, I had a sensation of being reunited after a long separation. I couldn't help myself and cried, because the two scenes – on the weathered rock and now in reality – both touched me. I didn't tell him where I'd been, because I felt that what I'd done was a secret between me and the rock.

Valodya didn't ask me anything. He just handed me a bowl of warm reindeer-milk tea. A good man never enquires where his woman has been.

That night Valodya held me ever so tightly, and Tatiana's gentle snoring echoed in the *shirangju* like a spring breeze. I merged with Valodya as naturally as a fish in water, dew drops on a flower, bird calls in a cool breeze, and the moon in the Milky Way.

And it was then that Valodya chanted in a low voice a song that he made up for me. His was different from Nihau's Spirit Song, for it was very comforting:

> *Morning dew wets the eye*
> *Midday sun warms the back*
> *Evenfall reindeer bells refresh the heart*
> *And night birds wing home forest-bound.*

Valodya patted my back softly as he sang the last line. This little pat made my eyes water. Fortunately it was night-time and he couldn't see my tears. I buried my head deep, deep in his embrace like a bird snuggling in its warm nest.

* * *

Ever since Zefirina's miscarriage she had not become pregnant again. She often went to Nihau's, her cheeks sallow, knelt before the *Malu*, and prayed earnestly. This scene recalled a younger Maria. Didn't she often go to Nidu the Shaman's to beg the Spirits to grant her a child? The difference was that Maria wrapped her head in a handkerchief, while Zefirina wore nothing on her head, not even a barrette.

Zefirina was probably sensitive about her imperfect mouth, so when she combed her hair she always coiled it towards the side of her mouth that wasn't crooked. Her hair looked like a thick cloud beside a crescent moon, covering her defect and endowing her entire face with a certain dignity.

Maria probably regretted forcing Zefirina to do away with her child back then, and when the antler-cutting season arrived and she saw fresh blood oozing from the reindeer horns, Maria's tears cascaded onto the ground again.

In 1950, one year after the founding of the People's Republic, a supply cooperative was established in Uchiriovo. The Han *anda* Xu Caifa managed it with his son Xu Rongda. The cooperative acquired products such as pelts and antlers, and supplied us with items like rifles, bullets, iron skillets, matches, salt, cloth, grain, tobacco, liquor, sugar and tea.

Vladimir brought an abandoned child back from Uchiriovo that summer.

After he and Dashi exchanged goods at the cooperative, they spent the night at a small inn. The next day they took breakfast and were about to set out when Dashi told Vladimir he wanted to ask Xu Caifa to help him get some medicine for Zefirina. Vladimir understood that Dashi was going to seek drugs to treat his wife's infertility.

Bored, Vladimir decided to go out for a stroll. As he passed by the stable next to the inn, he heard an infant's giggle. Vladimir wondered how the innkeeper could be so careless as to allow his child to crawl into the stable without realising it. What if a horse kicked the child!

Vladimir turned around and entered the inn. 'Your child has found its way into the horse stable. Shouldn't you be looking after it?'

'My son's old enough to help run the inn,' smiled the innkeeper, 'and my daughter's fourteen. So what child would that be? Sure your ears aren't fooling you?'

'No way. It sounded like a baby's giggle.'

'You must have heard wrong,' argued the innkeeper. 'The last few days none of our guests has been travelling with an infant! If there's really a baby in the stable, that child must be God, and that makes me God's Father. So what am I doing working like a dog running this inn?'

But Vladimir insisted his ears couldn't be wrong.

'Fine,' said the innkeeper. 'Let's go and take a look. But if there's no child, you forfeit your leather jacket to me!' Vladimir agreed.

When they entered the stable, they were mesmerised by the scene: an infant in swaddling clothes lay on the straw, and a silver-grey horse was licking the baby as if washing its face. It tickled so much that the baby kept giggling loudly.

The child was wrapped in a quilt with white blossoms against a blue background. Its face was a tender pink, and its jet-black eyes rolled about. One of the baby's hands had fought free of the swaddling clothes, and seeing people peering towards it, the baby waved and laughed even more energetically.

Vladimir said he fell at once for that child, because it was just too beautiful and adorable.

The innkeeper said the baby must have a defect, otherwise why would someone have abandoned it? First they inspected the infant's eyes, ears, nose, throat, tongue and hands, and found nothing abnormal; then they opened the swaddling clothes to see if any part of the body or limbs were incomplete. But a glance revealed everything was normal. It was then that they realised this was a little girl.

'Evil-doers!' cried the innkeeper. 'Such a bright and vivacious child. How could anyone not want her?'

'I want her,' said Vladimir.

'It looks like she's just a few months old; she should be breast-feeding. How will you keep her alive?'

'I'll feed her reindeer milk.'

The innkeeper had heard about Vladimir's emasculation. 'If you want her that would be perfect. It seems she's a gift to you from the Lord above. Raise her as your daughter and she'll look after you in your old age. Wouldn't that be a blessing?'

Hearing that someone had abandoned a child in the stable, the innkeeper's wife put aside her chores and came running. She said last night when she got up to relieve herself, she had heard the pounding of hooves stopping right outside the inn.

'At the time I wondered why a guest was arriving so late,' she recounted. 'I decided to wait until the guest knocked on the door before getting the lamp. I felt around for the matches, but no one knocked.

'Thinking I must have been mistaken, I went back to sleep on my heated *kang*. Just then I heard the sound of hooves again, but it grew faint, so the horseman must have left.'

There were still bandits on the run in the mountains, and the innkeeper's wife had suspected that a bandit was sizing up her inn. She eventually got up to latch the door, and only then was she able to go to sleep. But now it appeared that the rider had come expressly to abandon the infant.

There was no note in the swaddling clothes, so they couldn't tell where the child came from or when it was born. But since her milk teeth hadn't emerged, she must have been less than six months old. From her looks you could tell she wasn't of Evenki stock, because the bridge of her nose was set high, and she had big eyes, slightly curled lips and a fair complexion.

'The parents are probably Han. But why would they abandon their own flesh and blood?' wondered the innkeeper's wife.

'This is probably the illegitimate child of a young lady from a well-to-do family,' surmised her husband. 'Or else someone kidnapped an enemy's child for revenge.'

'If it was an act of revenge, why not just leave her in the mountains to be eaten by wolves?' said his wife. 'Obviously the horseman abandoned her in the stable to allow her to survive.'

Vladimir and Dashi carried her back into the mountains. No one had imagined that Vladimir would bring home an abandoned little girl! But everyone adored the child. She not only had comely eyebrows, she also loved to laugh and rarely cried.

Vladimir asked Valodya to name her. Valodya thought for a while. 'Since she was abandoned in a stable, and a horse watched over her for a night and didn't harm her, let's give her the Han family name *Ma*, for "horse". And since she loves to wave her arms and kick her feet, when she grows up she'll no doubt dance the *Ikan*, so let's call her Mai-kan.' *Ikan* means 'Circle Dance' or 'Bonfire Dance' in our language.

Maikan brought unmatched happiness to the whole *urireng*. Every day I milked the reindeer and took it to Vladimir's. He brought it to the boil, waited until it was neither hot nor cold, and then fed her. At times Vladimir fed her too quickly and she'd choke on the milk, so I often went over to help.

Berna was two and still nursing, so even though Nihau didn't have a lot of milk, she occasionally nursed Maikan too. But as soon as Nihau stuffed her nipple in Maikan's mouth, Berna behaved as if she had suffered some great injustice. She tugged at Nihau's lapels and wouldn't stop howling. So Nihau often nursed Maikan for just an instant and then she had to put her down and pick up Berna.

Zefirina adored Maikan. But when she held her, Zefirina's face was terribly forlorn, for she wanted a child of her own so badly.

Whenever Maria saw Maikan, her tongue twisted involuntarily as if Maikan were a flame scalding her tongue. '*Ai yoyo!*' she'd exclaim. 'I've never seen such a lovely child. A tiny fairy!'

But Yveline treated Maikan with indifference, barely even glancing at her.

In deep autumn, with an eye to obtaining a set of pretty winter clothing for Maikan, Vladimir put two roe-deer pelts under his arm, picked up the child and went to seek Yveline's aid, saying that only her handiwork was reliable.

That was the first time Yveline actually looked at Maikan. She threw her a glance, and said: 'Isn't this a ball of fire on water?'

Vladimir didn't get her meaning, so he just smiled. Then she added: 'A fish in the grass!'

Vladimir assumed that Yveline didn't want to make clothes for Maikan and was spouting nonsense to put him off. But just as he was about to leave, Yveline spoke again. 'Leave the furs and come back in three days.'

Three days later Yveline was finished. But it was a very odd garment. Without a collar or sleeves, it resembled a large bag with no holes for breathing, and Vladimir was so furious that he froze in an angry stare.

'Yveline is old now,' I said to Vladimir, 'her handiwork isn't as good as before, and she's a tad crazy too, so it's no surprise that she would make clothing like this.' I took it apart and sewed a new one whose sleeves and collar were embroidered with green silk. Vladimir was content so he didn't reproach Yveline.

* * *

Ivan didn't return to the mountains as promised, and Luni and I missed him a lot. That winter Xu Caifa came with horses transporting many goods, particularly grain, salt and liquor. He said Ivan had arranged for a Mongolian fellow in the trucking business to transfer money to the supply cooperative, and then Xu Caifa used that money to buy goods and bring them up to our *urireng*. Ivan sent word that he was stationed now at Jalannér, and told us not to worry about him. He'd come back to see us two years hence.

This was the first time that we had benefited from goods without exchanging pelts and antlers, and the unexpected gift made everyone happy. 'Ivan is really something. Now we get a share of his soldier's pay and rations!' said Hase.

'The way I see it,' said Xu Caifa, 'living off the military isn't as reliable as raising reindeer and eating food available in the mountains.'

When he finished speaking, Yveline came over and offered him a bowl of reindeer milk. It had been several years since Xu Caifa last saw her, and he couldn't have imagined that she'd become so wizened and stooped. 'Life in the mountains certainly ages you,' he sighed.

Xu Caifa heard that Vladimir had claimed an abandoned baby girl in Uchiriovo. 'Everyone says that little girl's looks rival those of a fairy. Bring her over and let me have a look.'

'Has anyone been looking for a child over the last half year?' asked Vladimir.

'An abandoned child is like spilled water,' said Xu Caifa. 'Who'd go looking for it?' His heart at ease, Vladimir brought Maikan out. He was always worried that whoever had abandoned Maikan would regret it, and show up at his *urireng* looking for her.

When Vladimir carried the child over, Xu Caifa clicked his tongue in admiration. 'Sure enough, she is truly lovely. A perfect wife for my grandson one day!'

Vladimir's expression altered immediately. 'Maikan is my daughter. When she grows up she won't be any man's wife!' Everyone chuckled at Vladimir's reaction.

'Outside the mountains they're carrying out land reform now,' said Xu Caifa. 'Those ruthless landlords are all as withered as if they'd been covered in frost. Their land, houses and livestock aren't their property any more, and they've been divided up among the poor.

'The peasants who once slaved away for those landlords are gleefully settling scores with them. They're paraded in the street with ropes around their necks and hands tied behind their backs, and they're so wretched that their toes stick out from their shoes. And as for those daughters of well-to-do households who once dressed in silk and satin, nowadays they can't marry themselves off to a *mafoo*. It's really a changing of the dynasties,' concluded Xu Caifa.

No one else had much to say about Xu Caifa's revelations, but Yveline cleared her throat and spoke. 'Bravo! Bravo! Nowadays you can even denounce landlords, so why not settle scores with the Soviets and Japanese too?'

No one seconded Yveline. She eyed us one by one, shook her head, got up slowly, and repeated Xu Caifa's words: 'Life in the mountains certainly ages you,' and then walked away hunched over.

That evening we lit a bonfire in the camp, roasted squirrel meat and downed it with *baijiu*. After we had drunk our fill, everyone circled the bonfire and danced. I stood at a distance and admired the red-orange flames as they trembled and jumped. The bonfire was so radiant that it not only illuminated the nearby forest, it even shone upon the curves of the distant mountain ridges.

If the Spirits above were on the hunt, then our bonfire was their prey. This prey brought happiness to the Spirits and to us. I believe that the Spirits were sweetly regaling themselves with their prey, and when the bonfire turned to ashes, didn't the smoke and flames float off into the Heavens?

Valodya discovered I was standing all alone. He crept up silently, circled my neck with his arms, pressed against my ears and said romantically: 'I am mountains, you are water. Mountains create water, and water nourishes mountains. Where mountains and water meet, earth and sky are eternal.'

If the Right Bank of the Argun where we live is a giant rooted in the earth and holding up the skies, then those waterways of all sizes are blood vessels criss-crossing his body, and mountain ranges form his skeleton. Those mountains belong to *Egdan*, the Greater Khingan Mountain Range.

Over the course of my life I've seen many a mountain and no longer recall all of them. In my eyes, every mountain on the Right Bank is a star sparkling on Mother Earth. During the spring and summer, these stars are green, in the autumn they are golden yellow, and silvery white in the winter.

I love them. They are like human beings with their own temperaments and physiques. Some are short and rounded, like a clay pot turned upside down; some stand tall and elegantly linked like the beautiful outstretched horns of a reindeer. In my eyes, the trees on the mountains are masses of flesh and blood.

Unlike rivers, most mountains have no name, but we have designated certain ones. For instance, we named one *Alanjak* for the way it towers from on high; one that reveals its white stones, *Kailaqqi*; *Yanggirqi* Mountain is covered with horsetail pines and lies between *Yaagi* River and the *Luddoy* Watershed. To the mountain on the northern slopes of the Greater Khingan Range where we once discovered a cow's skull, we gave the name *Hvhuldur*.

Mountain springs were numerous, and most were cool and sweet, but there was one mountain whose stream had an acrid taste, as if the mountain suffered from melancholy, so we named it *Slerkan*.

Puffball loved to name the mountains. When he saw a mountain where reindeer lingered, he called it *Morkofka*, 'the mountain where moss grows'. Seeing a mountain rich in astragalus, he'd style it *Aikusk*, for 'mountain covered in astragalus'. I still recall these names, but which particular mountain they refer to I don't remember. But there is one mountain whose name we shall always remember – *Listvyanka* Mountain in the Jiin Béra river basin.

In the spring of 1955 when the fawning season began, we decided to perform a marriage ceremony for Viktor and Lyusya, because Viktor had spent the entire spring polishing a deer-bone necklace for Lyusya. Without telling anyone, they often accompanied one another to pick wild fruits or hunt squirrels. Valodya said they were adults now and should be allowed to be together.

Just when we were worrying that if Nihau hosted the marriage ceremony she'd see Lyusya and, reminded of Juktakan's death, feel sad, news came that our Clan Chieftain had passed away. As our Clan Shaman, Nihau ought to preside over the chief's funeral, and could thus avoid Lyusya's marriage ceremony.

For the Chieftain's funeral rites, not only Nihau but also Luni, as our *urireng*'s Headman, had to go. When they left we didn't mention that we were going to perform a marriage ceremony for Viktor because we feared Nihau would object. Strictly speaking, given the death of our Chieftain, we should have delayed the marriage ceremony.

But I felt that's the way life is – there are births and there are deaths, sorrows and joys, marriages and funerals, and there needn't be so many taboos. So as soon as Nihau and Luni left, our *urireng* began wedding preparations.

Nihau and Luni left their son and daughter behind. Nihau instructed me to be sure to look after her children well, and I told her to put her heart at ease. My Tatiana, who was already nine, and her Berna, who was two years younger, were very close and virtually inseparable, so Nihau needn't fret over this pair of well-behaved young girls.

Maikan was also five then and Tatiana and Berna liked to play with her. They chased each other about in the camp like a trio of colourful butterflies flitting in the wind.

Nihau's son, Tibgur, was ten that year. He was a very sensible child, hardworking and diligent, and better liked than Grigori, who had died. When Nihau ate *khleb*, he always helped her spread bear fat on the bread, and when Luni wanted to drink tea, Tibgur would be off in a flash to boil the water. At eight he began hunting squirrels with Luni, and on the way back he always gathered faggots and carried them on his back. Valodya said that when Tibgur grew up he'd be a marvellous man with his gentleness and winning personality.

Tibgur loved the fawns and when Puffball and Vladimir were busy delivering them he always went to watch. At the moment of birth, he would wave his hands and cheer and jump for joy just like a playful fawn.

Sometimes the reindeer roamed far away to forage and the fawns went hungry, so the women had to leave camp, locate the does and bring them back to nurse their offspring.

Tibgur accompanied us on our searches. 'You were all nursed to adulthood by your mothers,' he'd say when we found the errant does. 'If they hadn't fed you back then, you'd have turned to dust long ago.'

On the third day after the departure of Nihau and her entourage, Valodya presided over the marriage of Viktor and Lyusya. It had rained the day before, so the air was fresh and the bird calls in the forest were especially cheerful.

We conducted the ceremony at the foot of a mountain on the banks of the Jiin. Slender Lyusya wore the wedding gown that I had sewn for her and sported a garland of wild flowers on her head.

Hanging from her neck was the deer-bone necklace painstakingly crafted for her by Viktor; she looked very pretty.

That day Puffball dressed very neatly. He had even shaved and seemed very pleased about this union. A smile never left his face. Ever since his self-mutilation, his voice had gone hoarse and his jowls sagged.

'A name should be given to this mountain to commemorate the marriage of Viktor and Lyusya,' Valodya said.

The mountain was covered in lush green pine trees. 'Let's call it Listvyanka Mountain,' said Puffball. *Listvyanka* means 'pine woodland'.

Once the mountain had a name, Valodya put it to immediate use. 'We gather here where reindeer fawns are delivered in order to bless your union,' he told Viktor and Lyusya. 'The surging waters of the Jiin Béra are the dewdrops of your love, and majestic Listvyanka Mountain is the cradle of your happiness. May the Jiin Béra forever encircle you, and may Listvyanka Mountain accompany you both in your dreams!'

Observing my Viktor's heroic bearing, I recalled Lajide, the first man in my life, and my eyes moistened. Although Valodya was gazing at me tenderly, I yearned passionately for Lajide at that moment. I suddenly comprehended that, in the lamp of my life, there was still oil left over from Lajide; his flame had been extinguished, but his energy was still there. Even though Valodya injected new oil, and lit it with tenderness, what he lit was a half-full lamp.

After the rites, everyone began to eat and drink, sing and dance. The banquet dishes were Zefirina's handiwork, and the sausages she cooked up were very popular. First, she minced roe-deer meat, mixed in green onions and *laosangqin*, and just the right amount of salt. She poured this mix into sausage casings and boiled them in an iron pot for three to five minutes. Then she took the sausages out and cut them into short sections. Indescribably delicious!

Zefirina also used the hanging pot to cook several wild ducks. She added chopped leek to the soup, and the duck tasted meaty but not greasy. Besides this, there also roe-deer head broth, reindeer-milk cheese, grilled fish fillets and lily bulb congee.

It's fair to say that of all the wedding feasts I attended, this was the most bountiful. Several times Valodya expressed his admiration for Zefirina's cuisine, and she blushed at his compliments.

Like Yveline, Maria was now entirely hunched over. Though the pair sat by the bonfire drinking *baijiu* to celebrate, no words passed between them and their eyes didn't even meet.

During those days Maria coughed from morning to night, and her long coughing spells left her gasping. But Maria's cough was glad tidings to Yveline. Her eyebrows rose contentedly and the hint of a smile appeared.

If the bonfire is a flower bud in the daylight hours, then in the dusk's indistinct light it begins to unfold bashfully. As the night approaches, its petals open wider, but in the deep of night, it blooms wildly.

By the time the bonfire was in full bloom, Puffball was already drunk and so was Kunde. Kunde's hand quivered as he drank, and when he sliced Zefirina's sausage, he cut his hand and blood flowed between his fingers.

Puffball consoled Kunde in his badly slurred speech. 'Have no fear! Just rub me into little pieces and sprinkle me on your wound, and the blood will stop flowing.'

His drunken babble made the dancers laugh, but Kunde was so

moved that he shed tears. 'My body is covered in wounds,' he replied. 'Thank goodness you're here, Puffball! How else could I stop the bleeding?'

Andaur rarely drank but he was happy for his brother's marriage and he also came over with a bowl of *baijiu* in his hand. Puffball patted him on the shoulder.

'If I had two daughters that'd be great, a big Lyusya and a little Lyusya. I'd marry one to Viktor, and the other to you!' said Puffball. 'Then you brothers could marry on the same day!'

'Which one would I marry?' Andaur asked earnestly. 'Big Lyusya or Little Lyusya?'

Even though Andaur was just about old enough to marry, his naïve temperament hadn't changed, and you can imagine how amusing everyone found his question.

That night a doe remaining in the camp gave birth to a fawn. But none of us could have imagined it would be deformed.

Generally speaking, black reindeer don't give birth to deformed fawns; it's the white ones that tend to. If the impaired offspring is female, it symbolises good fortune, while a male symbolises disaster.

Such a fawn doesn't live long, not usually more than three days. Yveline once described a deformed fawn as a 'little ghost' among the reindeer. When it dies, it can't be discarded as unceremoniously as a human child. Red and blue strips of cloth must be attached to its ear, neck, waist and tail. Then an upright birch tree is selected, the fawn is hung from it, and a Shaman is requested to perform a Spirit Dance for it.

The doe was pale grey, not pure white. But it bore a small, snow-white male. It had a head but no tail and only three legs, and a skewed face with one big eye and one small. When the members of the *urireng* heard that Vladimir had delivered a crippled fawn on the riverbank, they all stopped dancing and ran off to see.

The sight sobered up all of the adults. The fawn couldn't stand yet, and it lay curled up under its mother like a pile of melting snow.

'*Aiyo!*' exclaimed Maria upon seeing it. 'When will Nihau return?' Her voice was trembling. Although swaying from side to side, Maria was walking unaided when she arrived to view the fawn. But when she left, she had to lean on Dashi.

Valodya was concerned that the unfortunate fawn's birth would dilute the festive atmosphere of Viktor's wedding, so he told everyone a fairy tale. I didn't know then he was making it up on the spot.

'Long, long ago,' Valodya began, 'there was a lovely white swan that hatched a brood of little swans. All the little swans that broke through their egg shells were white, except for one that looked rather ugly, with short legs, a short neck too, and grey and black feathers all jumbled together.

'The other swans ignored it. But the white mother swan didn't look askance at her ugly offspring, and continued to carefully feed it. The little black swan grew day by day, and soon it could follow its mother to the river to catch fish. One day when the swan took her brood to play on the river, a strong wind began to blow and a fierce hawk swooped down and snapped the mother swan up in its beak.

'The young swans scattered out of fear, and only the ugly black swan went to rescue its mother. But it was too feeble to be of use, and could only watch helplessly as the hawk carried its mother away.

'When the wind calmed and the waves subsided, the little swans gathered once again to frolic. Only the ugly little swan was heartbroken, and it stood on the bank and made a mournful call.

'Its cry attracted a hunter just then passing by. "Why are you weeping?"

'"An old hawk snatched my mother, and now she's on a cliff across the river. My wings aren't strong enough to save her. I beg you, go and rescue my mother!"

'"If you wish to save your mother, you might lose your own life in turn. Aren't you afraid?"

'"If only my mother can escape from the hawk's beak, I'm willing to die in her place."

'The hunter forded the river and came to the foot of the mountain. He shot an arrow that struck the hawk so forcefully that the bird flipped backwards and hit the ground, and the mother swan was saved. But the ugliest of the little swans did indeed die on the opposite shore.

'When the hunter recounted all this to the mother swan, she cried. "Save my ugly little black swan," she begged the hunter.

'"But if it comes back to life, you will lose all those little white swans in the river," he cautioned. They were frolicking in the water, happy and carefree.

'"If only you can revive my ugly little swan, I am willing to sacrifice my other offspring."

'The hunter smiled, said nothing, turned and left. Suddenly the river waters rose high, and those snow-white little swans were struck so hard by the surging waves that they cried out in terror.

'Meanwhile the wings of the little black swan on the shore began to move, and it stood up slowly, alive again!

'Amazingly, the ugly black swan was transformed into a beautiful snow-white, long-necked little swan! But the dead little white swans turned grey and black, like a patch of rubbish scattered on the river.'

This tale touched everyone present and did away with their worries. Tibgur was especially happy. 'I'm sure that you'll be transformed into a darling fawn tomorrow morning!' he said to the misshapen young creature. 'Your eyes will be brighter than the stars, and your missing leg will grow like a rainbow after the rain!'

We were comforted by Tibgur's words, but then he said something that altered everyone's expression. 'If my *Eni* encounters danger, I'm willing to die for her just like that little black swan!'

The birth of the deformed fawn cast a dark shadow over the night of the marriage of Viktor and Lyusya. We knew it wouldn't live more than three days, and yearned for Nihau's return so that she could perform a Spirit Dance for it.

At midnight it rained again. It began with a drizzle but grew heavier. Rainfall on the day of a marriage is normally auspicious. So when I returned to our *shirangju* and heard the pattering rain, my heart that had been disturbed by the deformed fawn gradually calmed down.

Rain fell until dawn. Walking out of our *shirangju* I found myself in a fairyland. Mountains near and far were veiled in white mist, and the camp danced with twisting fog. The people standing across from me appeared indistinct, and I felt I had already left the ground and was wafting in the air.

Valodya rose earlier than I and went to the river. 'The waters of the Jiin are rising. Some willows on the shore are already submerged, and there's a thick fog floating over the river. If it rains another day, I'm afraid the water will overflow the banks,' he warned. 'There's no guarantee we can remain at this camp, so we have to be ready to move upstream to higher ground at any time.'

I was worried for the deformed fawn. 'Is it still alive?'

Valodya smiled and said it was not only alive but looked very energetic. It nursed on its mother's teat and even staggered forwards a few steps at a time.

I was startled. 'How can a three-legged fawn walk?'

'If you don't believe me, go see for yourself.'

When I arrived at the banks of the Jiin, the fog there was already thicker than over the mountains. You could hear the *hwa-hwa* sound of the river grumbling, but you couldn't see the water itself. Vladimir fitted a halter on the mother doe, and the deformed fawn was indeed taking wobbly steps.

'It seems enchanted with the fog over the water,' said Vladimir, 'and it keeps heading for the river. But it can't go far. Each time it takes three or four baby steps, it falls down.'

'Watch the fawn carefully. If it dies, carry it back to camp to await Nihau's return. No matter what,' I told Vladimir, 'don't let the ravens peck at it.'

The sun must be mist's enemy. At noon, the sun finally ripped through the face of the dark clouds. When the sky cleared, our hearts cleared too. As long as it didn't rain and cause the river to overflow, we could remain in the same camp. The moss in those mountains was copious, so the does who had just fawned needn't roam far for food, and for those of us who had to constantly bring them back to nurse their fawns, this meant much less trekking along winding paths.

The children adored the deformed fawn. As soon as the mist dispersed they all went running to watch it by the Jiin. Tatiana helped Berna and Maikan make a garland of blue-green grass. They placed it around the fawn's neck, and agreed that with the new garland, the fawn wasn't ugly at all. And Tibgur lit a fire to chase away the deer flies and mosquitoes that harassed the young reindeer.

It was dusk and we were busy cooking dinner back at the camp when Tibgur and the deformed fawn got into trouble.

Crying as they ran back from the Jiin, Tatiana and Berna said Tibgur and the fawn had been swept away by the river and lost from sight. Viktor was already paddling a birch-bark canoe in pursuit.

It transpired that when the sun began leaning to the west, Maikan said she was hungry and so Vladimir had carried her back to the camp to rustle up some food. Before he left, he instructed Tatiana and the others that if the fawn was in difficulty, they should fetch him at once.

At first, Tatiana and Berna stayed near the fawn with Tibgur and played. But then they spotted Viktor holding a fish spear. They knew he was going to fish for Lyusya so they ran over to watch. When the river rises there are more fish than usual. Viktor chose a bend in the river with a backwash, and the fish behaved like panicking birds that had just been shut inside a cage. They swarmed, jumping up and down, making them easy prey.

Viktor stood on a big stone in the middle of the current. He tossed each fish he speared onto the bank where Tatiana and Berna strung them on a willow branch.

Some of the fish hadn't been fatally speared, so after they were thrown ashore they shook their heads and wiggled their tails. A stream of giggles flowed from Tatiana and Berna as they strung the fish, because the more resilient ones brushed the girls' faces with a layer of sticky white slime.

Spearing a fish is a task that requires a quick eye and a deft hand, and Viktor performed it effortlessly. He speared them so steadily and accurately that they piled up higher and higher on the bank, and Tatiana and Berna had their hands full.

'There are so many fish that we should make a wreath for the fawn,' said Tatiana to Berna, 'and replace the grass one.'

'Good idea,' added Berna. 'Maybe with a fish wreath the fawn's face will right itself!'

And the girls giggled even more. But just then they heard Tibgur's scream: 'Come back! Come b-a-a-ck!'

Tibgur and the fawn were not too far downstream so Viktor, Tatiana and Berna could clearly see what was happening. The deformed fawn dashed along the bank, and in the blink of an eye, dived into the river. At that instant, the fawn seemed to transform into a big fish.

Shouting after the fawn, Tibgur raced right into the Jiin.

When they reached the centre of the river, the fawn and the boy encountered a whirlpool. They went round in circles, bobbing up and down until you couldn't distinguish between human and animal.

'*Tian ah!*' screamed Viktor, as he jumped hurriedly on shore and threw his fish spear down.

By the time Viktor, Tatiana and Berna began running downstream, Tibgur and the fawn had already been swept away by the torrential current.

Viktor dragged a *jawi* from the willow grove next to the bank, jumped into it and dashed off to rescue Tibgur. Meanwhile, Tatiana and Berna raced back to the camp to break the news.

We all ran to the banks of the Jiin. The sun had already descended halfway, dyeing the surface of the water to the west so that the river looked like it was split in two, one side deep blue-green, one a milky yellow.

Many years later when I entered that shop in Jiliu County, I saw two bolts of cloth, one bright and one dark, standing upright on the merchant's shelf. The Jiin River at dusk that day suddenly came to mind. Indeed, the river was just like two rolls of cloth lying next to one another, one bright, one dark. But the cloth was tightly rolled in the shop, while the cloth on the river was entirely spread out, extending to places we could not discern.

Valodya and Puffball carried another canoe to the river and went in search of Tibgur.

We waited anxiously on the riverbank, and no one made a sound except for Berna. 'That fawn must have grown another leg, we all saw it. It was running faster than Tibgur,' she said repeatedly to Tatiana. 'Now you tell me, if it didn't have four legs, it couldn't run so fast, could it?' She shivered as she said this, and we shuddered too.

The sun set for good, taking with it the beautiful interplay of light and shadow on the river surface. The Jiin now consisted of a single colour, but due to changes in the sky, its gold tint appeared greyish and faded. The rushing waters sounded *hwa-hwa*, as if someone were piercing our hearts with a knife, and each incision hurt acutely.

The stars appeared and so did the moon but those searching for Tibgur hadn't returned. Luni and Nihau, back at last from the Clan Chieftain's funeral, now stood silently behind us. 'There's no point in waiting,' Nihau said when her eyes met ours. 'My Tibgur has already departed.'

Just then the shadows of a pair of birch-bark canoes appeared, like two large fish swimming towards us. The boats contained four persons, three standing, and one lying down. The prone one would remain so for ever, and that was Tibgur.

Although Tibgur had been thoroughly scoured by the river, Nihau insisted on using water from the Jiin to cleanse his body, and then she changed his clothes. Valodya and I placed him in a white cloth bag and threw him on the south-east slopes of Listvyanka Mountain. This mountain was designated to commemorate the marriage of Viktor and Lyusya, but in my heart it is a cemetery.

Nihau said Tibgur died in order to save her. When she and Luni were riding their reindeer on the way back, keen to see their children as soon as possible, they took a shortcut along the hard-to-negotiate Baishilazi Trail, with its cramped, winding path. One side sticks closely to towering white cliffs, and the other opens onto a deep, deep ravine. Generally speaking, unless we had a particularly pressing reason, we never took that path. Even reindeer's legs tremble when they walk that narrow path.

Due to two recent heavy rainfalls, the surface was extremely slippery, so they reduced their speed and walked gingerly. But the path was simply too narrow and the rain had seeped into the soil, loosening the edges of the path.

At a bend, Nihau's reindeer stepped at the very edge of the path, inclined for an instant and then tumbled down with Nihau into the bottomless ravine.

Luni saw Nihau and her mount disappear in the blink of an eye, and his heart froze. There could be no happy ending for anyone that fell into a deep gulch like that.

But a miracle happened. The reindeer fell to its doom at the valley bottom, while Nihau found herself hanging from a black birch tree located just off the path. Luni lowered a rope and hauled Nihau back up.

As soon as Nihau arrived back on the path, she began crying. 'Tibgur must have had an accident,' she said. 'When that black birch blocked my fall, I saw the tree extend a pair of hands, and those hands were Tibgur's.'

*Tibgur* means black birch.

It was dusk when Nihau had her accident, and that was the same instant Tibgur was swept away by the river. Luni said he examined that birch again and again. It was strong and sturdy like Tibgur. But he couldn't find the pair of hands Nihau saw as she tumbled off the pathway. How sorely Luni wanted to grasp his son's warm little hands once more!

That deformed fawn did bring us bad luck after all.

On that night of extreme sorrow when everyone was mourning and had no appetite for food or drink, Yveline lit an open fire, roasted the wild duck Kunde shot earlier in the day, and ate and drank *baijiu*. The fragrance of that meat pierced our grieving hearts like a bullet.

She drank until the moon leaned to the west, and only then did she stand up on her quivering legs. As she walked towards her *shi-rangju*, she heard Nihau crying. Yveline stopped, looked up at the sky, cackled, clapped her hands and danced in celebration.

'Jindele, listen up! Who's that weeping? The maiden you wanted and the one you didn't want: is either living happily? I've never heard a lovelier sound than that weeping, Jindele!'

At that moment, Yveline was a true demon. The happiness that she expressed at the tragedy of those two women made your heart freeze over.

I was sitting with Maria's family around their fireplace. Yveline's cry of pleasure at another's misfortune so enraged Maria that she began to cough violently. Zefirina pounded Maria's back lightly with her fists.

Once her cough subsided, Maria grasped Zefirina's hands firmly. 'You must have a child for me,' she said, still panting. 'A good, healthy child! Dashi and you should get along well, and show Yveline how happy you are!'

I'd never have imagined that Yveline's increasingly intense hatred would cause Maria to forgive Zefirina. Dashi and Zefirina each held one of Maria's hands, and they were so moved that they cried.

I left Maria's and on the way back to our *shirangju*, I heard Nihau incant a Spirit Song:

> *O, earthly white cloth bag*
> *Why not store grain and jerky*
> *Instead of felling my Black Birch*
> *and crumpling my Little Lily*
> *To hoard in your filthy gut?*

We quickly left Listvyanka Mountain and Jiin River. But this time we didn't all go in one direction. We split into two, with Valodya leading one group, and Luni the other. Yveline's crazed cry that night had stung everyone's heart, and Luni said it was absolutely necessary to separate Yveline from Maria. Luni's group took Maria and her family, some of Valodya's clansmen, and my son Andaur. I wasn't keen to see him leave me, but it seemed he preferred Luni. Whatever children like, I respect their wishes.

Berna was the most reluctant to go with Luni for she couldn't stand to be apart from Tatiana and Maikan. When we left, Berna started to cry. 'Even though you'll be separated,' I said, 'they'll be close by, and you'll often have the chance to visit Tatiana.' Berna stopped crying.

Seeing Luni taking some members of the *urireng*, Maria's family among them, and the herd in another direction, Yveline resembled a warmonger about to be deprived of a foe. Her violent temper flared. She accused Luni of dividing the people and wronging his clan. Many years ago she had used the same tone to curse Lajide.

Luni paid her no heed. Then Yveline turned and pointed at Berna. 'If you go with them, do you think things will end well for you? As soon as Nihau does a Spirit Dance, you're dead!'

Berna had stopped crying earlier, but Yveline's terrible words unleashed her tears again. Nihau sighed and pulled Berna close. Even though the sun was shining bright on them, their faces seemed terribly pale.

Kunde had long since ceased speaking to Yveline, but at that instant he suddenly grabbed his hunting knife and waved it at her. 'Say one more word and I swear I'll cut off your tongue and feed it to the ravens!'

Yveline tilted her head to one side, gazed at Kunde, laughed darkly, and shut her mouth.

\* \* \*

The following spring Ivan returned. We hadn't seen him for several years, and he was much thinner and had aged considerably.

'*Aiyo!*' exclaimed Yveline. 'Can't get by on those soldier's rations, so you've come back to the mountains?'

Ivan told Kunde that he wasn't in the military any more. His personnel file – and thus responsibility for his livelihood – had been transferred to the local civilian authorities. Kunde asked if he'd been dishonourably discharged, but Ivan denied it.

'I just couldn't get used to the way everybody gathered round a table inside to eat, and at night they closed the door and windows so tight you couldn't even hear the wind blow,' he complained.

And what's more, the army kept trying to find him a wife, but those women might as well have been soaked in medicinal herbs. They weren't at all attractive to him. 'If I stayed there any longer, I'd have died before my time.'

He'd recently been transferred to a work unit in Mengkui. He even received a salary there, a sum that was many times greater than the monthly 'living allowance' – a modest cash payment – that was made to hunters still earning their living in the mountains.

Ivan told Valodya that he feared the mountain forests wouldn't be so peaceful in the future because many workers had arrived in Mengkui, and they were going to chop down trees and develop the Greater Khingan Mountains. The railway company had also arrived, and they would construct railways and roads in the mountains to ship felled timber to the outside world.

'Why do they chop down the trees?' asked Viktor.

'It's getting crowded outside the mountains, and people want houses to live in,' said Ivan. 'How can you build houses without wood?'

Everyone remained silent, for Ivan's arrival brought us no cheer. But Ivan didn't seem to sense our gloomy mood, and he rattled on about Wang Lu and Ludek, and also about Suzuki.

Ivan said that although Wang Lu and Ludek weren't executed, they were both sentenced to prison, one for ten years, and one for seven. When Ivan pronounced 'ten' and 'seven', he slurred his words a bit.

The story about Suzuki went like this. Word had it that he was captured while fleeing and was taken to the Soviet Union with many other Japanese prisoners of war. They worked on the construction of the Siberian Railway alongside German prisoners. Suzuki missed his hometown and his aged mother, and wanted to go back to Japan. To obtain permission to go home, one day he intentionally allowed a railway sleeper to sever his leg. Now lame, he couldn't work on the railway, so he was repatriated.

Kunde sighed at the end of the tale of Suzuki's misfortune. 'He'll be paying for the evil he did for the rest of his life!'

'I'd never have thought he'd become a "cripple" like me!' added Vladimir.

Ivan stayed just three days with us and then went to Luni's *urireng*.

I became a grandmother that year. Lyusya gave birth to a strong and healthy boy and asked me to name him. When I remembered that the flower and tree names Nihau gave her children were so fragile, I simply named him '*Youyin Biela*' – 'September' – since he was born in the ninth month of the year. I reckoned the Spirits could easily summon flowers and trees, but they couldn't reclaim the months. Each year, good or bad, there are twelve months, and none can be omitted.

What Ivan said turned out to be true. In 1957, forestry workers stationed themselves in the mountains. They were unfamiliar with the terrain and shouldering those building materials for their 'station' was hard work, so we not only acted as their guides, we also had to use our reindeer to transport their tents and other items. On three occasions Valodya led our *urireng* members to drive the reindeer hauling their goods. They were frequently away for two weeks at a stretch.

Thus commenced the din of logging. Once the snowy season arrived, you could hear axes and saws at work. One after another, those thick and sturdy pine trees fell, and one road after another was opened up to transport timber.

At the beginning horses were used to drag logs to the paved roads, but afterwards tractors roared in their place. They had more horsepower than horses themselves and could haul ten logs per trip. All the timber dragged from the deep forest was loaded onto long logging trucks and hauled to destinations beyond the mountains.

We and the reindeer craved quiet, so from then on as soon as the logging season began, we relocated more frequently. We sought secluded spots, but not every secluded spot could serve as a campsite. It depended if there was sufficient 'reindeer moss', and if the surrounding area was good for hunting. We cherished the springtime more than ever, for it marked the end of the tree-harvesting season when the forest regained its former tranquillity.

In 1959, the government built a few Russian-style wooden cabins for us in Uchiriovo. Some clansmen occasionally went there to live but never stayed long because they still preferred the mountain life. So those houses were generally vacant and only rarely did one spot smoke rising from their chimneys.

A primary school opened there and the children of Evenki hunters could study for free. Valodya suggested sending Tatiana to school.

Concerning education, Valodya and I were not of the same mind. He believed that children should go to a school to study, while it seemed to me that learning to recognise all sorts of plants and animals in the mountains, understanding how to get along with them harmoniously, and being able to understand the significance of changes in the wind, frost, snow and rain – all these were a kind of education.

I've never believed that you can obtain a bright and happy world via book learning. But for his part, Valodya said that only a person who possesses knowledge would have the vision to perceive the brightness present in our world.

But I felt that brightness was right there in the rock paintings next to the river, in the trees that mingled with one another, in the dewdrops on the flowers, in the stars at the tiptop of the *shirangju*, and in the reindeer's antlers. If that isn't brightness, what is?

Tatiana didn't go to school after all, but when he was free Valodya taught her and Maikan to read. Employing a branch as a writing utensil and the soil as paper, he traced *hanzi* on it and taught them how to pronounce them.

Tatiana loved to learn the characters, but Maikan was no good at them. She studied and studied, and then she'd doze off. Vladimir felt sorry for his Maikan and didn't insist she continue her studies.

'Valodya got his hands on some ants, and now he's stuffing them in Maikan's brain,' Vladimir said. 'I won't allow him to harm my darling daughter.'

Late in the autumn of 1959, Luni suddenly came looking for me and invited us to attend my Andaur's marriage ceremony.

One of the people allotted to Luni's group was a girl named Washia. A member of Valodya's clan, she was three years older than Andaur and taller than him too. She was a chatty girl, quick with a smile, and she loved to dress up. But Luni said no one had imagined Andaur and Washia as a couple because she was already engaged.

Early one summer morning three reindeer were missing from those that had just returned to the camp, so Luni mobilised the young members of the *urireng* to search for them. They left in the morning and returned in the afternoon, having located the reindeer but lost two people: now Andaur and Washia were missing.

Just when they had separated from the others, no one was sure. Luni said he knew that Andaur was a good child and wouldn't do anything improper, and Washia was already engaged to be married, so he reckoned that nothing would happen between them.

The pair came back in the evening. Andaur looked a bit listless, and he had a few small cuts on his face. But when asked, he just said he'd run into a patch of thorns.

As for Washia, she was very gay and resembled someone who had just drunk a bowl of deliciously cool spring water on a hot day. She told everyone that she and Andaur had taken the long way when the path forked, and that's why they had arrived later.

But a month or so later Washia began vomiting in the morning. People assumed she had something wrong with her digestion, and gathered wolf-tongue grass to make soup for her. By the autumn, however, her belly had grown big, and everyone recalled that day when Andaur and Washia came back alone.

Washia's father went looking for Andaur. 'Washia is already engaged,' he said. 'You've defiled my daughter! You might as well have pushed her off a cliff!' He pummelled Andaur and left his face black and blue.

Andaur didn't comprehend what he'd done wrong. He said he hadn't been keen to perform that stark-naked act, but Washia had said it was a thing of beauty. He even said that Washia had taken off her trousers and pulled him into her embrace.

'I didn't know what to do. Washia showed me,' Andaur said. 'She got so excited and happy that I thought she was going crazy. She shouted "Andaur! Andaur!" and grabbed at my face and scratched me until I bled!'

'Washia told me, if anyone asks about the cuts on your face, just say thorns pricked you.'

'But Washia told me a different story,' Luni said to me. 'She said she was forced. That Andaur raped her.'

'No matter what,' said Luni, 'Washia is pregnant with Andaur's child. Her earlier engagement is as good as broken, and Andaur must marry her.'

This was a union neither party desired. Andaur said he didn't want to marry a woman who fibbed, and Washia cried and said she didn't want to marry an idiot.

I went to Luni's and asked Andaur: 'Are you willing to live with Washia?'

'No. When she's excited she scratches you, and she even fibs.'

'But you got her pregnant, so you have to marry her!' Luni and I both told him.

Andaur covered his face with his hands and cried silently. Watching the tears flow out from between his fingers, I thought my heart was going to shatter. But after he cried he nodded at me, and agreed to swallow the bitter fruit he had sown.

When Nihau presided over the marriage, Andaur held his head down while Washia kicked her foot against the ground. Maria coughed and said to Washia: 'Watch that foot of yours or you'll lose your child.'

I didn't want Maria to let her mouth run because that would be even more awkward for Andaur, so I handed her a bowl of *baijiu*.

Maria really had grown old. She sipped at the bowl several times but only managed to drink half of it, and her hand quivered like a flame caught in an icy wind.

After Andaur's marriage ceremony, I returned to my *urireng*. But just one month later, after the first snow had covered the forest in a silver-white headscarf, Luni summoned me again. This time it was to take part in a funeral.

Maria was dead. As she lay dying, she held Zefirina's hand tightly for the longest time until she exhaled one last, long breath, and then slowly released her hand. Even when she died she had not set eyes on the grandson for whom she had yearned. She departed with her eyes wide open.

It was at that funeral that Luni told me that Nihau was pregnant again. When Luni pronounced those words, his lips quivered. For others, pregnancy was a joyful affair, but Luni and Nihau were shrouded in a deep sense of terror.

'In the future, treat your own children like someone else's, and treat other people's children like yours, and everything will be fine,' I advised Nihau.

Nihau got my meaning. 'But I can't stand by and watch my own children suffer and do nothing,' she said sadly.

I understood that what she referred to as 'my own children' actually meant 'other people's children'.

Maria ascended the Heavens. Meanwhile, Ivan descended the mountains to nurse the rheumatism he had contracted. His knees had become misshapen and he could hardly walk.

Two families in Valodya's clan who had been with Luni also left for Uchiriovo, leaving Luni's *urireng* rather cheerless.

'Maria is gone and her feud with Yveline has ended, so let's come back together,' I said to Luni. 'I'm speaking for the good of Andaur too. Washia seems flirtatious and overbearing, and this doesn't bode well for him. If Washia bullies Andaur, I can exercise my influence as her elder.'

Luni and Nihau also agreed to reunite the two *urireng* because ever since Berna had lost her partners in play, she had become increasingly withdrawn.

'Berna once caught a yellow butterfly,' recounted Nihau, 'and she said she was going to put it in her stomach and let it fly about and play with her. I thought it was just idle talk, but she really did so. Berna tossed the live butterfly in her mouth and closed it, squinted her eyes, and didn't speak for several hours. Luni and I were almost scared to death!'

When Luni led his *urireng* back to our camp, Yveline discovered that Maria and Ivan weren't there, and Washia and Nihau were both big-bellied.

'A pair departed and a pair set to arrive!' She snorted.

I explained that Ivan's departure was different than Maria's. Maria had ascended the Heavens to enjoy a happy life, while Ivan had left the mountains to recuperate.

Yveline was stunned for a moment, but she quickly regained her wits: 'Men who've lived off military rations are useless. They even get sick!'

But after Yveline bad-mouthed Ivan, her eyes suddenly blurred with tears. Her mouth spoke of Ivan, but her heart thought of Maria. Her tears proved that.

That evening, Kunde told me Yveline had not eaten.

The second day, she still didn't eat.

On the third day, she could no longer walk unaided. Leaning on a wooden stick, she proceeded with difficulty over to Hase's. 'Did you give Maria a wind-burial or a land-burial?'

Hase still despised Yveline. 'Maria can see the sun and the moon without lifting her head. Young squirrels with pine cones in their claws jump about her. You tell me: is she in the wind or in the ground?'

Yveline lowered her head. 'In the wind is best. Yes, in the wind.'

Yveline left Hase's and suddenly threw down her stick, folded one hand over the other, and bowed three times towards the sky. When she finished bowing, she picked up her staff and returned, trembling, to her *shirangju*.

Yveline resumed eating, but henceforth she couldn't manage without a walking stick.

Valodya and Hase came back from the supply cooperative in Uchiriovo where they traded for grain, and they told us that famine was ravaging the world outside. Grain supply was tight, so they only got four bags of flour and a bag of salt. For our entire *urireng*, such a small amount of grain was negligible. Since grain was insufficient, distilling liquor was also a problem, and the cost of *baijiu* rose. All the drinkers among us were listless.

But we had abundant stores of jerky and dried vegetables, and with an assured supply of ammunition, we could get our food by hunting. So no one panicked. We allotted the flour mainly to Luni and Andaur because their partners were pregnant.

After Washia and Andaur married, he stopped smiling. He didn't sleep with her and she found this intolerable. One time she came to complain. 'I have a bitter life,' she sobbed. 'Andaur doesn't even know how to sleep with a woman. He's truly the Number One Idiot under the sky!'

'You say Andaur doesn't know how to sleep with a woman.' I replied. 'Does that mean the thing swelling your belly was drummed up by the wind?'

Washia cried more fiercely. 'I have rotten luck. Andaur did that thing to me just once, and now I'm pregnant with his little monster.'

'You're pregnant, so for the safety of the child, you should refrain from sex. If the first child is aborted, you might turn out like Zefirina who has found it hard to get pregnant again.'

That set Washia jumping. 'I don't believe it!' she yelled. 'Three years ago my first foetus miscarried, but I got pregnant again this time, didn't I? Why do I have such rotten luck?'

When she finished her outburst, Washia realised she had misspoken. She covered her mouth but the horror and regret in her eyes betrayed her, and she said nothing more. I realised she had lost her innocence long before she met Andaur. Whom she had coupled with she didn't mention, and I didn't ask.

But after this, Washia was better behaved. In front of me, she stopped cursing Andaur for being an idiot, but she was still unhappy with her lot. When she saw women, her eyes were colourless like a dead fish's, but her eyelashes fluttered and eyebrows arched at the very sight of an adult male's silhouette. But men never paid her intimations any heed.

Once Valodya asked Andaur: 'Doesn't Washia please you?'

Andaur repeated his old reply. 'I despise her. When she's excited she scratches your face. Her hands are like an eagle's claws. She likes to fib, but nice girls don't tell lies.'

'And you don't care for the child she's carrying for you?' continued Valodya.

'The child hasn't come out yet. How do I know if it will be loveable?' Andaur's answer made me laugh.

In June of the following year, Washia gave birth to a boy in a meadow, and Valodya named him An'tsaur.

An'tsaur's arrival brought the shadow of a smile to Andaur's face. But Washia didn't care for An'tsaur. She didn't dare call Andaur an idiot again, but she married this appellation off to An'tsaur. 'My Little Idiot, drink your milk!' she said when she nursed him. And when she cleaned faeces from her baby's rump, she said angrily: 'How can this Little Idiot's shit stink so bad?'

After Washia gave birth to An'tsaur, she assumed that since Andaur was content with the child he'd naturally feel gratitude and tenderness towards her, and seek pleasure with her. But he still didn't sleep with her. 'You Little Idiot, you're ruining my life!' she moaned, venting her frustration on An'tsaur.

'Other people's children are their darlings. Why do you call your child an "idiot" from morning to night?' Vladimir reproached her. 'Even if he isn't an idiot, you'll end up talking him into one!'

'His *Ama* is one, so naturally he'll be an idiot too! Isn't that so? Except for useless men like you who don't know how marvellous a woman can be, what kind of man doesn't enjoy women? Only an idiot!'

Washia's words deeply stung Vladimir and the heart of every member of our *urireng*. From then on, no one was willing to converse with her. I hadn't imagined she could be so shameless, and I didn't want my Andaur to spend his life with her. It wasn't fair to him.

I discussed the matter with Valodya with an eye to dissolving their marriage. Valodya agreed. We brought Andaur over and told him our intention, but surprisingly he rejected it immediately.

'When Washia is excited she scratches you, and she likes to fib. If I let her go, she'll go and hurt another man! She's just a wolf. Since I know that she's a people-eater, if I let her go I'd be doing wrong! I'll keep her, watch over her, and not allow her to eat anyone else!'

As I recall, that's the longest string of words that Andaur ever uttered. And the most reasonable and the most resolute. In them, I saw the shadow of his father Lajide.

In August that year, as Nihau approached childbirth, ten reindeer went missing in one go: four fawns, two studs and four does. This was no trivial matter. The men split into three search groups. One group consisted of Valodya, Viktor and Andaur; one of Vladimir, Puffball and Dashi; and one of Luni, Kunde and Hase. After they left the campsite, we anxiously awaited their return.

The first evening, Vladimir's group returned empty-handed. The second evening, Valodya's group returned, faces full of disappointment. But on the third evening, Luni's group finally returned with our reindeer in tow.

The reindeer aside, Luni also brought back three unfamiliar Han men. Two were on foot behind Hase and Kunde, one tall and one short. The other lay feebly atop a reindeer.

'These three stole our reindeer,' said Luni. 'They planned to take them out of the mountains and slaughter them for the meat.'

When Luni caught up with them, they had already killed a fawn, so his group brought back just nine head.

As Luni recounted the tale, the tall man and the short one knelt before us and begged us to let them go and, above all, not to shoot them dead.

'The famine drove us to steal your reindeer,' they cried. 'We can't get enough to eat, and our parents and wives and children are all starving. We heard that you were herding reindeer in the mountains.'

Valodya asked them where they came from and what work they did. They just said they were from outside the mountains and didn't have jobs, but they wouldn't say anything more specific.

Then they pointed at the man stretched out on the reindeer. 'We beg you to save him. He's only sixteen and he hasn't even married!'

'A sixteen-year-old who steals things – what kind of future can he have?' mumbled Hase.

But he took the man stretched out on the reindeer and placed him on the ground. His eyes were closed, he had a round face, pale complexion, thick eyebrows and very thick lips, but like his face, those lips showed no sign of blood. He did indeed look like he was just fifteen or sixteen, his whiskers shallow, all fuzzy, like the green grass that grows on the sunny south-east slopes in the early spring, soft and tender.

His stomach bulged like a frog's. He was completely still and everyone took him for dead. Valodya crouched down and felt for his breath with his hand and discovered he was still exhaling. He told the kneeling pair to stand up.

'What illness does this boy have?' Valodya asked.

'We slaughtered a fawn, built a fire, and gathered around to roast the venison,' explained the tall one. 'But he was starving and while it was still half raw he ripped the meat apart and wolfed it down. When it was cooked through, he ate that too until his belly was all round.

'Then he said he was dying of thirst, so we gave him a flask of water. It's when he finished that off that he was in trouble.'

'It's not when he drank the water,' interrupted the short one. 'It's when he stood up, shot a stream of piss on a big tree and came stumbling back. He collapsed on to his bottom, sweat poured off his face, and then – *gudung!* – he toppled over.'

'How dare he pee on a big tree!' said Valodya. 'He must have offended the Mountain Spirit!'

'The Mountain Spirit is exacting its retribution,' said Kunde. 'There's no way he'll come out of this alive!'

The tall fellow and the short one knelt down together and kow-towed to us. 'We heard that you have many Immortals, so once we entered the mountains we were extra careful. We didn't dare sit on tree stumps or rocks, or even bend a blade of grass.

'But who'd have guessed that taking a pee would end up water-ing your Immortals? We didn't do it intentionally! It is said that you have a Sorceress who can commune with the Spirits. Please ask Them to forgive the boy.

'In the future even if we are dying of starvation, we won't dare steal! If he dies, how can we face his family on our return? We beg you, save him!'

Lyusya held September, Washia held An'tsaur, Tatiana held Berna's hand in one hand and Maikan's in the other, and they all surrounded the youth who lay on the ground. Nihau's body was bloated, and the *yataju* for childbirth had already been constructed.

As the two strangers implored, Nihau's body began to tremble and so did Luni. '*Tian ah!* Why did I bring them back with me?' he groaned, pulling Berna against his chest.

I didn't want to see Nihau and Luni lose their own beloved child again just to save the life of another. 'We have no Sorceress here!' I exclaimed. 'It doesn't look to me like this boy angered the

Immortals, he just ate too much. Take a look at his stomach. He must have swallowed half a fawn! Isn't that like asking to die? You all come up with a way to beat that venison out of his belly, and he'll be all right!'

'Things that have gone into the stomach are like things that have fallen into a deep well,' said the tall one. 'How can you drag them out?'

'Do you have any herbs that can make him throw up what he ate?' asked the short one.

We stood the youth up straight and stuck our fingers down his gullet, hoping to stimulate his throat and make him vomit, but he didn't react at all. Then we poured laxative down his throat in the hopes of getting him to discharge what he'd eaten, but that method didn't work either.

The sun sank behind the mountains and a few bands of reddish orange emerged on the horizon. Those were the sun's final breaths. Now the sky was the colour of dusk, and this colour caused spasms of pain in my heart, because it was at this time of the day that our Shamans normally commenced their Spirit Dance.

Valodya tested the man's breath again, and his hand quivered for a second. It looked like the youth had stopped breathing, so we might as well get rid of him. I felt an airy sense of relief; I reckoned his soul had already departed so we needn't try to save him.

But then Nihau bent down with difficulty and placed her hand on the youth's forehead. She stood up. 'Carry him into our *shirangju*, and slaughter a fawn,' she told Luni.

'Nihau, think of others' children first!' I shouted. I thought only she would understand the significance of 'others' children'.

Nihau's eyes moistened. 'My own child can be saved, how can I . . . ?'

Nihau didn't finish her thought, but everyone understood what she left unsaid.

Luni stood motionless, but he held Berna tightly. Valodya instructed Puffball to slaughter a fawn and dedicate it to the *Malu*. He and Hase carried the boy into Luni's *shirangju*.

This time Nihau didn't allow anyone to enter the *shirangju*. Just how difficult it was for her to don the heavy Spirit Robe, Spirit Skirt and Spirit Headdress, none of us knew. When the drumbeats began to sound, the true night approached. The reddish-orange band of colour that had briefly appeared at the edges of the sky was gone, swallowed up by the night.

We stood trembling with fear in the campsite, encircling Luni and Berna like water surrounding a little island.

'Everything will be all right,' said Luni to Berna. 'You don't need to be afraid.' We too comforted her with these words.

But not Washia. 'I've heard that when your *Eni* performs the Spirit Dance, a child must die. You're afraid to die, so why don't you flee? How stupid!'

Berna was already shivering and this just made her shake more. I took An'tsaur from Washia's arms, and told her: 'Please leave here at once!'

'Did I say something wrong?'

'Leave! Now!' I shouted.

Washia muttered something and turned and left, followed by Andaur. A few moments later, the *chala-chala* of the metallic totems on the Spirit Robe striking one another and even the thumping of the Spirit Drum were partially drowned out by the din of Washia's wailing and cursing. Andaur had tied Washia to a tree and was whipping her with a birch branch.

'She deserves it!' said Washia's parents, and no one went to dissuade Andaur.

After Washia made a ruckus for half an hour, the sounds of her weeping and swearing grew faint. They were a dark cloud, and once they dissipated, the drumbeats boomed clear like the limpid moon.

From their urgency, you could imagine how excitedly and powerfully Nihau was dancing. Her body was so petite and contained an infant awaiting birth. How could she bear it?

To our ears, the drum howled like winter's icy northern wind and it made you shiver.

The moon was already in the middle of the sky, and it was a half moon. In spite of its incompleteness, it looked bright and pure. The drumming had ceased, and it seemed the dance had too. Luni still held Berna close, and we all breathed a long sigh of relief.

'Do you hear that? The drumbeats have ended, and you're just fine,' I said to Berna.

Berna burst out noisily in tears as if she had been deeply humiliated. We comforted her and waited for Nihau to appear.

But even when Berna's tears dried, Nihau still had not appeared. Luni and I grew anxious and just as we were about to enter to see how Nihau was doing, a Spirit Song emerged from the *shirangju*. Her singing made me think of light – the moon's light on a frozen river.

> *O child, come back!*
> *Our world's brightness unseen*
> *You descend into darkness.*
> Eni *made you leather gloves*
> *And* Ama *a pair of snowshoes.*

*O child, come back!*
*The bonfire is lit*
*And the hanging pot is in its place.*
*Unless you return*
*Your parents shall crowd the hearth*
*Yet still feel cold.*
*Unless you return*
*They shall watch over a pot full of meat*
*Yet still feel hungry.*

*O child, come back!*
*Your feet bound in snowshoes*
*Follow the herd so near*
*For without you*
*Wolves will mangle*
*The lovely horns of the reindeer.*

Luni and I both understood what we were hearing. Nihau's Spirit Song was for the infant who was about to be born. We refused to believe it would die before birth.

Luni and I ran into the *shirangju*. Filled with the stench of blood and rotten flesh, the air stank. The fire in the hearth was almost out. Luni lit the bear-oil lamp, and we saw the boy curled up in the corner, sobbing quietly amidst the clumps of vomit that were scattered around him.

Nihau was seated next to the fireplace, head down, holding the new-born in her bosom. She had removed her headdress, and her sweat-drenched hair swung like a weeping willow above the dead infant's hair. Her Spirit Robe and Spirit Skirt were still on her.

Perhaps she hadn't the strength to remove them. Her Spirit Skirt was stained with fresh blood, and the metallic totems on her Spirit Robe were still twinkling.

The infant was a boy. Before he had seen a ray of light in our world, he had sunk into the darkness. He didn't even have a chance to be named, the only one of Nihau's children to remain nameless.

Once again Valodya and I picked up a white cloth bag and went to bury Luni's and Nihau's flesh and blood. But this time we didn't discard him haphazardly. We dug a hole with our hands and buried him in the soil baked hot by the blazing August sun. For us, he was a seed that would germinate and grow into a sky-bound tree.

In my eyes, among the lush greenery on the sunlit southeast slopes there grows a passionate plant, and that is sunlight. As my fingers and Valodya's dug the grave, they were encrusted with warm soil.

At one point, I unearthed a pink earthworm and unwittingly severed it.

The two parts continued to squiggle to their heart's content, boring into the dirt and then resurfacing. Its ability to survive is so great that a single earthworm's body houses several lives, and this touched me deeply. I couldn't help wondering: what if human beings possessed this ability?

Luni set fire to the *yataju* built by Nihau, the *yataju* that was never occupied by a mother-to-be, the *yataju* in which no child was born. The birthing hut resembled thick clouds that we had believed would bring rain and dew and coolness to the parched couple. Who could have foreseen those clouds would appear and then vanish in vain?

In the end we let the three Han go free. Valodya said that thievery engendered by famine is pardonable.

When they left the camp, a despondent Luni gave them some jerky to eat on their way. They knelt on the ground and kowtowed to us over and over, and swore with tears in their eyes that one day they would repay us for saving the boy's life.

Nihau rested in her *shirangju* for a week before she found the strength to step out. She had grown even thinner, and her cheeks were sunken, lips pale, and her grey hairs more numerous.

It seemed she feared the sunlight, and she shivered outside. Nihau resembled a wealthy person who once possessed a big granary, but famine had emptied it and shrivelled her belly.

We smelled an odd odour about her – the scent of musk.

The River Deer is the ugliest creature in the forest. It has coarse, brownish-yellow fur, but its chest sports a permanent band of white fur – a white towel ready to wipe away sweat, just in case it should be needed. With a small, pointed head that's all wrinkled, it's incredibly repugnant. But a buck is a rare catch, for located between his belly button and genitals lies a sac containing a glandular secretion that, once removed and dried, emits a special aroma – musk – so we call the animal 'Musk Deer'.

Musk is a valuable medicinal material, and whenever we kill a Musk Deer, it's a festive event for our *urireng*. Musk can be used to remedy food poisoning, and serves to restore consciousness and relieve nasal congestion.

These usages aside, it also functions as a contraceptive. Just a whiff of it inhibits fertility, so if a woman constantly keeps musk in her pocket, she'll never get pregnant.

Everyone understood why Nihau put musk in her clothing. Nihau's pregnancies were always associated with disaster. She was a bird that painstakingly constructed her nest, but just when it was complete an unforeseen storm knocked it down.

The scent of musk often causes women to shed tears, as if its odour burns our eyes. Luni didn't reproach Nihau for her behaviour, but deep in his heart he despaired. During that summer and autumn when Nihau carried musk on her, Luni frequently broke down crying in public. As he scrambled to wipe away the tears, he always said there was a smell that irritated his eyes.

I knew how badly Luni longed for a son. Grigori and Tibgur were two shooting stars that had crossed the sky in Luni's heart, and then disappeared without a trace.

Early that winter, the smell of musk on Nihau's body vanished abruptly. I reckon it was Luni's tears that chased it away. That fragrance was a thick mist, and Luni's tears were rays of sunlight that broke through to shine on Nihau.

After 1962, the famine outside the mountains eased but grain supply was still tight. Ivan came back in the autumn but moved with difficulty. He hired two horses and brought us *baijiu* and potatoes, and cheese he got from Mongols. Those huge hands of his were deformed, their joints protruding and twisted. Once able to crumble a rock, now they could barely crush a raven's eggshell.

Ivan told us he had heard that the government was cooking up a major plan: it was going to build another village and make the hunting peoples in the mountains relocate there.

'Even those few houses in Uchiriovo were never fully occupied. If they go and build another site, I bet it'll stay vacant too!' said Hase.

'If we leave the mountains, how will the reindeer survive?' wondered Dashi.

Vladimir echoed their sentiments. 'That's right. I still think it's best here in the mountains! There's a famine going on down there, and there are robbers and even thugs. Living outside the mountains – wouldn't that be like living in a den of thieves?'

In reality, Vladimir was unwilling to leave the mountains because of Maikan. He never took Maikan out of our *urireng* because he feared her real parents would reclaim her.

Maikan was truly lovely. Her beauty made flowers pale and out-shone the sun and moon. Vladimir's ears stood erect like a hound's whenever he heard horse hooves in the distance, and he became especially alert, certain someone had come to fetch Maikan.

The day Ivan returned everyone drank plenty of *baijiu*, and that evening I desperately desired to be with Valodya. Tatiana was already a young lady, and I feared that the wind-sounds we made at night would startle her, even though it's true she grew up with them.

But that evening was different because the drink was a flame that ignited our passion, and the collision of our passionate wind-sounds must have been much more intense than usual.

I nestled against Valodya's chest and we tried using conversation to restrain our passion. 'Are you willing to go and live outside the mountains?'

'You'd best ask the reindeer: are you willing to leave the mountains?' replied Valodya.

'They certainly won't agree.'

'Then we should obey our reindeer,' he urged.

But he sighed and went on. 'If the trees in the mountains continue to be chopped down like this, sooner or later – even if we aren't willing – we'll have to leave.'

'There are plenty of trees in the mountains, more than can ever be chopped down!' I said.

Valodya sighed again. 'The day will come when we must depart.'

'If I stay here in the mountains and the reindeer leave, what will you do?'

'I'll stay behind with you, naturally. The reindeer belong to everyone, but you're mine alone!' he said tenderly.

His words stimulated my desire, and we embraced more tightly, kissing until our passion finally burst like a thunderbolt behind thick clouds. Valodya lay over my body and melted me like intoxicating spring sunlight.

I am grateful for the wind-sounds provided by Mother Nature that night, because when we began to voyage on our hidden river of life, enjoying our own unique happiness, a fierce wind began to blow outside our *shirangju*.

Those wind-sounds were so sonorous that they seemed expressly intended to camouflage and accompany our passion. When my joy was complete and I lay cotton-like in his embrace, I felt Valodya was my mountain, ascending straight as a tower; and I was as ethereal as a cloud, a cloud floating beneath his body for eternity.

* * *

We passed two years in relative peace. In the summer of 1964, Nihau gave birth to a son, and Luni named him Maksym. His face was large and square with a wide forehead and mouth, big hands and feet, and when he was born his wail – a tiger's roar – shook the entire camp. Yveline was already hard of hearing, but even she heard it.

'The child's cry was so loud that he must have deep roots here on earth. No storm can blow him away!' Her words moved Luni to tears.

Maria's death made Yveline revert to her former self. But if she regained her former kind-heartedness, her body was unable to return to the past. When we relocated she had to ride a reindeer, and she couldn't take a step in the camp without her walking stick.

Kunde said Yveline rarely slept lying down. She always sat next to the hearth and napped, day and night, as if she were the Guardian Spirit of Fire.

But the happiness brought by Maksym's arrival hadn't accompanied us three months when the dark clouds of death once again massed above our *urireng*.

September is rutting season for the forest's wild deer. Bucks are short-tempered during this period and prefer to be on their own. They often stand alone on a hill in the early morning or evening, and make their long *yoo yoo* mating calls.

Among the deer that heed this call, some are does attracted by a buck's virility, while others are envious bucks. The former come for the joys of mating, the latter to do battle.

Our ancestors exploited the male deer's habitual long cry to invent a sort of deer whistle. They made it by hollowing out the middle of a naturally curved section of a larch tree root, and glued it with fish skin. The top is broader than the tail, but you can blow on either end. It sounds remarkably like a real deer call. We dub it '*uléwung*', but it is popularly known as a deer-call pipe.

Each *urireng* possesses several *uléwung*, most passed down from our ancestors. In the autumn, we use them to lure deer. When a boy turns eight or nine, an adult teaches him how to blow on the pipe. The women who stay behind in the camp might hear a *jrr-lu jrr-lu* sound, and we honestly can't distinguish a genuine wild deer call from one originating in a deer-call pipe.

When Maksym was more than two months old we moved again to the Jiin River basin, because that year wild deer were uncharacteristically active there. We didn't set up at the old campsite, and stayed far away from Listvyanka Mountain.

When the men went hunting, they usually divided into two or three small groups of three or four members each. By that time Ivan, like Yveline, required a walking stick. Since Maria's death, Hase increasingly showed his age and he was blurry-eyed, so he and Ivan stayed in the camp with us women and handled less demanding chores.

Those who went on the hunt were younger and more robust. Valodya liked to partner with Viktor, Kunde and Puffball, while Luni preferred to go with Vladimir, Dashi and Andaur.

The master deer whistlers were Puffball and Andaur. After Puffball castrated himself, during the dead of winter he liked to blow occasionally on the deer-call pipe, as if summoning his now distant virility. His call was terribly forlorn and touching. As for Andaur, his deer whistle had a gentle air to it. Who'd have imagined that these two mutually attractive sounds, instead of fusing melodiously, would end with the annihilation of the gentle by the forlorn?

During the autumn the falling leaves are dyed yellow or red by a succession of frosts. Frost can be light or heavy, so the dyed hues are unequally dark or light. Pine needles turn yellow, while the leaves of birch, poplar and oak turn yellow or red. Once their colour changes, the leaves become fragile and drop in the autumn breeze. Some fall in gorges, some onto the forest floor, and some into flowing waters. Those that fall in gorges will transform into soil, those that fall onto the forest floor will become umbrellas for the ants, and those that fall into flowing waters become fish that voyage downstream.

At dusk that day I was casting fish nets on the Jiin with Lyusya, she in the water and I on the bank. We were having rotten luck: three times we had hauled in the nets without a fish. September was playing with An'tsaur on the bank. They built one sand castle after another, and stuck straws in them.

The sun descended into the mountains. 'We've had bad luck today. The fish are all lingering at the bottom, so let's go back,' I said.

Lyusya walked out of the water and up onto the bank. When she'd entered the river she was wearing waterproof, genuine fish-skin trousers, and now they radiated a bright, moist yellow light thanks to the water and the setting sun. It looked as if she were coming ashore astride a pair of beautiful, plump goldfish.

We chatted as we brought in the nets. 'September is already eight years old, why not have another?' I said. 'I'd like a granddaughter.'

Washia and Lyusya were both my daughters-in-law, but I didn't speak like this to Washia. That Andaur didn't sleep with her was common knowledge.

Lyusya blushed. 'We've been trying, but no luck. It's strange. Perhaps September isn't fated to have a brother or sister.'

'If I'd known that earlier, I would have done like the Han and named him "Brother-bringer" or "Sister-bringer" instead of "September",' I said.

'Well, I see that he loves to play with sand, so naming him "Sand-bringer" wouldn't be unfair to him,' replied Lyusya. This thought tickled me.

It was Zefirina who brought the bad tidings. We hadn't finished laughing when we saw her running towards us crying. She smelled heavily of salt since she had been busy drying jerky for several days.

Zefirina said just one thing: 'Andaur has gone to drink water in the Heavens!' Then she collapsed on the riverside and began to wail.

In the small hours before the morning stars had retired, the men had broken into two groups, and carrying their pipes and shouldering their rifles, they went to hunt wild deer. We weren't up yet when they left.

Valodya led Viktor and Puffball towards the south-east, and Luni led Andaur, Dashi and Vladimir towards the south-west. Under normal circumstances, they wouldn't have encountered one another, but this was an odd coincidence.

The two groups passed the whole day in the mountains but didn't shoot a single deer. On the way home they both altered their original routes in the hopes of encountering a wild deer. As Valodya's group came to the foot of Listvyanka Mountain, they heard a deer call come from above, and thinking there was a buck on the crest, they halted.

Puffball blew on his *uléwung* and very quickly a wild deer's long reply travelled down from the mountaintop.

Valodya's team blew their pipe as they walked up towards the summit, and the source of the deer call they had heard at first came closer and closer. By this time Viktor had his rifle in his hands, ready to shoot the buck that might appear at any instant.

Valodya said he'd never heard such melodious deer calls, with each animal's call rising and falling like music, passionate and pure. He didn't want to make such a lovely sound disappear for ever; actually, he didn't even want Viktor to fire his weapon.

But just thirty to forty metres from their destination, the deer call opposite Valodya's team became even more heated. A *cha-cha* rustling sound emerged from a thicket, tree leaves stirred chaotically and a muddy yellow shadow flashed before their eyes. Viktor fired twice without hesitation.

But after the gun's report, a cry rang out: '*Tian ah! Tian ah!*' It was Vladimir.

'Oh no!' groaned Viktor, and he was the first to run across towards the voice.

He couldn't believe his eyes. He had shot his own younger brother, Andaur!

It transpired that when Luni's group passed by Listvyanka Mountain on the way back to the camp, Luni began thinking of his dead son Tibgur who was buried there. He wanted to go up and take a look, and Vladimir, Dashi and Andaur climbed with him to the summit.

The sun leaned to the west and Luni was weighed down with grief. He sighed. 'I wonder if there are any deer in the sun?' he said to Vladimir.

'I'll make a deer call,' replied Andaur, 'and then you'll know.' Whereupon he faced the setting sun and sounded his *uléwung*. He blew and blew, and lo and behold, there was a response from down the mountain.

Luni was very pleased. 'The sun is truly a Spirit. It knows that we desire a wild deer, and now it has dispatched one to us.'

Andaur and his group blew their deer-call pipe as they descended the mountain, while Valodya and his group blew theirs as they ascended. In fact, both were emitted by deer-call pipes, it's just that the mating calls whistled by Puffball and Andaur were too close to the real thing, so each team believed a deer awaited them.

The inevitable tragedy occurred at that instant. If only Andaur hadn't bent over and imitated a wild deer as he blew his deer whistle, and if he didn't happen to camouflage himself in buckskin that day, then sharp-eyed Viktor would have sensed something wasn't quite right, and wouldn't have fired so hastily.

But Viktor's marksmanship was spot on. One of the bullets struck Andaur's skull, the other went through his chin and hit his chest. Even before Viktor arrived Andaur ceased breathing.

My poor Andaur. At his last moment he must have figured the hunter was concealed in the setting sun from where the bullet came from. Perhaps being shot by a hunter in the setting sun was something worthy of pride, so Andaur's countenance was serene when he departed, a smile hanging from the corners of his lips.

We performed a wind-burial for Andaur on Listvyanka Mountain. The Greater Khingan Range comprises several mountains, but the only one imprinted on my heart is this one, because it shelters two members of my family. From then on, we never approached this mountain and no longer blew on our *uléwung*.

After we buried Andaur, we embarked on a major relocation that took three days. We hoped never to lay eyes on the Jiin again. It was a poisonous snake and we wanted to leave it far, far behind.

Snowflakes came in the midst of our move, for the winter arrives when it pleases. Yesterday's red and yellow forest was transformed instantly into silver. Shrouded in a vast expanse of snowflakes, we and the reindeer were their slaves. Their icy bodies lashed our faces incessantly.

The move was very depressing. Those mounted on reindeer were listless and those who were on foot hung their heads in dejection. Perhaps seeking to dilute this rueful ambience, Vladimir pulled out his *mukulén* and began to play. The *mukulén* possesses a sensitivity of sorts, and whatever mood the player is in, it also infects the instrument. Though its sound was moving, its timbre was bleak. The *mukulén* didn't blow away the dark clouds on our faces, but it did blow down our tears.

Only Washia was untouched by grief. Zefirina told me when she broke the news of Andaur's death, Washia was eating pine nuts. She spat out a cracked purple shell with a *pei!*, raised her eyebrows and said: 'Am I really that lucky?'

Washia's parents urged her to go to Listvyanka Mountain to take one last look at Andaur. 'I saw my fill of that idiot long ago!' she quipped.

And she really didn't bid farewell to Andaur. The day of his burial, back at the campsite she chewed jerky at her leisure while An'tsaur played in front of her. 'The Big Idiot is no more. When will the Little Idiot leave? Once you're both gone, I'll be free!'

She even told Zefirina that in the future she'd worship the deer-call pipe as a Spirit because it had brought light into her life.

I longed for Washia to leave us. I reckoned she'd remarry quickly: she certainly wouldn't mourn for Andaur for the customary three years. 'You can go your way whenever you like. Don't worry that An'tsaur will be a burden to you. You don't care for him, so leave him to me.'

'No need to remind me. I'll go when the time is right. After all, getting married to two men isn't a shameful thing. Didn't *Hadam'eni* do so?' said Washia sarcastically.

We address our mother-in-law as '*Hadam'eni*'. After Lyusya married Viktor, she always called me that, but not Washia. This was the only time she ever addressed me like this. Not out of respect, but to insult me.

'Andaur has departed. You're free, and I am not your *Hadam'eni* any more.'

After we pitched camp at the new site, the squirrel-hunting season arrived. All the men and women busied themselves except Viktor and Washia. After he shot Andaur, it was as if he'd been struck by lightning. Viktor looked vacant and remained silent all day, speaking neither to us nor to Lyusya. If he wasn't drinking then he was sleeping, and his eyes were red and puffy. He especially couldn't bear the sight of An'tsaur, Andaur's son. As soon as he saw the boy, tears would roll down his face like someone encountering a strong wind.

I assumed that Viktor would gradually recover from his low spirits since no wound remains unhealed, even though that old wound may still ache on rainy days. We didn't dissuade him when he drowned himself in drink.

Viktor gave the rifle that killed Andaur to Valodya, and said that even if he starved to death, he'd never hunt again. He didn't touch meat again either, and when he drank *baijiu* it was dried fish and prunes that he munched on. When we went squirrel hunting, he remained in the camp with the young and the elderly.

As for Washia, even though Andaur held no place whatsoever in her heart, when she sought an excuse to avoid the hunt she said that since Andaur had just died she was very sad and in no mood to kill squirrels.

One evening when Lyusya and I brought a few squirrels back, Viktor came to my *shirangju*. '*Eni*, it's probably better for Andaur that he died, for if he'd lived he would have suffered a lot.'

'It's better if you can see things like that,' I said.

Then Viktor told me haltingly that recently when he was drinking alone in his *shirangju*, Washia came looking for him. Seeing he was drunk, she snuggled up against him, kissed his neck and said she wanted to sleep with him.

When Viktor pushed her away, she said: 'Once you've slept with me and know the wonderful taste of a real woman, you'll forget that idiot!'

Furious, Viktor grabbed Washia by the hair. 'If you dare call Andaur an idiot again, I'll cut out your tongue!' Washia cursed him and his brother, and ran off crying.

I feared Washia would continue to harass Viktor, so after that incident I arranged for Lyusya to remain in the camp too. But my worries were unnecessary. A dozen or so days later, a horse trader came to our camp with four horses in the hopes of bartering them for two reindeer. We didn't make this trade because we didn't need horses; horses would conjure up painful memories. What's worse, he wanted the reindeer for their flesh. He had heard that reindeer meat was very tasty. How could we put our beloved reindeer in the hands of such a man?

The horse trader stayed one night in our camp, and early on the second day he gathered his horses and left. But he didn't leave alone – he left with Washia in tow.

From then on, An'tsaur lived in our *shirangju*.

* * *

In 1965, four men came to our camp: an Evenki hunter serving as a guide, a doctor and two men who had the air of cadres. One reason they came was to conduct a survey of the state of our health, and the other was to encourage us to resettle. They said the living environment in the mountains was poor and we had little access to medical treatment.

So after soliciting suggestions from the Evenki on how to proceed, the government established Jiliu Township at the meeting point of the Bistaré and the lower reaches of the Uldihitt Rivers, and began construction of a permanent settlement there.

We were all quite familiar with the location of Jiliu Township. The woods in that region were lush and the scenery was lovely, so it was well suited to human habitation.

But there was a problem: what about the reindeer? If the reindeer of all the *urireng* went there, they couldn't forage moss in the Bistaré River basin for ever. In the end, wherever they went, we had to follow them.

Valodya said residing there over the long term just wasn't feasible.

'What's the difference between these "four Dissimilars" you raise, and cows, horses, pigs and sheep?' asked the cadres. 'Animals aren't as picky as human beings. Your reindeer can eat tender branches in the summer, and hay in the winter. They won't starve.'

These words left us all exasperated.

'Do you take reindeer for cattle or horses?' asked Luni. 'Reindeer won't eat hay. They can forage hundreds of different foods in the mountains. If you make them eat just grass and branches, their souls will suffer and die!'

'How dare you compare reindeer with pigs!' said Hase. 'What

are pigs? It's not as if I haven't seen any in Uchiriovo. They're filthy things that even eat shit! In the summer, our reindeer walk among dewdrops. When they eat flowers, butterflies accompany them. When they drink they can see fish in the water. And in the winter, when they scrape away layers of snow to eat moss, they can even find red love-peas hidden in the snow beneath, and hear little birds chirping. How can pigs compare with them?'

The two cadres could see that everyone was angry. 'Reindeer are fine, reindeer are Spirit Deer!' they said hastily. Right from the start, many people had concerns about living in a fixed location because of their reindeer.

The doctor with the stethoscope around his neck also met with problems when he began conducting physical examinations.

When he had the men unbutton their upper garments and expose their chests, things went fairly smoothly, but when he did the same to the women, everyone except Yveline resisted.

'Except for Dashi, no one can ever expect to see my chest while I'm alive,' said Zefirina.

'If I let another man look at my chest, I wouldn't be able to look Viktor in the eye,' said Lyusya.

As for me, I didn't believe that ice-cold, round metal thing could diagnose my illnesses. In my eyes, the wind and the flowing waters and the moonlight can hear what ails me.

Sickness is a secret flower hidden in one's chest. All my life I've never been to a clinic to see a doctor. When I'm depressed, I stand in the wind for a while, and it blows away the gloomy clouds in my heart. When I am vexed, I go to the riverside to listen to the waters flow, and they soon bring serenity to my heart. I've lived to a ripe old age and that proves I didn't choose the wrong doctors. My doctors are the cool wind, flowing waters, sun, moon and stars.

After the doctor listened to Yveline's heart and lungs, she asked him hoarsely: 'How long do I have?'

'Your heartbeat sounds weak and you have murmurs in your lungs. When you were young did you like to eat raw meat?'

Yveline opened her mouth with difficulty, and bared her teeth. 'The Spirits gave me good teeth. Wouldn't it be a pity not to use them to chew raw flesh?'

The doctor said she might have tuberculosis and left her a packet of pills. Yveline took the pills, and leaning on her walking stick, she tottered over to Nihau's. 'In the future you won't have to perform the Spirit Dance to exorcise illness any more. Look, here's something to cure disease!'

Yveline revealed the packet of pills in her palm. 'From now on, your children are safe!' Her words brought tears to Nihau's eyes.

But Yveline didn't feel compassion for everyone, and she still treated Kunde unfeelingly.

When the season of fluttering, falling leaves arrived, the majority of roaming Evenki hunters in several clans drove their reindeer down to the Jiliu Township settlement. After Uchiriovo, this was our second historic, large-scale relocation to a permanent settlement. The government not only built houses for us there, it also built a school, health clinic, grain store, shops and a purchasing station for the goods we obtained through hunting.

From then on we didn't have to go to the supply cooperative in Uchiriovo to trade.

I didn't move to Jiliu Township and Vladimir didn't either. He told me that taking Maikan down from the mountain would be like placing a spotted deer in amongst a pack of wolves. The prettier Maikan grew, the more anxious he became.

Lyusya was caught in a dilemma. On the one hand, Andaur's death stiffened her husband Viktor's resolve to relocate to the settlement. But on the other, her father Puffball was accustomed to the good old days and roaming in the mountains with the reindeer was the only thing that felt right for him. In the end, Lyusya chose Viktor. Viktor was drunk so frequently that he needed looking after.

Luni's family didn't go either, and Nihau predicted that those who went to Jiliu Township would eventually come back one by one. For the aged like Ivan, Yveline, Kunde and Hase, their health grew worse with each passing day, so moving to the settlement was inevitable. Still hopeful that Zefirina might become pregnant, Dashi placed his trust in the doctors at the clinic, so he felt compelled to relocate too.

My daughter Tatiana was nineteen that year, a young lady keen on pursuing a modern lifestyle. 'The only way to know if a new way of living is good or not is to experience it,' she said to us. Valodya also went to Jiliu Township on account of Tatiana and his clansmen, but I knew he'd return.

A few days before they left, we allocated the reindeer. By that time we had more than one hundred head. We split them into bucks, does and fawns, and we let those who were leaving take a few of each down the mountains. It's not that we were mean — we just feared the reindeer couldn't adapt to the new environment.

I had my grandson An'tsaur remain at my side because I knew that in a crowded place with a large population, a simpleminded child would be subjected to other children's ridicule and pranks. I didn't want him to be humiliated like that. In the mountains, his simplicity was in harmony with the surroundings where mountains and water are simple by nature. A mountain remains seated in the same place, and water always flows downstream.

During the days when Valodya and Tatiana weren't around, An'tsaur was my lamp. He was very tranquil. He did whatever you told him to do without a fuss. From his earliest days he adored reindeer. If he heard cries of joy and laughter in the camp, he didn't react in the slightest. But if he heard the sound of reindeer bells coming, he ran out excitedly from the *shirangju* to greet them. He put salt in his palm, knelt down and fed the reindeer like a devout believer kowtowing before the Spirit he venerates.

He liked to follow me as I did my chores. His tongue was slow but his hands nimble, and he mastered his chores very quickly. At six he could milk reindeer, and at eight or nine he could set a *charka* to catch squirrels. He was so content when doing his daily tasks – I've never seen a child like him.

Valodya and the others left in the autumn but when winter arrived I had an inkling he'd return soon. So when we moved camp, I chopped the tree markers myself. On some of the markers I attached a piece of birch bark and drew a sun and crescent moon on it. One end of the crescent hooked towards the sun, as if hailing it. I believed that if Valodya saw those pieces of birch bark, he'd understand how I longed for his return.

And so Valodya came back with the fourth snowfall. He had cut his long hair and was considerably leaner, but his complexion was ruddy and he looked much younger.

I asked him, 'Why did you cut your long hair?'

'My clansmen have basically all moved to Jiliu Township. There's a Township Head there, so the position of Clan Chieftain should be abolished.'

I laughed. 'Who abolished you?'

He lowered his head. 'Time.'

He said many of his clansmen cried when he cut his hair. Each of them picked up a few strands to store them away, and said he would always be their Chieftain.

I feared he was hurt so I teased him. 'Did any women pick up your hair?'

'Of course.'

'Now, that's not right. I'll have nightmares.'

'Other women collect my hair, but the strands are dead,' said Valodya. 'The living things are growing all around you.'

His words were filled with such tenderness that we were especially intimate that night. When Valodya and I saw off that surge of tender wind-sounds, we discovered An'tsaur seated erect by the hearth, his head reflecting the red flames.

'Why aren't you sleeping?'

'The sound of a big wind woke me up,' he said. 'Is *Até* a Wind Spirit?'

The day Valodya returned, Luni, Vladimir and Puffball came over to greet him but left soon after. They probably wanted us to enjoy the reunion by ourselves. But the next day they came quite early to ask Valodya what Jiliu Township was like, and enquire about those who settled there and how the reindeer were faring.

Valodya said there was a Party Secretary for the township, a Han surnamed Liu, a friendly fellow in his forties with a fat wife and two very skinny children. The Township Head was Qigede, a former Headman of another Evenki clan in the mountains where we lived. Of the other two Deputy Township Heads, one was Han and one was Evenki.

Valodya said the day after they arrived at the settlement, the township leaders held a meeting for everyone. 'Now that you've come to live in the settlement,' said Party Secretary Liu, 'unity is the number-one priority. No one should cause conflicts or disagreements between clans. We're all living in one big family now.'

When Party Secretary Liu finished, Viktor, who was stinking drunk, asked: 'If we're all one big family, can we swap wives?'

His question almost spoiled the meeting because everyone was so busy laughing that no one listened any more to the Party Secretary or the Township Head. Secretary Liu also said that everyone should keep an eye on their rifles and drink moderately. And even if drunk, they shouldn't fight. They were to be 'New-style Socialist Hunters' behaving in a polite and civilised manner.

Valodya said there were two families to a building in Jiliu, an improvement over the first settlement at Uchiriovo. Poplars, common in that region, were planted around each house. Cotton-padded quilts were provided for each bedroom, but everyone felt suffocated sleeping under them so they stuck with their animal skins.

During the first few days after their arrival no one could sleep. They slipped out of their houses and wandered like sleepwalking ghosts. And it wasn't just the residents who did this; so did their hunting dogs. They were accustomed to guarding *shirangju* in the mountain forests, and those houses laid out in rows seemed unfamiliar, so the hounds lingered in the streets along with their masters. When strangers encountered strangers, they didn't speak. But when unfamiliar hunting dogs encountered one another, they weren't so restrained, barking and sometimes tearing into one another. So at the beginning of their time in the settlement, no creature knew peace in the middle of the night.

Valodya said Tatiana, Yveline and Kunde lived together, and Dashi's family and Viktor's family were in the same house. But Ivan was the beneficiary of special treatment by the government, so he had one house all to himself. Even the Party Secretary had heard tell of how Ivan fought the Japanese devils, and labelled him a 'Founding Hero of New China'.

The men continued hunting in the mountains, sometimes returning the same day, sometimes after several days. Managing the reindeer was still the women's main chore, but the reindeer didn't like to return to Jiliu. They preferred to stay in quiet, more open places, so the women enclosed a large space two or three *li* from the township where the reindeer could rest, and each day they had to carry some dried food for themselves and go and count the reindeer. If any were missing, they'd go out searching for them as in the old days.

'That cadre who came last time – didn't he say that in Jiliu Township the reindeer could eat hay and tree branches?' said Puffball. 'From what I hear, it seems they're living the same way as before.'

Valodya said when they had just arrived the reindeer were corralled on the shores of the lower Uldihitt River, west of the seat of the township government. The vet surnamed Zhang from the township's Veterinary Station, who wore a long blue robe and a pair of spectacles, stayed with the reindeer each day.

'Zhang wouldn't let them out and just fed them fodder and

manufactured bean pellets,' recounted Valodya. 'But the reindeer didn't care for that stuff, and except for licking a bit of salt and drinking a little water, they preferred to go hungry.'

Watching the reindeer grow thinner right before their eyes, the hunters stopped cooperating. 'They cursed that devilish vet, and some even wanted to give him a beating. When the township leaders realised the hunters were enraged, and the state of the reindeer wasn't good, they agreed to everyone's suggestions. So the reindeer won back their freedom.'

'But when the moss in that area grows sparse the reindeer will go elsewhere to search for food. In less than two years, those houses will be vacant again,' I said to Valodya. 'Because those houses are dead. They can't move like our *shirangju*, which are alive and can follow the reindeer.'

That winter the large-scale exploitation of the Greater Khingan Mountain Range began, and even more forestry workers were stationed in the mountains. Many logging sites were set up, and even more new roads were opened up to transport the timber.

The din of tree felling grew louder. The number of squirrels in the forest dropped and Valodya said this was because pine trees were being chopped down. Squirrels like to eat the nuts that mature on the pine, so each pine tree that was felled meant that much less food for the squirrels. People flee famine, and squirrels are no different. No doubt they raised their bushy tails high and escaped to the Left Bank of the Argun.

After two years, like migratory birds heading homeward, people from various clans who had resettled in Jiliu Township did return to the mountains, one group after another, on account of their reindeer. It seems that the old lifestyle was our eternal spring.

In our *urireng*, some members returned but others remained in Jiliu Township. Dashi and Zefirina were unwilling to come back because they still sought treatment in the hopes of having a child. Ivan's rheumatism was so bad that he now moved only with difficulty. His heart yearned to return but his body wouldn't permit it. And Lyusya had no choice but to stay behind on account of Viktor, and September who was already in primary school.

Those who did come back were the elderly Yveline, Kunde and Hase. They returned with reindeer that had not been well cared for and appeared as spiritless as these three.

Among the returnees only one was full of vigour, and that was my daughter Tatiana. With her ruddy face and a gentle light rippling from her eyes, she possessed a special beauty.

She brought gifts for each woman in the camp: for Nihau and me, blue headscarves, and for Berna and Maikan, a colourful handkerchief each. The night she returned she told Valodya and me that two men had requested her hand in marriage. Whose request should she accept?

One of her suitors was an elementary school teacher in Jiliu Township named Gao Pinglu, a Han who was six years older than Tatiana. The other was one of us Evenki named Suchanglin. He was the same age as Tatiana, and known in his clan as a superb marksman.

'Gao Pinglu is tall, on the thin side, fair-skinned, pleasantly tempered and educated. He has a stable income and plays the flute,' she said. 'As for Suchanglin, he's middling height, neither fat nor thin and muscular. He enjoys a good laugh and loves to eat meat raw.' And like us, he herded reindeer and hunted for a living.

'You should marry the one who eats raw meat,' I said.

'You should marry the one who plays the bamboo flute,' said Valodya.

'So whose words should I obey? *Eni*'s or *Ama*'s?'

'Listen to your heart,' said Valodya. 'Wherever your heart beckons, that is where you should go.'

Tatiana came back in the spring looking as happy as a little bird just out of its cage. She said she wasn't at all keen to return to Jiliu Township. Living in a *shirangju* was better after all.

Then in the summer she announced to Valodya and me: '*Eni*, *Ama*, I'm going to marry the one who likes raw meat.' We rushed to prepare her dowry and just two weeks later Suchanglin married Tatiana and took her away.

The day that Tatiana left the camp Valodya emitted a long, weighty sigh. I understood that he was not just feeling sad because Tatiana was leaving us; he also felt regret about the fellow who played the flute.

Just after Tatiana left, several guests arrived in the camp: a guide, the Deputy Jiliu Township Head, the vet from the Veterinary Station, and Gao Pinglu, the primary school teacher who courted Tatiana and played the flute.

Each visitor had his own goal. Deputy Head Chen came to conduct a census and register each family. The veterinarian came to check the reindeer for disease, and he said he also wanted to collect semen specimens to breed better reindeer, which earned him guffaws.

When Deputy Head Chen introduced Gao Pinglu, he said Gao was a scholar taking advantage of his summer vacation to collect Evenki folk songs, so he hoped we would sing for him often. The first thing Gao asked about was Tatiana, and when we told him she had just married and moved away, he said that was fine but looked very disappointed.

As soon as Vladimir learned that Deputy Head Chen had come to conduct a census, he tried to frighten Maikan. 'The people who want to take you away have come at last. You're not allowed to take a step out of our *shirangju*. Otherwise, you're dead!' Maikan gave her word.

But the sound of singing and dancing in the camp that night was too tempting, and Maikan slipped out of her *shirangju* and found her way among the dancers around the bonfire. Already as lovely as a dew-drenched lily, the seventeen-year-old maiden drew the gaze of all the visitors with her nimble and graceful dancing.

Maikan's sudden appearance was a bright crescent moon jumping out into the night, a rainbow rising over the mountains after the rain, a young fawn standing by the lakeshore at dusk. Her beauty took your breath away.

Deputy Head Chen rubbed his eyes. 'She wouldn't be a fairy, would she?' The vet gaped as if witnessing a dream. As for Gao Pinglu, at the start he was recording lyrics by the light of the fire, but when Maikan appeared, his head rose, pen stopped, and notebook fell into the fire and fused with the flames. Though he said nothing, his eyes helped him speak and tears flowed. Those tears made us believe he was no longer aching over Tatiana, because a cloud named Maikan had floated into Gao's heart and begun to stir up wind and rain.

When Vladimir realised that Maikan had come out, he shook with anger. If she was a sparkling pearl now, then Vladimir was the pearl's owner left grasping an empty jewellery box. Utter desolation and misery were written on his face. So while Maikan's legs spun happily, Vladimir's shoulders twitched painfully like a bird whose wings have been injured.

'This young lady isn't an Evenki, is she?' Deputy Head Chen asked Valodya. 'She's so beautiful and dances so well. In the future I must introduce her to the Arts Troupe. What a pity it would be for her talent to be buried here in the mountains!'

'She was abandoned and Vladimir raised her,' Valodya confided. 'She is his eyes; without her Vladimir would go blind.'

Deputy Head Chen straightened his neck, said 'Oh', and didn't speak again.

That evening a succession of tearful noises emanated from Vladimir's *shirangju*, first Vladimir's, then Maikan's. The next morning we discovered they were gone. Everyone understood that Vladimir considered those men wolves, and he had taken Maikan to seek a 'safe haven'.

And our assumption was correct. On the third day after our visitors left, Vladimir brought Maikan back. From then on, Maikan rarely spoke, and she didn't play with Berna any more either.

Each day at dusk, Maikan would begin singing softly. Her song was plaintive and melancholic. Valodya said Gao Pinglu had come to collect folk songs, and Maikan's song was certainly for him. She sang the same song each day. We became familiar with that melody, but the lyrics remained vague. It was only when Berna took flight that autumn and Maikan sang that song again, then the lyrics floated to the surface of the water like tadpoles.

It was Hase's life-threatening illness that drove Berna to leave us. A big mushroom took Hase away. When the autumn rain finally ceased, mushrooms of all sorts popped up in the forest. One grows quite oddly, for its cap is large and crimson and sports a layer of thick mucus. We call it the 'sticky mushroom'.

Sticky mushrooms don't seem to like light, and typically flourish in shaded, moist areas of the forest floor. Hase stepped smack on one, slipped and fell motionless on the ground. He wanted to get up but couldn't. By then he was already seventy.

When they carried him to his *shirangju*, he instructed Luni that he should not be treated under any circumstances. He was a bag of old bones, and saving him would be a waste.

'Hase, you've got a broken bone,' said Valodya, and he made preparations to take him to the clinic in Jiliu Township.

'I won't go!' said Hase. 'I want my bones cast in the mountains. Maria's are here.'

These sad words made our hearts ache. The day Hase slipped his faculties were still good, but the second day he began to babble and couldn't drink a drop. Luni looked at Nihau with tears in his eyes, and Nihau knew what Luni wanted him to do, but she gazed gloomily at Berna and Maksym. Maksym was still a child and ignorant of what had happened within his clan, and he continued playing happily with the wooden man that Luni had whittled for him. But Berna was scared white. She bit her lip, trembled, and looked as lonely and helpless as a fawn surrounded by wolves.

That very afternoon Berna took flight. We assumed she'd gone to gather mushrooms, for she relished mushrooms like the reindeer. But at dinner she still wasn't back. Everyone waited until nightfall and the stars came out, and then we realised something wasn't right and we split into groups to search for her. We searched all night but found no sign of her. Luni cried and so did Nihau.

Nihau buried her head in Luni's chest. 'Stop the search. Unless I die, she'll never come back!'

The second night after Berna's disappearance, Maikan sang that song of hers again. This time we heard the lyrics clearly. It seemed to be for the man who played the flute, but also for Berna and herself:

> *To the riverbank I came clothing to wash*
> *But a fish snatched my ring*
> *And dropped it on the riverbed.*
>
> *Down the mountain I came firewood to gather*
> *But the wind blew my hair*
> *And ensnarled it in the reeds.*
>
> *To the riverbank I came to claim my ring*
> *But the fish kept their distance.*
>
> *Down the mountain I came to claim my hair*
> *But the wind made me tremble.*

Hase struggled for three days and three nights and finally closed his eyes.

Luni went to Jiliu Township to inform Dashi of his father's death and to search for Berna. But he found no trace of her there.

When Luni brought back Dashi and Zefirina, he looked very sad. When he saw his son Maksym, he grabbed him and drew him to his chest and held him as tight as death itself. The boy squirmed and cried. Nihau rescued Maksym from Luni's embrace, and Maksym stopped crying, but Luni wept.

After Hase's burial, Dashi and Zefirina returned to Jiliu Township.

The scent of musk floated around Nihau again, and I knew this time the scent announced the end of her youth. Indeed, Nihau never mothered another child.

\* \* \*

In 1968, the year after she married, Tatiana gave birth to her beloved Irina. It was in Jiliu Township that I first saw my granddaughter, still in her swaddling clothes. Ironically, this happened at a funeral. Ivan's funeral, that is.

Who'd have imagined that both Dashi and Ivan would be struck down by calamities that fell from the sky? The roots of the disaster lay in the map that Commander Yoshida gave Vladimir when he left Kwantung Army Garrison for good decades ago.

By this time during the Cultural Revolution, Sino-Soviet relations had ruptured and Soviet revisionist spies were being arrested everywhere. Long filed away as military data, the map was rediscovered in a search conducted by a Rebel Faction of the Red Guards in the army. There was a sentence in Russian on the back of the map: 'The mountains are finite, the waters are infinite.' The rebels reckoned that a Soviet spy drew this map, and when its origins were investigated, Ivan's name emerged.

The rebels came rushing in a car, driving several hundred kilometres to Jiliu Township where they interrogated Ivan: 'Was this map obtained from the Soviets?'

Ivan said the map was given to him by Dashi, who in turn got it from Vladimir. So they brought Dashi in for questioning. When he heard the map was linked to the Soviets, Dashi said: 'How could that be? The Japanese gave the map to Vladimir.'

'We relied on that map later to locate and destroy several fortifications established by the Kwantung Army,' explained Ivan. 'A map like that could only have been drafted by the Japanese.'

'So how come there's a sentence in Russian on the back?' queried the Rebel Faction's interrogator.

Ivan asked the meaning of the Russian and once it was clarified, he continued. 'That Japanese named Yoshida despised the war. He must have been making an analogy between the mountains and Japan that was bound for defeat, and between the river and mighty China. That's why he wrote "The mountains are finite, the waters are infinite".

'As to why he used Russian to write it, he's probably the only one who can say,' said Ivan. 'But on the eve of Japan's surrender he committed hara-kiri on the banks of the Argun.'

'Anyway, how can there be so many Soviet spies running around now?' said Dashi. 'When I was trained at the Kwantung Army Garrison, I was even sent to the Soviet Union where I photographed the Soviets' railways and bridges for the Japanese. Based on what you say, doesn't that make me a spy too?'

Dashi's words only deepened the rebels' suspicions, and they hauled him and Ivan away the next day.

The third day after they were arrested, Township Head Qigede gathered a dozen or so hunters without discussing his plan with the County Party Secretary. Hunting rifles at their backs, they rode in horse-drawn carriages for one day and one night until they found the place where Ivan and Dashi were jailed.

'Either you lock us up with Dashi and Ivan,' said Qigede to the Rebel Faction, 'or you free them and let them join us again!'

In the end Dashi and Ivan were taken back to Jiliu Township, but by then both had been crippled. Ivan lost two fingers, and one of Dashi's legs was broken. Ivan bit off his own fingers when his outrage reached its limits during his interrogation, and the rebels fractured Dashi's leg.

After Ivan returned to Jiliu Township, he coughed up blood for two days, and then he departed. Before he died he was very lucid. 'Bury me in the earth with my head facing the Argun, and erect a cross before my grave.'

I understand that the cross was Nadezhda's embodiment. But if Nadezhda went to that world too, she'd certainly be upset about Ivan's missing fingers. She loved his hands so.

No one in Jiliu Township recognised the pair of fair maidens all in white who made a sudden appearance at Ivan's funeral. They said simply that they were Ivan's goddaughters, and, learning of his departure, they had rushed to send him off.

By that time Yveline was already so feeble that she couldn't even lean on a walking stick and needed someone's arm to support every step she took, but she insisted on coming to Jiliu Township to bid Ivan goodbye. We let her ride a reindeer.

Even though she was elderly, her intuition was still sharp. 'Those two maidens must be the pair of white foxes Ivan spared in the mountains when he was young,' she confided. 'They feel gratitude towards him, and knowing that his own children are unable to mourn him, they've disguised themselves as his goddaughters to reward his act of mercy.'

I wasn't entirely convinced, but it's a fact that after Ivan's burial the pair vanished miraculously from the gravesite.

When I first saw my granddaughter Irina sleeping in Tatiana's embrace, her tiny pink face lost in angelic sleep, I took her in my arms, and to my surprise she opened her eyes and smiled at me. Her eyes were so radiant. A child with such eyes will be blessed with good fortune.

Dashi and Zefirina returned to the mountains with us. Not only did they come back from Jiliu Township without a child, they lost a leg. When Vladimir saw Dashi appear in the camp leaning on a cane, he embraced him and cried.

Because of the Ivan affair, Qigede was stripped of his title and returned to the mountains. Not long thereafter, Party Secretary Liu brought a man wearing a Mao suit into the mountains to see Valodya. He said the hunting peoples intended to nominate Valodya as the new Head of Jiliu Township. What did Valodya think?

Valodya gestured to me. 'Never mind that I've cut my long hair. I'm still her Chieftain. If she doesn't leave the mountains, then this Chieftain must stay at her side.'

Qigede died that winter when he slipped and fell into an animal trap. His clansmen still treated him as their respected Clan Chieftain and held a solemn funeral for him.

I've already told too many tales of death, but it's unavoidable, because everyone will die. Each person's birth is similar, but each person's path to death is distinctive.

The year after Ivan passed away, in the summer of 1969 that is, Kunde died, followed by Yveline. Their deaths were expected because they were already in their seventies. By that time an old person resembles the setting sun about to drop into the mountains – no matter how sad you are, you can't stop its descent.

But the deaths of Kunde and Yveline were still unique. Imagine this: Kunde, who feared neither ferocious wolves nor almighty black bears, was scared to death in the end by a black spider.

An'tsaur was nine years old and he wasn't a naughty child. But that day in the forest he caught a big black spider the size of a jujube pit. He was intrigued by it, so he picked a long blade of grass, cut the grass into sections and tied up the spider with them, and then wandered about with his catch.

Kunde was seated outside his family's *shirangju* and squinting as he basked in the sun. 'Looks like you're dangling something there. What is it?' Kunde asked, his eyes widening as the boy passed by.

An'tsaur didn't say. Instead, he leaned over and suspended the spider right in front of Kunde so he could get a good look.

The spider was bound but its feelers were still waving freely in the air. '*Tian ah!*' moaned Kunde. Whereupon he gasped, his head tilted sharply, and he dropped dead.

Yveline was seated next to the hearth in the *shirangju* drinking reindeer-milk tea. When Nihau and I told her Kunde had been frightened to death by a big spider, Yveline chortled gleefully. She hadn't laughed for a long time now.

'So Kunde's chicken-heartedness killed him in the end? Years ago if he'd been brave enough to take that Mongolian maiden for his wife instead of me, he and I both would have led happy lives. Well, well. He lost his life thanks to his cowardice. Now that's fair!'

Kunde had long before instructed that he wanted to be buried with his clansmen. So when Kunde breathed his last, Luni dispatched a messenger to inform Kunde's clan of his death, and when they came, they brought a horse-drawn carriage to take his body to his clan's cemetery. The carriage stopped at the end of the road used to transport timber out of the mountains, but that was still some three or four *li* from our camp.

Luni and Valodya constructed a pine-pole stretcher and got ready to carry Kunde to the paved road. I still recall Yveline's last words as she saw off Kunde whose corpse, covered in white cloth, was about to begin its journey to its resting place in the soil: 'No matter how many times you whipped me, Kunde, you were just a coward. Good riddance!'

After Kunde's departure, Yveline seemed a bit more energetic. Leaning on her walking stick, she could walk again, though she swayed precariously. She used to love raw meat, but in her last days, like Viktor she refused to smell or touch animal flesh. She drank a little reindeer milk every day, and An'tsaur collected fallen flower petals for her. She said she wouldn't live much longer, but before she departed she wanted to clean out her gut.

An abscess festered on the neck of five-year-old Maksym. It ached so much that he cried all day long. At dusk we were seated beside the hanging pot cooking fish when Yveline arrived.

'Why is he crying?' she asked, gesturing towards Maksym in Nihau's arms.

'Out of pain,' said Nihau. 'Maksym has a boil on his neck.'

Yveline pursed her lips. 'Why didn't you say so sooner? I'm a widow now, so if I blow a few breaths of air on the wound, won't it heal right away?'

In our clan there is an old saying that wherever a child has a boil, if a widow draws three circles around it with her index finger and then blows three puffs of air on it – three times over – then the sore will heal.

Nihau carried Maksym over to Yveline. Yveline's hand shook as she extended her index finger that resembled a wizened tree branch. She drew circles on Maksym's neck and then blew on the abscess with all her might. After each puff of air she had to lower her head and inhale deeply again. She trembled as she blew the last puff and suddenly dropped airily by the hearth. The firelight quivered against her face, making her look as though she still wanted to open her mouth and say something.

Indeed, after Yveline's funeral the abscess on Maksym's neck did heal.

It was in that year that a man on a horse suddenly arrived in our camp. He brought us liquor and sweets. But if he hadn't said it himself, we wouldn't have recognised him as the Han youth who stole our reindeer and caused Nihau to lose the infant still in her womb. He was a mature man now.

'You gave me back my life. I want to return the favour,' he said to Nihau.

'My daughter Berna has run away. If one day you can find her and bring her back for my funeral, that will do.'

'If Berna is still alive, I'll find her for sure.'

We lived in relative tranquillity for the next few years. An'tsaur was a big child and could go hunting now with Luni. Maksym grew tall too and especially loved to play with the fawns. He'd bend over and pose like a reindeer, announcing he wanted to lock antlers. You could see that his hornless head would be no match for a horned adversary, but Maksym's playfulness brought us all much joy.

Valodya and I grew older day by day. Even though we slept

together, we lacked the passion to make wind-sounds. It seems the real Wind Spirit resides in the Heavens. The two rock paintings I made those years were both associated with the Wind Spirit. The Wind Spirit I painted had no facial features and you could say it was a man or a woman, and it had especially long hair, as long as the Milky Way.

Using the excuse that he was documenting our folk songs during winter and summer vacation, the Jiliu Township teacher Gao Pinglu came again and again to visit Maikan and propose marriage.

But whenever Vladimir heard talk of a match for Maikan, he'd start to howl. No matter who came to our camp to ask for her hand, Vladimir shook his head. He always said Maikan was just a child, even though she was already a young woman in her twenties.

* * *

After Dashi returned with a broken leg, he was cheerless. He couldn't go out hunting as before. He often said he was useless, and could only stay behind in the camp and do lighter chores of which he was capable. Each time Luni, Puffball and Valodya came back from the hunt and gave him his share of the catch, Dashi's face creased in sorrow. He often cursed Zefirina for no reason, but since she knew the bitterness in his heart, no matter how he insulted her, she tolerated it.

In the autumn for 1972 our hunting luck was especially good, and our chores were heavier because of the large catch. Typically, after the men brought back their kill, it was up to the women to skin it, separate the meat from the carcass and tan the hide. While the women toiled, the men loved to smoke and sip tea recounting the day's hunting exploits.

As Dashi could only do chores along with the women, he helped us to skin the catch and strip the meat. But he handled the tanning on his own.

On this particular day, as the men recounted the tale of how they had shot the wild deer, Dashi sat on the ground skinning it. The more exciting their tale, the gloomier he grew.

After Dashi had skinned the catch and stripped the meat off the bones, Nihau and I began to cook it. When the meat was half cooked and we called Dashi to come and eat, a rifle shot rang out from nearby. No one had imagined that Dashi would use a hunting rifle to make himself his last kill! Excellent marksman that he was, he used just one bullet.

Poor Zefirina! When she saw Dashi's blood-drenched head, she knelt down and, treating it like a piece of fruit blown to the ground by a strong wind, she held it tenderly in her arms and kissed it.

She gently licked clean the splattered blood on his face. And while we were occupied with cleaning his body and dressing him for burial, she slipped away into the forest and swallowed a handful of poisonous mushrooms so she could join Dashi.

We buried them together. The autumn leaves danced and Vladimir used the sound of his mouth harp to see off his dear friend. It was a heart-wrenching melody. That was the last time I heard Vladimir blow on it. He stuck it at the head of the grave of Dashi and Zefirina, and that *mukulén* became their tombstone.

The members of our *urireng* were fewer and fewer and we were deeply shrouded in death's shadow. If it hadn't been for An'tsaur, our lives would have been even more depressed. But An'tsaur's simple-mindedness resembled bright rays of sunlight that pierced the dark clouds and brought us light and warmth.

One day not long after we buried Dashi and Zefirina, An'tsaur was in high spirits. 'At last the *mukulén* on the grave has been rescued!' he said to Valodya and me.

I asked him what he meant.

'Ever since the *mukulén* was stuck on the grave, the weather has been dry. I thought it might die of thirst. But now the rain has come and nourished it, so it'll grow again.'

I asked him what the *mukulén* would grow.

'The sound that came out was so nice to hear. At least a flock of little birds will grow out of it!'

How could such words fail to bring a smile to our hearts?

* * *

But our happiness didn't continue for long. In 1974, Valodya left me for ever. This tragedy began with a comedy.

That summer a travelling cinema came into the mountains to cheer up the forestry workers. They travelled between logging sites and tree farms showing films. We had never seen a film, and when Valodya heard the news, he discussed it with Luni. They contacted two neighbouring *urireng*, and, liquor and meat in hand, they went to invite the cinema troupe to play films for us.

The forestry workers were very friendly, and once they heard we'd never seen a film, they agreed. There were two people in the travelling cinema troupe: the projectionist and his assistant. But the assistant had diarrhoea, so the workers dispatched only the projectionist. Our reindeer transported the two big boxes containing the film projector and electricity generator.

'The projectionist is an intellectual sent down to the countryside for re-education,' explained a forestry worker. 'He used to be an assistant history professor at a university, and he's under supervision.' They instructed that after the film we should escort him back safely, and we must ensure that nothing went wrong.

We hadn't had such a merry get-together for many a year. Members of two neighbouring *urireng*, more than forty in all, crowded into our camp. They brought liquor and meat from a fresh kill, and we lit a bonfire and ate and drank, sang and danced.

The projectionist looked to be in his forties with a very pale face that rarely smiled, and he said little. Everyone toasted him, but at first he declined. Later on he cautiously moistened his lips with *baijiu*, then sipped at it, and in the end gulped it down heartily.

When he came among us he was a piece of wet kindling, but our enthusiasm and joy quickly dispelled the air of gloom about him. We ignited him and he transformed into a joyful flame.

When the sky had been rubbed black, the projectionist instructed us to hang the white curtain on a tree. With the electricity generator rumbling, he set up the projector and started the film as we seated ourselves on the ground. When the first rays of silver white light were projected onto the screen, we cried out in amazement, and even the hounds curled up behind the screen began yelping in terror.

Shadows of buildings, trees and people appeared miraculously on the screen, everything in colour. The people up there not only moved about freely, they could speak and sing. It was really unimaginable. I forgot the storyline long ago, because the people inside the film talked and talked, struck poses and sang 'Y*ee-yee Ya-ya*' endlessly.

We didn't understand the lyrics so we watched the film in a state of some confusion. But we were still excited about it, because after all we could glimpse an unlimited vista on a tiny screen.

'Films nowadays aren't as interesting as older ones,' said the projectionist. 'There are just a handful and they're mostly revolutionary "model operas". Earlier films were in black and white, but they had a more human feeling to them and they were worth watching again.'

Puffball got angry. 'Since there are beautiful ones to watch, why do you play ugly ones for us? Aren't you just cheating our eyes?'

The projectionist hurried to explain. 'The more interesting ones from before have all been judged "poisonous weeds", and locked away for safe-keeping. They can't be screened.'

'You're lying. Why would they lock away beautiful films? And anyhow, you can't eat a film, so how could they be "poisonous weeds"? You're bullshitting us!'

Puffball was all riled up and wanted to punch the projectionist. Valodya rushed over to dissuade him. 'I'll only forgive him if he empties a bowl of *baijiu* in one go,' said Puffball.

So the projectionist had little choice but to take the bowl and finish it off.

The film was over but the fun continued. We circled the bonfire and began a round of singing and dancing. Encouraged by the drink in our stomachs, everyone wanted the projectionist to sing us a song. Thanks to the bowl of *baijiu* forced on him by Puffball, he was already dead drunk. Swaying from side to side, he slurred his words but managed to explain that he didn't know how to sing. Could he recite a poem instead? Yes, he could.

The projectionist recited just one verse:

> *Eastward flows the mighty river,*
> *Washed away by its waves are those*
> *Gallant heroes of bygone millennia*

Whereupon he suddenly fell over, lost to the world. The contrast between the grand verse he recited and his sudden collapse set everyone laughing. We began to appreciate the projectionist, because only an honest fellow would allow others to get him drunk like this.

We revelled until the moon leaned to the west, and then members of the two neighbouring *urireng* began to take their leave. It was entirely on account of their reindeer that they rushed back, because if the animals returned in the early morning and found their masters absent, they'd be anxious.

I rose the next morning to find An'tsaur busy making breakfast and brewing reindeer-milk tea. Normally we make just one pitcher, but that day he poured the first brew into a birch-bark bucket, put the lid on and heated another. I thought he wanted to drink a bit more than usual, so I didn't ask why. But when he cooked the third pitcher, I thought it was odd.

'Those people who came to watch the film last night have left, so now we have just one guest, the projectionist,' I said. 'And no matter how much he drinks, he won't finish three pitchers!'

'It's true they left, but a lot of people arrived last night in the film,' said An'tsaur earnestly. 'Men and women, young and old, a whole bunch! I went looking for them just now but I couldn't find them. I wonder where they slept last night. When they come back later, won't they want to drink reindeer-milk tea too?'

An'tsaur's words amused me, but he seemed a little ill at ease as I laughed. 'Could it be that the people in the film have gone away?' he mumbled. 'They sang until midnight and left with their stomachs empty. Will they have enough energy to reach wherever they are going?'

I went back to our *shirangju* and repeated An'tsaur's words to Valodya, and he laughed too. But then we fell silent because our hearts were filled with a sweet-and-sour emotion.

The projectionist didn't rise until past nine because he had indulged in too much drink. He said his head ached, he felt thirsty and his legs were weak.

'Never mind,' said Valodya. 'Have some reindeer-milk tea and you'll naturally feel better.'

An'tsaur brought the pitcher over and poured the projectionist a bowl. He drank it, and then he said that his head really didn't ache so, and his legs had regained their strength. Valodya told An'tsaur to refill his bowl.

'Last night I saw a fairy-like maiden,' said the projectionist. 'She didn't look an Evenki. Who is she?'

Valodya realised he was asking about Maikan. But Vladimir was ill disposed towards any man who took an interest in Maikan. 'You were drunk. You must've been seeing things.'

The projectionist drank three bowls until his face displayed the colours of the dawning sun, and then he enjoyed a piece of our *khleb* too.

'Next time you visit an Evenki camp, you'd better bring medicine for a hangover,' joked Valodya.

'I really envy your lifestyle. It's so harmonious, a kind of lost paradise like the "Peach Orchard Spring" in the famous fable.'

Valodya emitted a long sigh. 'Where on this earth is there such a paradise?'

At around ten o'clock, we packed the projection equipment in cases, loaded them on reindeer and saw the projectionist off back to the tree farm. Both Luni and Valodya should have escorted him, but Maksym suddenly got a stomach ache, so Puffball volunteered to go in Luni's stead. Puffball had been very drunk the previous night and his face was still red and his breath reeked of liquor.

The projectionist feared Puffball and kept his distance. But Puffball could tell, and he patted the projectionist warmly on the shoulder. 'Brother, the next time you come to show a film, bring some of those interesting "poisonous weeds" along!'

'Absolutely! Absolutely!' assured the projectionist. 'Sooner or later "poisonous weeds" become "fragrant grass"!'

Five reindeer and three men left the camp. Each man rode a reindeer with the other two hauling the projection equipment. If I'd realised that I was parting with Valodya for good, I'd have hugged him tight and kissed him tenderly. But I had no inkling whatsoever.

Perhaps Valodya had a premonition. As I watched him mount his reindeer, he suddenly joked: 'If I come back as a character in a film, don't let me go hungry!'

Indeed, he did turn himself into a character in a film. That evening he returned to the camp on his back. They had encountered a bear on their way, and in order to protect Puffball and the projectionist, he departed from the mountains and rivers of our world, and left me for eternity.

I came to know Lajide because I was pursued by a black bear, an event that brought happiness to my side; and my eternal separation from Valodya was also due to a black bear. It seems this creature was both the beginning and the end of my happiness.

Generally speaking, bear mishaps occur in the spring. Having just crawled out from a tree hollow, black bears are terribly hungry, but since wild fruits haven't yet matured, they search everywhere for game. That's why most instances of bears harming humans happen then.

By summertime, there are plenty of edibles, such as various insects and wild fruits, so the black bears are fairly quiescent. Unless provoked, they rarely attack. But if aggravated, they will put a man in death's corner.

Hibernating black bears choose a tree hollow as their hiding place. If the hole faces the sky, we call it a *tiancang*, or 'sky cache', but if the hole faces straight ahead or down, we call it a *dicang*, or 'earth cache'.

By summertime both *tiancang* and *dicang* are empty and squirrels amuse themselves crawling in and out of them.

Puffball told me it was because of such an 'earth cache' that the tragedy occurred.

After they left camp and proceeded three hours or so, they stopped to rest. Puffball and the projectionist sat on the forest floor taking a smoke while Valodya went off to relieve himself.

They had just begun chatting when Puffball spotted a squirrel's head poking out of a nearby *dicang*. He raised his rifle and fired. But it was a bear cub that he hit, not a squirrel!

It seems that a squirrel had gone inside the *dicang* to play. But when it discovered a bear cub there, it made a quick exit. The cub jumped out of its lair to snag the panicked squirrel, and Puffball's bullet struck it dead.

The cub tumbled onto the forest floor, and Puffball turned to the projectionist. 'Lucky you! You'll have something delicious to eat in just a little while!'

But just as he was about to pick up the cub, a rustling sound emerged from the dense forest. It transpired that the she-bear had heard the rifle shot, realised her cub was in trouble, and come running over to the tree hollow. Puffball lifted his rifle and shot right at her, but his aim was off. He fired again, but again the bullet veered.

Now the mother bear made a mad charge for them, but when Puffball went to shoot again, the rifle chamber was empty. He hadn't brought many bullets since this wasn't a hunting trip.

If Valodya hadn't fired at the animal from behind just in the nick of time and made her change the direction of her attack, said Puffball, he and the projectionist would have been done for.

The she-bear stood up and charged at Valodya. She was moving rapidly and Valodya fired again, and this bullet pierced her abdomen and tore open her intestines. But she was not cowed. She stuffed her guts back inside, and pressing the wound with one of her paws, rushed furiously at Valodya.

When Valodya shot his third round, the bear was already near him, but that bullet missed its target. Before he could get off the fourth round, the she-bear extended her blood-soaked forepaws, pulled Valodya towards her chest and then cast him down violently on the ground.

The projectionist fainted from fright while Puffball, rifle in hand, ran towards Valodya. But it was too late, for by then the she-bear had already ripped open Valodya's skull.

She picked up Valodya's gun, and grasping it like a tenacious soldier, proceeded towards Puffball. But her intestines came rippling out again, and, unable to withstand the pain, she put her front paws down and released the rifle. She crawled a few steps with great difficulty, and then stopped. Puffball ran forward and smashed her head with his rifle butt.

Puffball and Valodya were both good marksmen, and if he himself hadn't drunk so much after happily watching the film the previous night, his hand wouldn't have trembled, and Valodya wouldn't have died in the bear's paws.

And that is how the very last Clan Chieftain of our people departed.

We gave Valodya a wind-burial and there were many mourners. When his clansmen heard that he had ascended to the Heavens, they flocked from Jiliu Township and campsites scattered in the region. Nihau presided over his burial. The wind blew fiercely, and if it weren't for Tatiana supporting me, I'd certainly have been knocked down by the gale.

Valodya's departure left a blank spot in the ensuing months and years. I remember that once I missed Valodya so badly that my heart ached, but when I felt for my heart I discovered that my chest had turned into a hard rock. I threw off my clothes, grabbed my painting stick, and sketched freely on my chest. I painted and painted and a feeling of humiliation came over me. I cried. Just then

Nihau entered my *shirangju* and she wiped clean my face and tears and the colours on my chest, and dressed me.

'You painted a bear on your chest,' she told me later.

\* \* \*

In 1976 Viktor died from constant drunkenness. I didn't attend his funeral in Jiliu Township because I didn't care to see off a spineless man, even if he was my son. They buried him next to Ivan.

Viktor's son September began working as a mailman for the Jiliu Township post office, and that year he fell in love with a Han maiden, Lin Jinju, who worked at a store in the township.

I went to the township again for their marriage in the autumn of 1977. Lyusya took me to the store to see Lin Jinju, and there on the shelves I saw two rolls of cloth displayed, one a bright milky yellow, and the other a deep blue-green.

The colours of Jiin River at dusk when Tibgur was swept away by the torrential current flashed before my eyes. These are the two colours of the river of my life. Sentimental memories flooded my heart and tears criss-crossed my face.

My tears made Lin Jinju uneasy. 'Doesn't Grandmother want me to be her grandson's bride?'

I asked Lyusya to explain to her that I was just recalling a river.

After September's marriage, Lyusya returned to my side. She still wore the deer-bone necklace Viktor had polished for her, and every month at the full moon she cried, for that's when Viktor traditionally sought pleasure with her. I learned this secret soon after they married, because each month when the moon was full Viktor's blissful cries rang out from their *shirangju*.

In 1978, Tatiana and Suchanglin moved back to our *urireng* with their new-born daughter Soma. Irina was already ten, and Tatiana sent her to primary school in Jiliu Township where September and Lin Jinju looked after her. Tatiana told me that she yearned for a son. Prior to Soma she had been pregnant in the mountains, but in her sixth month she tripped and fell and miscarried. It was a boy, and she and Suchanglin were so distressed they couldn't eat for days.

An'tsaur arrived at the marriageable age too. I never thought any maiden would be keen on him, because his simple-mindedness was common knowledge. But one named Yolien took a fancy to him.

Yolien's *urireng* was nearby, and once Puffball went there and recounted the amusing tale of how An'tsaur brewed several pitchers of reindeer-milk tea for the film's cast.

Everyone chortled, except Yolien. '*Eni*, An'tsaur is so kind and his heart is so pure. You can count on a man like that for a lifetime. I'm willing to marry him,' she told her mother.

Yolien's *Eni* repeated these words to Puffball, and Puffball was overjoyed. He ran back immediately and conferred with us about An'tsaur's marriage, and we quickly held a wedding for them.

At the beginning Nihau and I worried that An'tsaur didn't understand about what went on between a man and a woman. But not long after their marriage Yolien became pregnant and we were truly overjoyed.

Yolien didn't rely on An'tsaur's kind heart for a lifetime, however, for the following year when she gave birth to a pair of twins, she haemorrhaged badly and died.

We usually bury a woman who dies in childbirth the very next day. But An'tsaur wouldn't allow it. He stayed at her side and didn't permit mourners to approach. One day passed, then a second, third and fourth, and despite the cool autumn weather, her corpse began to rot. The stench attracted throngs of ravens.

'Don't think that Yolien has died,' I said to An'tsaur. 'She has actually become a seed, and if you don't bury her in the soil, she won't be able to sprout, grow and bloom.'

'What kind of flower will Yolien bloom into?'

I recounted the legend Yveline had told me. 'Lotus flowers blossom all across Lake Lamu, and Yolien will be one of them.' Only then did An'tsaur permit us to bury his Yolien.

From then on, when spring arrived An'tsaur would ask me: 'Has Yolien bloomed yet?'

'One day when you find Lake Lamu, you'll see her.'

'When will that be?'

'One day you'll surely find it. Our ancestor came from there, and in the end, we shall all return there.'

'Yolien will become a lotus blossom. And what about me?'

'If you're not a blade of grass next to the lotus,' I said, 'then you'll be a star that shines down on its blossom!'

'I won't be a star. I want to be a blade of grass so I can kiss the lotus blossom and smell its lovely fragrance.'

An'tsaur chose names for the twins left behind by Yolien. He named one Beriku, and one Sakhar. '*Beriku*' is a basket carried on the back, and '*Sakhar*' means 'sugar' in our tongue. It seemed that An'tsaur was totally immersed in the fantasy in which Yolien became a lotus blossom, and he paid their real-life offspring no heed. So responsibility for raising his twins fell on my shoulders.

In 1980, thirty-year-old Maikan became pregnant out of wedlock.

Maikan's tragedy was directly related to Vladimir. No matter who came to request Maikan's hand in marriage, Vladimir always replied that she was still a child.

More than once Nihau and I advised him: 'Maikan is almost thirty. If she doesn't get married, aren't you wasting her precious time? She was an abandoned child and her life has been a sad one. She should be permitted a bit of happiness.'

But Vladimir's answer never varied: 'She's still just a child.'

And if Maikan herself implored him and said she yearned to be like other young women who marry and have children, then Vladimir would have a big, noisy cry. This delicate and charming blossom named Maikan faded as the days passed by amidst Vladimir's wailing.

After Gao Pinglu's repeated proposals were rejected, he stopped coming to document our folk songs, and had long since taken a wife and had children.

When Vladimir heard that Gao Pinglu had married, he said to Maikan: 'Don't you see? Affection. Romance. Which one is real? They are all just clouds and smoke that float past your eye! And what about that Han teacher? Didn't he go and get married too? Everyone will abandon you – except your *Ama*!'

By that time Maikan had learned how she had been abandoned in the stable at an inn in Uchiriovo, and she cried.

'*Ama*, if I marry one day,' she said when her tears stopped, 'then it will certainly be with an Evenki!'

During the spring of her thirtieth year, Maikan suddenly disappeared. Vladimir normally watched over her very closely and never let her go out alone. She'd never even been to Jiliu Township. She was the loneliest flower blooming in the deepest of ravines.

And yet in its thirtieth year this flower suddenly transformed into a butterfly and fluttered out of the valley. Vladimir just about went crazy with anxiety.

Luni and Suchanglin each led a band of men to search for her. One group went towards Jiliu Township, the other towards Uchiriovo, while Vladimir waited back in the camp, crying until his eyes nearly dried up. He didn't eat, drink or sleep for several days running. He simply sat next to the hearth, his eyes bloodshot, his face a sickly yellow, crying out Maikan's name despondently.

Nihau and I were very concerned that if Maikan didn't return, Vladimir couldn't go on living. But on the fifth day of her disappearance, before the search party that had taken the route to Uchiriovo returned, Maikan came back by herself. She looked very calm and was dressed in the same clothes as when she left, but there was something new in her hair, and that was a pastel-coloured handkerchief that tied her hair back.

'Where have you been?' asked Vladimir.

'I lost my way.'

Vladimir just about fainted out of anger. 'You lost your way? How come there's not a tear in your clothes but you've got a handkerchief in your hair? Where did you get it?'

'I picked it up on the path when I lost my way,' she replied.

Vladimir realised she was telling him a tall tale, and he cried. In reality, he had no more tears to cry, so he just bawled.

Maikan knelt down in front of him. '*Ama*, I won't ever leave you again. I will remain with you in the mountains for ever.'

Not long after her return, Maikan began to vomit. At first it didn't occur to us she might be with child, but her pregnancy became evident in the summer. Vladimir, who had just calmed down, was beside himself with rage.

He beat Maikan with a birch branch, cursed at her and interrogated her: what man did that thing to her?

'He's Evenki, and I was willing.'

'You're still just a child. How could you do such a shameless thing!'

'*Ama*, I'm not a child,' she said, her voice quivering. 'I'm thirty years old.'

During that period Vladimir seemed to be under an evil spell. Each day he went to beg Nihau to perform a Spirit Dance and rid Maikan of the child in her body.

'I only save people. I don't kill them.'

Left with no choice, Vladimir ordered Maikan to do heavy manual tasks, praying it would cause a miscarriage. But the child was very sturdy and survived. When winter arrived, she gave birth to a boy and named him Shiban. At two, Shiban could already eat meat and *khleb*, and he looked exceptionally strong and healthy.

Maikan weaned her son. Then she jumped off a cliff.

Only then did we comprehend that Maikan had found a substitute for herself to accompany Vladimir. She had probably long since lost the will to live, but fearful that Vladimir would be lonely with no one to look after him, she had a child. Shiban was Maikan's very last present to Vladimir.

Maikan's death just about made Vladimir go blind from crying. From then on his vision was fuzzy. He often wailed in pain when he was drunk, as if someone were trying to cut his heart out with a knife. Meanwhile, we looked after Shiban for him as he grew day by day.

\* \* \*

My granddaughter Irina attended school in Jiliu Township, but during winter and summer vacations Suchanglin brought her back. She was a clever and lively girl. She loved the reindeer, and during one summer she pleaded with Suchanglin to let her follow them into the mountains in the afternoon and return with them early next morning. So Suchanglin had little choice but to take his roe-deerskin sleeping bag and camp with her under the sky. Whenever Irina came back we rarely lost any reindeer, for she was like a Reindeer Guardian Spirit.

Now twelve or so, Irina came back again for her summer vacation. At that time our *urireng* was hunting on the move along the banks of the Argun, and one afternoon I brought along my painting sticks made of red ochre clay, led her to a patch of weathered cliffs along the river, and taught her to paint.

When the figure of a reindeer appeared on the bluish-white cliff face, Irina began to jump about. 'So a rock can give birth to a reindeer!' she exclaimed.

Then I painted flowers and little birds, and she started jumping again. 'The rock must be soil and sky. How else could flowers bloom and birds fly on it?'

I handed her a painting stick. First she drew a reindeer and then a sun. I was surprised at how vivid her rock paintings were. The reindeer I painted was subdued, but hers was playful. Her reindeer leaned its head, lifted its front hoof and tried to kick the bell around its neck. Its horns were asymmetrical, with seven prongs on one side and just three on the other.

'How come I've never seen a reindeer like the one you've painted?' I asked her.

'This is a Spirit Reindeer. Only a rock can grow a reindeer that looks like this.'

From then on, Irina became fascinated with painting. When she went back to school in Jiliu Township, she became exceptionally keen on her painting class. And when she returned to the mountains, she brought a pile of her pencil sketches.

Those sketches featured people as well as animals and scenery. The people she drew were all rather curious; if they weren't tilting their heads and gnawing on bones, then they were dangling a cigarette butt as they tied their shoelaces. Her animal drawings were mainly of reindeer. Among her drawings of scenery, one type was mainly houses and streets in Jiliu Township, and another was bonfires, rivers and mountains. Even though they were all grey pencil drawings, I felt as if I could see the orange-red hue where the bonfire burned hottest, and the bright light radiating from the waters of the moonlit river.

Each time Irina returned she confided that she missed the riverside cliffs. Painting on them was much more fascinating than on paper. So I'd pick a fine day for us to go rock painting.

'Pretty, isn't it?' she asked after each painting.

'Let the wind be your judge, for the wind's eyes are sharper than mine.'

Irina smiled. 'The wind says: "One day I shall blow the cliff apart, and your painting will become grains of sand in the river!"'

'And how do you answer the wind?' I asked.

'Fine. They will turn into grains of sand in the river, and the sand will become gold!'

But Irina's return meant Maksym wouldn't be happy. He was

also over ten, but each time Luni took him to school in Jiliu Township, he would run back to our *urireng*. He said the sight of books made his head hurt. So when Irina returned, Maksym was very annoyed because Irina liked school. They furtively competed to win the support of the other children.

Back then Sakhar, Beriku, Shiban and Soma were all still very young. When Irina was absent, Maksym exercised total hegemony – whatever he ordered, they did. Maksym liked to speak our people's language, so he used only Evenki with other children. But Irina spoke Han quite fluently, so when she came back she taught them to speak it.

This angered Maksym. 'If you learn how to speak Han, your tongue will rot,' he said to frighten them. But except for Shiban, they didn't believe Maksym and continued to learn Han from Irina.

Maksym developed other means to assert his dominance. He'd take a pile of woodblocks and whittle human figures, so naturally the kids were delighted and hung around with him.

But Irina was not one to admit defeat easily. She'd grab a pencil and sketch a portrait of one of the children, and they'd be under her spell again.

Irina's portraits brought us a lot of joy, too. Take Soma, for instance. When she saw her likeness on white paper, she thought she was facing a looking glass. She pointed at the paper and said: 'Mirror! Mirror!'

Since the twins were identical, Irina drew just one portrait for Beriku and Sakhar. They fought over it endlessly, each claiming the person in the drawing was himself. Being a wee bit naughty, Irina would add a few strokes here and there to make it look like the boy was taking a pee. Then each of the twins would argue that it *wasn't* him.

It was when Maksym was whittling wooden figures that we discovered Shiban's penchant for eating bark. He stripped the bark off the woodblocks, put it in his mouth, and chewed it with gusto. He loved to munch on birch and poplar bark because they are both moist and sweet.

From then on, Shiban chewed on bark every few days. He grasped the trunk of a birch or poplar, tilted his head and gnawed on the bark like a young mountain goat.

Vladimir treated Shiban very coldly, as if he was the one who pushed Maikan off the cliff. But once Shiban took to munching on bark, Vladimir gradually grew fond of him. 'That Shiban is really something. His food grows on trees, so famine won't bother him!'

Like Maikan's, Shiban's origins were a mystery. I once thought such riddles would never be solved, but the year that Irina passed the entrance exam for a Beijing art institute, Tatiana and I accompanied her to Jiliu Township to see her off, and Maikan's origins were revealed.

When Irina finished middle school, she went to Uchiriovo, now known as Qiqian in Heilongjiang Province, for high school. Then she passed the national university entrance exam, the first university student ever produced by our branch of the Evenki tribe of reindeer-herders. The fact that Irina gained entrance to a fine arts institute in Beijing attracted the attention of the world at large.

A reporter in his early thirties named Liu Bowen came all the way from Hohhot, Inner Mongolia, just to interview her. Afterwards, he mentioned he was also going to Qiqian to enquire on behalf of his father about a baby girl abandoned there over three decades ago. Liu Bowen didn't bring up the subject intentionally, but Tatiana and I immediately thought of Maikan.

'What year was the baby girl abandoned, and how old was she at the time?'

'Back then my grandfather was a well-known landlord in Jalannér. His family owned many houses and lots of land, and employed many long-term hired hands. During the land reform when they held "struggle sessions" against landlords, Grandfather hanged himself.

'Grandfather had two women and my father was the son of the first wife, but Grandfather also had a concubine of jade-like beauty. His concubine was pregnant when Grandfather ended his life. After she gave birth in nineteen fifty, she threw herself into a well. But before she committed suicide, she entrusted the infant to my grandmother, and instructed her to give the infant girl away. It could be rich or poor, but it must be a kindhearted family that could ensure a quiet life for her.

'My grandmother took out a gold bracelet she had hidden away, gave the baby to a horse trader and entreated him to find a good home for her. He had travelled widely and was worldly wise, and he reckoned that since Uchiriovo was a remote location the locals were plain, kind people. So with no regard to the distance involved, he took the infant to Uchiriovo and abandoned her in an inn's stable.

'When he passed by Jalannér later, the horse trader told my grandmother that he'd left the infant in Uchiriovo and heard that a kindly Evenki had taken her into the mountains. Before my grandmother died, she held her son's hand and told him to go in search of his sister who was twenty years younger than him. After all, they shared the same father.'

After I heard Liu Bowen's story, I knew the person he sought was Maikan. 'There's no need to go to Qiqian because that girl jumped off a cliff years ago. But she left a son named Shiban. If you want to see someone, go see Shiban.'

Tatiana and I recounted Maikan's story to Liu Bowen and he cried. Then he followed us into the mountains.

When I told Vladimir that Maikan was Liu Bowen's aunt, Vladimir took Shiban tightly in his arms. 'Shiban isn't Maikan's son. He was abandoned and I raised him.'

I understood that for Vladimir Shiban and Maikan were the same. Shiban was his pair of eyes, and losing him would be like going blind.

Liu Bowen stayed two days and took photographs of Shiban, and then Puffball escorted him out of the mountains. Luni had originally arranged for Suchanglin to do so, but Puffball volunteered. At that time Lyusya's son September had his own son, July, and Lyusya often left the mountains to see the two, but Puffball rarely had such an opportunity to visit his grandson and great-grandson.

Puffball might be an old man, but his legs were still limber and his marksmanship just as sharp.

By that time there were more and more tree farms and logging stations in the mountains, and the pathways for moving the logs were increasingly interconnected. Wild game, however, grew more and more scarce.

Each time he came back from a hunt empty-handed, Puffball cursed those logging stations. 'They're like tumours growing in the mountains that scare off the animals.'

Puffball loved to drink on the road. He said that walking and drinking allowed you to appreciate both the scenery and the liquor. Puffball drank continuously as he escorted Liu Bowen down the mountain.

'We left early in the morning and had walked fifteen kilometres by noon, when we reached an extension of Mangu Road that was just three or four kilometres from Jiliu Township,' recalled Liu Bowen.

'There were a lot of logging trucks on that road. When Puffball saw the unloaded trucks entering the mountains he had no reaction, but the sight of the long trucks loaded with logs rumbling by got him all riled up. He pointed at them and swore: "Sons of bitches!"

'But as luck would have it that day a slew of trucks were leaving the mountains. As soon as one passed another followed right behind. When the fourth logging truck went by with its load of larch, Puffball finally lost control. He raised his hunting rifle, aimed at the tyres and sprayed them with bullets. His aim was spot on. Several tyres punctured immediately, and the tilting logging truck came to a halt.

'Out jumped the driver and his assistant. The driver charged over and grabbed Puffball's deerskin overcoat. "Drunkard! Are you lookin' to die?" he cursed.

'His assistant, a young fellow, delivered a punch to Puffball's head. "You savage in animal clothes!" he shouted.

'That punch left Puffball reeling. "You . . . savage . . ." he repeated forlornly. He staggered a few steps, dropped his rifle, and then he collapsed.'

We knew that Puffball didn't care for noisy places, and we intended to bury him in a secluded spot, but Lyusya didn't agree. 'Puffball died on the way to visit the younger generation, so he should be buried in Jiliu Township where September and July can regularly make offerings to his soul. Places that seem secluded now will probably be less so in a few years, so it would be better for him to return to the side of his relatives in Jiliu Township.' So we buried him next to Ivan and Viktor.

People of my generation had just about all departed for another world. As the nineties began, time seemed to fly. Beriku and Sakhar were adults now and frequently left the mountains. Sakhar loved to drink, and if he didn't go and smash store windows, then he damaged desks and chairs in the school, or else he went and punctured tyres on government vehicles.

September told me that as soon as Sakhar appeared in Jiliu Township, everybody at the police station would get nervous. They informed the owners of the bars that he frequented: 'Sakhar's come down from the mountains, so keep an eye out.'

Beriku liked to go to Hohhot in Inner Mongolia and visit Irina. He loved dancing and dreamed that one day she'd help him join the theatre troupe and he could become a performer and travel with them.

By that time Irina had graduated from the fine arts institute in Beijing and was working as a production artist for a publishing house in Hohhot. She married a worker in a cement factory, but got divorced one year later.

After Irina divorced, so did Liu Bowen. 'They live together,' Beriku told me. 'But they argue a lot.'

'What do they argue about?'

'I don't know,' he said. 'But each time they finish quarrelling, Liu Bowen smashes things and Irina gets drunk.'

Each year Irina made sure to come back and visit me, and she always brought her artist's tools. Painting aside, she just liked to be with the reindeer. There were colours in her paintings. She rubbed oil paints of every hue on her canvases, but I don't care for oils. They're very pungent.

She wasn't as happy as before. I used to find her sitting alone on the bank, washing her paintbrushes and colouring the river. Her paintings were often published in art magazines. Each time she returned she brought those magazines to show me. Amidst all sorts of paintings, I could always recognise hers right away. They never lacked reindeer, bonfires, rivers and snow-capped mountains.

Irina usually became irritable after living with us for a month or two. She found the mountains too isolated and inconvenient for keeping in touch with the outside. Accompanied by Shiban, she'd go to Jiliu Township occasionally just to make a phone call to a friend.

Irina liked Shiban. She rarely drew people but she did several portraits of him. If Shiban wasn't gnawing on tree bark in those paintings, then he was squatting in the camp starting a smoky fire to chase the insects away from the reindeer, or carving characters on a woodblock.

Shiban had two great loves: creating Evenki pictographs, and making birch-bark handicrafts. He preferred to speak Evenki, and when he learned that the language didn't have a written form, he decided to invent one.

'Such a lovely language without a script. What a pity!' he said to us.

'Would it be so easy to create one?' we wondered.

'If I put my mind to it, I'm sure I can create a way to write Evenki words.'

Maksym was good at woodcutting, so Shiban had him make stacks and stacks of woodblocks. Shiban liked to sit next to the fireplace and invent pictographs. Once he imagined a new word, he wrote it on his palm with a ballpoint pen. Shiban asked us to look at each pictograph, and if everyone agreed it was appropriate, then he'd have Maksym solemnly carve it into a woodblock.

The pictographs he invented were concise. Take 'river', for instance. It was just one perfectly straight horizontal line; lightning, a curving horizontal line; rain, a broken vertical line; the wind, two wave-shaped vertical lines; clouds, a pair of linked semicircles; and a rainbow was a semicircle.

Since he was always sketching on his palm, he washed his hands especially carefully, fearful that he would unwittingly wash away a newly created word.

Pictographs aside, Shiban also liked to create all sorts of *mata*, or birch-bark handcrafted items. He mastered various drawing and engraving skills, and carved images of flying birds, reindeer, flowers and trees on birch-bark cigarette cases, penholders, tea-leaf containers and jewellery boxes. His preferred motifs were waves and clouds with thunderbolts.

Shiban's birch-bark items were very popular, and tourists from afar snapped them up from the shelves of shops in Jiliu Township. Shiban used the money he earned to buy us all sorts of things, and this made Vladimir incomparably proud. Shiban's greatest dream was to render our Evenki language in a concrete written form and ensure that it could be passed on to future generations.

But whenever Sakhar returned and found Shiban racking his brain to create pictographs, he ridiculed him and called him an idiot.

'Who wants to speak Evenki among young people nowadays, anyhow?' said Sakhar. 'Those written words you invent, aren't they destined to be buried in a grave?'

Shiban never took offence. He had a mild temperament and many people said he resembled An'tsaur. Tatiana once confided to me that Maikan had probably been pregnant with An'tsaur's child.

'How could that be? Maikan was missing for several days before she came back, and An'tsaur didn't leave the camp then.'

'Maybe Maikan tricked An'tsaur into making love with her first, and then she pretended to run away in order to confuse everyone,' said Tatiana.

I thought Tatiana's words were totally unfounded. That is, until one day two years ago when I was helping An'tsaur put things in order. I discovered a pastel handkerchief, and only then did I realise Tatiana's guess might just be right.

I gestured at the handkerchief. 'Did Irina leave this behind?'

'Maikan gave it to me as a gift,' An'tsaur said. 'She has one and I have one. She said when the wind blows and makes me cry, I can use it to wipe my tears.'

Right away I recalled the handkerchief on Maikan's head upon her return. How did Maikan get her hands on this pair of pastel-coloured handkerchiefs? I couldn't imagine. In reality, our lives conceal countless secrets, and there is nothing bad about the days we live with those unknowns. So I didn't feel like exploring Shiban's parentage.

When Irina became restless in the mountains, she would put her paintings on her back and return to the city. But she'd be back again before long. On each return she was excited, saying that everywhere the city was full of people in motion, buildings, vehicles and dust, and it was really a bore.

'It's wonderful to come back to the mountains where I can be with the reindeer, sleep at night with stars in my eyes, hear the wind, and fill my eyes with mountains, brooks, flowers and birds. It's so refreshing.'

But in less than a month's time, once again she'd be frustrated that there was no bar here, and no phone, no cinema and no bookshop. She'd get drunk, and afterwards direct her fury at the paintings she hadn't finished, say they were rubbish, and toss them in the fire.

Tatiana was often terribly anxious. Even though Irina had brought her worldly honour and everyone admired that her family had produced a painter, her daughter's internal contradictions and pain still made her uneasy.

As for Soma, she hated school like Sakhar. When she studied in Jiliu Township, she skipped class two days out of three.

Soma liked to make friends with boys, and at fourteen, she announced to Tatiana that she wasn't a virgin any more. Tatiana was so enraged that she brought Soma back into the mountains, forbade her to leave and made her herd reindeer every day.

But Soma despised reindeer. 'It would be great if they all caught the plague. Then we'd all have to leave the mountains.' Her curse aroused much aversion.

One day Irina finally quit her job and returned to us with luggage in tow.

'Why did you leave?' I asked her.

'I'm tired of work, the city and men. I've finally grasped the fact that the only things one never tires of are reindeer, trees, rivers, the moon and the cool wind.'

After that, she stopped painting with oils and began using animal fur to create collages. According to their different hues, she cut the furred hides of reindeer and elk into different shapes, and then stitched them together to form a 'fur mosaic'.

This sort of collage featured light brown and pale grey as the main colours. There were sky and clouds at the top, mountains rising and falling or rivers meandering at the bottom, and in the middle there were always reindeer in myriad poses.

To be frank, from the day that Irina began to make those fur mosaics, my heart was not at peace. I felt the pelts had souls, and while they might be willing to help people cover themselves against the rain and keep themselves warm, once you shredded them to amuse the eye and made them into a decoration to be hung, those furred hides might become cross.

At first Irina stated she wouldn't take her paintings out of the mountains, but after she created two mosaics, she couldn't resist rolling them up and taking them into the city. She looked like someone in search of a kind owner for her two dogs.

Two months later she came back with a TV reporter. She looked so excited. 'Those two tableaux created a sensation in the art world. A gallery accepted one for its collection, and somebody bought up the other one for big money.'

The TV crew came solely on her account. They filmed the *shirangju*, the reindeer, the bonfire, Shiban creating pictographs, and old Nihau and her Spirit Robe and Spirit Drum.

They wanted to shoot me too. 'We hear that you're the wife of this people's last Clan Chieftain. Can you chat with us about what you've experienced?'

I turned and walked away. Why should I tell them my story?

In early spring 1998 a big fire occurred in the mountains. The fire crept slowly over from the northern branch of the Greater Khingan Range. Those years the spring had been dry, the winds strong and the grasses parched, and there were frequent fire disasters. Some resulted from lightning strikes, while others were started by a smoker carelessly discarding his cigarette butt.

In order to prevent the possibility of an unextinguished cigarette destroying the forest, we invented a substitute: a unique kind of 'mouth tobacco'. It combined three ingredients: ground tobacco, tea leaves and charcoal dust. You don't need to light it. You just take a pinch and stick it up against your gums, and while your mouth enjoys the flavour of tobacco, it also refreshes the mind. Each spring and summer, we used mouth tobacco as a substitute for cigarettes.

Two forestry workers who carelessly discarded their cigarette butts started that fire. We had just relocated by the banks of the Argun when the fire dragon swept down upon us. Smoke billowed above the forest, and one flock of birds after another cried in panic as they escaped from the north. Their plumage was already tinted grey-black, so you can imagine the fire's ferocity.

The Township Party Secretary and Deputy Township Head drove a jeep into the mountains. At each of the Evenki camp-grounds, they showed us how to construct fire buffer zones and protect our reindeer. Helicopters flew back and forth in the sky to artificially induce rain. But the cloud cover wasn't thick enough, so we heard the rumble of thunder but felt no raindrops.

It was then that Nihau donned her Spirit Robe, Spirit Headdress and Spirit Skirt, and drumstick in hand, prepared to perform a Rain Dance for the last time. Her back was bent, and her cheeks and eye sockets sunken. She used two wooden woodpeckers as ritual items to pray for rain, one grey with a red tail, one black with a red fore-head. She placed them in shallow water near the bank, ensured their bodies were submerged and their beaks opened towards the sky, and then began her dance.

As Nihau danced thick clouds roiled in the sky and the reindeer herd stood, heads down, on the bank of the Argun. The drum beat feverishly, but Nihau's feet were not as nimble as before. She danced and danced, and then she coughed. She was stooped at the start, but when she coughed she bent over even further. Her Spirit Skirt dragged on the forest floor and collected dirt.

We couldn't bear to watch her arduous movements as she prayed for rain, so one by one we moved away and mingled with the reindeer. Except for Irina and Luni, no one had the heart to observe the ritual to its end.

But after Nihau had danced for an hour, dark clouds appeared; one hour later, thick clouds shrouded the sky; after yet another hour of dancing, bolts of lightning appeared. Nihau stopped. Swaying from side to side, she walked to the bank of the Argun, picked up the pair of soaked woodpeckers, and hung them from a sturdy pine. Just then thunder rumbled and a bolt of lightning lit up the sky, and rain poured down.

In the middle of the downpour, Nihau intoned her final Spirit Song, but collapsed before she could finish:

> O, *Argun River*
> *Flow towards the Milky Way.*
> *Our parched mortal world . . .*

The mountain fires extinguished, Nihau departed. She hosted many a funeral in her lifetime, but she was unable to see herself off.

Long-lost Berna returned for Nihau's funeral. With her was the very same youth who once stole our reindeer, but now they were both middle-aged. Where he found Berna, and how they learned of

Nihau's death, we didn't bother to ask. Nihau's last wish was realised anyhow, for Berna returned to take part in her funeral. Nihau
needn't perform any more Spirit Dances, and the terror in Berna's
heart was banished for ever.

About six months after Nihau's departure, Luni left too. Maksym said Luni looked just fine that day. He was sipping leisurely at
his tea. 'Give me a piece of candy,' he said to Maksym out of
the blue.

Suddenly his head tilted sharply, and his breathing ceased.

I believe that the world where Luni and Nihau went is a jovial
one, because Grigori, Juktakan and Tibgur are all there.

To Irina, the scene of Nihau praying for rain was unforgettable.
'At that instant I saw a century of the storms that have engulfed our
people. It was inspiring. I must capture this on canvas.'

At first she used a fur collage to express it, but half-way through
she said that animal fur was too frivolous a material; oils would be
more solemn.

She fixed the canvas against a piece of wood again, dipped her
brush in the oils and continued painting. She painted very slowly
with great emotion, often painting until she broke down in tears.

That painting took two years to complete. It expressed a bold
vision. At the top are thick, swirling clouds and black-green mountains shrouded in smoke. Nihau is dancing and reindeer surround
her in the middle of the tableau. The Shaman's face is fuzzy, but the
Spirit Robe and Spirit Skirt are so vivid that if the wind were to
blow ever so lightly, those twinkling metallic totems would *kling*
and *klang*. At the bottom are the desolate Argun and our people
standing on the bank with heads drooped, praying for rain.

We thought that painting had long ago been finished, but Irina kept saying no, it wasn't. She painted so delicately and in such detail that it seemed she was reluctant to finish.

It wasn't until we celebrated the first spring of the new millennium that Irina announced she had completed the tableau. At the time we were delivering fawns on the banks of the Bistaré. To celebrate the painting's completion, we organised a bonfire gathering.

Irina drank a lot. She didn't dance, but because she walked as if on air, she gave everyone the impression of dancing.

That was the night that Irina departed.

After she had drunk her fill, she returned to her *shirangju*, grabbed a handful of paintbrushes and walked towards the Bistaré, swaying from side to side. 'I'm going to wash my brushes,' she said as she passed. It was just a five-minute walk, and we watched her proceed towards the river.

'When Irina's finished cleaning her brushes, she'll go and paint something new for sure,' said Tatiana. 'But she'd better not spend another two years on a single painting. How could she bear it?'

'Irina is stupid,' said Soma. 'Two years just for one painting. That's long enough to have two kids!'

Soma's words made us laugh.

We chatted about Irina and her Rain Dance painting, and we didn't notice that it had grown late and Irina hadn't returned.

'Go and see why your elder sister hasn't returned,' said Tatiana to Soma.

'Tell Shiban to go!'

Shiban was squatting next to the open fire, head down, inventing pictographs while Maksym carved them on woodblocks. Shiban heard Soma. 'No, you go. I'm busy inventing our script.'

'Whoever it is that Irina draws in her paintings, that person should go look for her!'

'Uh,' said Shiban. He stood up. 'That's me. I'll look for her.'

About twenty minutes later Shiban returned with a handful of brushes. They were all dripping wet, rinsed perfectly clean by the Bistaré.

'What about Irina?' asked Tatiana.

'There are just brushes, no Irina.'

At noon the next day we found Irina downstream. If it weren't for several bushy willows that stopped her at a bend in the river, who knows where she would have floated. But I hate those meddling willow trees, because Irina was a fish and she should have kept floating on the Bistaré towards a far-off place that we cannot see.

When Irina returned to the camp prostrate in a birch-bark canoe, the setting sun had dyed the surface of the water golden, as if the Heavens knew that she liked paintings, so they splashed an oil painting on the river and embedded her in it.

Just then Vladimir was helping deliver a snow-white fawn. It was certainly from the sky above because it resembled a cloud. Vladimir named the fawn after his unforgettable mouth harp: *Mukulén*.

On the bank where Irina washed up, I selected a stretch of white rock and painted a lamp for her. I hoped that it would light her way as she drifted on dark, moonless nights. I knew that would be the last rock painting of my life. When I finished, I put my head against it and cried. My tears seeped into the lamp and filled it with oil to burn.

When we left the Bistaré, Shiban fastened a pair of golden bells around *Mukulén*'s neck. As they echoed crisply and melodiously in the wind, they awoke memories of years past. They were the sun and the moon in the sky, illuminating the paths we left on the Right Bank of the Argun – 'Evenki trails', as they are called – those paths trod into existence by our feet and the plum-blossom hooves of our reindeer.

PART FOUR

# THE LAST QUARTER OF THE MOON

*

The day is just about over. The sky is dark and I've almost finished my tale.

Tatiana and the others must have arrived in Busu by now.

Jiliu Township is a ghost town and none of our people are there. But that tiny township was a big, big city in my eyes. I'll never forget the two rolls of cloth that I saw in the store, one milky yellow, one deep blue-green. They stood there, one dark and one bright, like the night and the dawn.

Irina's death made Tatiana despise life in the mountain forests, and Suchanglin descended into the depths of pain too. He began to get drunk regularly. One day he finished off his baijiu and told Vladimir to go down the mountain and buy him some more. When Vladimir refused, Suchanglin took an axe to Vladimir's head. If Shiban hadn't pulled them apart, Vladimir might not have escaped alive.

Vladimir shouted in pain all night.

Because of all the logging, trees have grown sparser in recent years and there's less and less game too, while the wind blows stronger by the day. Meanwhile, the annual decline in edible moss means that we are forced to relocate more frequently with our reindeer.

The third year after Nihau left us, Maksym began exhibiting bizarre behaviour. He slit his wrist with a hunting knife, and tossed red-hot embers in his mouth. On rainy days, he took to running outside and shouting at the top of his lungs, and in arid weather he covered his head and wailed at the sight of zigzagging crevices in the soil.

We knew what this signified.

But the tragic fate of Nidu the Shaman and Nihau made us

unwilling to witness the birth of a new Shaman. Tatiana took the Spirit Robe, Spirit Skirt and Spirit Headdress left by Nihau and donated them to the Folk Museum in Jiliu Township, and we kept just the Spirit Drum. We wanted to isolate Maksym from that mysterious and gloomy ambience.

And, day by day, he did become more normal. Except during spells of drought when he occasionally behaved a bit oddly, he was an ordinary person.

From the moment it came into being, Jiliu Township was never fully occupied. People treated it like a rest stop where they could take a break, and it became shabbier by the day.

I am truly worried that the place Tatiana and the others are bound for – Busu – will turn into another rest stop.

Sakhar is behind bars now. The year before last, he recruited a few unemployed ex-convicts, and they entered the mountains to cut down trees inside a government-protected wildwood. They planned to smuggle the logs out and sell them on the black market for big money. But before the timber had even left the mountains, they were stopped at a checkpoint and their trucks were seized. Sakhar got three years in prison.

Despite Tatiana's strict supervision of Soma, she often ran off to other campgrounds for romantic liaisons. She said it was too lonely in the mountains, and only those things that occur between a man and a woman brought her a moment of joy.

Every time Soma left the mountains it was for an abortion. Tatiana was worried sick about the matter of her daughter's marriage. Whenever she introduced her daughter to a prospective spouse, the response was contemptuous. 'Soma? She goes out with everybody. How could she be somebody's wife?'

Later on, three scavengers in rags – the sort that couldn't eat their fill *or take a wife – arrived in Jiliu Township. But they'd heard that the local Evenki girls had trouble getting married off – and since the girls benefited from a government living allowance, the scroungers had decided to drop in and take a look!*

*This was no less of a shock to Tatiana than the death of her daughter Irina. 'Eni, these scavengers want to collect our maidens like pieces of trash! We've got to leave this damn place!'*

*Tatiana started agitating for the construction of a new settlement for the Evenki. She complained that Jiliu Township was too isolated, transport was inconvenient and medical treatment wasn't guaranteed. Our children weren't being educated at a senior level, and they'd have trouble getting jobs later. Our people were facing a future in which we were moving backwards rather than progressing.*

*She joined forces with several* urireng *and presented the Jiliu Township government with a petition calling for the Evenki to relocate to a permanent settlement outside the mountains. It was this petition that brought about the large-scale relocation to Busu.*

*There are fewer than two hundred Evenki living in the mountains now, and only six or seven hundred reindeer. Apart from me, everyone in our* urireng *voted in favour of resettling in Busu. When he heard I had voted against the move, the newly appointed Jiliu Township Party Secretary came into the mountains specifically to carry out the task of persuading me.*

*Secretary Gu said that if we left the mountains with our reindeer, it would also be a way of protecting the forest. Roaming reindeer damaged the vegetation and disturbed the balance of the ecosystem. And anyway, wild animals are protected now so hunting is prohibited.*

*Only a people that is willing to lay down its hunting rifles, he added, is a truly civilised people with a promising future.*

*I really wanted to tell him that our reindeer have always kissed the forest. Compared to the loggers who number in the tens of thousands, we and our animals are just a handful of dragonflies skimming the water's surface. If the river that is this forest has been polluted, how could it be due to the passage of a few dragonflies?*

*But I didn't say any of that to him. I sang a song for him, one that Nihau once sang, a Spirit Song for a Bear Burial passed down in our clan:*

> O, Bear Grandmother
> You have fallen down.
>
> Sleep sweetly!
> Feasting on your flesh
> Are those black, black ravens.
>
> Reverently, we place your eyes in the trees
> As if hanging Spirit Lamps!

*I've remained behind and An'tsaur has too, and that will do. I had hoped Shiban might stay, for he loves to munch on bark and he hasn't completed his Evenki script. But he's a filial boy, and wherever Vladimir goes, he goes. I reckon Vladimir's days are numbered. His tongue is twisted and his speech indistinct. If Vladimir passes away, then Shiban will return for certain.*

*We don't need to leave a trail of tree markers any more when we relocate. There are more and more paved roads in the mountains now. When there were none, we'd lose our way; there are many roads now, but we still lose our way because we don't know which road to choose.*

*When the moving van drove into the campground at dawn this morning, I could see that the expressions of those who were leaving were not entirely happy. Their eyes also revealed a bleak, confused look.*

*Especially the white fawn that was born when Irina left us. No matter what was said it wouldn't board the truck. But Shiban can't live without it. Shiban shook the pair of reindeer bells around its neck. Mukulén, he said, get on the truck quickly. If you don't like Busu and can't bear being fenced in, we'll come back! Only then did Mukulén obey.*

*I've spent the whole day telling my tale, and I'm tired. I didn't tell you my name because I don't want to leave my name behind. I've already instructed An'tsaur: when Até leaves, don't bury her in the ground. Bury her in a tree, in the wind. It's a pity that nowadays finding four suitably spaced trees isn't so easy.*

*I don't actually know how things ended for some people. The woman who abandoned her daughter Lyusya and her husband Puffball, for instance, or Washia, or Nihau's daughter Berna who vanished mysteriously after her mother's burial. My tale must come to an end, but not everyone gets an epilogue.*

*An'tsaur comes in and adds a few pieces of kindling to the fire. This fire given me by Mother is aged now, but its face is still animated and youthful.*

*I step out of my shirangju.*

*The moist air filled with the delicate fragrances of plants makes me sneeze, a refreshing sneeze that sweeps away my fatigue.*

*The moon has risen, but it's not round. A quarter moon of flawless white jade. It bends over gently like a fawn lapping water. Beneath the moon extends the road that leads out of the mountains. I look at that road full of sadness. Suddenly, a fuzzy grey-white shadow appears at the far end of the road. I can hear the faint ring of a reindeer bell as the shadow proceeds towards our campground.*

*Até, Mukulén has come home! shouts An'tsaur.*

*I don't dare believe my eyes, even though the jingle is increasingly distinct.*

*I lift my head and gaze at the moon, and it looks like a snow-white fawn running towards us. When I look again at the fawn that is nearer and nearer to us, it feels as if the pale-white crescent has fallen to the ground. I'm crying, because I can no longer distinguish between heaven and earth.*

## VINTAGE EARTH

Change the story.

Vintage Earth is a collection of transformative novels brimming with the power and beauty of the natural world. Each one is a work of creative activism, a blast of fresh air, a seed from which change can grow. Discover great writing on the most urgent story of our times.

| | |
|---|---|
| *The Overstory* | Richard Powers |
| *Solar* | Ian McEwan |
| *The Last Quarter of the Moon* | Chi Zijian |
| *The Tusk That Did the Damage* | Tania James |
| *The Man with the Compound Eyes* | Wu Ming-Yi |
| *The Man Who Planted Trees* | Jean Giono |
| *The Mermaid of Black Conch* | Monique Roffey |
| *The Wall* | Marlen Haushofer |

*A Note on Our Sustainability Commitments*

The books in the Vintage Earth series have been
created with the environment in mind.

We have minimised the carbon impact of our books by printing
with a low carbon FSC™ certified paper based in Sweden, and only
using cover boards and finishes that are fully recyclable and FSC™
certified. All titles are then printed locally in the UK.

Whilst we have minimised our environmental impact,
we understand that the production of our books will still
contribute to carbon emissions. Therefore, we have offset
the remainder of this book's carbon emissions to support
land conservation initiatives in Brazil.

For more information on our sustainability commitments,
please visit greenpenguin.co.uk.

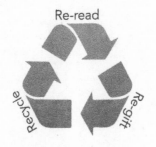

# **VINTAGE** CLASSICS

Vintage launched in the United Kingdom in 1990, and was originally the paperback home for the Random House Group's literary authors. Now, Vintage is comprised of some of London's oldest and most prestigious literary houses, including Chatto & Windus (1855), Hogarth (1917), Jonathan Cape (1921) and Secker & Warburg (1935), alongside the newer or relaunched hardback and paperback imprints: The Bodley Head, Harvill Secker, Yellow Jersey, Square Peg, Vintage Paperbacks and Vintage Classics.

From Angela Carter, Graham Greene and Aldous Huxley to Toni Morrison, Haruki Murakami and Virginia Woolf, Vintage Classics is renowned for publishing some of the greatest writers and thinkers from around the world and across the ages – all complemented by our beautiful, stylish approach to design. Vintage Classics' authors have won many of the world's most revered literary prizes, including the Nobel, the Man Booker, the Prix Goncourt and the Pulitzer, and through their writing they continue to capture imaginations, inspire new perspectives and incite curiosity.

In 2007 Vintage Classics introduced its distinctive red spine design, and in 2012 Vintage Children's Classics was launched to include the much-loved authors of our childhood. Random House joined forces with the Penguin Group in 2013 to become Penguin Random House, making it the largest trade publisher in the United Kingdom.

@vintagebooks

penguin.co.uk/vintage-classics